Anna
Karenina

Leo Tolstoy

Anna Karenina

COMPACT EDITIONS

PHOENIX

A PHOENIX PAPERBACK
COMPACT EDITIONS

This paperback edition, a condensed version of the original,
first published in Great Britain in 2007
by Phoenix,
an imprint of Orion Books Ltd,
Orion House, 5 Upper St Martin's Lane,
London WC2H 9EA

1 3 5 7 9 10 8 6 4 2

A CIP catalogue record for this book
is available from the British Library.

ISBN 978-0-7538-2267-8

Printed and bound in Great Britain by
Clays Ltd, St Ives plc

The Orion Publishing Group's policy is to use papers
that are natural, renewable and recyclable products and
made from wood grown in sustainable forests. The logging
and manufacturing processes are expected to conform to
the environmental regulations of the country of origin.

www.orionbooks.co.uk

Contents

About Leo Tolstoy

Leo Tolstoy was born in 1828 at Yasnaya Polyana, province of Tula, the fourth son of Count Nikolay Tolstoy. His mother died soon after, in 1830. When Tolstoy was nine the family moved to Moscow where his father died in the same year. In 1844 Tolstoy began studying law and oriental languages at Kazan University where his teachers described him as being both 'unwilling and unable to learn'. He left before completing his degree and went back to Yasnaya Polyana. He began to lead a life typical of men of his class, focused on cards, wine and women. However, he was already becoming preoccupied with politics.

Disillusioned with the emptiness of his life, he joined an artillery unit based in Chechnya in 1851. A year later, he published his first story, *Childhood*, which was immediately successful and helped to establish him as part of the Russian literati – Tsar Alexander II was said to have praised his work in this period.

Having got his commission and taken part in fighting against the Turks and the defence of the Fourth Bastion, Tolstoy left the army, sickened at what he had seen. Between 1856 and 1861 Tolstoy wrote and travelled abroad extensively. He returned with a sense of revulsion for what he considered to be European materialism. In 1859 he started a school for peasant children at Yasnaya and in 1862 he founded a magazine in which he contended that it was the peasants who should teach the intellectuals, rather than the other way round.

At the age of fifty Tolstoy had a mid-life crisis. He declared that he had to find the meaning of life or would commit suicide. This crisis was followed by a religious conversion, although his interpretation of Christianity had Buddhist overtones.

In 1862 he married Sophia Andreyevna Behrs who gave him

thirteen children, five of whom died in childhood. She was a devoted wife and mother who gave Tolstoy a great deal of help with his literary endeavours. It is well known that she copied out *War and Peace* (1868–9) seven times. For fifteen years the marriage was extremely happy but Tolstoy's increasingly radical political stance at the end of his life alienated his wife. He frequently dispensed huge sums of money to beggars and drew up a will relinquishing his copyrights. Such behaviour led to frequent disputes with Sophia. Finding it impossible to continue living a comfortable life with his family whilst preaching communism, he left Yasnaya in 1910, with one of his daughters and his doctor, for an unknown destination. He died on the journey and was buried in a simple peasant's grave.

Chronology of Tolstoy's Life

Year	Life
1828	Born on 28 August* in Yasnaya Polyana, a province in Tula
1830	Mother dies
1837	Death of father, Count Nikolay Tolstoy Leo Tolstoy is brought up by relatives
1847	Leaves University of Kazan after three years without a degree
1851	Visits Caucasus with elder brother Enlists in army Starts work on *Childhood*
1854	Receives his commission. On active service in Wallachia; gets posted to Sevastopol *Boyhood* published
1855	Returns to St Petersburg
1857	Travels around Western Europe In August returns to Yasnaya Polyana
1859	Creates school for peasant children on his estate *Three Deaths* and *Family Happiness* published
1860–1	Travels again to Western Europe, examining educational methods
1861	As Arbiter of the Peace, he negotiates land settlements following emancipation of serfs
1862	Marries Sophia Behrs. Together they have 13 children, eight reach adulthood

Chronology of His Times

Year	Literary Context	Historical Events
1828	Birth of Meredith Birth of D.G. Rossetti.	
1830	Tennyson, *Poems,* *Chiefly Lyrical*	Cholera hits Russia
1831		Polish rebellion against Tsar Nicholas I fails
1847	C. Brontë, *Jane Eyre* E. Brontë, *Wuthering Heights*	
1851	Ruskin, *The Stones of Venice* Melville, *Moby Dick*	St Petersburg–Moscow railway opens
1853	C. Brontë, *Villette*	Outbreak of Crimean War between Russia and the Alliance of France, Britain and the Ottoman Empire
1854	Dickens, *Hard Times*	
1855	Elizabeth Gaskell, *North and South*	Death of Nicholas I Alexander II becomes Tsar Censorship is relaxed and public access to books and periodicals increases
1857	Flaubert, *Madame Bovary* Trollope, *Barchester Towers*	
1859	Darwin, *Origin of Species* Mill, *On Liberty*	
1860	Collins, *The Woman in White* Eliot, *The Mill on the Floss*	
1861	Dickens, *Great Expectations*	Emancipation of serfs American Civil War begins
1862	Turgenev, *Fathers and Sons*	

Year	Life
1863	*The Cossacks* published Begins work on *War and Peace* Birth of first child, Sergey
1869	Completes *War and Peace* and final volumes published
1870	Takes up Greek
1872	*A Prisoner in the Caucasus* published
1873	Begins work on *Anna Karenina*
1877	Completes *Anna Karenina*
1879	Begins work on *A Confession*
1881	Writes to Tsar Alexander III asking for clemency for assassins of Alexander II
1882	*What Men Live By* published
1883	Meets Chertkov who becomes his leading disciple.
1885	Founds *The Intermediary*
1886	*The Death of Ivan Ilyich* published
1891–2	Organizes relief for victims of ongoing famine
1894	
1899	*Resurrection* published
1901	Excommunicated by Russian Orthodox Church. Seriously ill. Meets Chekhov and Gorky in Crimea
1902	*What is Religion?* completed
1905	
1906	Favourite daughter Masha dies of pneumonia Tensions between Tolstoy and his wife Sophia increase
1908	*I Cannot Be Silent* published
1909	Relationship with Sophia worsens Makes will handing over copyrights to his work to public
1910	Dies 7 November* at Astapovo railway station, aged 82

* In the Julian Calendar, which was used in Russia during Tolstoy's life

Year	Literary Context	Historical Events
1863	Mill, *Utilitarianism* Eliot, *Romola* Death of Thackeray	Polish revolt Slavery abolished in USA
1867	Marx, *Das Kapital*	
1869	Blackmore, *Lorna Doone* Mill, *Subjection of Women*	
1870	Death of Dickens	Fall of Napoleon Birth of Lenin
1873	Death of Mill	
1877	Turgenev, *Virgin Soil*	Russo-Turkish war begins
1879	Ibsen, *A Doll's house*	Birth of Trotsky and Stalin
1881	Dostoevsky dies	Reformist Tsar Alexander II is assassinated The more repressive reign of Alexander III begins
1882	Death of Darwin and Trollope	
1883	Turgenev dies	
1885	D.H. Lawrence born	
1886	James, *The Bostonians*	
1891	Hardy, *Tess of the D'Urbervilles*	Famine in Volga Basin begins
1894		Death of Alexander III Nicholas II becomes Tsar
1899		Boer War begins
1901		Death of Queen Victoria
1902	Lenin, *What Is To Be Done?*	
1904	Chekhov, *The Cherry Orchard*	Russo-Japanese war begins
1905		1905 Revolution Nicholas II forced to grant a constitution and establish the Duma
1906		Stolypin Reforms begin

List of Principal Characters

Oblónsky, Prince Stephen Arkádyevich ('Stiva')

Oblónskaya, Princess Dárya Alexándrovna ('Dolly'), *Stiva's wife; eldest daughter of Prince Shcherbátsky*

Matthew, *a valet*

Karénina, Anna Arkádyevna

Karénin, Aléxis Alexándrovich, *Anna's husband*

Tánya, *Stiva's daughter*

Grísha, *Stiva's son*

Nikítin, Philip Ivánich,

Grinévich, Michael Stanislávich, } *colleagues of Oblónsky's*

Lévin, Constantine Dmítrich ('Kóstya')

Koznyshév, Sergius Ivánich, *Lévin's half-brother*

Shcherbátsky, Prince Alexander Dmitrich

Shcherbátskaya, *the Princess, his wife*

Shcherbátskaya, Princess Catherine Alexándrovna ('Kitty'), *their youngest daughter*

Shcherbátsky, *Dolly's cousin*

Lvóva, Princess Nataly Alexándrovna, *Prince Shcherbátsky's second daughter*

Lvov, Prince ('Arsény')

Lévin, Nicholas, *Constantine's brother*

Vrónsky, Count Alexis Kirílovich

Countess Nórdston

Countess Vrónskaya, *Vrónsky's mother*

Karénin, Sergéy Alexéyich, *Anna's son* ('Serézha', 'Kútik')

Mariette, *Serézha's governess*

Krítsky, *an acquaintance of Nicholas Lévin's*

Mary Nikolávna ('Másha'), *living with Nicholas*

Agatha Mikháylovna, *Lévin's housekeeper*

Kuzmá, *Lévin's man-servant*

Vasíly Fédorich, *Lévin's steward*

Ánnushka, *Anna's maid*

Countess Lydia Ivánovna, *Karénin's friend*

Kondráty, *the Karénins' man-servant*

Princess Elisabeth Fédorovna Tverskáya (Betsy)

Captain Kameróvsky

Démin, *Colonel of Vrónsky's regiment*

Prince Alexander Vrónsky

Princess Myágkaya

Prince Tverskóy

Councillor Stremov

Yáshvin, Captain Prince, *Vrónsky's friend*

Bryánsky

Cord, *the English trainer*

List of Principal Characters

Slyúdin, Michael Vasílich, *Karénin's secretary*

Rtíshcheva, Mary Evgényevna

Mlle Várenka

Mme Stahl

Petróv, *an invalid artist*

Petróva, Anna Pávlovna, *his wife*

Titus, *peasant on Lévin's estate*

Serpukhovskóy, General Prince

Sviyázhsky, Nicholas Ivánich, *a Marshal of the Nobility*

Iván, *a cowman*

Kornéy Vasílich, *Karénin's valet*

Turóvtsyn, Theodore Vasilyevich, *a visitor at Oblónsky's*

Chírikov, *Lévin's friend*

Goleníshchev, *Vrónsky's friend*

Mikháylov, *an artist*

Masha, *Kitty's maid*

Vasíly Lukích, *a tutor to Serézha*

Várya, *Vrónsky's sister-in-law*

Princess Barbara Oblónskaya, *Anna's aunt*

Tushkevich, *a friend of Princess Betsy's*

Philip, *Lévin's coachman*

Vasíly Fédorich, *Vrónsky's steward*

Snetkóv, Michael Stepánich, *an old Marshal of the Nobility*

Nevédovsky, *the new Marshal of the Nobility*

Flérov, *a member of the Nobility*

Gágin, *a visitor at the club*

Vorkúyev, Iván Petróvich, *a publisher*

Peter Dmítrich, *a doctor*

Michael,

Peter,

Jules Landau (Count Bezzúbov), *a Frenchman*

Dmítry ('Mítya'), *Lévin's son*

Mikháylich, *a beekeeper*

Iván, *Lévin's coachman*

Anna
Karenina

Vengeance is Mine;
I Will Repay

PART ONE

1

All happy families resemble one another, each unhappy family is unhappy in its own way.

Everything was upset in the Oblonskys' house. The wife had discovered an intrigue between her husband and their former French governess, and declared that she would not continue to live under the same roof with him. This state of things had now lasted for three days, and not only the husband and wife but the whole household suffered from it. The wife kept to her own rooms; the husband stopped away from home all day; the children ran about all over the house uneasily; the English governess quarrelled with the housekeeper; the cook had gone out just at dinner-time the day before and had not returned; and the kitchen-maid and coachman had given notice.

On the third day after his quarrel with his wife, Prince Stephen Arkadyevich Oblonsky—Stiva, as he was called in his set in Society—woke up at his usual time, eight o'clock, not in his wife's bedroom but on the morocco leather-covered sofa in his study. He let down his legs, felt about with his feet for his slippers and from nine years' habit stretched out his arm towards where his dressing-gown usually hung in their bedroom. And then he suddenly remembered that, and why, he was not sleeping there but in his study. The smile vanished from his face and he frowned.

'Oh dear, dear, dear!' he groaned, recalling what had happened.

'No, she will never forgive me! And the worst thing about it is, that it's all my own fault; and yet I'm not guilty! That's the tragedy of it!' he thought despairingly, as he recalled the most painful details of the quarrel. The worst moment had been when, returning home from the theatre merry and satisfied, he saw her in her bedroom with the unlucky note which had betrayed him in her hand.

She sat there: the careworn, ever-bustling, and (as he thought) rather simple Dolly—with the note in her hand and a look of terror, despair, and anger on her face.

'What is this? This?' she asked, pointing to the note.

At the moment he had not had time to assume an expression suitable to the position in which he stood toward his wife now that his guilt was discovered and he involuntarily smiled his usual kindly and therefore silly smile.

He could not forgive himself for that silly smile. Dolly, seeing it, shuddered as if with physical pain, and rushed from the room. Since then she had refused to see him.

'It's all the fault of that stupid smile,' thought Oblonsky. 'But what am I to do?' he asked himself in despair, and could find no answer.

2

Oblonsky could not feel repentant that he, a handsome amorous man of thirty-four, was not in love with his wife, the mother of five living and two dead children and only a year younger than himself. He repented only of not having managed to conceal his conduct from her. He had a vague notion that his wife had long suspected him of being unfaithful and winked at it. He even thought that she, who was nothing but an excellent mother of a family, worn-out, already growing elderly, no longer pretty, and in no way remarkable, ought to be lenient to him. It turned out that the very opposite was the case.

'How awful! Oh dear, oh dear, how awful!' Oblonsky kept repeating to himself. 'And how well everything was going on till now—how happily we lived! Of course it's not quite nice that *she* had been a governess in our house. There's something banal, a want of taste, in carrying on with one's governess—but as long as she was in the house I never took any liberties. The worst of the matter is, that she is already ... Why need it all happen at once? Oh dear, dear, dear! What am I to do?'

He could find no answer, except life's usual answer to the most complex and insoluble questions. That answer is: live in the needs of the day, that is, find forgetfulness.

'We'll see when the time comes,' thought Oblonsky, and got up, put on his grey dressing-gown lined with blue silk, and went with his usual firm tread toward the window, drew up the blind and rang loudly. The bell was answered immediately by his old friend and valet, Matthew, who brought in his clothes, boots, and a telegram. He was followed by the barber with shaving tackle.

'Any papers from the Office?' asked Oblonsky, as he took the telegram and sat down before the looking-glass.

'They're on your table,' answered Matthew.

Oblonsky glanced at Matthew's face in the looking-glass. From their looks, as they met in the glass, it was evident that they understood one another.

Oblonsky tore open the telegram and his face brightened.

'Matthew, my sister Anna Arkadyevna is coming to-morrow,' he said, motioning away for a moment the shiny plump hand of the barber.

'The Lord be thanked!' said Matthew, proving by his answer that he knew just as well as his master the importance of this visit: namely, that Anna Arkadyevna, Stephen Arkadyevich's favourite sister, might help to reconcile the husband and wife.

'Is she coming alone, or with Mr. Karenin?'

Oblonsky could not answer as the barber was busy with his upper lip; but he raised one finger.

'Alone. Would you like one of the upstairs rooms got ready?'

'Ask Darya Alexandrovna. See what she says.'

Oblonsky was washed and his hair brushed when Matthew re-entered the room. The barber was no longer there.

'Darya Alexandrovna told me to say that she is going away. "He may do as he pleases"—that is, as you please, sir,' he said, laughing with his eyes only; he gazed at his master. Oblonsky remained silent, then a kind and rather pathetic smile appeared on his handsome face.

'Ah, Matthew!' he said, shaking his head.

'Never mind, sir—things will shape themselves.'

'Do you think so?—Who's that?' asked Oblonsky, hearing the rustle of a woman's dress outside the door.

'It's me, sir,' answered a firm and pleasant woman's voice, and Matrena Filimonovna, the children's nurse, thrust her stern pockmarked face in at the door.

'What is it, Matrena?' asked Oblonsky, stepping out to her.

'Won't you go and try again, sir? By God's grace you might make it up! She suffers dreadfully; it's pitiful to see her, and everything in the house is topsy-turvy. You should consider the children ...'

'But she won't admit me!'

'Do your part—God is merciful. Pray to Him, sir, pray to Him!'

'All right—now go,' said Oblonsky, suddenly blushing.

'I must get dressed,' said he, and threw off his dressing-gown.

3

When he was quite dressed Oblonsky, in spite of his misfortune, went with a slight spring in each step into the dining-room where his coffee stood ready. Beside the coffee lay letters and papers from the Office.

He read the letters, one of which concerned the sale of a forest on his wife's estate, and came from a dealer. This forest had to be sold; but until he was reconciled with his wife the sale was quite out of the question. The idea that he might be biased by that consideration, might seek a reconciliation in order to sell the forest, offended him. Having looked through his letters, Oblonsky began to drink his coffee.

At the same time he unfolded the still damp morning paper, and began reading. Oblonsky subscribed to and read a Liberal paper that expressed the opinions of the majority. And although neither science, art, nor politics specially interested him, he firmly held to the opinions of the majority and of his paper on those subjects.

Oblonsky's tendency and opinions were not his by deliberate choice: they came of themselves, just as he did not choose the fashion of his hats or coats but wore those of the current style. Living in a certain social set, he was obliged to hold views, just as he was obliged to have a hat. If he had a reason for preferring Liberalism to the Conservatism of many in his set, it was because it suited his manner of life better. The Liberal Party maintained that everything in Russia was bad, and it was a fact that Oblonsky had many debts and decidedly too little money. The Liberal Party said that marriage was an obsolete institution which ought to be reformed; and family life really gave Oblonsky very little pleasure. The Liberal Party hinted that religion was only good as a check on the more barbarous portion of the population; and Oblonsky really could not understand why one should use all that high-flown language about another world while one can live so merrily in this one.

Thus Liberalism became habitual to Oblonsky, and he loved his paper as he loved his after-dinner cigar, for the slight mistiness it produced in his brain. He read the leading article, in which hits were made at the Ministry. With his natural quickness of perception he understood the meaning of each hit, whence it came, for whom it was meant and what had provoked it, and this as usual gave him a certain satisfaction. But to-day the satisfaction was marred by the memory of Matrena Filimonovna's advice, and of the fact that there was all this trouble in the house.

Having finished the paper, his second cup of coffee, and a buttered roll, he got up and smiled the smile of a healthy digestion. But that joyful smile at once brought everything back to his mind, and he grew thoughtful.

Then he heard the sound of two childish voices outside the door, and recognized them as the voices of his eldest daughter, Tanya, and of his little boy Grisha. They were dragging something along, and had upset it.

'I told you not to put passengers on the roof,' the girl shouted in English. 'Now pick them up!'

'Everything is disorganized,' thought Oblonsky and going to the door he called them in. They left the box, which represented a train, and came to their father.

The girl, her father's pet, ran boldly in, embraced him, and hung laughing on his neck.

'How's Mama?' he asked, passing his hand over his daughter's smooth delicate little neck, as he smilingly said 'Good morning' in answer to the little boy's greeting.

'Mama? She's up,' said the girl.

'Yes, but is she cheerful?' he added.

'I don't know,' she said. 'She said we were not to have any lessons, but must walk to Grandmamma's.'

'Well, you may go, my little Tanyakin. ... Oh, wait!' he said, still holding her and stroking her delicate little hand.

Taking a box of sweets from the mantelpiece, he chose two sweets which he knew she liked best, a chocolate and a coloured cream.

'For Grisha?' she asked, holding out the chocolate.

'Yes, yes,' and stroking her shoulder he kissed her hair at the roots and her neck, and let her go.

'The carriage is ready,' said Matthew.

Oblonsky took his hat and paused to consider whether he had forgotten anything. He found he had forgotten nothing but what he wanted to forget: his wife.

'Oh yes!' His head dropped, and his handsome face became worried.

'To go, or not to go?' he asked himself; and his inner consciousness answered that he ought not to go: that it could only result in hypocrisy; that it was impossible to restore their relations because it was impossible to render her attractive and capable of exciting love.

'Nevertheless it will have to be done sooner or later. Things can't remain as they are,' he said, and crossing the drawing-room with rapid steps, he opened the door which led into his wife's bedroom.

4

Darya Alexandrovna was there in a dressing-jacket, with her large frightened eyes, made more prominent by the emaciation of her face, and her knot of thin plaits of once luxurious and beautiful hair. The room was covered with scattered articles, and she was standing among them before an open wardrobe. Hearing her husband's step she stopped and looked at the door, vainly trying to assume a severe and contemptuous expression. She was afraid of the impending interview. She was trying to do what she had attempted ten times already during those three days, to sort out her own and her children's clothes to take to her mother's; she must do something to punish and humiliate him, and to revenge herself if only for a small part of the pain he had caused her. She still kept saying that she would leave him, but felt that this was impossible because she could not get out of the habit of regarding him as her husband and of loving him.

On seeing her husband she thrust her arms into a drawer of the wardrobe as if looking for something, and only when he had come close to her did she turn her face toward him. But her face, which she wanted to seem stern and determined, expressed only perplexity and suffering.

'Dolly!' he said in a soft, timid voice. He drew his head down, wishing to look pathetic and submissive, but with a rapid glance she took in his fresh and healthy figure. 'Yes, he is happy and contented,' she thought, 'but what about me? … And that horrid good-nature of his which people praise so, how I hate it!'

'What do you want?' she said quickly.

'Dolly,' he repeated unsteadily, 'Anna is coming to-morrow.'

'What's that to do with me? I can't receive her!' she exclaimed.

'But after all, Dolly, you really must,' said he.

'Go away, go away, go away!' she cried, as if in physical pain.

Oblonsky could think calmly of his wife, could hope that 'things would shape themselves' as Matthew had said, and could calmly read his paper and drink his coffee, but when he saw her worn, suffering face, and heard her tone, resigned and despairing, he felt a choking sensation. A lump rose to his throat and tears glistened in his eyes.

'Oh, my God! What have I done? Dolly—for heaven's sake! … You know …' His throat was choked with sobs.

She slammed the doors of the wardrobe and looked up at him.

'Dolly, what can I say? … Only forgive me! Think, nine years. … Can't they atone for a momentary—a momentary …'

Her eyes drooped and she waited to hear what he would say, as if entreating him to persuade her somehow that she had made a mistake.

'A momentary infatuation, …' he said, and was going on; but at those words her lips tightened again as if with pain.

'Go away—go away from here!' she cried in a still shriller voice, 'and don't talk to me of your infatuations and all those horrors!'

'Dolly!' he said, now actually sobbing, 'for heaven's sake think of the children—they have done nothing! Punish me—make me suffer for my sin! Tell me what to do—I am ready for anything. I am the guilty one. ... But, Dolly, forgive me!'

She sat down and he could hear her loud, heavy breathing. He felt unutterably sorry for her. She tried again and again to speak and could not. He waited.

'You think of our children when you want to play with them, but I am always thinking of them, and know they are ruined now,' she said. 'I do not know how to save them—whether by taking them away or by leaving them with a dissolute—yes, a dissolute father. ... Tell me, do you think it possible for us to live together after what has happened? Is it possible?' she repeated, raising her voice. 'When my husband, the father of my children, has love affairs with his children's governess?'

'But what's to be done?—what's to be done?' said he, in a piteous voice, and sinking his head lower and lower.

'You are horrid and disgusting to me!' she shouted, getting more and more excited. 'Your tears are—water! You never loved me; you have no heart, no honour! To me you are detestable, disgusting—a stranger, yes, a perfect stranger!'

He looked at her and the hatred he saw in her face frightened and surprised him. He did not understand that his pity exasperated her.

At that moment a child began to cry in another room. Darya Alexandrovna listened, and her face softened suddenly. She rose quickly and moved toward the door.

'After all, she loves my child,' he thought, noticing the change in her face when the baby cried; '*my* child—then how can she hate me?'

'Dolly, just a word!' he said, following her.

'If you follow me, I shall call the servants and the children! I'll let everybody know you are a scoundrel! I am going away to-day, and you may live here with your mistress!'

She went out, slamming the door.

For a few seconds Oblonsky stood alone; then he wiped his eyes, sighed, and went out of the room.

'Well, perhaps things will "shape themselves",' he thought.

'Matthew!' he called, 'will you and Mary arrange everything for Anna Arkadyevna in the little sitting-room?' he added when Matthew appeared.

'Yes, sir.'

Oblonsky put on his fur coat, and went out into the porch.

'Will you be home to dinner, sir?' said Matthew.

'I'll see. ... Oh, and here's some money,' said he, taking a ten-rouble note out of his pocket-book. 'Will it be enough?'

'Enough or not, we shall have to manage, that's clear,' said Matthew, closing the carriage door and stepping back into the porch.

Meanwhile Darya Alexandrovna after soothing the child, knowing from the sound of the carriage wheels that her husband had gone, returned to her bedroom. She sat down. Locking together her thin fingers, on which her rings hung loosely, she went over in her mind the whole of their conversation.

'Gone! But how did he finish with *her*?' she thought. 'Is it possible that he still sees her? Why didn't I ask him? No, no! It's impossible to be reunited. ... Even if we go on living in the same house, we are strangers—strangers for ever!' she repeated. 'And how I loved him! Oh God, how I loved him! ... How I loved—and don't I love him now? The most terrible thing ...' She did not finish the thought, because Matrena Filimonovna thrust her head in at the door.

'Hadn't I better send for my brother?' she said. 'After all, he can cook a dinner;—or else the children will go without food till six o'clock, as they did yesterday.'

'All right! I'll come and see about it in a moment. ... Has the milk been sent for?' and Darya Alexandrovna plunged into her daily cares, and for a time drowned her grief in them.

5

Oblonsky's natural ability had helped him to do well at school, but mischief and laziness had caused him to finish very low in his year's class. Yet in spite of his dissipated life, his unimportant service rank, and his comparative youth, he occupied a distinguished well-paid post as Head of one of the Government Boards in Moscow. This post he had obtained through Alexis Alexandrovich Karenin, his sister Anna's husband, who held one of the most important positions in the Ministry to which that Moscow Board belonged. But even if Karenin had not nominated his brother-in-law for that post, Stiva Oblonsky would have obtained this or a similar post with a salary of some 6000 roubles a year, which he needed because in spite of his wife's substantial means his affairs were in a bad way.

Half Moscow and half Petersburg were his relations or friends. He was born among those who were or who became the great ones of this world. One third of the official world, the older men, were his father's friends and had known him in petticoats, he was on intimate terms with another third, and was well acquainted with the last third. Consequently the distributors of earthly blessings, such as government posts, grants, concessions, and the like, were all his friends.

Oblonsky was not only liked by every one who knew him for his kind and joyous nature and his undoubted honesty, but there was something in him that had a physical effect on those he met, making them feel friendly and cheerful.

Oblonsky had won not only the affection but also the respect of all who had anything to do with him. The chief qualities that had won him this general respect in his Office were, first, his extreme leniency, founded on a consciousness of his own defects; secondly, his true Liberalism which made him treat all men alike whatever their rank or official position; thirdly and chiefly, his complete indifference to the business he was engaged on, in consequence of which he was never carried away by enthusiasm and never made mistakes.

Having arrived at his destination, Oblonsky, respectfully followed by the door-keeper bearing his portfolio, entered his little private room, put on his uniform, and came out into the Office. The clerks and attendants all rose and bowed cheerfully and respectfully. Oblonsky walked quickly, as was his wont, to his place, shook hands with the Members, and sat down. He chatted and joked just as much as was proper and then turned to business. No one could determine better than he the limits of freedom, simplicity, and formality, necessary for the pleasant transaction of business.

'Well, gentlemen ...' said Oblonsky and the sitting commenced.

It was not quite two when the large glass doors suddenly swung open and some one came in. All the Members, glad of some distraction, looked toward the door; but the door-keeper at once turned out the intruder and closed the glass doors behind him.

When the Report had been read, Oblonsky rose to go to his private room. Two of his colleagues—Nikitin, an old hard-working official, and Grinevich, a Gentleman of the Bedchamber—followed him out.

'Who was it came in?' Oblonsky asked the door-keeper.

'Some man came in without permission, your Excellency. He asked for you. I told him, "When the Members come out, then ..."'

'Where is he?'

'That's him,' said the door-keeper, pointing to a strongly-built broad-shouldered man with a curly beard, who, without taking off his sheep-skin cap, was running lightly and quickly up the worn steps of the stone staircase. Oblonsky's kindly face, beaming over the gold-embroidered collar of his uniform, grew still more radiant when he recognized the man who was coming up.

'Yes, it's he! Levin, at last!' he said, scrutinizing the approaching Levin with a friendly mocking smile. 'How is it you deign to look me up in this _den_?' he asked; and not contented with pressing his friend's hand, he kissed him. 'Been here long?'

'I've only just arrived, and am very anxious to see you,' answered Levin, looking round with constraint, and yet crossly and uneasily.

'Well then, come into my room,' said Oblonsky, who knew his friend's self-conscious and irritable shyness.

Levin and Oblonsky were almost of the same age. Levin had been his comrade and friend in early youth, and they were fond of one another in spite of the difference in their characters and tastes. Yet, as often happens between men who have chosen different pursuits, each thought that his own way of living was real life, and that the life of his friend was—illusion. Oblonsky could not repress a slightly sarcastic smile at the sight of Levin. How many times he had already seen him arriving in Moscow from the country, where he did something, though what it was Oblonsky could never quite understand or feel any interest in. Levin came to Moscow always excited, always in a hurry, rather shy and irritated by his own shyness, and usually with totally new and unexpected views about things. Oblonsky laughed at all this, and yet liked it. Similarly, Levin in his heart despised the town life his friend was leading, and his official duties which he considered futile and ridiculed. But the difference was that Oblonsky, doing as every one else did, laughed with confidence and good-humour, while Levin laughed uncertainly and sometimes angrily.

'We have long been expecting you,' said Oblonsky entering his private room. 'I'm very, very glad to see you!' continued he. 'Well, how are you, eh? When did you arrive?'

Levin looked silently at the faces of Oblonsky's colleagues, and especially at the hands of the elegant Grinevich, who had such long white fingers and such long yellowish nails curving at the points. Oblonsky at once noticed Levin's look and smiled.

'Oh, of course! Let me introduce you,' he said. 'My colleagues: Philip Ivanich Nikitin; Michael Stanislavich Grinevich,' then turning to Levin, 'Constantine Dmitrich Levin, an active member of the Zemstvo, one of the new sort—a gymnast who lifts a hundredweight and a half with one hand, a cattle-breeder, a sportsman,—my friend and a brother of Sergius Ivanich Koznyshev.'

'Very pleased ...' said the old official.

'I have the honour of knowing your brother,' said Grinevich, holding out his narrow hand with the long fingernails.

Levin frowned, shook hands coldly, and immediately turned to Oblonsky. Though Levin had great respect for his half-brother, an author known throughout Russia, he hated to be regarded not as Constantine Levin but as a brother of the famous Koznyshev.

'No, I am no longer on the Zemstvo—I have quarrelled with the lot of them, and don't attend their meetings any more,' said he.

'Quick work!' said Oblonsky, smiling. 'What was it all about?'

'To put it in a nutshell, I have come to the conclusion that there is and can be, no such thing as Zemstvo work,' he said, speaking as if some one had just offended him. 'On the one hand they play at being a parliament, and I am neither young enough nor old enough to amuse myself with toys. On the other hand ...' he hesitated, 'it is a means of getting unearned salaries!' he went on as warmly as if he had just been contradicted.

'Aha! I see you've reached another new phase—a Conservative one this time!' said Oblonsky. 'However, we'll talk about that later.'

'Yes, later! ... But it is very, very important for me to have a talk with you. ... However, it's nothing particular,' said Levin, and his face became almost vicious in his efforts to overcome his shyness.

'What are the Shcherbatskys doing? All going on as usual?'

Oblonsky smiled very slightly and his eyes sparkled merrily.

'Excuse me a moment ...'

The Secretary came in, approached Oblonsky with some papers, and began to explain some difficulty. Oblonsky, without hearing him to the end, put his hand in a kindly way on the Secretary's sleeve and, softening his remark with a smile, said:

'No; please do it as I said,' and, having in a few words explained his view of the matter, he pushed the paper away.

The Secretary went out, abashed. Levin, who during Oblonsky's talk with the Secretary had quite overcome his shyness, stood leaning both arms on the back of a chair and listening with ironical attention.

'I don't understand it at all!' he remarked, shrugging his shoulders. 'How can you do it seriously?'

'Why not?'

'Because there's nothing to do!'

'That's how it seems to you, but we're overwhelmed with work.'

'—On paper! But all the same I admire your dignity and am proud that my friend is such a great man! But all the same you've not answered my question,' he added, making a desperate effort to look Oblonsky straight in the face.

'All right! All right! About what you were asking: nothing has changed, but it's a pity you've stopped away so long.'

'Why?' asked Levin in alarm.

'Oh, nothing—' answered Oblonsky. 'We'll talk it over later on. Let's see,—if you want to meet them, you'll be sure to find them in the Zoological Gardens from four to five. Kitty skates there. Go there, and I'll call for you and we'll dine somewhere together.'

'Splendid! Well then, *au revoir!*' said Levin and left the room, only recollecting when already at the door that he had not taken leave of Oblonsky's colleagues.

6

The Levins and the Shcherbatskys, two old aristocratic Moscow families, had always been on intimate and friendly terms. Their ties were drawn still closer during Levin's University days. He had prepared for and entered the University together with young Prince Shcherbatsky, Dolly's and Kitty's brother. At that time Levin often visited the Shcherbatskys, and fell in love with the whole family—especially the feminine half of it. He could not remember his mother, and his sister was much his senior, so that in the Shcherbatskys' house he saw for the first time the family life of a well-educated and honourable family of the old aristocracy—a life such as he had been deprived of by the death of his own father and mother.

In his student days he very nearly fell in love with the eldest daughter, Dolly; but a marriage was soon after arranged between her and Oblonsky. Then he began falling in love with the second daughter. But Nataly married the diplomat, Lvov. Kitty was still a child when Levin finished at the University. Young Shcherbatsky who entered the navy was drowned in the Baltic; and after that, in spite of his friendship with Oblonsky, Levin's intercourse with the Shcherbatskys became less frequent. But when he had come to Moscow early in the winter of this year and met them, he knew at last which of the three sisters he was really fated to love.

It would seem that nothing could be simpler than for him, a man of good family, rich rather than poor, and thirty-two years of age, to propose to the Princess Shcherbatskaya. But having spent two months in Moscow, living as in a fog, meeting Kitty almost every day in Society which he began to frequent in order to meet her, he suddenly made up his mind that it was impossible, and returned to the country.

Levin's conviction that it was impossible rested on the idea that from her relatives' point of view he was not a good or suitable match for the delightful Kitty, and that Kitty herself could not love him. From her parents' standpoint (it seemed to him) he had no settled occupation or position in the world. He was merely a country squire, spending his time breeding cows, shooting snipe, and erecting buildings—that is to say, a fellow without talent. Of course the mysterious, enchanting Kitty could not love a plain fellow, such as he considered himself to be, a man so ordinary and undistinguished. He thought a plain kindly fellow like himself might be loved as a friend, but to be loved with the kind of love he felt for Kitty, a man must be handsome, and above all remarkable.

But after spending two months alone in the country, he became convinced that he could not live unless the question whether she was to be his wife or not were decided; also that his despair had been the outcome of his own fancy, and that he had no proof that he would be rejected. So he had now come to Moscow determined to propose to her, and dared not think what would happen if she refused him.

7

Having reached Moscow by a morning train, Levin went to stay at the house of his half-brother Koznyshev, who was older than he, and after changing his clothes entered his brother's study, intending to tell him why he had come and to ask his advice. But his brother was not alone. A well-known professor of philosophy was with him, who had come specially from Kharkov to settle a dispute that had arisen between them on an important philosophical question: whether a definite line exists between psychological and physiological phenomena in human activity; and if so, where it lies?

When Levin entered, Sergius Ivanich greeted him with the coldly affable smile he bestowed on everybody and, having introduced him to the professor, went on with the discussion.

When the professor had gone, Koznyshev turned to his half-brother.

'I am very glad you have come. Are you here for long? How do you get on with your farming?'

Levin knew that farming did not interest his brother and that the question was merely a concession; therefore he replied generally as to the sale of wheat and money matters. He wanted to tell his brother of his intended marriage and to ask his advice. He had even firmly made up his mind to do so, but when he noticed the patronizing tone in which he asked him about the business of their estate (this estate which they had jointly inherited from their mother had not been divided, and Levin was managing the whole of it), he felt that his brother would not look at the matter as he wished him to.

'Well, and how is your Zemstvo getting on?' asked Koznyshev, who took a keen interest in the rural administration.

'I really don't know. I resigned,' answered Levin, 'and don't attend the Meetings any more.'

'That's a pity!' said Koznyshev, and frowned. 'Do you know that Nicholas is here again?'

Nicholas was Constantine Levin's elder brother, and Koznyshev's half-brother. He was a ruined man who had squandered the greater part of his fortune, mixed with the strangest and worst society, and quarrelled with his brothers.

'How do you know?' cried Levin, horror-struck.

'Prokofy met him in the street.'

'Here, in Moscow? Where is he? Do you know?' Levin rose from his chair as if meaning to go at once.

'I am sorry I told you,' said Koznyshev. 'I sent to find out where he is living, and this is the answer I received.'

Koznyshev took a note from under a paper-weight and handed it to his brother.

'I humbly beg you to leave me alone. That is all I demand of my dear brothers.—NICHOLAS LEVIN.'

When Levin had read the note, a struggle was going on within him between the desire to forget his unfortunate brother for the present, and the consciousness that this would be wrong.

'He evidently wants to offend me,' continued Koznyshev, 'but he cannot do that. I wish with all my heart I could help him, but I know it can't be done.'

'Yes, yes,' said Levin, 'I understand, and appreciate your attitude toward him; but personally I shall go to see him.'

'Go if you like, but I don't advise it,' said Koznyshev. 'It's impossible to help him. However, do as you please!'

'It may be impossible to help him, but I feel—especially at this moment ... but that's a different matter—I feel that I cannot be at peace ...'

'Well, I don't understand that,' said Koznyshev. 'But what I do understand is a lesson in humility. I have begun to look differently, more leniently, at what is called rascality, since brother Nicholas became what he is. Do you know what he has done?'

'Ah, it's dreadful, dreadful!' Levin repeated.

Having got the address from Koznyshev's footman Levin thought of going at once to see his brother; but, on reflection, decided to put off the visit till the evening. To obtain peace of mind it was necessary first of all to decide the business that had brought him to Moscow. He therefore went to Oblonsky's office, and having received news of the Shcherbatskys he drove to the place where he was told he could see Kitty.

8

At four o'clock that afternoon Levin, conscious that his heart was beating rapidly, got out of the hired sledge at the Zoological Gardens and went down the path leading to the ice-hills and skating lake, sure of finding Kitty there, for he had noticed the Shcherbatskys' carriage at the entrance.

It was a clear frosty day. Carriages, private sledges, sledges for hire, and mounted police stood at the entrance. He walked along the path leading to the skating lake, and kept repeating to himself: 'I must not be excited. I must be quiet!' But the more he tried to be calm, the more laboured grew his breath. An acquaintance called to him, but Levin did not even notice who it was. A few more steps brought him to the skating lake, and among all the skaters he at once recognized her. He knew she was there by the joy and terror that took possession of his heart. She stood talking to a lady at the other end of the lake, as easy for Levin to recognize in that crowd as to find a rose among nettles. Everything was lit up by her. She was the smile that brightened everything around.

'Can I really step down on to the ice, and go up to her?' he thought. The spot where she stood seemed to him an unapproachable sanctuary, and there was a moment when he nearly went away, he was so filled with awe. He had to make an effort and reason with himself that all sorts of people were passing near her and he himself might have come just to skate.

On that day of the week and at that hour, people belonging to the same set and acquainted with one another, met on the ice. Nicholas

Shcherbatsky, Kitty's cousin, in a short jacket, tight trousers, with skates on his feet, was sitting on a bench, and seeing Levin, called out to him.

'Hullo, you Russian champion skater! When did you come? The ice is splendid—put on your skates!'

'I haven't any skates,' answered Levin, wondering at such boldness and freedom of manner in her presence, and not losing sight of her for a moment although not looking at her. He felt the sun approaching him. She was turning a corner, her little feet, shod in high boots, kept close together, and she was skating timidly toward him. She glided straight up to Shcherbatsky, and catching hold of him with her hand, nodded smilingly to Levin. She was more beautiful than he had imagined her.

When he thought about her he could vividly picture to himself her entire person, and especially the charm of her small, fair-haired head, so lightly poised on the shapely girlish shoulders, and the childlike brightness and kindness of her face. But what always struck him afresh as unexpected was the expression of her eyes—mild, calm, and truthful,—and above all her smile, which filled him with tenderness.

'Have you been here long?' she said, shaking hands with him.

'I? No, not long—since yesterday ... I mean to-day ...' replied Levin, in his excitement not quite taking in her question. 'I wanted to come and see you,' he went on, and then, remembering the reason why he wanted to see her he became abashed, and blushed. 'I did not know that you skated, and so well.'

She looked at him as if wishing to understand his confusion.

'*Your* praise is valuable. There is a tradition here that you are the best skater,' she said.

'Yes, I used to be passionately fond of skating. I wanted to be perfect at it.'

'You seem to do everything passionately,' she remarked with a smile. 'I should so like to see you skate. Put on a pair and let us skate together.'

'Skate together! Can it be possible?' thought Levin looking at her.

'I'll go and put them on at once,' he said, and went to hire some skates.

'You've not looked us up for a long time, sir,' said one of the attendants as, holding up Levin's foot, he bored a hole in the heel of his boot. 'Since you left we have had no gentleman who is such a master at it as you! Is that right?' he added, pulling the strap tight.

'Yes, that's right, that's right! Please be quick!' answered Levin, trying to restrain the happy smile which appeared on his face. 'Yes,' he thought, 'this is life—this is joy! She said, "*Together: let us skate together*"! Shall I tell her now? But that's just why I'm afraid of speaking. Now I am happy, if only in my hopes—but then? ... But I must ... I must ... I must ...! Away with this weakness!'

He stood up, took off his overcoat, and having given himself a start on the rough ice near the shelter, glided down to the smooth surface of the lake, increasing and diminishing his speed and shaping his course as if by volition only. He approached Kitty timidly, but her smile again tranquillized him.

She gave him her hand and they went on together, increasing their speed, and the faster they went the closer she pressed his hands.

'I should learn quicker with you; for some reason I feel confidence in you,' she said.

'And I am confident of myself when you lean on me,' he answered, and was immediately frightened of what he had said, and blushed. And in fact, as soon as he had uttered these words her face lost its kind expression: a wrinkle appeared on her smooth forehead.

'Has anything unpleasant happened ...? But I have no right to ask,' he said hurriedly.

'Why? ... No, nothing unpleasant has happened,' she answered, but he thought there was an intentionally quiet manner in her affability and he felt sad.

'Have you come for long?' asked Kitty.

'I don't know,' he answered, without thinking of what he was saying. 'It all depends on you,' he said, and was at once terrified at his own words.

Whether she had not heard his words or did not wish to hear them, anyhow, after slightly stumbling and striking her foot twice against the ice, she skated hurriedly away from him toward the little house where the ladies took off their skates.

'My God! What have I done? O Lord, help me and teach me!' prayed Levin, and feeling at the same time a need of violent exercise, he got up speed and described inner and outer circles.

Just then a young man, the best of the new skaters, came out of the coffee-room and taking a run, descended the steps leading to the lake, clattering with his skates as he jumped from step to step. He then flew down the slope and glided along the ice without so much as changing the easy position of his arms.

'Oh, that's a new trick!' said Levin, and at once ran up to try it.

Levin went up the path as far back as he could to get up speed, and then slid downwards, balancing himself with his arms in this unaccustomed movement. He caught his foot on the last step, but, scarcely touching the ice with his hand, made a violent effort, regained his balance, and skated away laughing.

'Good! Dear man!' thought Kitty who was just coming out of the little house, looking at him with a smile of gentle tenderness. 'Can I really be guilty—have I really done anything wrong? I know it's not him I love, but still I feel happy with him, he is so charming! Only why did he say that?' she thought.

When he saw Kitty who was going away, and her mother who had met her on the steps, Levin, flushed with the violent exercise, stood still and considered. He then took off his skates and overtook mother and daughter at the gates of the Gardens.

'Very pleased to see you,' said the Princess. 'We are at home on Thursdays, as usual.'

'And to-day is Thursday!'

'We shall be glad to see you,' said the Princess drily.

Kitty was sorry to hear that dry tone and could not resist the desire to counteract her mother's coldness. She turned her head and said smilingly: '*Au revoir!*'

Just then Oblonsky, his hat tilted on one side, with radiant face and eyes, walked into the Gardens like a joyous conqueror. But on approaching his mother-in-law he answered her questions about Dolly's health with a sorrowful and guilty air. After a few words with her in a subdued and mournful tone, he took Levin's arm.

'Well, shall we go?' he asked. 'I kept thinking about you, and am very, very glad you've come,' he went on, looking significantly into Levin's eyes.

'Yes, yes! Let's go,' answered the happy Levin, still hearing the voice saying: '*Au revoir!*' and still seeing the smile with which it had been said.

'The Angleterre, or the Hermitage?'

'I don't care.'

'Well then, the Angleterre,' said Oblonsky, choosing the Angleterre because he was deeper in debt to that restaurant than to the Hermitage, and therefore considered it wrong to avoid it. 'Have you a sledge? … That's a good thing, because I've sent my coachman home.'

9

When they entered the restaurant Oblonsky took off his overcoat, and with his hat on one side walked into the dining-room, giving his orders to the Tartar waiters, in their swallow-tail coats, with napkins under their arms, who attached themselves to him.

'This way, please, your Excellency! This way—no one will disturb your Excellency here,' said a specially officious waiter.

'If you please, your Excellency,' he said, turning to Levin. In a moment he had spread a fresh cloth on a round table and stood with a napkin and menu awaiting the order.

'We've some fresh oysters in, sir.'

'Ah—oysters!' Oblonsky paused and considered. 'But are the oysters really fresh?'

'They only arrived yesterday.'

'Well then, shall we begin with oysters, eh?'

'I don't mind. Whatever you choose will suit me, I've been skating and I shall be glad of a good dinner.'

'I should think so! Say what you like, it is one of the pleasures of life!' said Oblonsky. 'Well then, my good fellow, bring us two—or that will be too little, ... three dozen oysters, and vegetable soup. ... Then turbot with thick sauce; then ... roast beef (and mind it's good!); and then capon, shall we say? Yes, and stewed fruit.'

The waiter, as if moved by springs, put down the bill of fare in one cardboard cover, and seizing another containing the wine-list held it out to Oblonsky.

'What shall we have to drink?'

'Whatever you like ... Champagne!' said Levin.

'What, to begin with? Why not? The white seal. Yes, bring us that with the oysters, and then we'll see.'

The Tartar darted off, his coat-tails flying; and five minutes later rushed in again, with a dish of opened oysters in pearly shells and a bottle between his fingers.

Levin could eat oysters, though he preferred bread and cheese. But it gave him more pleasure to watch Oblonsky. Even the Tartar, who having drawn the cork and poured the sparkling wine into the thin wide glasses was straightening his white tie, glanced with a smile of evident pleasure at Oblonsky.

'You don't care much for oysters?' said Oblonsky, emptying his glass—'or perhaps you're thinking of something else. Eh?'

'I? Yes, I am preoccupied—and besides, you can't imagine how strange it all seems to me who lives in the country—while we try to get over our meals as quickly as we can, so as to be able to get on with our work, here you and I try to make our meal last as long as possible, and therefore eat oysters.'

'Well, of course,' said Oblonsky. 'The aim of civilization is to enable us to get enjoyment out of everything.'

'Well, if that is its aim, I'd rather be a savage.'

'You are a savage as it is. All you Levins are savages.'

Levin sighed. He remembered his brother Nicholas and frowned, feeling ashamed and distressed; but Oblonsky started a subject which at once distracted his thoughts.

'Well, are you going to see our people to-night? The Shcherbatskys, I mean,' he said, pushing away the rough and now empty oyster shells while his eyes glittered significantly.

'Yes, certainly I shall go. Though the Princess appeared to ask me rather unwillingly.'

'Not a bit of it! What humbug! It's just her manner. … Come, bring us that soup, my good fellow! … It's her *grande dame* manner,' said Oblonsky. 'What a strange fellow you are, though! How do you explain your sudden departure from Moscow? The Shcherbatskys asked me again and again. Yet all I know is that you never do things as anyone else does!'

'Yes,' said Levin slowly and with agitation. 'You are right, I am a savage. Only my savagery lies not in having gone away then, but rather in having come back now.'

'Well, and why have you come to Moscow? …'

'Don't you guess?' answered Levin, the light shining deep in his eyes as he gazed steadily at Oblonsky.

'I do, but *I* can't begin to speak about it,—by which you can judge whether my guess is right or wrong,' said Oblonsky, looking at him with a subtle smile.

'Well, and what do you say to it?' asked Levin with a trembling voice, feeling that all the muscles of his face were quivering.

Oblonsky fixed his eyes on Levin.

'There is nothing I should like better,' said he, 'nothing! It is the best that could happen.'

'But suppose a refusal is in store for me?'

'Why do you think so?' said Oblonsky, smiling at Levin's excitement. 'Every girl is proud of an offer.'

'Yes, *every* girl, but not she.'

Oblonsky smiled. He knew that for Levin all the girls in the world were divided into two classes: one class included all the girls in the world except her, and they had all the usual human failings and were very ordinary girls; while the other class—herself alone—had no weaknesses and was superior to all humanity.

Levin said, 'Understand that for me it is a question of life and death. I have never spoken to any one about it, and can speak to no one else about it. Now you and I are quite different in everything but I know you like me and understand me, and so I am awfully fond of you. But for God's sake be quite frank with me!'

'I am telling you what I think,' said Oblonsky smiling. 'And I'll tell you something more. My wife is a most wonderful woman ...' He sighed, remembering his relations with his wife; then after a minute's pause he continued: 'And she is—on your side.'

'How do you know?'

'In this way—she not only likes you, but says that Kitty is sure to be your wife.'

At these words a sudden smile brightened Levin's face, the kind of smile that is not far from tears of tenderness.

'She says that?' he cried. 'I have always thought her a jewel, your wife! But enough—enough about it!' and he got up.

'All right, but sit down!'

But Levin could not sit still.

'Try and realize,' he said, 'that this is not love. I have been in love but this is not the same thing. It is not my feeling but some external power that has seized me. I went away, you know, because I had come to the conclusion that it was impossible—you understand? Because such happiness does not exist on earth. But I have struggled with myself, and found that without that there's no life for me. And it must be decided ...'

'Then why did you go away?'

'Wait a moment! Oh, what a crowd of ideas! How many things I have to ask! Listen. You can't imagine what you have done for me by saying what you did! But there is one awful thing about it. You who are married, know the feeling ... it is awful that we—who are comparatively old and have pasts ... not of love but of sin ... suddenly we come into close intimacy with a pure innocent being! And therefore one can't help feeling oneself unworthy.'

'Well, there haven't been many sins in your past!'

'Ah, but all the same,' said Levin, 'looking back at my life, I bitterly regret. ... Yes! My one consolation is that prayer that I like so much: "Not according to my deserts but according to Thy mercy!" And she too can only forgive me that way.'

Levin emptied his glass and they were silent for a while.

'There is one thing more that I must tell you,' began Oblonsky. 'You know Vronsky?'

'No, I don't. Why do you ask?'

'Vronsky is one of your rivals. He is one of Count Ivanovich Vronsky's sons, and a very fine sample of the gilded youth of Petersburg. Awfully rich, handsome, with influential connections, an aide-de-camp to the Emperor, and at the same time very good-natured—a first-rate fellow. As I have got to know him, he turns out to be both educated and very clever—a man who will go far.'

Levin frowned and was silent.

'Well, so he came here soon after you left, and as far as I can make out is in love with Kitty; and you understand that her mother ...'

'Pardon me, but I understand nothing,' said Levin dismally.

'You just wait a bit, wait!' said Oblonsky, smiling and touching Levin's arm. 'I have told you what I know, and I repeat that, as far as anyone can judge in so delicate and subtle a matter, I believe the chances are all on your side.'

Levin leant back in his chair. His face was pale.

'But I should advise you to settle the question as soon as possible,' Oblonsky continued, filling Levin's glass.

'No, thanks! I can't drink any more,' said Levin pushing his glass aside, 'or I shall be tipsy. ... Well, and how are you getting on?' he continued, evidently wishing to change the subject.

'One word more! I advise you to decide the question quickly, but I shouldn't speak to-day,' said Oblonsky. 'Go to-morrow morning and propose in the classic manner, and may heaven bless you!'

'You have so often promised to come and shoot with me—why not come this spring?' said Levin.

He now repented with his whole heart of having begun this conversation with Oblonsky. His personal feelings had been desecrated by the mention of some Petersburg officer as his rival, and by Oblonsky's conjectures and advice.

Oblonsky smiled.

'I'll come some day,' he said. 'Ah, old chap, women are the pivot on which everything turns! Things are in a bad way with me too, very bad and all on account of women. Tell me quite frankly ...'

He took out a cigar, and with one hand on his glass he continued:

'Supposing you were married and loved your wife, but had been fascinated by another woman ...'

'Excuse me, but really ... it's quite incomprehensible to me. It's as if I, after eating my fill here, went into a baker's shop and stole a roll.'

Oblonsky's eyes glittered more than usual.

'Why not? Rolls sometimes smell so that one can't resist them!' he said with a subtle smile and Levin himself could not help smiling.

'Tell me, what am I to do? My wife is getting old, and I am full of vitality. A man hardly has time to turn round, before he feels that he can no longer love his wife in that way, whatever his regard for her may be. And then all of a sudden love crosses your path, and you're lost, lost!' said Oblonsky with despair. 'But what am I to do?'

Levin smiled.

'Don't steal rolls.'

Oblonsky burst out laughing.

'Oh, you moralist! But just consider, here are two women: one insists only on her rights, and her rights are your love, which you cannot give her; and the other sacrifices herself and demands nothing. What are you to do? How are you to act? It is a terrible tragedy.'

'If you want me to say what I think of it, I can only tell you that I don't believe in the tragedy.' Here Levin recollecting his own sins and the inner struggle he had lived through added unexpectedly, 'However, maybe you are right. It may very well be. But I don't know, I really don't know.'

'Well, you see *you* are very consistent,' said Oblonsky. 'It is both a virtue and a fault in you. You have a consistent character yourself and you wish all the facts of life to be consistent, but they never are. For instance you want the activity of each separate man to have an aim, and love and family life always to coincide—and that doesn't happen. All the variety, charm, and beauty of life are made up of light and shade.'

Levin sighed and did not answer. He was thinking of his own affairs and not listening to Oblonsky.

10

Princess Kitty Shcherbatskaya was eighteen, and this was her first season. Her success in Society was greater than that of her two elder sisters, and greater even than her mother had expected. Two serious suitors presented themselves for her that very first winter: Levin and, immediately after his departure, Count Vronsky.

Levin's arrival at the beginning of the winter, his frequent visits and evident love for Kitty gave rise to disputes between her parents. The Prince took Levin's part and said he desired nothing better for Kitty. The Princess with a woman's way of talking round the question said that Kitty was too young; but she did not say the most important things, namely that she expected a better match for her daughter, that she did not like Levin and did not understand him. When he suddenly left, the Princess was pleased. When Vronsky appeared she was still more pleased and was strengthened in her opinion that Kitty ought to make a brilliant match.

In the mother's eyes there was no comparison between Levin and Vronsky. She did not like Levin's awkward manner in Society which she attributed to pride, and what she considered his strange way of life in the country; in particular she did not like the fact that when he was in love with her daughter he came to the house for six weeks and did not understand that, if he visited at a house where there was a marriage-able girl, he ought to declare his intentions. And then suddenly he left without proposing!

Vronsky satisfied all the mother's desires: he was very rich, clever, distinguished, with a brilliant military career before him, a position at Court, and altogether was an enchanting man. Nothing better could be desired.

Vronsky was openly attentive to Kitty when they met at balls, danced with her, and came to the house, so there could be no doubt as to the seriousness of his intentions. But in spite of this the mother was in a dreadful state of anxiety and agitation all that winter.

And now she was afraid that Vronsky might content himself with merely flirting with her daughter. She saw that Kitty was in love with him, but consoled herself with the thought that Vronsky was an honest man and therefore would not act in such a way. At the same time she knew how lightly men regarded an offence of that kind. The week before, Kitty had repeated to her mother a conversation she had had with Vronsky while dancing the mazurka with him. This conversation had partly reassured the Princess; but she could not feel quite at ease. Vronsky had told Kitty that he and his brother were so used to comply with their mother's wishes that they never made up their minds to take an important step without consulting her. 'And I am now especially happy looking forward to my mother's arrival from Petersburg,' he had said.

Kitty had narrated this without attaching any special meaning to the words. But to her mother they appeared in a different light. She knew that the old lady was expected any day, and would approve of her son's choice; and though she thought it strange that he should delay propos-ing for fear of hurting his mother, she so desired the marriage, and especially relief from her own anxiety, that she believed it.

Hard as it was to see the misfortune of Dolly, her eldest daughter (who thought of leaving her husband), the Princess's anxiety as to her youngest daughter's fate, now about to be decided, entirely absorbed her. Levin's arrival that day gave her further cause for anxiety. She was afraid that her daughter who had once seemed to have a certain affection for Levin might be led by an exaggerated feeling of loyalty to reject Vronsky, and she feared that in general Levin's arrival might cause complications and delays in matters now so near conclusion.

11

During the interval between dinner and the beginning of the evening party, Kitty could not fix her thoughts on anything.

She felt that this evening, when those two men were to meet for the first time, would decide her fate; and she kept picturing them to herself, now individually and now together. When she thought of the past, she dwelt with pleasure and tenderness on her former relations with Levin. Memories of childhood and of Levin's friendship with her dead brother lent a peculiar poetic charm to her relations with him. His love for her, of which she felt sure, flattered and rejoiced her, and she could think of him with a light heart. With her thought of Vronsky was mingled some uneasiness, though he was an extremely well-bred and quiet-mannered man; a sense of something false, not in him, for he was very simple and kindly, but in herself; whereas in relation to Levin she felt herself quite simple and clear. On the other hand when she pictured to herself a future with Vronsky a brilliant vision of happiness rose up before her, while a future with Levin appeared wrapped in mist.

At half-past seven, as soon as she had come down into the drawing-room, the footman announced 'Constantine Dmitrich Levin!' The Princess was still in her bedroom, nor had the Prince yet come down.

'So it's to be!' thought Kitty and the blood rushed to her heart.

She felt sure that he had come so early on purpose to see her alone and to propose to her. And now for the first time the matter presented itself to her in a different and entirely new light. Only now did she realize that in a moment she would have to wound a man she cared for, and to wound him cruelly. ...

'Oh God, must I tell him so myself?' she thought. 'Must I really tell him that I don't care for him? That would not be true. What then shall I say? Shall I say that I love another? No, that's impossible! I'll go away. Yes, I will.'

She was already approaching the door when she heard his step. 'No, it would be dishonest! What have I to fear? I have done nothing wrong. I'll tell the truth, come what may! Besides, it's impossible to feel awkward with him. Here he is!' she thought, as she saw his powerful diffident figure before her and his shining eyes gazing at her. She looked straight into his face as if entreating him to spare her, and gave him her hand.

'I don't think I've come at the right time, I'm too early,' he said gazing round the empty drawing-room. When he saw that his expectation was fulfilled and that nothing prevented his speaking to her, his face clouded over.

'Not at all,' said Kitty and sat down at the table.

'But all I wanted was to find you alone,' he began, still standing and avoiding her face so as not to lose courage.

He glanced at her; she blushed and was silent.

'I told you that I did not know how long I should stay ... that it depends on you.'

Her head dropped lower and lower, knowing the answer she would give to what was coming.

'That it would depend on you,' he repeated. 'I want to say ... I want to say ... I came on purpose ... that . .... to be my wife!' he uttered hardly knowing what he said; but feeling that the worst was out he stopped and looked at her.

She was breathing heavily and not looking at him. She was filled with rapture. Her soul was overflowing with happiness. She had not at all expected that his declaration of love would make so strong an impression on her. But that lasted only for an instant. She remembered Vronsky, lifted her clear, truthful eyes to Levin's face, and noticing his despair she replied quickly:

'It cannot be ... forgive me.'

How near to him she had been a minute ago, how important in his life! And how estranged and distant she seemed now!

'Nothing else was possible,' he said, without looking at her, and bowing he turned to go.

But just at that moment the Princess came in. An expression of terror appeared in her face on seeing them alone together and noticing their troubled looks. Levin bowed to her and said nothing. Kitty sat with downcast eyes.

'Thank heaven she has refused him,' thought the mother, and her face brightened into the usual smile with which she greeted her visitors on Thursday evenings. She sat down and began questioning Levin about his life in the country. He too sat down until the arrival of other guests should enable him to get away unnoticed.

Five minutes later Kitty's friend the Countess Nordston, who had married the year before, came in.

She was a thin, sallow, nervous, ailing woman with shining black eyes.

She was fond of Kitty, and she wished to see her married to Vronsky. She always disliked Levin, whom at the beginning of the winter she had often met at the Shcherbatskys.

The Countess at once attacked Levin.

'Ah, Mr. Levin! So you have returned to our depraved Babylon!' she said, holding out her tiny yellow hand and repeating the words he had used early in the winter when he had called Moscow 'Babylon,'—'Has Babylon improved or have you deteriorated?' she added, and turned toward Kitty with a sarcastic smile.

'I am much flattered that you remember my words so well, Countess,' replied Levin who had had time to recover his self-possession, resuming by force of habit his banteringly hostile relation with her. 'They evidently produced a strong impression on you.'

'Why, of course, I always write them down. Well, Kitty, have you been skating again?'

She began to talk with Kitty. Awkward as it would have been for Levin to leave just then, he would have preferred doing so to remaining in the house for the rest of the evening in sight of Kitty, who now and then glanced at him but avoided catching his eye. Another lady entered the room and Levin rose and as he turned he saw an officer who had come into the room behind the lady.

'That must be Vronsky,' he thought, and looked at Kitty to make sure. She had already glanced at Vronsky and then turned toward Levin. And by the look of her eyes which had involuntarily brightened Levin realized that she loved this man, realized it as surely as if she had told it him in so many words.

It was not difficult to see what was good and attractive in Vronsky: a dark sturdily-built man of medium height, with a good-natured, handsome, exceedingly quiet and firm face. Everything about his face and figure—from his black closely-cropped hair and freshly-shaven chin to his wide, brand-new uniform—was simple and at the same time elegant. Having stepped aside to let a lady pass, Vronsky approached first the Princess and then Kitty. When he moved toward her his fine eyes brightened with a special tenderness, and carefully and respectfully bending over her with a scarcely-perceptible, happy, and (as it seemed to Levin) modestly-triumphant smile, he held out to her his hand.

Having greeted and spoken a few words to every one else, he sat down without having once looked at Levin, who had not taken his eyes off him.

'Let me introduce you,' said the Princess indicating Levin. 'Constantine Dmitrich Levin, Count Alexis Kirilovich Vronsky.'

Vronsky rose and looking cordially into Levin's eyes pressed his hand.

'I was to have dined with you earlier this winter,' he said with his simple frank smile, 'but you unexpectedly went away to the country.'

'Mr. Levin despises and hates the town and us townspeople,' said Countess Nordston.

Vronsky glanced at him and at the Countess, and smiled.

'And do you always live in the country?' he asked. 'Isn't it dull in the winter?'

'No, not when one is busy: nor need one be dull in one's own company,' replied Levin abruptly.

'I am fond of the country,' said Vronsky, noticing, but pretending not to notice, Levin's tone.

'But I hope, Count, you would not consent always to live in the country,' said the Countess Nordston.

'I don't know, I never tried it for long. I have experienced a curious feeling,' he went on. 'Nowhere have I felt so homesick for the country, our Russian country, as when I spent a winter with my mother in Nice ...'

He was addressing both Kitty and Levin, his quiet and friendly glance passing from the one to the other. He was evidently speaking quite sincerely and frankly. Noticing that the Countess Nordston wished to say something, he stopped without finishing what he was saying, and listened attentively to her.

The conversation did not flag for a moment, so that Countess Nordston had no opportunity to tease Levin.

Levin wished to join in the general conversation, but found it impossible.

Just as he was about to go, the old Prince came in, and having greeted the ladies he turned to Levin.

'Ah!' said he heartily. 'Been here long? I did not even know that you had arrived; very glad to see you.'

He embraced Levin, and speaking to him did not catch sight of Vronsky who rose and stood quietly waiting until the Prince should notice him.

Kitty was conscious that, after what had taken place, her father's cordiality oppressed Levin. She also noticed how coldly her father at last responded to Vronsky's bow, and she blushed.

Vronsky began talking to the Countess Nordston about the ball that was to take place the next week.

'I hope you will be there,' he said to Kitty.

As soon as the old Prince had turned away from him Levin went out unobserved, and his last impression was Kitty's happy smiling face as she answered Vronsky's question about the ball.

12

After the guests had gone Kitty told her mother of her conversation with Levin, and in spite of all her pity for him she was pleased by the thought that she had had a proposal. She did not doubt that she had acted rightly, yet for a long time she lay in bed unable to sleep. One image pursued her relentlessly. It was Levin's face with his kind eyes looking mournfully from under his knit brows as he stood listening to her father and glancing at her and at Vronsky, and she felt so sorry for him that tears rose to her eyes. But she immediately remembered for whom she had exchanged him. She vividly pictured to herself that strong manly face, that well-bred calm and the kindness toward everybody he always showed: she remembered the love the man she loved bore her, and again became joyful and with a happy smile put her head on her pillow. 'It is a pity, a pity, but I am not to blame,' she said to herself, but an inner voice said something different and her happiness was troubled by doubts.

'Lord have mercy, Lord have mercy, Lord have mercy,' she repeated to herself till she fell asleep.

Meanwhile below in the Prince's little study her parents were having one of their frequent scenes about their favourite daughter.

'What? I'll tell you what!' shouted the Prince. 'You have no pride, no dignity, you disgrace and ruin your daughter by this vile idiotic match-making.'

'For goodness' sake, Prince, what in heaven's own name have I done?' said the Princess almost in tears.

After her talk with her daughter she had come in, happy and contented, to say good-night to the Prince as usual, and though she did not intend to speak to him about Levin's proposal and Kitty's refusal she hinted to him that she thought the matter with Vronsky was quite settled and would probably be definitely decided as soon as his mother arrived. And when she said that, the Prince suddenly flared up and began to shout rudely: 'What have you done? Why this: first of all you *entice* a suitor. All Moscow will talk about it and with reason. If you give a party invite everybody and not only selected suitors. Have a pianist and let them dance; but don't have the sort of thing we had to-night—these suitors and this pairing off. It makes me sick to see it, simply sick, and you have had your way and have turned the child's head. Levin is a thousand times the better man.'

'I know this much,' the Princess interrupted him, 'that if I were to listen to what you say we should never see our daughter married, and we had better go and live in the country.'

'So we had!'

'Wait a bit! Do I draw them on? No, certainly not, but an excellent young man falls in love with Kitty, and she too seems …'

'Seems indeed! And suppose she really falls in love with him while he intends to marry about as much as I do. … Oh, I wish my eyes had never seen it. …'

'But why do you suppose such a thing?'

'I don't suppose, I know! I can recognize a man who has serious intentions—such as Levin—and I can see through a weathercock like that popinjay who only wishes to amuse himself.'

'Oh well, when you once get a thing into your head …'

'And you'll find it out, but too late, just as with poor Dolly.'

'All right. All right, don't let's talk,' said the Princess, interrupting him and remembering the unfortunate Dolly.

'Very well then, good-night.'

And having made the sign of the cross over one another and kissed, feeling that each of them retained their individual opinions, the couple separated for the night.

The Princess had been firmly convinced that there could be no doubt as to Vronsky's intentions; but her husband's words disturbed her, and when she reached her room, in terror of the uncertainty of the future, she mentally repeated, just as Kitty had done: 'Lord have mercy, Lord have mercy, Lord have mercy!'

13

Vronsky had never known family life. His mother in her youth had been a brilliant Society woman, and during her married life and especially in her widowhood had had many love affairs, known to everybody. He hardly remembered his father, and had been educated in the Cadet Corps.

On leaving that Corps as a very young and brilliant officer he at once joined the swim of the wealthy military Petersburg set. Though he occasionally went into the highest Petersburg Society, all his love interests lay outside it.

In Moscow, he experienced for the first time the delight of intimacy with a sweet, innocent Society girl who fell in love with him. It never entered his head that there could be any wrong in his relations with Kitty. At balls he danced chiefly with her and he visited her at her home. Though he never said anything to her which could not have been said before everybody he was conscious that she was becoming more and more dependent upon him, and the more he felt this the pleasanter it was, and the more tender became his feelings toward her. He did not know that his behaviour toward Kitty had a name of its own, that it was decoying a girl with no intentions of marrying her, and is one of the evil actions common among brilliant young men like himself.

If he could have heard what her parents said that night, if he could have known her family's point of view and learnt that Kitty would be unhappy if he did not marry her, he would have been much surprised and would not have believed it. Even less could he have believed that he ought to marry.

Marriage had never presented itself to him as a possibility. Not only did he dislike family life, but in accordance with the views generally held in the bachelor world in which he lived he regarded the family, and especially a husband, as something alien, hostile, and above all ridiculous. But although Vronsky had no suspicion of what Kitty's parents were saying, he felt, as he left the Shcherbatskys' house that night, that the secret spiritual bond which existed between him and Kitty had so strengthened during the evening that some action ought to be taken. But what this should or could be he could not imagine.

'That's what is so delightful,' he thought as he left the Shcherbatskys' house, carrying away from there, as usual, a pleasant feeling of purity and freshness (partly due to the fact that he had not smoked at all that evening) and deeply touched by a new sense of tender joy in the consciousness of her love for him. 'That is what is so delightful, that nothing was said either by me or by her, yet we so well understand one another in that subtle language of looks and tones that to-day more plainly than ever she has told me that she loves me. And how sweetly, simply, and above all trustfully! I feel myself better and purer, I feel I have a heart and that there is much that is good in me. Those dear loving eyes! when she said, "and very much".'

'Well, and what of it? Nothing, of course. It's pleasant for me and for her,' and he considered where he should finish his evening.

At eleven o'clock next morning Vronsky drove to the Petersburg railway station in Moscow to meet his mother, and the first person he saw on the steps of the large portico was Oblonsky, who was expecting his sister by the same train.

'Hallo, your Excellency!' exclaimed Oblonsky. 'Whom are you after?'

'My mother,' replied Vronsky, shaking hands and smiling as they went up the steps together. 'She is coming from Petersburg to-day. And whom have you come to meet?' he asked.

'I? A lovely woman,' answered Oblonsky. 'My sister Anna!'

'Oh! Mrs. Karenina!' said Vronsky.

'I expect you know her?'

'I think I do. But perhaps not. ... I really can't remember,' answered Vronsky absent-mindedly.

'But you are sure to know Alexis Alexandrovich Karenin.'

'Yes, I know him by repute and by sight. I know he is clever, learned, and by way of being religious, but you know it is not my ... *not in my line*,' he added in English.

'Oh yes, he is a very remarkable man, a bit conservative, but a splendid fellow,' said Oblonsky, 'a splendid fellow.'

'Well, so much the better for him,' and Vronsky smiled. 'Ah, you are here!' he went on, turning toward his mother's old footman who was standing by the door. 'Come in here.'

Besides liking Oblonsky, as everybody did, Vronsky latterly had felt still more drawn to him because he was connected in his mind with Kitty.

'Well, are we to give a supper to the diva next Sunday?' he asked smilingly, taking Oblonsky's arm.

'Certainly, I will collect subscriptions. I say, did you make the acquaintance of my friend Levin last night?' asked Oblonsky.

'Of course. Only he left very early.'

'Levin is sometimes very charming. His is such an honest, straightforward nature, and he has a heart of gold. But yesterday there were special reasons,' continued Oblonsky with a significant smile, quite forgetting the sincere sympathy he had felt for his friend the day before, 'why he had to be either specially happy or specially unhappy.'

Vronsky stopped and asked him straight out: 'What do you mean? Did he propose to your *belle sœur* last night?'

'Perhaps,' said Oblonsky. 'I seemed to noticed something of the kind yesterday. Oh yes, if he left early it must be that. ... He has been in love with her so long, and I am very sorry for him.'

'Dear me! ... But I should think she may make a better match,' said Vronsky, and again moved forward. 'However, I don't know him,' he added. 'Yes, it is a painful position! But here's the train.'

A few moments later the platform shook as the train puffed in; the steam spread low in the frozen air, the connecting rods slowly and rhythmically pushed and pulled. The engine with the tender behind it moved slowly into the station, gradually slowing down and making the platform tremble still more.

The sprightly guard blew his whistle and jumped off while the train was still moving, and impatient passengers began to descend one after another.

Vronsky, as he stood by Oblonsky and watched these passengers coming out of the carriages, quite forgot about his mother. What he had just heard about Kitty excited and delighted him.

'The Countess Vronsky is in that compartment,' said the sprightly guard, addressing Vronsky.

His words roused Vronsky from his reverie and reminded him of his mother and of the coming meeting.

In the depths of his heart he did not respect his mother and (though this he never acknowledged to himself) did not love her, but in accordance with the views of the set he lived in, and as a result of his education, he could not imagine himself treating her in any way but one altogether submissive and respectful; the more submissive and respectful he was, the less he honoured and loved her in his heart.

14

Vronsky followed the guard to the carriage and had to stop at the entrance of the compartment to let a lady pass out.

The trained insight of a Society man enabled Vronsky with a single glance to decide that she belonged to the best Society. He apologized for being in her way and was about to enter the carriage, but felt compelled to have another look at her, not because she was very beautiful nor because of the elegance and modest grace of her whole figure, but because he saw in her sweet face as she passed him something specially tender and kind. When he looked round she too turned her head. Her bright grey eyes which seemed dark because of their black lashes rested for a moment on his face as if recognizing him, and then turned to the passing crowd evidently in search of some one. In that short look Vronsky had time to notice the subdued animation that enlivened her face and seemed to flutter between her bright eyes and a scarcely-perceptible smile which curved her rosy lips. It was as if an excess of vitality so filled her whole being that it betrayed itself against her will, now in her smile, now in the light of her eyes.

Vronsky entered the carriage. His mother, a thin old woman with black eyes and curled hair, screwed up her eyes as she recognized her son and her thin lips smiled slightly. She rose from the seat, and giving her hand-bag to her maid held out her small dry hand to her son, then lifting his head which had been bent to kiss her hand kissed him on his face.

'Have you had a good journey?' asked her son, sitting down on the seat beside her. The lady he had met as he entered the carriage was again entering the compartment.

'Well, have you found your brother?' asked Vronsky's mother.

Vronsky understood now that this was Mrs. Karenina.

'Your brother is here,' he said rising. 'Excuse my not recognizing you before. Our acquaintance was so slight,' he said with a bow, 'that I am sure you do not remember me.'

'Oh yes, I should have recognized you, especially as I believe your mother and I have talked of nothing but you all the way,' said she, at last allowing the animation she had been trying to suppress to reveal itself in a smile. 'But my brother is not here yet.'

'Go and call him, Alexis,' said the old Countess.

Vronsky went out on to the platform and shouted, 'Oblonsky! Here!'

Mrs. Karenina did not wait for her brother to come in, but, on seeing him, descended from the carriage with a firm light step. As soon as her brother came up to her she gave him a vigorous kiss. Vronsky did not take his eyes off her, and kept smiling, he knew not why. But remembering that his mother was waiting for him he went back into the carriage.

'She is very charming, isn't she?' said the Countess, referring to Mrs. Karenina. 'We talked all the way.'

Mrs. Karenina again entered the carriage.

'There, Countess, you have met your son and I my brother,' she said, 'and I have exhausted my stock of stories and should have had nothing more to tell you.'

'No, no,' said the Countess holding her hand, 'I could travel round the world with you and not be dull. You are one of those charming women with whom it is nice to talk, and nice to be silent. But please don't fret about your son, you can't expect never to be parted.'

Mrs. Karenina stood very erect and her eyes were smiling.

'Anna Arkadyevna Karenina has a son who, I think, is eight years old,' explained the Countess, 'and she has never before been separated from him and so she is worried at having left him.'

'Yes, the Countess and I have talked all the time—I about my son and she about hers,' said Mrs. Karenina, and a smile brightened her face, a kind smile on his account. She turned to the old Countess.

'Thank you very much. I hardly noticed how the time passed. *Au revoir*, Countess.'

'Good-bye, dear!' answered the Countess. 'Let me kiss your pretty face. I'm an old woman and say what I mean, and tell you frankly that I've lost my heart to you.'

Conventional as the phrase was, Mrs. Karenina was pleased. She blushed, stooped a little, and held out her face for the Countess to kiss, then she stood up again, and with the same smile hovering between her lips and eyes held out her hand to Vronsky. He pressed the little hand, and the firm grip with which she shook his gave him unusual pleasure. She went out with that brisk tread which carried her rather full figure with such wonderful ease.

'Very charming,' said the old lady.

Her son thought so too. He followed her with his eyes as long as he could see her graceful form, and his face retained its smile.

'Well, *maman*, are you quite well?' he said, turning toward his mother.

'Quite, everything is all right. Alexander was very nice, and Varya looks very handsome. She is most interesting.'

And she began to tell about what interested her most, her grandson's christening, for which she had gone to Petersburg, and the special favour the Emperor had shown to her eldest son.

'Here is Lavrenty at last,' said Vronsky looking out of the window. 'We can go now if you like.'

The old major-domo, who had accompanied the Countess on her journey, came in and announced that everything was ready, and the Countess rose to go. Vronsky gave his arm to his mother, but, just as they were coming out of the carriage, several people ran past them with frightened faces. The station-master with his peculiar coloured cap also ran past them.

Evidently something unusual had happened. The people were running back from the train.

'What? ... What? ... Where? ... Thrown himself under ... Run over ...' shouted the passers-by.

Oblonsky, with his sister on his arm, also turned back, and, avoiding the crowd, stood with frightened faces beside the carriage. The ladies re-entered the carriage, while Vronsky and Oblonsky followed the crowd, to find out about the accident.

A watchman, either tipsy or too much muffled up because of the severe frost, had not heard a train that was being shunted, and had been run over.

Before Vronsky and Oblonsky returned the ladies had heard this from the major-domo.

Oblonsky and Vronsky had both seen the mangled corpse. Oblonsky was evidently suffering. His face was puckered and he seemed ready to cry.

'Ah, how terrible! Oh Anna, if you had seen it! And his wife was there. ... It was dreadful to see her. She threw herself on the body. They say he was the sole support of a very large family.'

'Can nothing be done for her?' said Mrs. Karenina in an agitated whisper.

Vronsky glanced at her and at once went out. 'I will be back directly, *maman*,' he added, turning at the doorway.

When he returned a few minutes later Oblonsky was already talking to the Countess about the new opera singer, while she was impatiently glancing at the door in expectation of her son.

'Now let's go,' said Vronsky as he came in.

They went together, Vronsky walking in front with his mother, Mrs. Karenina following with her brother. At the exit the station-master overtook them, and said to Vronsky:

'You gave my assistant 200 roubles. Please be so kind as to say whom you intended it for.'

'For the widow,' said Vronsky, shrugging his shoulders.

'You have given it!' exclaimed Oblonsky behind Vronsky, and pressing his sister's arm he added, 'Very kind, very kind! Isn't he a fine fellow? My respects to you, Countess,' and he remained behind with his sister, seeking her maid.

When they came out, the Vronskys' carriage had already started.

Mrs. Karenina got into her brother's carriage, and Oblonsky noticed with surprise that her lips were trembling and that it was with difficulty she kept back her tears.

'What is the matter with you, Anna?' he asked when they had gone a few hundred yards.

'It's a bad omen,' she replied.

'What nonsense!' said Oblonsky. 'You're here, and that is the chief thing. You can't think how my hopes rest on you.'

'And have you known Vronsky long?' she asked.

'Yes. Do you know we hope he will marry Kitty?'

'Yes?' said Anna softly. 'But let us talk about your affairs,' she added, shaking her head as if she wished physically to drive away something superfluous that hampered her. 'Let us talk of your affairs. I've received your letter and have come.'

'Yes, all my hopes are fixed on you,' said her brother and began his story.

On reaching his house, he helped his sister out of the carriage, pressed her hand, and drove off to his office.

15

When Anna arrived Dolly was sitting in her little drawing-room giving a fair-haired, plump little boy (who already resembled his father) a French reading-lesson. She was knitting, a piece of work begun long ago, to which she always returned in times of trouble. Dolly was overpowered by her sorrow and was quite absorbed by it. Nevertheless, she remembered that her sister-in-law, Anna, was the wife of one of the most important men in Petersburg, and thanks to that circumstance she did not carry out her threat to her husband, and did not forget that her sister-in-law was coming.

'After all, it is not in the least Anna's fault,' thought she. 'She has never shown me anything but kindness and friendship. If only she does not try to console me!'

Dolly knew that, one way or other, she would tell Anna everything, and now it pleased her to think how she would say it, and then she felt vexed to have to speak of her humiliation to her—his sister—and to hear from her set phrases of consolation.

As it often happens, though she kept looking at the clock, waiting for Anna, she let the moment when her visitor arrived go by without even hearing the bell.

When she heard soft steps and the rustle of petticoats already in the doorway, she rose and embraced her sister-in-law.

'Dolly, I am so pleased to see you!'

'And I am pleased too,' said Dolly with a feeble smile, trying to guess from Anna's expression how much she knew. 'She must know,' she thought, noticing the look of sympathy on Anna's face.

'Come, let me take you to your room,' she went on, trying to put off as long as possible the moment for explanation.

'This is Grisha? Dear me, how he has grown!' said Anna, and kissed him. 'Why, dear me, here is Tanya! You're just the same age as my little Serezha,' she added, turning to the little girl who had run into the room, and, taking her in her arms, Anna kissed her. 'Sweet girlie! darling! Let me see them all.'

Having looked at the children they returned to the drawing-room and, being now alone, sat down to coffee at the table. Anna took hold of the tray, but then pushed it aside.

'Dolly,' she said, 'he has told me!'

Dolly looked coldly at Anna. She expected now to hear word of insincere sympathy: but Anna said nothing of the kind.

'Dolly dear!' she began, 'I do not wish to take his part or console you; that would be impossible, but, dearest, I am simply sorry for you, sorry from the bottom of my heart!'

'It is impossible to console me. Everything is lost after what has happened, everything destroyed!'

As soon as she had said it her face softened. Anna lifted Dolly's dry thin hand, kissed it, and said:

'But what is to be done, Dolly, what is to be done? What is the best way of acting in this dreadful position?'

'Everything is at an end,' said Dolly. 'And the worst of it is, you understand, that I can't leave him: there are the children, and I am bound. Yet I can't live with him; it is torture for me to see him.'

'Dolly, my darling, he has spoken to me, but I want to hear it from you. Tell me everything.'

Dolly looked at her inquiringly.

Sincere sympathy and affection were visible in Anna's face.

'If you like,' said Dolly suddenly, 'but I'll begin from the beginning. With the education Mama gave me, I was not merely naïve, but silly! I knew nothing. I know they say husbands tell their wives how they have lived, but Stiva ...' She corrected herself. 'But Stephen Arkadyevich never told me anything. You will hardly believe it, but up to now I thought I was the only woman he had ever known. In this way I lived for nine years. Only think, that I not only did not suspect him of unfaithfulness, but thought it impossible. To be fully convinced of one's happiness and suddenly ...' continued Dolly, suppressing her sobs, 'to read a letter, his letter to his mistress, my children's governess. No, it is too horrible!' She suddenly drew out her handkerchief and hid her face in it.

'I could perhaps understand a momentary slip,' she went on after a pause, 'but deliberately, cunningly to deceive me ... and with whom? To go on living with me as my husband, and with her at the same time ... it's awful; you cannot realize ...'

'Oh yes, I do, I do understand, Dolly dear, I do understand,' said Anna, pressing her hand.

'And do you think he realizes the horror of my situation?' continued Dolly. 'Not at all! He is happy and contented.'

'Oh no,' Anna quickly interrupted. 'He is pitiable, he is overwhelmed with remorse ...'

'Is he capable of remorse?' interrupted Dolly, looking searchingly into her sister-in-law's face.

'Oh yes, I know him. I could not look at him without pity. We both know him. He is kind-hearted, but he is proud too, and now he is so humiliated. He kept saying, "No, no, she will not forgive me!"'

Dolly, gazing beyond her sister-in-law, listened thoughtfully.

'Yes, I understand that his position is dreadful; it is worse for the guilty than for the innocent one,' she said, 'if he feels that the misfortune all comes from his fault. But how can I forgive him, how can I be a wife to him after her? ...' Sobs cut short her words.

But as if intentionally every time she softened, she again began to speak of the thing that irritated her.

'You know she is young, she is pretty,' she said. 'You see, Anna, my youth and my good looks have been sacrificed, and to whom? For him and his children. I have served his purpose and lost all I had in the service, and of course a fresh, good-for-nothing creature now pleases him better. It is terrible, my soul has so revolted that instead of love and tenderness for him I have nothing but anger left, yes, anger.'

'Dolly dearest! I understand, but don't torture yourself. You are so deeply hurt that you see many things in the wrong light.'

Dolly was silent, and for a moment or two neither spoke.

'What am I to do? Think it over, Anna, help me! I have turned over in my mind everything I could think of, and can find nothing.'

Anna could not think of anything, but her heart responded to every word and every look of Dolly's.

'All I can say is,' began Anna, 'I am his sister and I know his character,' she made a gesture with her hand in front of her forehead, 'that capacity for letting himself be completely carried away, but on the other hand for completely repenting. He can hardly believe now—can hardly understand—how he could do it.'

'No, he understands and understood,' Dolly interrupted. 'And I ... you forget me ... Does it make it easier for me?'

'Wait a bit. When he was speaking to me, I confess I did not quite realize the misery of your position. I saw only his side and I was sorry for him, but now having spoken with you I see your suffering and I cannot tell you how sorry I am for you. But, Dolly dearest, there is one thing I do not know. I do not know how much love there still is in your soul—you alone know that. Is there enough for forgiveness? If there is—then forgive him.'

'No,' Dolly began, but Anna stopped her and kissed her hand.

'I know the world better than you do,' she said. 'I know men like Stiva and how they see these things. These men may be unfaithful, but their homes, their wives, are their holy places. They manage in some way to hold these women in contempt and don't let them interfere with the family. I do not understand it, but it is so.'

'Yes, but he kissed her ...'

'Dolly, wait a bit. I have seen Stiva when he was in love with you. You know we used to laugh at him because his every third word was, "Dolly is a wonderful woman." You have been and still are his divinity, and this infatuation never reached his soul ...'

'And you, would you forgive?'

'I do not know, I cannot judge. ... Yes, I can,' said Anna, after a minute's consideration. Her mind had taken in and weighed the situation, and she added, 'Yes, I can, I can. Yes, I should forgive. I should not remain the same woman—no, but I should forgive, and forgive it as utterly as if it had never happened at all.'

'Well, of course ...' Dolly put in quickly as if saying what she had often herself thought, 'or else it would not be forgiveness. If one is to forgive, it must be entire forgiveness. Well now, I will show you your room.' She rose, and on the way embraced Anna. 'My dear, how glad I am you came! I feel better now, much better.'

16

The whole of that day Anna remained at the Oblonskys' house, and did not receive anybody, although several of her acquaintances who had heard of her arrival came to see her. She spent the earlier part of the day with Dolly and the children, and sent a note to her brother to be sure and come home to dinner.

Oblonsky dined at home, the conversation was general, and his wife addressed him familiarly in the second person singular, which she had not done all these days. There was still the same estrangement in their manner to each other, but no longer any question of separating, and Oblonsky saw that reconciliation was possible.

Immediately after dinner Kitty came. She knew Anna, but only slightly, and came to her sister's not without fear of how she might be received by this Petersburg Society woman whom everybody admired so much. But she noticed at once that Anna liked her. Anna was not like a Society woman or the mother of an eight-year-old son. The flexibility of her figure, her freshness, and the natural animation of her face appearing now in her smile, now in her eyes, would have made her look more like a girl of twenty had it not been for a serious and some-times even sad expression in her eyes which struck Kitty and attracted her.

After dinner, when Dolly had gone to her own room, Anna got up quickly and went to her brother who was just lighting a cigar.

'Stiva,' she said to him with a merry twinkle in her eye and making the sign of the cross over him as she indicated the door with a look. 'Go, and may God help you.' He understood, threw down his cigar, and disappeared through the door.

When Oblonsky had gone, she returned to the sofa where she had been sitting surrounded by the children.

'And when is the ball to be?' said Anna, turning to Kitty.

'Next week, and it will be a delightful ball. One of those balls which are always jolly.'

'There are no more jolly balls for me,' said Anna, and Kitty saw in her eyes that peculiar world which was not yet revealed to her. 'There are some that are not as difficult and dull as the rest.'

'Will you go to that ball?' asked Kitty. 'I should so like to see you at a ball.'

'Well, then, if I have to go, I shall console myself with the reflection that it will give you pleasure. ... Now, children, run away, run away to tea,' she went on, disengaging herself from the children and dispatching them to the dining-room. 'But I know why you are asking me to go to that ball. You're expecting much from it, and would like everybody to be there and have a share in it.'

'How do you know? Well, yes!'

'I know something—Stiva told me and I congratulate you. I like him very much,' Anna continued. 'I met Vronsky at the railway station. I travelled yesterday with his mother,' she continued, 'and she talked about him all the time. He is her favourite son.'

'What did his mother tell you?'

'Oh very much! but anyone can see he is full of chivalry. ... For in-stance she told me that he wished to give all his property to his brother, that already as a boy he had saved a woman from drowning. In a word, he is a hero,' said Anna, smiling and remembering the 200 roubles he had given away at the station.

But she did not mention the 200 roubles. For some reason she did not like to think of them. She felt that there had been something in it relating personally to her that should not have been.

'Well, thank heaven Stiva is stopping a long time with Dolly,' she added, dissatisfied with something, Kitty thought.

17

Dolly came out of her room for the grown-up people's tea. Oblonsky did not appear. He had probably left his wife's room by the other door.

'I'm afraid you will be cold upstairs,' remarked Dolly to Anna. 'I want to move you down, and then we shall be nearer to one another.'

'Oh, please don't trouble about me,' said Anna, scrutinizing Dolly's face and trying to discover whether a reconciliation had taken place.

'What are you talking about?' asked Oblonsky, entering the room from his study and addressing his wife with a slight smile.

From his tone both Kitty and Anna gathered that a reconciliation had taken place.

'Yes, a full, a full reconciliation, quite complete. Thank God!' thought Anna, and pleased to have been the means of bringing it about, she went up to Dolly and kissed her.

All that evening Dolly maintained her usual slightly bantering manner toward her husband, and Oblonsky was contented and cheerful, but not to the extent of seeming to forget his guilt after having obtained forgiveness.

At half-past nine an unusually pleasant and happy family conversation round the Oblonskys' tea-table was disturbed by an apparently very ordinary occurrence which yet struck them all as strange. While they were talking about their mutual Petersburg acquaintances Anna rose suddenly.

'I have her photo in my album,' said she, 'and I'll show you my Serezha's too,' she added with a mother's proud smile.

For toward ten o'clock—the time when she generally said good-night to her son and often put him to bed herself before going to a ball—she felt sad at being so far from him, and, whatever they talked about, her thoughts kept returning to her curly-headed Serezha. She longed to look at his portrait and to talk about him. Seizing the first opportunity she rose and, stepping firmly and lightly, went out to fetch her album. As she was coming out of the drawing-room there was a ring at the door.

'Who can it be?' asked Dolly.

A footman ran up to announce the new arrival, who stood at the foot of the stairs under a lamp. Anna looked down from the landing where she stood and at once recognized Vronsky, and a strange feeling of pleasure mixed with fear suddenly stirred in her heart.

He stood in his overcoat, feeling for something in his pockets. When Anna was half-way up the top flight, he lifted his eyes and saw her, and a look of something like embarrassment and fear came into his face. She bowed slightly and went on. She heard Oblonsky's loud voice downstairs asking him to come in, and Vronsky's low, soft voice refusing.

When Anna returned with her album he had already gone, and Oblonsky was saying that Vronsky had called to inquire about a dinner they were giving next day to a celebrity who was visiting Moscow, but that he could not be induced to come in.

Kitty blushed. She thought that she alone understood why he had come to the house and why he would not come in. 'He has been to our house,' she thought, 'and not finding me in he guessed that I was here. And he would not come in because Anna is here, and he thought it too late.'

They all glanced at one another and said nothing but began examining Anna's album.

There was nothing extraordinary in the fact that a man had called at half-past nine at a friend's house to ask about a dinner they were planning and that he would not come in; but it seemed strange to all of them. To Anna in particular it seemed strange and not right.

18

The ball had only just begun when Kitty and her mother ascended the broad staircase which was deluged with light, decorated with flowering plants, and occupied by powdered footmen in red liveries. From the ball-room came the regular sound of movement, and while they were arranging their hair and dresses before a mirror on the landing between the plants, they heard the accurate measured sound of the orchestra violins just beginning the first waltz.

Although Kitty's gown and coiffure and all her other adornments had given her much trouble and thought, she now entered the ball-room in her complicated dress of white net over a pink slip, as if she had been born in this net and lace and with that high coiffure and the rose and its two leaves on the top.

It was one of Kitty's happy days. Her dress did not feel tight anywhere, the lace round her bodice did not slip, the bows did not crumple or come off, the pink shoes with their high curved heels did not pinch but seemed to make her feet lighter. The thick rolls of fair hair kept up as if they had grown naturally so on the little head. All three buttons on each of her long gloves, which fitted without changing the shape of her hand, fastened without coming off. The black velvet ribbon of her locket clasped her neck with unusual softness. Her bare shoulders and arms gave her a sensation as of cold marble, a feeling she liked very much. Her eyes shone and she could not keep her rosy lips from smiling at the consciousness of her attractive appearance. Before she had reached the light-coloured crowd of women in tulle, ribbons, and lace, who were waiting for partners, she was already asked for the waltz and asked by the best dancer, the famous *dirigeur* and Master of Ceremonies, a handsome stately married man, George Korsunsky. He noticed Kitty just coming in. He approached her at that peculiar free and easy amble natural only to Masters of Ceremonies, bowed, and, without even asking her consent, put his arm round her slim waist. She looked about for some one to hold her fan and the mistress of the house took it from her with a smile.

'It is a rest to waltz with you,' he said as he took the first slow steps of the dance. 'What lightness and precision! it's delightful!' he remarked, saying to her what he said to almost all the dancing partners whom he really liked.

She smiled at his praise, and over his shoulder continued to survey the ball-room. She saw that the élite of the company were grouped in the left-hand corner of the room. and there Kitty's eyes found Stephen, and then the lovely head and beautiful figure of Anna, in a black velvet dress. And *he* was there. Kitty had not seen him since the day she had refused Levin. She recognized him at once and even noticed that he was looking at her.

'Shall we have another turn? You are not tired?' asked Korsunsky who was a little out of breath.

'No more turns, thank you.'

'Where may I take you?'

'I believe Anna Arkadyevna Karenina is here, take me to her.'

'Wherever you please.'

And Korsunsky bowed, straightened his broad shirt front, and offered Kitty his arm to conduct her to Anna.

Anna was in a low-necked black velvet dress which exposed her full shoulder and bosom that seemed carved out of old ivory, and her rounded arms with the very small hands. Her dress was richly trimmed with Venetian lace. In her black hair, all her own, she wore a little garland of pansies, and in her girdle, among the lace, a bunch of the same flowers. Her coiffure was very unobtrusive. The only noticeable things about it were the wilful ringlets that always escaped at her temples and on the nape of her neck and added to her beauty.

Kitty had been seeing Anna every day but now saw her in a new and quite unexpected light. She now realized that Anna's charm lay precisely in the fact that her personality always stood out from her dress, that her dress was never conspicuous on her. And her black velvet with rich lace was not at all conspicuous, but served only as a frame; she alone was noticeable—simple, natural, elegant and at the same time merry and animated. She was standing among that group, very erect as usual, and was talking to the master of the house with her head slightly turned toward him, when Kitty approached. At once she turned to Kitty with a tender protecting smile.

'You even come into the room dancing,' she said.

'She is one of my most faithful helpers,' said Korsunsky, turning to Anna whom he had not yet seen. 'The Princess helps to make a ball gay and beautiful. Anna Arkadyevna, shall we have a turn?' he added, stooping toward her.

'I don't dance if it is possible not to,' she said.

'But to-night it is not possible,' he rejoined.

At that moment Vronsky approached.

'Well, if it is impossible not to dance to-night, let us dance,' she said taking no notice of Vronsky's bow and quickly putting her hand on Korsunsky's shoulder.

'Why is she displeased with him?' thought Kitty, noticing that Anna had intentionally taken no notice of Vronsky's bow. He came up to Kitty, reminding her of the first quadrille and regretting that he had not seen her for such a long time. Kitty, while gazing with admiration at Anna waltzing, listened to him, expecting him to ask her to waltz, but he did not do so and she glanced at him with surprise. He blushed and hurriedly asked her to dance.

19

Vronsky and Kitty waltzed several times round the room and then Kitty went to her mother, but hardly had she exchanged a few words with the Countess Nordston before Vronsky returned to fetch her for the first quadrille. Nothing special was said during the quadrille: it seemed to her that the mazurka would settle everything. That he did not ask her for the mazurka while they were dancing the quadrille did not disturb her. She was sure that she would dance the mazurka with him as at previous balls, and she refused five other partners for that dance, saying that she was already engaged. The whole ball up to the last quadrille was for Kitty an enchanted dream. But while dancing the last quadrille with one of the youthful bores whom it would not do to refuse, she happened to be *vis-à-vis* to Anna and suddenly noticed that she was elated with success, intoxicated by the rapture she had produced. She knew the feeling and knew its symptoms, and recognized them in Anna.

'Who is the cause?' she asked herself. 'All or only one?' And as she watched, her heart sank more and more.

'No, it is not the admiration of the crowd that intoxicates her, but the rapture of one, and that one is ... can it be *he*?'

Every time he spoke to Anna the joyful light kindled in her eyes and a smile of pleasure curved her rosy lips. She seemed to make efforts to restrain these signs of joy, but they appeared on her face of their own accord. 'But what of him?' Kitty looked at him and was filled with horror. What she saw so distinctly in the mirror of Anna's face, she saw in him. His face had an expression which she had never seen before.

A mist came over the ball and the whole world in Kitty's soul. Only the thorough training she had had enabled and obliged her to do what was expected of her, that is, to dance, to answer the questions put to her, to talk, and even to smile. But before the mazurka began Kitty was for a moment seized with despair. She had refused five men who had asked for the mazurka and now she had no partner for it. She had not even a hope of being asked again just because she had too much success in Society for anyone to think that she was not already engaged for the dance. She felt herself quite broken-hearted.

She went to the far end of a little drawing-room and sank into an easy chair. Her heart was crushed with terrible despair.

'But perhaps I am mistaken, perhaps it was nothing of the kind?' And she again recalled all that she had witnessed.

'Kitty, what does this mean?' asked the Countess Nordston, coming up inaudibly over the carpet. 'I don't understand it.'

Kitty's nether lip trembled, and she rose quickly.

'Kitty, are you not dancing the mazurka?'

'No, no,' said Kitty in a voice tremulous with tears.

'He asked her for the mazurka in my presence,' said the Countess, knowing that Kitty would understand whom she meant by 'him' and 'her'. 'She asked, "Are you not dancing with the Princess Shcherbatsky?"'

'Oh! it's all the same to me!' replied Kitty. No one but herself understood her situation, because no one knew that she had only a few days ago refused a man whom she perhaps loved, and refused him because she trusted another.

The Countess Nordston, who was engaged to Korsunsky for the mazurka, told him to ask Kitty instead.

Kitty danced in the first pair, and luckily for her she was not obliged to talk, because Korsunsky ran about all the time giving orders in his domain. Vronsky and Anna sat almost opposite to her. She saw them close by, too, when they met in the dance, and the more she saw of them the surer she was that the blow had fallen. She saw that they felt as if they were alone in that crowded ball-room. On Vronsky's face, usually so firm and self-possessed, she noticed that expression of bewilderment and submission which had so surprised her—an expression like that of an intelligent dog when it feels guilty.

Anna smiled—and the smile passed on to him; she became thoughtful—and he became serious. Some supernatural power attracted Kitty's eyes to Anna's handsome, animated face,—everything about her was enchanting, but there was something terrible and cruel in her charm.

Kitty felt herself crushed and her face expressed it.

Anna did not wish to stay to supper, but the master of the house tried to persuade her to do so.

'No, I won't stay,' answered Anna, smiling, looking round at Vronsky who stood beside her. 'I must rest before my journey.'

'So you really are going to-morrow?' said Vronsky.

'Yes, I think so,' Anna replied as if surprised at the boldness of his question; but the uncontrollable radiance of her eyes and her smile burnt him as she spoke the words.

Anna did not stay for supper, but went away.

20

'Yes, there is certainly something objectionable and repellent about me,' thought Levin after leaving the Shcherbatskys'. 'I do not get on with other people. They say it is pride! No, I am not even proud. If I had any pride, I should not have put myself into such a position.' And he pictured to himself, Vronsky, happy, kind, clever, calm, and certainly never placing himself in such a terrible position as he, Levin, had been in that evening. 'Yes, she was bound to choose him. What right had I to imagine that she would wish to unite her life with mine? Who and what am I? A man of no account, wanted by no one and of no use to anyone.' And he remembered his brother Nicholas, and kept his mind gladly on that memory. Levin went up to a lamp-post and read his brother's address which he had in his pocket-book, and then hired a sledge. On the long way to his brother's he recalled how despite the ridicule of his fellow-students his brother had lived like a monk while at the University and for a year after, strictly observing all the religious rites, attending service, fasting, avoiding all pleasures and especially women; and then how he suddenly broke loose, became intimate with the vilest people and gave himself up to unbridled debauchery. He remembered the night which Nicholas had spent in the police cells for disorderly conduct, and the disgraceful proceedings he had instigated against his brother Sergius Ivanich, whom he accused of not having paid out to him his share of his mother's fortune: and lastly, the time when his brother took an official appointment in one of the Western Provinces and was there arrested for assaulting an Elder. ... It was all very disgusting, but Levin remembered that when Nicholas was passing through his pious stage of fasting, visiting monks, and going to church; when he was seeking in religion for help to curb his passionate nature, not only did no one encourage him, but every one, and Levin among them, made fun of him. He was teased and called 'Noah' and 'monk', and then when he broke loose no one helped him, but all turned away from him with horror and disgust.

Levin felt that his brother Nicholas, in his soul, despite the depravity of his life, was no worse than those who despised him. It was not his fault that he was born with his ungovernable temper, and with a cramped mind. He always wished to do right. 'I will tell him everything, I will get him to tell me everything. I will show him that I love and therefore understand him,' Levin decided in his mind, as toward eleven o'clock he drove up to the hotel of which he had the address.

'Upstairs, Nos. 12 and 13,' said the hall porter in reply to Levin's question.

The door of No. 12 was ajar, and from within, visible in the streak of light, issued dense fumes of inferior and weak tobacco. Levin heard a stranger's voice, but knew at once that his brother was there, for he heard him coughing.

Constantine Levin glanced into the room, which was beyond a partition, and saw that the speaker was a young man with an enormous head of hair, who wore a workman's coat, and that a young, pock-marked woman in a woollen dress without collar or cuffs was sitting on the sofa. No one noticed him, and, as he took off his galoshes, he overheard what the man in the workman's coat was saying. He was talking about some commercial enterprise.

'Oh, let the privileged classes go to the devil,' said his brother's voice, with a cough.

'Masha, get us some supper and bring the wine if any is left, or send for some.'

The woman rose, came out from behind the partition, and saw Constantine.

'Here is a gentleman, Nicholas Dmitrich,' she said.

'Whom do you want?' said Nicholas Levin's voice angrily.

'It is I,' answered Constantine Levin, coming forward into the lamp-light.

'Who's I?' said the voice of Nicholas Levin still more angrily.

He was even more emaciated than three years before, when Constantine Levin had last seen him. He was wearing a short coat, and his hands and broad bones appeared more immense than ever. His hair was thinner, but the same straight moustache covered his lips; and the same eyes with their peculiar, naïve gaze looked out at the new-comer.

'Ah! Kostya!' he said suddenly, recognizing his brother, and his eyes lit up with joy. But at the same moment he turned to look at the young man and convulsively jerked his head and neck as if his neck-tie were strangling him, a movement Levin knew well, and quite another expression—a wild, suffering, and cruel look—settled on his haggard face.

'I wrote both to you and to Sergius Ivanich that I do not know you and do not wish to know you. What is it? What do you want?'

'I do not want anything of you specially,' he answered meekly; 'I have simply come to see you.'

His brother's timidity obviously softened Nicholas.

'Ah! You have come just for that?' he said. 'Well, come in, sit down. Will you have some supper? Masha, get supper for three. No, wait a little. Do you know who this is?' he added, turning to his brother and pointing to the man in the workman's coat. 'It is Mr. Kritsky, my friend ever since my Kiev days, a very remarkable fellow.

'And this woman,' said Nicholas Levin, pointing to her, 'is my life's companion, Mary Nikolavna; I took her out of a house ...' and as he said this he again jerked his neck. 'But I love and respect her and beg all those who wish to know me,' he added, raising his voice and scowling, 'to love and respect her. She is just the same to me as a wife. So now you know whom you have to deal with, and if you fear you will be degraded—there is the door.'

And again his eyes glanced questioningly around.

'Why should I be degraded? I don't understand.'

'Well, Masha, order supper for three, with vodka and wine ...'

21

'So you see, ...' Nicholas Levin continued with an effort, wrinkling his brow and twitching. It is the beginning of a new business we are undertaking. The business is to be a Productive Association ...'

Constantine hardly listened. He kept glancing at his brother's sickly, consumptive face, and felt more and more sorry for him, nor could he force himself to pay attention to what Nicholas was telling him about the Association. He realized that this Association was merely an anchor to save his brother from self-contempt.

'You know that capitalism oppresses the workers. Our society has so shaped itself that the more the people work the richer the merchants and landowners will become, while the people will remain beasts of burden for ever. And this system must be changed,' he concluded, with an inquiring look at his brother.

'Yes, of course,' said Constantine, looking intently at the flush which had appeared on his brother's face.

'And so we are starting a Locksmiths' Association, in which all the products and the profits and, above all, the instruments of production will be common property.'

Constantine sighed and at the same time looked round the room which was dismal and dirty. The sigh seemed to irritate Nicholas still more.

'But what is the good of talking? Why have you come here? You despise it, well, that is all right—then go away. Go, go in God's name!' he exclaimed, rising from his chair. 'Go, go!'

'I do not despise it at all,' Constantine replied meekly.

Meanwhile Mary Nikolavna had come back. Nicholas gave her an angry look. She hurried up to him and said something in a whisper.

'I am not well and have grown irritable,' said Nicholas, breathing heavily and quieting down.

Kritsky rose and took up his hat.

'Don't you want any supper? Well, good-bye. Come to-morrow and bring the locksmith.'

As soon as Kritsky had gone out, Nicholas smiled and winked.

'He is not much good,' he remarked. 'I can see ...'

But at that moment Kritsky called him from outside the door.

'What do you want now?' said Nicholas and went out into the passage.

Left alone with Mary Nikolavna, Levin spoke to her.

'Have you been long with my brother?' he asked.

'Yes, it is the second year now. His health is very bad, he drinks vodka, and it is bad for him.'

'Much vodka?' whispered Levin.

'Yes,' she said looking timidly toward the door, just as Nicholas returned.

'What were you talking about?' he asked frowning and looking from one to the other with frightened eyes. 'What was it?'

'Nothing,' replied Levin in confusion.

'If you do not wish to tell me, do as you please. Only you have no business to talk to her. She's a street girl, and you are a gentleman,' he continued, again raising his voice.

'Nicholas Dmitrich, Nicholas Dmitrich,' whispered Mary Nikolavna, again approaching him.

'Well, all right, all right! … and how about supper? Ah, here it is,' he said noticing a waiter who was bringing in a tray. 'Here, here, put it down here,' he said crossly, and at once poured out a wine-glass full of vodka and drank it greedily. 'Have a drink, will you?' he said to his brother, brightening up at once. 'Well, I am glad to see you, anyhow. Whatever one may say, after all, we are not strangers. Come, have a drink. Tell me what is happening in Pokrovsk. … Mind, don't change anything in the house, but get married soon and set things going again as they used to be. Then I will come to you if you have a good wife.'

'Come to me at once,' said Levin. 'How well we might settle down there!'

'I would come if I were sure I should not find Sergius Ivanich there.'

'You won't find him there. I live quite apart from him.'

'Still, say what you will, you must choose between him and me,' said Nicholas with a timid look at his brother.

His timidity touched Constantine.

'I take no side in your quarrel with Sergius Ivanich. You are both to blame. You more in external matters and he more in essential ones.'

'Ah, ah! Then you have grasped it, you have grasped it!' joyfully exclaimed Nicholas.

'But personally, if you care to know it, I value your friendship more because …'

'Why, why?'

Constantine could not tell him that it was because Nicholas was unfortunate and needed friendship. But Nicholas understood that he meant just that, and frowning, again took hold of the vodka bottle.

'Enough, Nicholas Dmitrich!' said Mary Nikolavna, stretching out her plump arm with its bare wrist to take the bottle.

'Let go! Leave me alone! I'll thrash you!' shouted he.

Mary Nikolavna gave a mild, kindly smile, which evoked one from Nicholas, and she took away the bottle.

Oh heavens, how senseless everything is in this world!' he suddenly exclaimed. 'All these new institutions, these magistrates, these Zemstvos. … What a confusion it all is!'

And he began to relate all his encounters with these new institutions. Constantine Levin listened to him, and the condemnation of the social institutions, which he shared with him and had often expressed, was unpleasant to him when he heard it from his brother's lips.

His speech began to grown confused and he jumped from one subject to another. With Masha's help Constantine succeeded in persuading him not to go out anywhere, and got him into bed quite tipsy.

Masha promised to write to Constantine in case of need, and to try to persuade Nicholas to go and live with him.

22

Next morning Constantine Levin left Moscow and toward evening he reached home. On his way back in the train he felt oppressed by discontent with himself and a vague sense of shame. But when he got out of the train at his station and by the dim light from the station windows saw his one-eyed coachman, Ignat, with his coat-collar turned up, and his sledge with its carpet-lined back, his horses with their tied-up tails, and the harness with its rings and tassels, Levin felt his shame and self-dissatisfaction pass. He felt this at the mere sight of Ignat and the horses; but when he had put on the sheep-skin coat that had been brought for him and, well wrapped up, had seated himself in the sledge and started homeward, he saw what had befallen him in quite a different light. He felt that he was himself and did not wish to be anyone else. He only wished now to be better than he had been formerly. First of all he decided that he would no longer hope for the exceptional happiness which marriage was to have given him, and consequently he would not underrate the present as he had done. He had always felt the injustice of his superfluities compared with the peasant's poverty, and now decided, in order to feel himself quite justified, that though he had always worked hard and lived simply, he would in future work still more and allow himself still less luxury. And it was with cheerful hopes for a new and better life that he reach his house toward nine o'clock in the evening.

A light fell on the snow-covered space in front of the house from the windows of the room of his old nurse, Agatha Mikhaylovna, who now acted as his housekeeper. She had not yet gone to bed, and Kuzma, whom she had roused, came running out into the porch. Laska, a setter bitch, ran out too, almost throwing Kuzma off his feet, and whined and rubbed herself against Levin's knees, jumping up and wishing but not daring to put her front paws on his chest.

'You have soon come back, sir,' said Agatha Mikhaylovna.

'I was home-sick, Agatha Mikhaylovna,' he replied, and went into his study.

A candle just brought in gradually lit up the study and its familiar details became visible: the stag's horns, the book-shelves, the looking-glass, the hot-air aperture of the stove with its brass lid, which had long been in need of repair, his father's couch, the large table on which were an open volume, a broken ash-tray, and an exercise-book in his hand-writing. He went to the corner where two thirty-six pound dumb-bells lay and began doing gymnastic exercises with them to invigorate himself. He heard a creaking of steps at the door and hurriedly put down the dumb-bells.

His steward entered and said that, 'the Lord be thanked,' everything was all right, but that the buckwheat had burned in the new drying kiln. This news irritated Levin. The new kiln had been built and partly invented by him. The steward had always been against the new kiln. Levin felt quite certain that if the buckwheat had been burnt it was only because the precautions about which he had given instructions over and over again had been neglected. He was vexed, and he reprimanded the steward. But the steward had one important and pleasant event to report. Pava, his best and most valuable cow, had calved.

'Kuzma, bring me my sheep-skin. And you tell them to bring a lantern. I will go and have a look at her,' he said to the steward.

The sheds where the most valuable cattle were kept were just behind the house. There was a warm steaming smell of manure when the frozen door opened, and the cows, astonished at the unaccustomed light of the lantern, began moving on their clean straw. The bull, Berkut, with a ring through his nose, snorted a couple of times as they passed by. The red beauty Pava, enormous as a hippopotamus, turned her back, hiding her calf from the new-comers and sniffing at it.

Levin entered the stall and examined Pava, who, becoming excited, was about to low, but quieted down when Levin moved the calf toward her, and sighing heavily began licking it with her rough tongue. The calf fumbled about, pushing its nose under its mother's belly and swinging its little tail.

'Like its mother,' he said, 'although the colour is its father's; very fine, big-boned and deep-flanked. Vasily Fedorich, isn't she fine?' he said, turning to the steward, and quite forgiving him for the buckwheat under the influence of his satisfaction about the calf.

'Whom could she take after, not to be good? Simon, the contractor, came the day after you left. We shall have to employ him, Constantine Dmitrich,' said the steward.

This one question led Levin back to all the details of his farming, which was on a large and elaborate scale. He went straight from the cow-shed to the office, and after talking things over with the steward and with Simon the contractor, he returned to the house and went directly upstairs to the drawing-room.

23

It was a large old-fashioned house, and though only Levin was living in it, he used and heated the whole of it. He knew this to be foolish and even wrong, and contrary to his new plans, but this house was a whole world to Levin. It was the world in which his father and mother had lived and died. Levin could scarcely remember his mother. His conception of her was to him a sacred memory, and in his imagination his future wife was to be a repetition of the enchanting and holy ideal of womanhood that his mother had been. And now he had to renounce marriage.

When he had settled in the arm-chair in the little drawing-room where he always had his tea, and Agatha Mikhaylovna had brought it in for him and had sat down at the window with her usual remark, 'I will sit down, sir!' he felt that, strange to say, he had not really forgotten his dreams and that he could not live without them. With *her*, or with another, they would come true. He read his book, and followed what he read, stopping now and then to listen to Agatha Mikhaylovna, who chattered indefatigably; and at the same time various pictures of farming and future family life arose disconnectedly in his mind. He felt that in the depth of his soul something was settling down, adjusting and composing itself.

He lifted his head and pondered. Old Laska, who had not yet quite digested her joy at her master's return and had run out to bark in the yard, now came back, bringing a smell of fresh air with her into the room and, wagging her tail, she approached him and putting her head under his hand whined plaintively, asking to be patted.

'She all but speaks,' said Agatha Mikhaylovna. 'She is only a dog, but she understands that her master has come back feeling depressed.'

'Why depressed?'

'Oh, don't I see? Never mind, my dear, as long as you have good health and a clean conscience!'

Levin looked at her intently, surprised that she knew so well what was in his mind.

'Shall I bring you a little more tea?' she said and went out.

Laska kept on pushing her head under his hand. He patted her a little, and she curled herself up at his feet with her head on her outstretched hind paw. And to show that all was now well and satisfactory, she slightly opened her mouth, smacked her sticky lips, and drawing them more closely over her old teeth lay still in blissful peace. Levin attentively watched this last movement of hers.

'And it is just the same with me!' he said to himself. 'It is just the same with me. What does it matter. ... All is well.'

24

Early in the morning after the ball Anna sent a telegram to her husband to say that she was leaving Moscow that same evening.

'Really I must, I must go,' she said, explaining her altered plans to her sister-in-law in a tone suggesting that she had suddenly remembered so many things she had to do.

Stephen Oblonsky was not dining at home, but promised to be back at seven to see his sister off.

Kitty also had not come, but had sent a note to say that she had a headache. Anna spent the whole morning preparing for her departure: writing notes to her Moscow acquaintances, making up accounts, and packing. It seemed to Dolly that Anna was in a state of anxiety that Dolly knew well from her own experience, a state which generally hides dissatisfaction with oneself. After dinner Anna went to her room to dress, and Dolly followed her.

'How strange you are to-day!' said Dolly.

'I? Do you think so? I am not strange, but wicked. It sometimes happens to me. I feel ready to cry. It is very silly, but it will pass,' said Anna hurriedly. 'I did not want to leave Petersburg, and now I do not want to leave here.'

'You came here and did a good action,' said Dolly, scrutinizing her attentively.

Anna looked at her with her eyes wet with tears.

'Do not say that, Dolly. I have done and could do nothing. There was enough love in your heart to forgive ...'

'But for you, God only knows what would have happened! How lucky you are, Anna,' said Dolly. 'Everything in your soul is clear and good.'

'Every one has a skeleton in their cupboard, as the English say.'

'What skeleton have you? Everything about you is so clear.'

'I have one!' said Anna, and unexpectedly following her tears, a sly, humorous smile puckered her lips.

'Well, at least your skeleton is a funny one and not a dismal one,' said Dolly smiling.

'No, it is a dismal one. Do you know why Kitty did not come to dinner? I was the cause of the ball being a torture instead of a pleasure to her. But really, really I was not to blame, or only a very little,' she said, drawling out the word 'very' in a high-pitched voice.

'Yes, Stiva told me that you danced the mazurka with Vronsky, and that he ...'

'You cannot think how queerly it came about,' Anna interrupted her. 'I only thought of arranging the match, and—suddenly it all came out quite differently. ... Perhaps against my own will I ... But I should be in despair if there were anything serious in it on his side. I am sure that it will all be forgotten, and Kitty will no longer hate me.'

'Well, do you know, Anna, to tell you the truth, I am not very anxious that Kitty should marry him if he, Vronsky, is capable of falling in love with you in a day.'

'Oh, my goodness! How stupid it would be,' said Anna, and a deep flush of pleasure suffused her face at hearing the thought that occupied her mind expressed in words. 'So I am going away having made an enemy of Kitty, of whom I am so fond.'

Dolly could hardly repress a smile. She was fond of Anna, but it was pleasant to find that she too had a weakness.

Oblonsky, smelling of wine and cigars, with his face red and happy, came in late, just as she was about to start.

Anna's emotion had spread to Dolly, who as she embraced her sister-in-law for the last time whispered: 'Remember that I love and always shall love you as my best friend!'

'I do not know why you should,' said Anna, kissing her and trying to hide her tears.

'You understood and understand me. Good-bye, my sweet one!'

25

'Well, that's all over, thank heaven!' was Anna's first thought when she had taken leave of her brother, who stood to the last moment obstructing the entrance to the railway carriage.

She sat down beside her maid Annushka, and peered round the dimly-lit sleeping compartment. 'Thank heaven, to-morrow I shall see Serezha and Alexis Alexandrovich again, and my good accustomed life will go on as of old.'

With the same preoccupied mind she had had all that day, Anna prepared with pleasure and great deliberation for the journey. With her deft little hands she unlocked her red bag, took out a small pillow which she placed on her knees, and locked the bag again; then she carefully wrapped up her feet and sat down comfortably. An invalid lady was already going to bed. Anna asked her maid to get out her reading-lamp, fixed it to the arm of her seat, and took a paper-knife and an English novel from her handbag. For a while the bustle of people moving about disturbed her, and when the train had finally started it was impossible not to listen to the noises; then there was the snow, beating against the window on her left, to which it stuck, and the sight of the guard, who passed through the carriage closely wrapped up and covered with snow on one side—but at last Anna began to read and to follow what she read. Annushka was already dozing, her broad hands, with a hole in one of the gloves, holding the red bag on her lap.

Anna put down her book, leaned back, and clasped the paper-knife tightly in both hands. She called up all her Moscow memories. They were all good and pleasant. She recalled the ball and Vronsky and his humble, enamoured gaze, and their relations with one another; there was nothing to be ashamed of. And yet at that very point of her recollections when she remembered Vronsky, a feeling of shame grew stronger. 'Well, what of it?' she finally said to herself with decision, changing her position on the seat. 'What does it signify? Just as if there existed, or could exist, between me and this officer-lad any relations differing from those with other acquaintances.' She smiled disdainfully and again took up her book; but now she absolutely could not understand what she was reading. They stopped at a station and she asked Annushka to give her the cape she had removed and a shawl, and putting them on she moved to the door.

'Are you going out?' asked Annushka.

'Yes, I want a breath of air. It is so hot in here.'

She opened the carriage door. The snow and wind rushed toward her and had a tussle with her for the door. She went out. The wind seemed only to have waited for her: it whistled merrily and tried to seize and carry her off, but she held on to the cold door-post and held down her shawl, then stepping on to the platform she moved away from the carriage.

Two gentlemen passed her with glowing cigarettes between their lips. She took a deep breath and had already drawn her hand out of her muff to take hold of the handrail and get into the train, when another man wearing a military overcoat came close between her and the wavering light of the lamp. She turned round, and instantly recognized Vronsky. With his hand in salute, he bowed and asked whether he could be of any service to her. For some time she looked into his face without answering, and, though he stood in the shade she noticed, or thought she noticed, the expression of his face and eyes. It was the same expression of respectful ecstasy that had so affected her the night before. She had assured herself that Vronsky in relation to her was only one of the hundreds of everlastingly identical young men she met everywhere, and that she would never allow herself to give him a thought; yet now, at the first moment of seeing him again, she was seized by a feeling of joyful pride.

'I did not know that you were going too. Why are you going?' she asked. Her face beamed with a joy and animation she could not repress.

'Why am I going?' he repeated, looking straight into her eyes. 'You know that I am going in order to be where you are,' said he. 'I cannot do otherwise.'

The awfulness of the storm appeared still more beautiful to her now. He had said just what her soul desired but her reason dreaded. She did not reply, and he saw a struggle in her face.

'Forgive me if my words displease you,' he said humbly.

He spoke courteously and respectfully, but so firmly and stubbornly that she was long unable to reply.

'What you are saying is wrong, and if you are a good man, I beg you to forget it, as I will forget it,' she said at last.

'Not a word, not a movement of yours will I ever forget, nor can I ...'

'Enough, enough!' she cried, vainly trying to give a severe expression to her face, into which he was gazing eagerly. She took hold of the cold handrail, ascended the steps, and quickly entered the little lobby leading into the carriage. But in that little lobby she stopped, going over in her imagination what had just taken place. Though she could remember neither his nor her own words, she instinctively felt that that momentary conversation had drawn them terribly near to one another, and this both frightened her and made her happy. After standing still for a few seconds she went into the carriage and sat down. She did not sleep at all that night, but the strain and the visions which filled her imagination had nothing unpleasant or dismal about them; on the contrary they seemed joyful, glowing, and stimulating. Toward morning Anna fell into a doze; when she woke the train was approaching Petersburg. At once thoughts of home, her husband, her son, and the cares of the coming day and of those that would follow, beset her.

When the train stopped at the Petersburg terminus and she got out, the first face she noticed was that of her husband.

'Great heavens! What has happened to his ears?' she thought, gazing at his cold and commanding figure, and especially at the gristly ears which now so struck her, pressing as they did against the rim of his hat. When he saw her, he came toward her with his customary ironical smile and looked straight at her with his large tired eyes. An unpleasant feeling weighed on her heart when she felt his fixed and weary gaze, as if she had expected to find him different.

'Yes, as you see. Here is a devoted husband; devoted as in the first year of married life,—consumed by desire to see you,' said he in his slow, high-pitched voice and in the tone in which he always addressed her, a tone which ridiculed those who could use such words in earnest.

'Is Serezha well?' she asked.

'And is this all the reward I get,' he said, 'for my ardour? He is quite well, quite well …'

26

Vronsky did not even try to sleep that night. He sat in his place but he neither saw nor heard anyone. He felt himself a king, not because he believed that he had made an impression on Anna—he did not yet believe that—but because the impression she had made on him filled him with happiness and pride.

What would come of it all he did not even consider. He felt that all his powers, hitherto dissipated and scattered, were now concentrated and directed with terrible energy toward one blissful aim. This made him happy. He knew only that he had told her the truth: that he would go where she went, that all the happiness of life and the only meaning of life for him now was in seeing and hearing her. When he had got out of the train at Bologoe station to drink a glass of seltzer water and had seen Anna, he had involuntarily at once told her just what he was thinking about it. He was glad he had said it to her, and that she now knew it and was thinking about it.

When he got out of the train at Petersburg he felt, despite his sleepless night, as fresh and animated as after a cold bath. He stopped outside the carriage, waiting till she appeared. 'I shall see her again,' he thought and smiled involuntarily. 'I shall see her walk, her face ... she will say something, turn her head, look at me, perhaps even smile.' But before seeing her he saw her husband, whom the station-master was respectfully conducting through the crowd. 'Dear me! the husband!' Only now did Vronsky for the first time clearly realize that the husband was connected with her, especially when he saw that husband with an air of ownership quietly take her hand.

When he saw Karenin, with his fresh Petersburg face, his sternly self-confident figure, his round hat and his slightly rounded back, Vronsky believed in his existence, and had such a disagreeable sensation as a man tortured by thirst might feel on reaching a spring and finding a dog in it, drinking the water and making it muddy. Karenin's gait particularly offended Vronsky, who acknowledged only his own unquestionable right to love Anna. But she was still the same, and the sight of her still affected him physically, exhilarating and stimulating him and filling him with joy. He ordered his German valet, who had run up from a second-class carriage, to get his luggage and take it home, and he himself went up to her.

'No, she doesn't and can't love him,' he decided mentally.

While he was approaching her from behind he observed with joy that she became aware of his approach and was about to turn but, on recognizing him, again addressed her husband.

'Did you have a good night?' he inquired, bowing toward them both, and leaving it to Karenin to recognize him, or not.

'Yes, quite comfortable, thank you,' she replied.

Her face seemed tired but just for an instant as she looked at him she saw a gleam in her eyes and, though the spark was at once extinguished, that one instant made him happy. She glanced at her husband to see whether he knew Vronsky. Karenin looked at him with displeasure, absently trying to recall who he might be.

'Count Vronsky,' said Anna.

'Ah! I believe we have met before,' said Karenin, extending his hand with indifference. 'You travelled there with the mother and came back with the son,' he said, uttering every word distinctly as though it were something valuable he was giving away. He said to his wife in his playful manner: 'Well, were many tears shed in Moscow over the parting?'

By addressing himself thus to his wife he conveyed to Vronsky his wish to be alone with her, and turning to Vronsky he touched his hat. But Vronsky, addressing Anna, said:

'I hope to have the honour of calling on you.'

Karenin glanced at him with his weary eyes.

'I shall be very pleased,' he said coldly. 'We are at home on Mondays.' Then having finally dismissed Vronsky he said to his wife in his usual bantering tone: 'But I must thank you once again, my dear, for having made me the present of a day. Our dear Samovar will be in ecstasies.' (He called the celebrated Countess Lydia Ivanovna *samovar* because she was always getting heated and boiling over about something.) 'She was asking after you. And, do you know, if I may advise, you should go and see her to-day. Her heart is always aching about somebody. At present, in addition to all her other worries, she is concerned about the Oblonskys' reconciliation.'

Countess Lydia Ivanovna was Anna's husband's friend, and the centre of that set in Petersburg Society with which Anna, through her husband, was most closely connected.

'But I wrote to her.'

'Yes, but she wants the particulars. Go and see her, my dear, if you are not too tired. ... Kondraty is here with the carriage for you, and I must be off to the Committee. Now I shan't have to dine alone,' he went on, no longer in a bantering manner. 'You can't think how I used ...' and with a long pressure of her hand and a special kind of smile he helped her into the carriage.

27

The first person to meet Anna when she reached home was her son. He ran down the stairs to her regardless of his governess's cries, and with desperate delight called out: 'Mama! Mama!' When he reached her he clung round her neck.

Her son, like his father, produced on Anna a feeling akin to disappointment. Her fancy had pictured him nicer than he was in reality. She had to come down to reality in order to enjoy him as he was. But even as he was, he was charming, with his fair curls, blue eyes, and plump shapely legs in tight-fitting stockings. Anna experienced an almost physical pleasure in feeling his proximity and his caresses, and a moral solace when she met his simple, trustful, and loving gaze and heard his naïve questions. She unpacked the presents which Dolly's children had sent him.

Before Anna had time to finish her coffee the Countess Lydia Ivanovna was announced. The Countess was a tall, stout woman with a sickly sallow complexion and beautiful, dreamy, black eyes. Anna was fond of her, but to-day she seemed to see her for the first time with all her defects.

'Well, my dear! did you take the olive branch?' asked the Countess as soon as she entered the room.

'Yes, it's all over; but the whole affair was not as serious as we thought,' Anna replied.

But the Countess, who was interested in everything that did not concern her, had a habit of never listening to what interested her, and she interrupted Anna:

'Ah, yes! There is much sorrow and evil in the world, and to-day I am terribly worried.'

'Why! What is the matter?' asked Anna.

'This is all just as it was before, but how is it that I never noticed it before?' said Anna to herself. 'Or is it that she is specially irritated this morning? But it is really funny; her aim is to do good, she is a Christian, and yet she is always angry and always has enemies—all on account of Christianity and philanthropy!'

After the Countess had left, a friend—a high official's wife—arrived and gave Anna all the Petersburg news. At three she also left.

Karenin was at the Ministry. Anna, left alone, spent part of the time before dinner in seeing her son have his dinner, in putting her things in order, and in reading and answering the notes and letters that had accumulated on her table.

The feeling of causeless shame she had felt during the journey, and her agitation, had quite vanished. In her accustomed conditions of life she again felt firm and blameless.

She thought with wonder of her state the day before. 'What had happened? Nothing! Vronsky said some silly things, to which it will be easy to put a stop, and I said what was necessary. It is unnecessary and impossible to speak of it to my husband. To speak of it would be to give it an importance that does not belong to it.' She remembered how she had once told her husband about one of his subordinates who very nearly made her a declaration, and how Karenin had answered that every woman living in Society was liable to such things, but that he had full confidence in her tact and would never degrade himself and her by being jealous. 'So there is no need to tell him! Besides, thank heaven, there is nothing tell!' she said to herself.

28

Karenin returned from the Ministry at four o'clock, but, as often happened, he had no time to go up and see his wife. He went straight to his study to receive some petitioners and sign a few documents brought by his private secretary. At the Karenins' dinners there were usually about three visitors. This time there came an old lady, a cousin of Karenin's; the Director of a Department; the Director's wife; and a young man who had been recommended to Karenin for a post under him. Anna went into the drawing-room to entertain them. Exactly at five Karenin entered in evening dress with a white tie and two stars on his coat, as he had to attend an official meeting directly after dinner. He entered the room, greeted everybody, and quickly sat down, smiling at his wife.

'So my solitude has come to an end. You wouldn't believe how uncomfortable'—he put special emphasis on the word *uncomfortable*—'it is to dine alone!'

At dinner he spoke a little about Moscow affairs with his wife, asking with an ironical smile after Stephen Oblonsky; but for the most part the conversation dealt with Petersburg affairs. After dinner he spent half an hour with his guests, and then, having again with a smile pressed his wife's hand, went away to the Council. That evening Anna went neither to see the Princess Betsy Tverskaya, who having heard of Anna's return had invited her, nor to the theatre, where she had a box for that evening. Instead she went to the nursery and spent the evening with her son. She put him to bed herself, made the sign of the cross over him, and tucked him up. She felt light-hearted and tranquil, and saw clearly that what in the train had appeared so important had merely been an ordinary and trivial incident of Society life, and that there was no reason for her to feel ashamed. She sat down by the fire with an English novel and awaited her husband. Exactly at half-past nine there was a ring at the front door, and he entered the room.

'Here you are at last!' she said, holding out her hand to him.

He kissed it, and seated himself beside her.

'In general, I see that your journey has been a success,' said he.

'Yes, quite,' she replied, and related everything that had happened from the beginning: her journey with the Countess Vronskaya, her arrival, the accident at the railway station. Then she spoke of her pity, first for her brother and then for Dolly.

'I don't think that one can excuse such a man, even though he is your brother,' remarked Karenin, severely.

Anna smiled. She knew he had said that in order to show that no consideration of kinship could hinder the expression of his sincere opinion. She knew and liked that trait in her husband's character.

'I am glad it has all ended satisfactorily and that you are back again,' he continued.

Having finished his second cup of tea and cream and his bread and butter, he rose and went into his study.

'And have you not been out anywhere? You must have been dull,' he said.

'Oh no!' she answered, rising, and slipping her hand under his arm walked with him to the study door. She knew his habit, which had become a necessity, of reading in the evening. She knew that in spite of his time being almost entirely absorbed by the duties of his post, he considered it incumbent on him to follow everything of importance that appeared in the world of thought. She also knew that really he was interested in political, philosophic, and theological books, and that art was quite foreign to his nature, yet in spite of this—or rather because of it—he never ignored anything that caused a stir in that sphere, but considered it his duty to read everything.

'Well, God bless you!' she said at the door of the study, where a shaded candle and a bottle of water had been placed ready for him beside his arm-chair; 'and I will go and write to them in Moscow.' He pressed her hand and again kissed it.

'After all, he is a good man: truthful, kind, and remarkable in his own sphere,' said Anna to herself when she had returned to her room, as if defending him from some one who accused him and declared it was impossible to love him. 'But why do his ears stick out so? Or has he had his hair cut?'

Exactly at midnight, when Anna was still sitting at her writing-table finishing a letter to Dolly, she heard the measured tread of slippered feet, and Karenin entered, freshly washed, his hair brushed, and a book under his arm.

'It's time! It's time!' said he with a peculiar smile, going into their bedroom.

'And what right had he to look at him as he did?' thought Anna, remembering how Vronsky had looked at Karenin.

When she was undressed she went into the bedroom, but on her face there was not a trace of that animation which during her stay in Moscow had sparkled in her eyes and smile.

29

When he went to Moscow, Vronsky had left his large flat on the Morskaya to his friend and favourite comrade, Petritsky.

Petritsky was a young lieutenant, not of very aristocratic birth, and not only not wealthy but heavily in debt, tipsy every evening, and often under arrest for amusing or improper escapades, but popular both with his comrades and superiors. Arriving home from the station about noon, Vronsky recognized a hired brougham at the front door. When he rang the bell, while still outside, he heard men's laughter, a woman's lisping voice.

Vronsky told the servants not to announce his arrival, and softly entered the first room. Petritsky's friend, the Baroness Chilton, her lilac satin dress and pink and white face glistening, and like a canary filling the whole room with her Parisian voice, was seated at the round table making coffee. Petritsky in his greatcoat, and Captain Kamerovsky in full uniform, sat on each side of her.

'Vronsky! Bravo!' exclaimed Petritsky jumping up and noisily pushing back his chair. 'The master himself! Baroness, some coffee for him out of the new coffee-pot. ... Well, this is unexpected! I hope you are pleased with this ornament to your study,' he added, pointing to the Baroness. 'Of course, you know one another?'

'I should think so!' replied Vronsky with a merry smile, as he pressed the Baroness's small hand. 'Of course: quite old friends.'

'You have returned from a journey?' said the Baroness. 'Oh, I'll be off home this very moment if I am in the way.'

'You are at home where you are, Baroness,' said Vronsky. 'How do you do, Kamerovsky?' he added, coldly shaking hands with the Captain.

'There now! You never manage to say such pretty things,' said the Baroness to Petritsky.

Vronsky listened with pleasure to the merry prattle of the pretty young woman. In his Petersburg world his set were above all well-bred, generous, bold, gay, and had to abandon themselves unblushingly to all their passions and laugh at everything else.

Just for a moment Vronsky was staggered, having brought back from Moscow the impression of a totally different world, but immediately, as though he had put his foot into an old slipper, he re-entered his former gay and pleasant world.

Having heard all the news, Vronsky, with the help of his valet, put on his uniform and went to report himself. After that he intended to go to see his brother and to see Betsy, and to pay a few calls in order to begin visiting the set in which he could meet Anna Karenina. As usual in Petersburg, he left the house not to return till late at night.

PART TWO

1

Toward the end of the winter a consultation was held at the Shcherbatskys' which was intended to ascertain the state of Kitty's health and to decide what should be done to restore her failing strength. She was ill, and with the approach of spring grew worse. Their doctor prescribed cod-liver oil, then iron, and then nitrate of silver, but as none of them did her any good he advised her to go abroad for the spring.

Kitty pretended to be cheerful. She often now, almost always, had to pretend.

'Really, Mama! I am quite well. But if you wish to travel, let us go!' and trying to appear interested in the journey she began to talk about the preparations for it.

Just after the doctor had left, Dolly came, though she had only recently got up after a confinement (she had given birth to a daughter at the end of the winter), and had many troubles and cares of her own.

'Well, how is she?' she said, entering the drawing-room. They tried to tell her what the doctor had said, but the only thing of interest was that it had been decided they should go abroad.

Dolly could not suppress a sigh. Her best friend, her sister, was going away; and as it was, her life was not a bright one. Her relations with her husband after their reconciliation had become humiliating. Oblonsky was hardly ever at home, there was hardly ever any money, and suspicions of his infidelity continually tormented Dolly, but she let herself be deceived, despising him, and especially herself, for such weakness.

'And how are you all getting on?' asked her mother.

'Ah, Mama, we have plenty of trouble of our own. Lily has fallen ill, and I'm afraid it's scarlet fever. I have come out to-day to hear the news, because I shall not come out at all if (which God forbid!) it really is scarlet fever.'

The old Prince came out of his study and, after giving his cheek to Dolly and greeting her, he turned to his wife:

'Well, have you made up your minds to go? And what are you going to do with me?'

'I think you should stay behind, Alexander,' replied his wife.

'Mama, why should not Papa come with us?' said Kitty. 'It would be pleasanter for him and for us too.'

'Well, Dolly,' he said, turning to his eldest daughter, 'and what is your prodigal about?'

'Nothing particular, Papa,' answered Dolly, understanding that he referred to her husband. 'He is always out, I hardly see him,'—she could not resist adding with an ironical smile.

'And has he not yet gone to the country to sell the forest?'

'No, he is always preparing to go.'

'Dear me!' said the Prince. 'And so I am also to prepare? I'm all obedience,' he said, as he sat down again. 'And look here, Kate,' he went on, turning to his youngest daughter: 'You must wake up one fine morning and say to yourself: "Why, I am quite well and happy, and will go out to walk in the frost again with Papa." Eh?'

Her father's words seemed very simple, but they made Kitty feel as confused and flurried as a detected criminal. 'Yes, he knows and understands it all, and in these words is telling me that, though I am ashamed, I must get over my shame.' She could not gather spirit enough to reply. She made an attempt, but suddenly burst into tears and ran away.

The Princess flew at her husband: 'That comes of your jokes. You always ...' and she began reproaching him.

The Prince listened for some time to her rebukes in silence, but his face frowned more and more.

'She is so pitiful, poor thing, and you don't feel that every allusion to what has caused it hurts her. Oh dear, oh dear, to be so mistaken in anyone!' said the Princess, and from the change in her tone both Dolly and the Prince knew that she was thinking of Vronsky.

'Oh, it makes me sick to hear it!' muttered the Prince gloomily, rising as if he meant to go away. 'Since you have invited it I will tell you who is at fault for it all: you, and no one but you!'

The Prince appeared to have much more to say, but as soon as the Princess heard his tone she, as always happened in serious cases, gave in and became repentant.

'Alexander, Alexander,' she whispered, bursting into tears.

As soon as she began to cry the Prince came up to her.

'That will do, that will do! You suffer too, I know. It can't be helped! There's no great harm done. God is merciful ... thank you ...' he went on, and after responding to his wife's wet kiss which he felt on his hand, he went out.

When Kitty, in tears, had left the room, Dolly mentally rolled up her sleeves, prepared for action. When her father left the room she was ready for the chief thing needful, which was to go to Kitty and comfort her.

'I wanted to tell you something long ago, Mama. Do you know that Levin wished to propose to Kitty when he was here last? He told Stephen.'

'Well, what of that? I don't understand ...'

'Perhaps Kitty rejected him? ... Did she not tell you ...?'

'No, she told me nothing about either—she is too proud. But I know it is all because of that ...'

'Yes, and just imagine if she refused Levin—and she would not have refused him if it had not been for that other. I know. ... And then ... the other deceived her so dreadfully.'

It was too dreadful for the Princess to think how much she was to blame in regard to her daughter, and she grew angry.

'Oh! I can't make anything out! Nowadays girls all want to trust to their own reason. They don't tell their mothers anything ...'

'Mama, I will go to her.'

'Go. Am I preventing you?' said the mother.

2

On entering Kitty's little snuggery, a pretty pink room, decorated with *vieux saxe* figures, Dolly remembered how light-heartedly and with what love they two had arranged that room the year before. Her heart grew chill when she saw Kitty sitting on the low chair nearest the door, her eyes fixed on a corner of the carpet.

'I am going home now and shall have to shut myself up, and you won't be able to come to me,' said Dolly, sitting down beside her sister. 'I want to talk to you.'

'What about?' asked Kitty quickly, lifting her face in alarm.

'What but your troubles?'

'I have no troubles.'

'Come now, Kitty. Do you think I can help knowing? I know everything. And believe me it is so unimportant. ... We have all passed through the same.'

Kitty was silent and her face looked stern.

'He is not worthy of your suffering for him,' continued Dolly, going straight to the point.

'No, because he has despised me,' said Kitty with a shaking voice.

'But who told you so? Nobody says so! I am sure he was in love with you and is still in love, but ...'

'Oh dear! these commiserations are what I dread most of all!' cried
Kitty, suddenly flaring up. Dolly knew how apt Kitty was to forget
herself when in a passion and to say much that was unpleasant and
had better not have been said. She tried to pacify her; but it was too
late.

'What do you want me to feel, what?' said Kitty quickly. 'That I was
in love with a man who wouldn't have anything to do with me, and that
I am dying for love of him?

'There is nothing for me to grieve for or seek comfort about. I have
enough pride never to let myself love a man who does not love me.'

'But I am not suggesting it. … Only, tell me frankly,' said Dolly, taking her by the hand, 'did Levin speak to you?'

The mention of Levin seemed to deprive Kitty of the last fragments
of self-control: she jumped up from her chair, and rapidly gesticulating
with her hands she began:

'What has Levin to do with it? I don't understand why you need torment me! I have said and I repeat I will never, _never_ do what you are
doing—returning to a man who has betrayed you and has loved another
woman. I can't understand it! You may do it, but I can't.'

Having said these words she looked at her sister and seeing that Dolly
remained silent with her head bowed sadly, Kitty, instead of leaving the
room as she had intended to do, sat down by the door, and hiding her
face in her handkerchief let her head sink down.

For a minute or two there was silence. Dolly was thinking about herself. The humiliation of which she was always conscious was peculiarly
painful when her sister touched on it. She had not expected such cruelty
from her, and was angry with her. But suddenly she heard the rustle of
a dress and a burst of suppressed sobbing. A pair of arms encircled her
neck from below and Kitty was kneeling before her.

'Dolly dear, I am so, so unhappy!' she whispered guiltily. And the
sweet tear-stained face hid itself in the folds of Dolly's dress.

Kitty knew that what she had said in her anger about the unfaithfulness of Dolly's husband and about her humiliation had cut her poor
sister to the depths of her heart, but that she was forgiven; while Dolly
understood that Kitty's grief, her hopeless grief, was really caused by the
fact that Levin had proposed to her and that she had rejected him, and
now that Vronsky had deceived her, she was prepared to love Levin and
to hate Vronsky. Kitty did not say a word of this; she spoke only of her
state of mind.

'I have no troubles whatever,' she said when she had grown calm,—
'but can you understand that everything has become horrid, disgusting

and coarse to me, and above all I myself? You can't think what horrid thoughts I have about everything.'

'But what horrid thoughts can you have?' asked Dolly smiling.

'The very nastiest and coarsest. How am I to tell you?'—she continued, noticing perplexity in her sister's eyes:—'Papa began to speak to me just now. ... It seems to me that he thinks that all I need is to get married. Mama takes me to a ball: and it seems to me she only takes me there to marry me off as quickly as possible and get rid of me. I know it is not true, but I can't get rid of the idea. I can't bear to see the so-called eligible men. I always think they are taking my measure. I feel ashamed and uncomfortable. Well, what is one to do? I only feel comfortable with children, only in your house.'

'What a pity you can't come to see us!'

'But I will come. I have had scarlet fever, and I will persuade Mama to let me.'

And Kitty insisted on having her own way. The two sisters nursed all the six children successfully through the illness, but Kitty's health did not improve, and in Lent the Shcherbatskys went abroad.

3

The highest Petersburg Society is really all one: all who belong to it know and even visit one another. But this large circle has its sub-divisions. Anna Arkadyevna Karenina had friends and close connections in three different sets. One of these was her husband's official set, consisting of his colleagues and subordinates; but (in spite of admonitions and advice from the Countess Lydia Ivanovna) this bureaucratic circle of male interests could not interest Anna, and she avoided it.

Another circle with which Anna was intimate was that through which Karenin had made his career. The centre of that circle was the Countess Lydia Ivanovna. It consisted of elderly, plain, philanthropic and pious women and clever, well-educated, ambitious men. Karenin set great value on this circle, and Anna, who knew how to get on with every one, had during the first part of her life in Petersburg made friends in it too. But now, on her return from Moscow, it seemed to her that she, and all of them, were only pretending, and she felt so bored and uncomfortable in that Society that she visited Lydia Ivanovna as rarely as possible.

The third circle with which Anna was connected was the Society of balls, dinner-parties, brilliant toilettes, the Society which clung to the Court with one hand lest it should sink to the *demi-monde*, for this the members of that Society thought they despised, though its tastes were not only similar but identical with their own. Anna was connected with this set through the Princess Betsy Tverskaya, the wife of her cousin, and who, from the time Anna first appeared in Society, had made much of her, and drawn her into her own set, making fun of that to which the Countess Lydia Ivanovna belonged.

At first Anna had avoided the Princess Tverskaya's set as much as she could, because it demanded more expense than she could afford; and also because she really approved more of the other set; but after her visit to Moscow all this was reversed. She avoided her moral friends and went into grand Society. There she saw Vronsky, and experienced a tremulous joy when meeting him. She met him most frequently at Betsy's, who was his cousin. Vronsky went everywhere where he had a chance of meeting Anna, and spoke to her of his love whenever he could. She gave him no encouragement, but every time they met there sprang up that feeling of animation which had seized her in the train on the morning when she first saw him. She was aware that when they met joy lit up her eyes and drew her lips into a smile, but she could not hide the expression of that joy.

At first Anna sincerely believed that she was displeased with him for allowing himself to persecute her; but soon after her return from Moscow, having gone to a party where she expected to meet him but to which he did not come, she clearly realized, by the sadness that overcame her, that she had been deceiving herself and that his persecution supplied the whole interest of her life.

Princess Betsy had scarcely time to order tea to be served in the big drawing-room, before one carriage after another began to arrive at the door of her immense house on the Great Morskaya. The visitors passed beneath the broad portico, and the hall porter noiselessly opened the door to admit them.

Almost at one and the same time the hostess, her hair rearranged and her face freshened up, entered at one door and the visitors at another of the large, dark-walled drawing-room, with its thick carpets and brightly-lit table, shining in the candle-light with white table-cloth, silver samovar and translucent china.

The company settled down, separating into two circles: one with the hostess round the samovar, the other, at the opposite end of the room, round the wife of an ambassador, a beautiful woman with black sharply-outlined eyebrows, in a black velvet dress.

The Princess Betsy's husband, a fat, good-natured man, an enthusiastic collector of engravings, hearing that his wife had visitors, entered the drawing-room before going to his club. Stepping silently on the thick carpet, he approached the Princess Myagkaya.

'How did you like Nilsson?' he inquired.

'Oh, how can you steal on one like that? How you frightened me!' said she in reply. 'Please don't talk to me about the opera—you know nothing of music. I had better descend to your level and talk about your majolica and engravings. Come now, tell me about the treasures you have picked up lately at the rag fair!'

'Shall I show you? But you don't understand them.'

'Yes, let me see them. I have learnt from those—what is their name?—the bankers. . . . They have some splendid engravings.'

'What? Have you been to the Schuzburgs'?' asked the hostess.

'I have, *ma chère*. They asked my husband and me to dinner, and I was told that the sauce alone at that dinner cost a thousand roubles,' said the Princess Myagkaya loudly, feeling that everybody was listening. 'And a very nasty sauce it was too, something green! We had to invite them, and I gave them a sauce that cost eighty-five kopeks, and satisfied every one.'

The effect produced by the Princess Myagkaya's words was always the same; and the secret of that effect lay in the fact that although she often—as at that moment—spoke not quite to the point, her words were simple and had the effect of a most witty joke.

While she was speaking everybody listened to her and the conversation in the circle round the ambassador's wife stopped; the hostess wished to make one circle of the whole company, and turning to the ambassador's wife, said:

'You should come and join us here.'

'No, we are very comfortable here,' replied the ambassador's wife smiling, and she continued the interrupted conversation. They were disparaging the Karenins, husband and wife.

'Anna has changed very much since her trip to Moscow. There is something strange about her,' said a friend of Anna's.

'The chief change is that she has brought back with her the shadow of Alexis Vronsky,' said the ambassador's wife.

'A woman with a shadow generally ends badly,' said Anna's friend.

'A murrain on your tongue!' suddenly remarked the Princess Myagkaya, hearing these words. 'Anna Karenina is a splendid woman. I don't like her husband, but I am very fond of her.'

'Why don't you like her husband? He is such a remarkable man,' said the ambassador's wife. 'My husband says there are few statesmen like him in Europe.'

'My husband tells me the same, but I don't believe it,' replied the Princess Myagkaya. 'If our husbands didn't talk, we should see things as they really are; and it's my opinion that Karenin is simply stupid. Formerly, when I was told to consider him wise, I kept trying to, and thought I was stupid myself because I was unable to perceive his wisdom; but as soon as I said to myself, he's stupid (only in a whisper of course), it all became quite clear! Don't you think so?'

'How malicious you are to-day!'

'Not at all. I have no choice. One of us is stupid, and you know it's impossible to say so of oneself.

'But the point is, that I won't abandon Anna to you. She is so excellent, so charming! What is she to do, if every one is in love with her and follows her about like a shadow?'

'But I don't even think of blaming her!' Anna's friend said.

'If no one follows us about like a shadow, that does not prove that we have a right to judge her.'

Having snubbed Anna's friend handsomely, the Princess Myagkaya rose with the ambassador's wife and joined those at the table, where there was a general conversation about the King of Prussia.

'Whom were you backbiting there?' asked Betsy.

'The Karenins. The Princess was characterizing Karenin,' replied the ambassador's wife with a smile, seating herself at the table.

'It's a pity we did not hear it!' said the hostess. 'Ah! Here you are at last!' she added, addressing Vronsky as he entered the room.

Vronsky not only knew everybody in the room, but saw them all every day, so he entered in the calm manner of one who rejoins those from whom he has parted only a short time before.

4

Steps were heard at the entrance, and the Princess Betsy, knowing that it was Anna, glanced at Vronsky. He gazed joyfully, intently, and yet timidly at the lady who was entering, and slowly rose from his seat. Anna entered the room holding herself, as usual, very erect, and approached her hostess, walking with that quick, firm yet light step which distinguished her from other Society women. She shook hands, smilingly, and with the same smile looked round at Vronsky. He bowed low and moved a chair toward her.

Anna responded only by an inclination of the head, though she blushed and frowned. But immediately, nodding rapidly to her acquaintances and pressing the hands extended to her, she turned again to her hostess:

'I have just been at the Countess Lydia's and could not get away.'

The conversation, interrupted by her entrance, again burnt up like the flame of a lamp that has been blown about.

'And it is true that the younger Vlasyeva is going to be married to Topov.'

'Yes; I am surprised at her parents. They say it's a love match.'

'Love match! What antediluvian ideas you have! Who talks of love nowadays?' said the ambassador's wife.

'What's to be done? That silly old fashion hasn't died out yet!' said Vronsky.

'So much the worse for those who follow the fashion! I know of happy marriages, but only such as are founded on reason.'

'Yes, but how often the happiness of marriages founded on reason crumbles to dust because the very passion that was disregarded makes itself felt later,' said Vronsky.

'But by "marriages founded on reason", we mean marriages between those who have both passed through that madness. It's like scarlet fever: one has to get it over.'

'No, joking apart, I believe that to understand love one must first make a mistake and then correct it,' said the Princess Betsy. 'What do you think?' she asked, addressing Anna, who with a scarcely discernible resolute smile was listening to this conversation.

'I think,' replied Anna, toying with the glove she had pulled off, 'I think ... if it is true that there are as many minds as there are heads, then there are as many kinds of love as there are hearts.'

Vronsky had gazed at Anna and with sinking heart waited to hear what she would say. He sighed when she had uttered these words.

Suddenly Anna addressed him:

'I have received a letter from Moscow. They write that Kitty Shcherbatskaya is very ill.'

'Really?' said Vronsky, frowning.

Anna glanced sternly at him. 'It does not interest you?'

'On the contrary, it interests me very much! What exactly do they write, if I may ask?' he inquired.

Anna rose and went up to Betsy. 'Give me a cup of tea,' she said, stopping behind Betsy's chair.

While Betsy was pouring out the tea, Vronsky went up to Anna. 'What do they write?' he asked again.

'I often think men don't understand honour, though they are always talking about it,' said Anna, without answering his question. 'I have long wanted to tell you,' she added, and, moving a few steps to a side-table, she sat down, 'that you have behaved very badly.'

'Don't I know that I behaved badly? But who was the cause?'

'Why say that to me?' she asked, looking severely at him.

'You know why,' he answered boldly and joyously, meeting her look and continuing to gaze at her.

It was not he, but she, who became abashed.

'That only proves you have no heart,' she said. But her look said that she knew he had a heart and that she therefore feared him.

'What you have just referred to was a mistake, and not love.'

Anna shuddered, and said: 'Don't you remember that I forbade you to mention that word, that horrid word?' But then she felt that the word *forbade* showed that she claimed certain rights over him, thereby encouraging him to speak of love. 'I have long wanted to say that to you,' she went on, looking resolutely into his eyes, her face all aglow and suffused with a burning blush, 'and to-day I came on purpose, to tell you that this must stop! I have never till now had to blush before anyone, but you make me feel as if I were guilty of something.'

'What do you want of me?' he asked, simply and seriously.

'If you love me as you say you do,' she whispered, 'behave so that I may be at peace.'

His face brightened.

'Don't you know that you are all my life to me? ... But peace I do not know, and can't give to you. My whole being, my love ... yes! I cannot think about you and about myself separately. And I do not see before us the possibility of peace either for me or for you. I see the possibility of despair, misfortune ... or of happiness—what happiness! ... Is it impossible?' he added with his lips only, but she heard.

She exerted all the powers of her mind to say what she ought; but instead she fixed on him her eyes filled with love.

'This is it!' he thought with rapture. 'Just as I was beginning to despair, and when it seemed as though the end would never come ... here it is! She loves me! She acknowledges it!'

'Do this for me: never say such words to me, and let us be good friends.'

'Friends we shall not be; but whether we shall be the happiest or the most miserable of human beings ... rests with you.'

She wished to say something, but he interrupted her.

'I ask only one thing: I ask the right to hope and suffer as I do now; but if even that is impossible, command me to disappear, and I will do it. You shall not see me if my presence is painful to you.'

'I don't want to drive you away.'

'Only don't change anything. Leave everything as it is!' he said with trembling voice. 'Here is your husband.'

Indeed, just at that moment Karenin, with his deliberate, ungraceful gait, entered the drawing-room.

He glanced at his wife and Vronsky, went up to the hostess, and having sat down with a cup of tea began talking in his deliberate and always clear tones, in his usual ironical way ridiculing somebody.

But the Princess Betsy could not bear that tone of his: so, like a clever hostess, she at once led him into a serious conversation on universal military service. Karenin was immediately absorbed.

Vronsky and Anna remained sitting at the little table.

Nearly all those present in the drawing-room, even the Princess Myagkaya and Betsy herself, several times glanced across at the pair who had gone away from the general circle. Only Karenin did not once glance that way and was not distracted from the interesting conversation in which he was engaged.

Noticing the unpleasant impression produced on every one, the Princess Betsy manœuvred for some one else to take her place and to listen to Karenin, and she herself went up to Anna.

'I am always amazed at your husband's clearness and exactitude of expression,' she said. 'The most transcendental ideas become accessible to me when he speaks.'

'Oh yes!' said Anna, radiant with a smile of happiness and not understanding a single word of what Betsy was saying; and going across to the big table she joined in the general conversation.

After half an hour's stay Karenin went up to his wife and suggested that they should go home together; but, without looking at him, she answered that she would stay to supper. Karenin bowed to the company and went away.

The hall-porter stood with his hand on the outer front door, Anna with her deft little hand was disengaging the lace of her sleeve which had caught on a hook of her fur coat, and with bent head was listening with delight to what Vronsky, who accompanied her, was saying.

'Granted that you have not said anything! I don't demand anything,' he was saying, 'but you know that it is not friendship I want! Only one happiness is possible for me in life—yes, love ...'

'Love,' she slowly repeated to herself, and suddenly, while releasing the lace, she added aloud: 'The reason I dislike that word is that it means

too much for me, far more than you can understand,' and she looked
him in the face. '*Au revoir!*'

She gave him her hand, and with her quick elastic step went past the
hall-porter and vanished into the carriage.

Her glance and the touch of her hand burnt him. He kissed the palm
of his hand where she had touched it, and went home happy in the
knowledge that in this one evening he had made more progress toward
his aim than he had during the previous two months.

5

Karenin did not see anything peculiar or improper in his wife's conversing animatedly with Vronsky at a separate table, but he noticed that
others in the drawing-room considered it peculiar and improper, and
decided to speak to his wife about it.

When he reached home he went to his study as usual, seated himself
in his easy-chair, and opened a book. At the usual hour he rose and
prepared for bed. Anna had not yet returned. With the book under his
arm he went upstairs; but to-night, his mind was full of his wife and of
something unpleasant that had happened concerning her. Contrary to
his habit he did not go to bed, but with his hands clasped behind his
back started pacing up and down the rooms.

He was not of a jealous disposition. Jealousy in his opinion insulted a
wife, and a man should have confidence in his wife. Why he should have
confidence—that is, a full conviction that his young wife would always
love him—he never asked himself; but he felt no distrust, and therefore
had confidence, and assured himself that it was right to have it. Now,
though his conviction that jealousy is a shameful feeling, and that one
ought to have confidence, had not been destroyed, he felt that he was
face to face with something illogical and stupid, and he did not know
what to do. Karenin was being confronted with life—with the possibility
of his wife's loving somebody else. It was the first time that possibility
had occurred to him, and he was horrified.

He paced up and down with his even step on the resounding parquet
floor of the dining-room. From time to time he stopped and thought:
'Yes, it is necessary to decide and to stop it: to express my opinion of it
and my decision.' Then he turned back again. 'But express what? What
decision?' he asked himself, and could find no answer. 'What is it that
has happened? Nothing at all. She had a long talk with him—Well?
What of that? Are there not plenty of men with whom a woman may

talk? Besides ... to be jealous is to degrade myself and her,' he said to himself. But a voice seemed to whisper that it was not so, and that if others noticed, that showed that there must have been something for them to notice.

'I must think it over, come to a decision, and throw it off,' he said aloud. 'The question of her feelings, of what has taken place or may take place in her soul, is not my business; it is the business of her conscience and belongs to religion,' said he. 'My duty is clearly defined. As head of the family I am the person whose duty is to guide her, and who is therefore partly responsible; I must show her the danger which I see, warn her, and even use my authority. I must speak plainly to her.'

A woman's steps were heard ascending the stairs. Karenin, aware of her approach, felt some apprehension of the coming explanations.

6

Anna walked in with bowed head, playing with the tassels of her hood. On seeing her husband she lifted her head and, as if awakening from sleep, smiled.

'You're not in bed? What a wonder!' she said, throwing off her hood, and without pausing she went on to her dressing-room. 'Alexis Alexandrovich, it's high time!' she added from beyond the door.

'Anna, I must have a talk with you.'

'With me?' she said with surprise, coming back from the other room and looking at him. 'What is it? What about?' she asked.

Anna, hearing her own words, was astonished at her capacity for deception. How simple and natural her words sounded.

'Anna, I must warn you,' said he.

'Warn me?' she asked; 'what about?'

She looked so naturally and gaily at him, that one who did not know her could not have noticed anything strange in the intonation or the meaning of her words. But for him, who knew that when he went to bed five minutes late she noticed it and asked the reason—knew that she had always immediately told him all her joys, pleasures, and sorrows—for him, her reluctance to notice his state of mind, or to say a word about herself, meant much. He saw that the depths of her soul, till now always open, were closed to him. More than that, he knew from her tone that she was not ashamed of this.

'I wish to warn you,' he said in low tones, 'that you may, by indiscretion and carelessness, give the world occasion to talk about you. Your too animated conversation to-night with Count Vronsky' (he pronounced the name with quiet deliberation) 'attracted attention.'

'You are always like that,' she replied, as if intentionally taking notice only of his last words. 'One day you dislike my being dull, another day my being happy. I was not dull. Does that offend you?'

Karenin started and bent his hands to crack his fingers.

'Oh, please don't crack your fingers! I dislike it so!' she said.

'Anna, is this you?' said he softly, refraining from moving his hands.

'But whatever is the matter?' she asked in a tone of comical surprise and sincerity. 'What do you want of me?'

Karenin paused and rubbed his forehead and eyes.

'This is what I intended to say,' he continued coldly and calmly, 'and I ask you to listen to me. As you know, I consider jealousy an insulting and degrading feeling and will never allow myself to be guided by it; but there are certain laws of propriety which one cannot disregard with impunity. I did not notice it this evening, but, judging by the impression created, all present noticed that you behaved and acted not quite as was desirable.'

'Really, I don't understand at all,' said Anna, shrugging her shoulders. 'It is all the same to him!' she said to herself. 'But Society noticed, and that disturbs him!' She rose and was about to pass out of the room, but he moved forward as if to stop her.

His face looked plainer and gloomier than she had ever yet seen it.

'Well, I'm listening! What next?' said she quietly and mockingly.

'I have not the right to inquire into all the details of your feelings, and in general I consider it useless and even harmful to do so,' began Karenin. 'Your feelings concern your own conscience, but it is my duty to you, to myself, and to God, to point out to you your duties. Our lives are bound together not by men but by God. This bond can only be broken by a crime, and that kind of crime brings its punishment.'

'I don't understand anything. ... Oh dear! And as ill-luck will have it, I am dreadfully sleepy!' said she.

'Anna, for God's sake don't talk like that!' he said mildly. 'Perhaps I am mistaken, but believe me that what I am saying I say equally for my own sake and for yours. I am your husband, and I love you.'

For an instant her head had drooped and the mocking spark in her eyes had died away, but the word 'love' aroused her again. 'Love!' she thought, 'as if he can love! He does not know what love is.'

'Alexis Alexandrovich, I really do not understand,' she replied.

'Allow me to finish. I love you. But I am not talking of myself. The chief persons concerned are our son and yourself. I repeat—perhaps my words may seem quite superfluous to you; perhaps they result from a mistake of mine. In that case I ask your pardon! But if you feel that there are any grounds, however slight, I beg you to reflect, and if your heart prompts you to tell me ...'

'I have nothing to say. Besides ...' she added, rapidly, and hardly repressing a smile, 'it really is bedtime.'

Karenin sighed, and without saying anything more went into the bedroom.

When she went there he was already in bed. His lips were sternly compressed and his eyes did not look at her. Anna got into her bed, and every moment expected that he would address her. But he remained silent. She lay waiting and motionless for a long time, and then forgot him. She was thinking of another; she saw him, and felt her heart fill with excitement and guilty joy at the thought.

From that time a new life began for Karenin and his wife. Nothing particular happened. Anna went into Society as before, frequently visiting the Princess Betsy, and she met Vronsky everywhere. Karenin noticed this, but could do nothing. She met all his efforts to bring about an explanation by presenting an impenetrable wall of merry perplexity. Externally things seemed as before, but their intimate relations with one another were completely changed. Karenin, strong as he was in his official activities, felt himself powerless here. Every day he prepared himself to have a talk with her. But each time he began to speak with her he felt the same spirit of evil and falsehood which had taken possession of her master him also, and he neither said the things he meant to, nor spoke in the tone he had meant to adopt. He spoke in his habitual half-bantering tone which seemed to make fun of those who said such things seriously; and in that tone it was impossible to say what had to be said to her.

7

That which for nearly a year had been Vronsky's sole and exclusive desire, supplanting all his former desires: that which for Anna had been an impossible, dreadful, but all the more bewitching dream of happiness, had come to pass.

'Anna, Anna,' he said in trembling voice, 'Anna, for God's sake!'

But the louder he spoke the lower she drooped her once proud, bright, but now dishonoured head.

'My God! Forgive me!' she said, sobbing and pressing Vronsky's hand to her breast.

She felt so guilty, so much to blame, that it only remained for her to humble herself and ask to be forgiven. Looking at him, she felt her degradation physically, and could say nothing more. He felt what a murderer must feel when looking at the body he has deprived of life. The body he had deprived of life was their love, the first period of their love. There was something frightful and revolting in the recollection of what had been paid for with this terrible price of shame. The shame she felt at her spiritual nakedness communicated itself to him.

Vronsky covered her face and shoulders with kisses.

She held his hand and did not move. 'Yes, and this hand is the hand of my accomplice.' She lifted his hand and kissed it. At last, as though mastering herself, she sat up and pushed him away. Her face was as beautiful as ever, but all the more piteous.

'It's all over,' she said. 'I have nothing but you left. Remember that.'

'I cannot help remembering what is life itself to me! For one moment of that bliss ...'

'What bliss?' she said with disgust and horror. 'For heaven's sake, not another word!'

She rose quickly and moved away from him.

'Not another word!' she repeated, and with a look of cold despair, strange to him, she left him. She felt that at that moment she could not express in words her feeling of shame, joy, and horror at this entrance on a new life, and she did not wish to vulgarize that feeling by inadequate words. But every time the thought of what she had done, and of what was to become of her and of what she should do, came to her mind, she was seized with horror.

8

When Levin first returned from Moscow, and while he still started and blushed every time he remembered the disgrace of the refusal, he had said to himself, 'Time will pass, and I shall become indifferent.'

But three months passed and he had not become indifferent to it, and to think of it still hurt him as it had done in the first days. He could not find peace, because he had so long dreamed of family life and felt so ripe for it, but was still unmarried and further than ever from marriage.

These wounds never closed up. And among these recollections stood the memory of her refusal and the pitiful rôle he must have played in the eyes of the others that evening. But time and work told. The painful memories became more and more covered over by the commonplace but important events of country life. Every week he thought less and less about Kitty. He waited impatiently to hear that she was married or was getting married soon, hoping that such news, like the drawing of an aching tooth, would quite cure him.

In February he had received a letter from Mary Nikolavna to say that his brother Nicholas's health was getting worse, but that he would not submit to any treatment. In consequence of this news Levin went to Moscow, saw his brother, and managed to persuade him to consult a doctor and go to a watering-place abroad. He had that winter begun writing a book on agriculture, the basis of which was that the character of the labourer was treated as a definite factor, like climate and soil. So that in spite of his solitary life, or rather because of it, his time was completely filled up; only occasionally he felt an unsatisfied desire to share with some one besides Agatha Mikhaylovna the thoughts that wandered through his brain—for even with her he often discussed physics, agricultural theories, and especially philosophy, which last was her favourite subject.

The spring had set in late. Easter found snow still on the ground; but on Easter Monday a warm wind began to blow, the clouds gathered, and for three days and nights warm stormy rain poured down. On the Thursday the wind fell and a thick grey mist rose as if to hide the secret of the changes nature was carrying on. On the first Sunday after Easter toward evening the mists dissolved, the clouds dispersed, the sky cleared, and real spring was there. In the morning the bright rising sun quickly melted the thin ice on the river and the warm air all around vibrated with the vapour given off by the awakening earth.

Spring had come.

Levin put on his high boots and, for the first time, a cloth coat instead of a fur, and went out to attend to his farm. Stepping now on a piece of ice, now into the sticky mud, he crossed the stream of dazzling water.

First of all he went to the cattle-yard. The cows had been let out there, and, warmed by the sunshine, their glossy new coats glistening, they were lowing to be let out into the fields. After he had for a while admired his cows, all familiar to him to the minutest detail, Levin gave orders for them to be driven into the field and for the calves to be let out into the yard. The cowherd ran away merrily to get ready. The dairymaids, with twigs in their hands, holding their skirts up over their bare white legs, not yet sun-burnt, splashed through the puddles into the yard, driving the calves, who were mad with the joy of spring.

Having gazed with admiration at the exceptionally fine calves born that year—the older ones were as big as peasants' cows, and Pava's three-month-old calf was as big as a yearling—Levin gave orders to bring a trough of food for them and to put some hay into the racks outside. But it turned out that the racks, which had been put up in the yard and not used during winter, were broken. He sent for the carpenter, who was under contract to be with the threshing-machine, but it turned out that he was mending the harrows, which should have been mended the week before Lent. This was very annoying to Levin. It was vexing that the careless farm management, against which he had struggled so many years with all his might, still continued. Levin sent for the steward, but instead of waiting went at once to look for him himself.

'Why is the carpenter not with the threshing-machine?'

'Oh, I meant to tell you yesterday that the harrows need mending. It's time to plough, you know.'

'Why wasn't it done in winter?'

'What is one to do with such people!' said the steward, waving his arm.

'It's not a case of such people, but of such a steward!' said Levin flaring up. 'Tell me what I keep you for!' he shouted; but remembering that this would not help matters, he stopped in the middle of what he was saying and only sighed. 'Well, can we begin sowing?'

'It will be possible, beyond Turkino, to-morrow or the day after.'

'And the clover?'

'I have sent Vasily, he and Mishka are sowing. Only I don't know if they will get through, it's very sticky.'

'How many acres?'

'Sixteen.'

'Why not the lot?' shouted Levin.

That they were only sowing sixteen instead of fifty acres with clover was still more annoying.

'There is no one to do it. What are you to do with such people?'

'Well then, you should have let the straw wait.'

'So I have.'

'But where are the men?'

'Five are making compote' (he meant compost) 'and four are turning the oats over. They might begin sprouting, Constantine Dmitrich.'

Levin understood very well that 'might begin sprouting' meant that the English seed-oats were already spoiling. Here again his orders had not been obeyed.

'Don't worry, it will all be done in good time.'

Levin waved his hand angrily and went to the barn. The oats were not yet spoilt, but the men were turning them over with shovels whereas they should have let them run down from the loft. Levin ordered them to do this, sent two of the men to help sow the clover, and got over his vexation with the foreman. Indeed, the day was so beautiful one could not long remain angry.

'Ignat!' he called to the coachman, who with sleeves rolled up was washing a carriage at the pump, 'saddle me Kolpik.'

'Yes, sir.'

While the horse was being saddled Levin again called the steward, who was hanging about within sight, in order to make it up with him, and began to talk about the spring work that lay before them.

The foreman listened attentively but his face still wore that hopeless and despondent expression so familiar to Levin.

Nothing grieved Levin so much as this manner, but all the same he could not but continue the struggle.

'But don't I know,' he added laughing, 'that you always want less of everything and worse? However, this year I will not let you have your way. I'll see to everything myself.'

'You don't sleep much as it is, I think. It's always pleasanter for us when the master's eye is on us ...'

'Then it's down in the Birch Valley that they are sowing the clover? I'll ride over and see,' said Levin, mounting the little light bay horse, Kolpik, which the coachman had brought.

If he had felt light-hearted in the cattle and farm yards, Levin felt still more so in the fields. Gently swayed by the ambling pace of his good little horse, and drinking in the warm smell with the freshness of snow and air in it, he rode through the forest over the crumbling sinking snow that melted at each footstep, and rejoiced at the sight of each one of his trees with its swelling buds and the moss reviving on its bark. When he had passed the forest, a vast expanse of velvety green unrolled before him without a single bare spot.

The further he went the happier he felt, and all sorts of plans for his estate, each better than the last, presented themselves to him.

Carefully guiding his horse so as not to trample down his young growth, he rode up to the labourers who were sowing the clover. The cart with the seed was standing in a field of winter-wheat, which was being cut up by the wheels and trampled by the horse's feet. Both the labourers were sitting on the narrow path between the fields, probably sharing a pipe of tobacco. On seeing the master the labourer Vasily moved toward the cart, and Mishka began to sow. This was not right, but Levin seldom got angry with the hired men. When Vasily came up Levin told him to take the cart and horse on to the border.

'It won't matter, sir, the wheat will recover.'

'Please don't argue,' said Levin, 'but do as you are told.'

'Yes, sir,' answered Vasily, and took hold of the horse's head.

'But the sowing, Constantine Dmitrich, is getting on first-rate,' he said making up to the master. 'Only the walking is dreadful. You drag half a hundredweight on your boots.'

'And why has not the earth been sifted?' said Levin.

'Oh, but we crumble it up,' said Vasily, taking a handful and rubbing the earth between his palms.

Vasily was not to blame that they had given him unsifted earth, but still it was annoying. Having more than once successfully tested a patent remedy for conquering vexation and making all that seemed wrong right again, Levin employed it now. He dismounted, took the seed-basket from Vasily, and prepared to sow.

'Where did you stop?'

Vasily pointed to a mark with his foot and Levin began scattering the seeds and earth as best he could. It was hard walking, and having done a row Levin, wet with perspiration, stopped and gave back the basket.

'Mind, sir, and don't scold me for this row when summer comes,' said Vasily.

'Why?' said Levin merrily, feeling that his remedy was acting well.

'Oh, you'll see when the summer comes. You'll distinguish it. You just look where I sowed last spring, how regularly I scattered it over. Why, Constantine Dmitrich, I don't think I could try harder if I was working for my own father. I don't like to do things badly myself, and I see that others don't. What's good for the master is good for us too. When one looks over there it makes one's heart rejoice,' said Vasily, pointing to the field.

'Well, mind and rub the lumps,' said Levin, going up to his horse, 'and keep an eye on Mishka, and if the clover comes up well you shall have fifty kopeks for each desyatina.'

'Thank you kindly. We are very grateful to you as it is.'

Levin mounted his horse and rode to the field where clover had been sown the year before.

It was already reviving and steadily growing green among last year's wheat stubble. The ploughed land was in excellent condition; it would be possible to harrow and sow it in a couple of days. Everything was beautiful and gay. Levin rode back by the way that led across the brook, scaring two ducks in so doing. 'There must be some snipe too,' he thought, and just at the turning to his house he met the keeper, who confirmed his supposition. Levin rode on at a trot, so as to have dinner and get his gun ready for the evening.

9

As Levin, in the highest spirits, was nearing the house he heard the sound of a tinkling bell approaching the main entrance.

'Why, that must be some one from the station,' he thought. 'They would just have had time to get here from the Moscow train.' He touched up his horse and, having passed the acacia trees, saw a hired three-horse sledge coming from the station and in it a gentleman in a fur coat. 'Ah,' he cried, joyfully lifting both arms, 'here's a welcome guest! Well, I am glad to see you!' he exclaimed, recognizing Oblonsky.

'I shall know now for certain whether she is married or when she will be,' thought Levin. And on this lovely day he felt that the memory of her did not hurt him at all.

'You did not expect me, eh?' said Oblonsky, getting out of the sledge with mud on his nose, cheek, and eyebrows, but beaming with cheerfulness and health. 'I have come to see you, that's one thing,' he said, embracing and kissing Levin, 'to get some shooting, that's two, and to sell the Ergushevo forest, that's three.'

'Well, I am very, very glad to see you,' said Levin with a sincere smile, joyful as a child's.

He showed his guest into the spare bedroom, and leaving him to wash and change Levin went to the office to give orders about the ploughing and the clover. Agatha Mikhaylovna met him in the hall with questions about dinner.

'Do just as you please, only be quick,' he said.

When he returned, Oblonsky, fresh and clean, with hair brushed, and face radiant with smiles, was just coming out of his room, and they went upstairs together.

'How glad I am to have come to you! Now I shall be able to understand what the mysteries you perpetrate here consist of. But, seriously, I envy you. What a house, and everything so splendid, so light, so gay!' said Oblonsky, forgetting that it was not always spring and bright weather there, as on that day.

'And your nurse! quite charming!'

Not a word did Oblonsky say about Kitty or about any of the Shcherbatskys; he only delivered greetings from his wife. Levin was grateful to him for his delicacy and was very glad of his visit. Oblonsky, always pleasant and quick at understanding everything from a hint, was specially pleasant on this visit; there was a new trait in him which Levin noticed and was flattered by—a kind of respect and a sort of tenderness toward him. The efforts of Agatha Mikhaylovna and the cook to make the dinner specially nice resulted only in both the hungry friends sitting down to a snack and having to appease their hunger with *hors d'œuvres* of bread and butter, smoked goose, and pickled mushrooms, and in Levin's ordering the soup to be served without waiting for the pasties with which the cook intended to astonish the visitor. But Oblonsky, though used to very different dinners, found everything delicious.

'Splendid, splendid!' he said, as Agatha Mikhaylovna came.

'Ah, Agatha Mikhaylovna,' said Oblonsky, kissing the tips of his plump fingers; 'what smoked goose you have, what herb brandy! ... But what d'you think, Constantine, is it not time?' he added.

Levin glanced out of the window at the sun which was setting behind the bare trees of the forest.

'High time, high time! Kuzma, tell them to harness the trap,' he said, and ran downstairs.

Oblonsky went down and himself carefully took the canvas cover off the varnished case, opened it, and set to work to put together his valuable gun, which was of the newest type.

'Constantine, please leave word that if the dealer Ryabinin comes they should ask him in and let him wait.'

'Are you selling the forest to Ryabinin?'

'Yes. Do you know him?'

'Of course I know him. I have had dealings with him, positively and finally.'

Oblonsky laughed. 'Positively and finally' were the dealer's favourite words.

'Yes, he does speak very funnily. She knows where the master is going,' he added, patting Laska, who was whining and jumping round Levin, now licking his hand, now his boots and his gun.

The trap was standing at the door when they went out. Oblonsky sat down, wrapped a rug round his legs, and lit a cigar. 'Ah, this is life! How delightful! This is how I should like to live.'

'But who prevents you?' Levin remarked, smiling.

'No—you are a lucky fellow! You have got all you are fond of. You like horses—you have them; hounds—you have them; shooting—you get it; farming—you get it too.'

'Perhaps it is because I am glad of what I get, and don't grieve about what I haven't,' said Levin, thinking of Kitty.

Oblonsky understood and looked at him but said nothing.

10

The place where they were going to shoot was not far away, by a stream among young aspen trees. When they had reached the wood Levin got down and led Oblonsky to the corner of a mossy and marshy glade, already free from snow. He himself went to a forked birch on the other side.

The old grey-haired Laska, following close on his heels, sat down warily in front of him and pricked up her ears. Levin stood listening, and gazing down now on the wet mossy ground, now at the attentive Laska, now at the sea of bare tree-tops stretched out before him at the foot of the hill, and now at the darkening sky streaked with fleecy clouds. A hawk flew leisurely past, high above the distant forest; another followed in the same direction and vanished. A cuckoo called beyond the river. It called twice in its usual note, then hoarsely and hurriedly and got out of time.

'Fancy a cuckoo already!' said Oblonsky, appearing from behind a bush.

'Yes, I heard,' answered Levin, reluctant to disturb the silence of the wood. 'They won't be long now.'

Oblonsky's figure again disappeared behind the bush.

They heard a shrill whistle in the distance, and after the two seconds' interval so familiar to sportsmen, another followed, and then a third, and after the third whistle came a cry.

Levin looked to the right and to the left, and there before him against the dull light-blue sky, over the lower branches of the aspen tops, appeared the birds flying straight toward him; the sound of their cry seemed close to his ears; the long beak and neck of a bird were quite visible, and just as Levin took aim a red flash came from behind the bush where Oblonsky was standing and the bird descended like an arrow and then fluttered up again. Another flash, followed by a report, and the bird, flapping its wings as if trying to keep up in the air, remained stationary for a moment and then with a heavy thud fell on the swampy ground.

Oblonsky brought down two more birds, and Levin brought down two, of which one was not recovered. It began to get dark.

They were now standing some fifteen yards apart.

'Stephen!' said Levin suddenly and unexpectedly; 'why don't you tell me whether your sister-in-law is married, or when she will be?'

Levin felt so strong and calm that he thought the answer, whatever it might be, could not agitate him.

'She has not thought, and is not thinking, of getting married, but she is very ill and the doctors have sent her abroad. They are even afraid for her life.'

'You don't mean it!' exclaimed Levin. 'Very ill? What's the matter with her? How did she? ...'

But at that moment both men heard a shrill whistle that seemed to smite on their ears; they both seized their guns and there were two flashes and two reports at the same moment. The woodcock that was flying high up instantly folded its wings and fell into the thicket, bending down the thin young shoots.

'That's good! It belongs to both!' cried Levin and ran into the thicket with Laska to look for the bird. 'Found? good dog!' he said, taking the bird from Laska's mouth and putting it into his well-filled game-bag.

'We've found it, Stephen!' he shouted.

11

On their way home Levin inquired the particulars of Kitty's illness and of the Shcherbatskys' plans, and though he would have been ashamed to confess it, what he heard was agreeable to him. It was agreeable because there was still hope for him, and even more because she was suffering, she who had made him suffer so much. But when Oblonsky began to speak of what caused Kitty's illness and to mention Vronsky's name, Levin interrupted him:

'I have no right whatever to know such family details, and frankly I am not interested in them either.'

Oblonsky gave a scarcely perceptible smile on noticing the quick change, so familiar to him, in Levin's face, which became as gloomy as it had been bright a moment before.

'Have you settled with Ryabinin about the forest?' asked Levin.

'Yes, I have. I'm getting a splendid price for it: thirty-eight thousand roubles. No one would give more.'

'The fact is you are giving the forest away,' said Levin moodily. 'The forest is worth at least five hundred roubles a desyatina.'

'Oh, you country gentlemen!' said Oblonsky jokingly. 'And your tone of contempt for us poor townfolk! ... But when it comes to getting business done, we do it better than anyone. Believe me, I have reckoned it all out,' continued he, 'and have sold the forest so well that I am afraid he may change his mind. You know it's not timber but, for the most part, only fit for fuel,' said he, 'and it will not yield more than ten sazhens of wood to the desyatina ... and he is paying me at the rate of two hundred roubles.'

Levin smiled contemptuously.

'I should not try to teach you the things you scribble about at your office,' he said, 'but in case of need would come to you for advice about them, but you are firmly convinced that you understand all this forest lore. Have you counted the trees?'

'How can one count the trees?' said Oblonsky, still anxious to dispel his friend's ill-humour.

'Well, Ryabinin's lofty mind is able to do it. And no dealer will ever buy without first counting. I know your forest. I go shooting there every year, and it is worth five hundred roubles a desyatina cash down, and he is paying you two hundred on long term. That means that you have made him a present of about thirty thousand roubles.'

'Come, don't get so carried away,' said Oblonsky piteously. 'Why did no one offer more?'

'Because he and the other dealers are in league, and he has bought them off. I have had dealings with them all, and I know them. He would not consider a deal which would bring him in ten or fifteen per cent.; he waits till he can buy at a fifth of the value.'

Ryabinin was already in the house and met the two friends in the hall. He was a tall, spare, middle-aged man, with a moustache, a prominent shaven chin, and prominent dim eyes. He wore a long-skirted blue coat with buttons very low down at the back, high boots drawn quite straight over the calves of his legs and crinkled round the ankles, and over them he had on a pair of large galoshes. He held out his hand to Oblonsky as if he were trying to catch something.

'Oh, so you have come,' said Oblonsky taking his hand.

'I dared not disobey your Excellency's commands, though the roads are quite too bad. But I have arrived in time. ... Constantine Dmitrich, my respects to you!' he said turning to Levin and trying to catch his hand too. But Levin pretended not to see the hand, and began taking the snipe out of the game-bag.

'Would you like to go into my study?' said Levin, frowning moodily, and addressing Oblonsky in French.

'That would do very well,—or wherever you like,' remarked Ryabinin with contemptuous dignity, as if to show them that though others might find it difficult to know how to behave, for him no difficulty of any kind could ever exist.

On entering the study Ryabinin glanced at the book cupboards and book-shelves, smiled contemptuously, and shook his head disapprovingly.

'Well, have you brought the money?' asked Oblonsky.

'There won't be any difficult about the money. I've come to see you and to talk matters over.'

'Talk what matters over? But take a seat.'

'I can do that,' said Ryabinin, sitting down and putting his arm on the back of his chair in a most uncomfortable way. 'You must let me off something, Prince. You're wronging me. As to the money, it is all ready to the last kopek. There will be no delay about the money.'

Levin, who had been putting away his gun in a cupboard, was just going out of the door, but on hearing the dealer's words he stopped.

'As it is you are getting the forest for next to nothing,' he said. 'He came to me too late, else *I* would have fixed the price.'

Ryabinin rose and smiled silently, surveying Levin from his feet to his head. 'He is very close, is Constantine Dmitrich,' he said, addressing Oblonsky with a smile.

'Well, have you settled the business or not? If you have, there's no use bargaining, but if not,' said Levin, 'I will buy the forest myself.'

The smile vanished from Ryabinin's face, which assumed a hawk-like, rapacious, and cruel expression. With his bony fingers he rapidly unfastened his coat, and quickly took out a thick old pocket-book.

'If you please, the forest is mine,' he said, rapidly crossing himself and holding out his hand. 'Take your money, the forest is mine. That's the way Ryabinin does business, no fussing about kopeks.'

Levin went out and slammed the door. Ryabinin looked at it and smiled, shaking his head. An hour later the dealer, with the agreement in his pocket, seated himself in his little cart and drove home.

Oblonsky went upstairs, his pockets bulging with the treasury-bills payable in three months' time with which Ryabinin had paid him. The forest transaction was completed, he had the money in his pocket, the shooting had been fine, he was in the best of spirits, and therefore all the more anxious to dispel Levin's ill-humour. He wanted to finish the day at supper as pleasantly as he had begun it.

Levin really was in a bad humour, and in spite of his desire to behave kindly and amiably to his charming guest he could not master himself. The intoxication of the news that Kitty was not married was beginning little by little to take effect on him.

Kitty was unmarried and ill, and ill for love of the man who had slighted her. This insult seemed to fall upon him. Vronsky had slighted her and she had slighted him, Levin. But Levin did not think all this and was angry not with what had upset him but with everything that presented itself to him. The stupid sale of the forest, the swindle Oblonsky had fallen a prey to, which had been perpetrated in his house, irritated him.

'Well, have you finished?' he said when he met Oblonsky upstairs. 'Will you have some supper?'

'I won't say no. What an appetite I get in the country, wonderful! Why did you not offer Ryabinin something to eat?'

'Let him go to the devil!'

'Well, really, how you treat him!' said Oblonsky. 'You did not even give him your hand. Why not shake hands with him?'

'Because I do not shake hands with the footman, and the footman is a hundred times better than he.'

'What a reactionary you really are!' said Oblonsky.

'I have really never considered what I am. I am Constantine Levin, that's all.'

'And Constantine Levin is in a very bad temper,' said Oblonsky, smiling.

'Yes, I am in a bad temper, and do you know why? Because, excuse me, of your stupid sale. You have not counted the trees but Ryabinin has! Ryabinin's children will have the means to live and get an education, while yours may not have!'

'Well, forgive me, but there is something petty in all this counting. We have our occupation and they have theirs, and they have to make a profit. Anyway the thing is done. And here come the fried eggs, just the way I like them best. And Agatha Mikhaylovna will give us some of that excellent herb brandy ...'

Try as Levin would to control himself, he remained morose and silent. There was one question he wanted to put to Oblonsky, but could not bring himself to ask. When Oblonsky had gone down to his room and, after again washing, had put on his frilled nightshirt and got into bed, Levin still lingered in his room talking about various trifles and unable to ask what he wanted to know.

'Yes, by the by, where is Vronsky now?' he asked suddenly.

'Vronsky?' said Oblonsky. 'He is in Petersburg. He left soon after you did, and has not been in Moscow once since then. And do you know, Constantine, I will tell you quite frankly,' he said, 'it was your own fault. You were frightened of a rival. But as I told you then, I do not know who had the better chance. Why did you not make a dash for it? I told you at the time that ...' He yawned, but only with his jaw, without opening his mouth.

'Does he, or does he not, know that I proposed?' thought Levin, and feeling himself blush, he gazed in silence straight into Oblonsky's eyes.

'If there was anything on her side at that time, it was only the external attraction,' continued Oblonsky. 'You know his being a perfect aristocrat and his future position in Society had an effect, not on her but on her mother.'

Levin frowned. The insult of the refusal he had had to face burned in his heart like a fresh, newly-received wound. But he was at home and the walls of home are helpful.

'Wait, wait,' he began, interrupting Oblonsky. 'You talk of his being an aristocrat. But I should like to ask you what is Vronsky's or anyone else's aristocracy that I should be slighted because of it? You consider Vronsky an aristocrat. I don't. A man whose father crawled up from nothing by intrigues and whose mother has had relations with heaven knows whom. ... No, pardon me, I consider myself and people like me aristocrats: people who can point back to three or four honourable generations of their family, all with a high standard of education (talent and intelligence are a different matter), who have never cringed before anyone, never depended on anyone, but have lived as my father and my grandfather did. We are the aristocrats.'

'But whom are you driving at? I agree with you,' said Oblonsky sincerely and cheerfully, 'though much of what you say is not true of Vronsky, I am not speaking about that. I want to tell you candidly that if I were you, I'd come to Moscow now with me, and ...'

'No ... I don't know if you knew it or not and I don't care, but I will tell you: I proposed and was refused, and your sister-in-law is now only a painful and humiliating memory to me.'

'Why? What nonsense!'

'But don't let us talk about it! Forgive me, please, if I have been rude to you,' said Levin. Now that he had spoken out he became once more as he had been in the morning. 'You are not angry with me, Stiva? Please don't be angry,' he said smiling.

'Oh no, not at all! There was nothing to be angry about.'

12

Though Vronsky's whole inner life was absorbed by his passion, his external life ran unalterably and inevitably along its former customary rails of social and regimental connections and interests. The interests of the regiment occupied an important place in his life, because he was fond of his regiment and still more because the regiment was fond of him.

It goes without saying that he spoke to none of them about his love, nor did he betray himself even in the wildest drinking-bouts (indeed, he never drank so as to lose all self-control). And he silenced any of his thoughtless comrades who tried to hint at the liaison. But in spite of this, his love affair was known to all the town: everybody guessed more or less correctly what his relations with Anna Karenina were.

Vronsky's mother, on hearing of the matter, was at first pleased, both because in her opinion nothing gave such finishing touches to a brilliant young man as an intrigue in the best Society, and also because this Anna Karenina was after all such as the Countess Vronsky expected all handsome and well-bred women to be. But latterly she had heard that her son had refused a post of importance for his career, merely to remain with his regiment and be able to see Anna Karenina, and that exalted persons were dissatisfied with him for it, so she changed her opinion, and through her eldest son she sent him word to come and see her.

The elder brother was also dissatisfied with the younger. He, the father of a family, kept a ballet girl, and was therefore lenient in these matters: but he knew that it was a love affair which displeased those whom it is necessary to please, and he therefore disapproved of his brother's conduct.

Besides his military and social interests Vronsky had another one, namely horses, of which he was passionately fond.

That year there was to be an officers' steeplechase, and Vronsky had put down his name, bought an English thoroughbred mare, and, in spite of his love, was passionately, though restrainedly, concerned about the coming races.

On the day of the Krasnoe Selo races Vronsky came earlier than usual to the regimental mess-room. He sat waiting with his elbows on the table and his coat unbuttoned over a white waistcoat, and while waiting for the beefsteak he had ordered he looked at the pages of a French novel that lay on his plate. He only looked at the book in order not to have to talk to the officers who came in and out of the room while he was thinking.

He thought of Anna, who had promised to meet him after the races. But he had not seen her for three days and, as her husband had returned from abroad, he did not know whether she could keep the appointment to-day or not, and he did not know how to find out. He had seen her last at his cousin Betsy's country house. He went to the Karenins' country house as seldom as possible, but now he meant to go there and was considering how to do it.

'Of course I can say that Betsy sent me to find out if she will be at the race. Yes, of course I will go,' he decided, lifting his eyes from the book, and a vivid sense of the joy of seeing her made his face radiant.

'Send to my house and tell them to harness three horses to the *calèche* at once,' he said to the waiter who had brought him a beefsteak on a hot silver plate; and drawing the plate nearer to him he began to eat.

At that moment Captain Yashvin, a tall man with a fine figure, entered the room, and came up to Vronsky.

'Ah, here he is!' he exclaimed, and with his big hand gave Vronsky a sharp slap on his shoulder-strap.

Yashvin, a gambler, a rake, a man not merely without principles but with bad principles, was Vronsky's best friend in the regiment. Vronsky respected and liked Yashvin, particularly because he felt that the latter liked him, not for his name and money but for himself. Among all the people Vronsky knew Yashvin was the only one to whom he would have liked to talk about his love. He felt that Yashvin knew all about it and understood it rightly, and it was pleasant to him to read this in Yashvin's eyes.

'Well, and what were you doing last night? Winning?' asked Vronsky.

'Eight thousand. But three of them doubtful. I do not expect he will pay up.'

'Well, then, you can afford to lose on me,' said Vronsky, laughing. (Yashvin had staked heavily on Vronsky.)

'I am sure not to lose. Makhotin is the only dangerous one.' The conversation turned to the forecast of the day's race, the only subject Vronsky could now think about.

'Let us go. I have finished,' said Vronsky, and he rose and moved toward the door. Yashvin rose also and he and Vronsky went out together.

13

Vronsky had his quarters in a roomy, clean, Finnish peasant cottage, divided in two by a partition. Here in camp also, Petritsky was asleep when Vronsky and Yashvin entered.

'Get up, you've slept enough!' said Yashvin, stepping behind the partition and shaking by the shoulder the dishevelled Petritsky, who suddenly sprang to his knees and looked round.

'Your brother has been here,' he said to Vronsky. 'He woke me up, devil take him! ... He said he would come back.' And drawing up his blanket he threw himself back on his pillow.

Vronsky put on the overcoat his servant had handed him.

'Where to now?' asked Yashvin. 'Here are the horses,' he added as he saw the *calèche* drive up to the door.

'To the stables, and then I have to go to Bryansky about the horses,' said Vronsky.

He had really promised to go to Bryansky's, who lived seven miles from Peterhof, and pay him for the horses, and he hoped to make time to call there too. But his friends understood at once that it was not only there that he was going.

'Mind and don't be late!' was all Yashvin said.

'Wait!' shouted Petritsky to Vronsky, who was already going out. 'Your brother left a letter for you and a note. Here they are.'

Vronsky took the letter and his brother's note. It was just what he had expected: a letter from his mother reproaching him for not having come to see her, and a note from his brother saying that they must talk things over. Vronsky knew that it all referred to the same subject. 'What business is it of theirs?' thought he, and crumpling up the letters he pushed them in between the buttons of his coat.

He went out and got into the *calèche*.

'To the stables!' he said, and was taking out the letter to read, but then changed his mind, not wishing to be upset before examining his horse. 'Later will do! ...'

The temporary stable, a wooden structure, had been built close to the racecourse, and it was there his mare was to have been brought the day before. He had not yet been to look at her. During these last days he had not exercised her himself, but had entrusted it to the trainer. Hardly had he stepped out of the *calèche* before his groom, who had recognized it from a distance, had called out the trainer. Cord, a lean Englishman in top boots and a short jacket, with only a tuft of beard left under his chin, came to meet him with the awkward gait of a jockey, swaying from side to side with his elbows sticking out.

'Well, how is Frou-Frou?' asked Vronsky in English.

'All right, sir,' came the answer from somewhere inside the man's throat. 'Better not go in,' he added, touching his cap. 'I have put a muzzle on her, and she is fidgety.'

'No, I'll go in. I want to have a look at her.'

'Come along,' said the Englishman frowning and he led the way.

They entered a little yard in front of the shed. Five horses stood in the horseboxes, and Vronsky knew that his principal rival, Makhotin's sixteen-hand chestnut, Gladiator, was to have been brought that day and should be standing there too. Vronsky was even more anxious to have a look at Gladiator, but he knew that horse-racing etiquette not only forbade his seeing it, but made it improper for him even to ask about it.

'Here is the horse of Mak … Mak … I never can pronounce his name,' said the Englishman over his shoulder, pointing with his black-nailed thumb to Gladiator's box.

'Makhotin's? Yes, that is my only serious rival,' said Vronsky.

'If you were riding him, I would back you,' said the Englishman.

'Frou-Frou is the braver, but the other is the more powerful horse,' said Vronsky, smiling at the compliment to his riding.

'In a steeplechase everything depends on the riding and on pluck,' said the Englishman.

Vronsky was firmly convinced that no one in the world could have more pluck than he had.

'Are you quite sure that more training was unnecessary?'

'Quite unnecessary,' said the Englishman. 'Please don't talk loud. The mare is nervous,' he added.

He opened the door, and Vronsky entered the box. When he had got used to the dim light of the box, Vronsky again instinctively took in at one comprehensive glance all the points of his favourite mare. Frou-Frou was of medium size and slenderly built. Her chest, though well arched, was narrow. Her hind-quarters tapered rather too much, and her legs, especially her hind legs, were perceptibly bowed inwards. But she possessed in the highest degree a characteristic which made one forget all her defects. This was her thoroughbred quality—the kind of blood that *tells*, as they say in English. The muscles, clearly marked beneath the network of sinews, stretched in the fine, mobile skin, which was smooth as satin, seemed hard as bone. Her whole appearance, more especially about the head, was spirited yet gentle. To Vronsky at any rate it seemed that she understood all he was feeling while looking at her.

'Oh, you darling!' said Vronsky, stepping toward the horse and soothing her. He stroked her firm neck and brought his face close to her dilated nostrils, delicate as a bat's wing.

'Be quiet, darling, be quiet!' he said, again stroking her flank, and left the box with a joyful conviction that the horse was in the very best condition.

'Well then, I rely on you,' said Vronsky to the Englishman. 'You will be on the spot at half-past six.'

'All right,' said the Englishman. 'And where are you going, my lord?' he asked unexpectedly.

Vronsky raised his head, surprised at the boldness of the question. But realizing that the Englishman in asking the question regarded him not as an employer, but as a jockey, he replied:

'I have to see Bryansky, but I shall be home in an hour.'

The Englishman looked at him attentively and, as if he knew where he was going, added: 'The chief thing before a race is to keep cool: don't be put out or upset.'

'All right,' said Vronsky smiling, and jumping into the *calèche*, he told the coachman to drive to Peterhof.

He had not gone many yards before the clouds, which had been threatening since morning, broke, and there was a downpour of rain.

'This is bad!' thought Vronsky, raising the hood of the *calèche*. 'It was muddy before, but now it will be a swamp.' He drew out his mother's letter and his brother's note and read them through.

Yes, it was the same thing over and over again. They all, his mother and his brother and everybody, considered it necessary to interfere with his intimate affairs. This interference roused him to anger, a feeling he rarely experienced. 'What business is it of theirs? If it were an ordinary, empty Society intrigue they would let me alone. They feel that it is something different, and that this woman is dearer to me than life. That is incomprehensible, and therefore it vexes them. They do not know that without love there is no happiness or unhappiness for us, for there would be no life,' he thought.

He was angry with everybody for their interference, just because he felt in his soul that they were right. He felt all the torment of his and her position, all the difficulties they were surrounded by in consequence of their station in life, which obliged them to hide their love, to lie and deceive, and again to lie and deceive, to scheme and constantly think about others while the passion that bound them was so strong that they both forgot everything but their love.

And for the first time the clear idea occurred to him that it was necessary to put an end to all this falsehood, and the sooner the better. 'Throw up everything and let us two conceal ourselves somewhere alone with our love,' said he to himself.

14

The downpour did not last long, and as Vronsky approached his desti-nation the sun appeared again. He no longer thought about the shower spoiling the racecourse, but was glad, because, thanks to the rain, he was sure to find Anna at home and alone, for he knew that Karenin, who had recently returned from a watering-place abroad, had not moved from Petersburg.

Vronsky, as usual, to attract less attention, alighted before crossing the little bridge that led to the house and walked on. He did not go straight to the entrance from the street but passed through the yard.

'Has your master returned?' he asked a gardener.

'No, sir. The mistress is at home. Go in at the front door; the servants are there and will open it,' replied the man.

'No, I will go through the garden.'

Having made sure that she was alone, and wishing to take her by surprise, he went, holding up his sword and stepping carefully along the sand-strewn flower-bordered path to the verandah facing the garden. Vronsky had now forgotten all his thoughts on the way, about the hard-ness and difficulty of his situation. He only thought that he would see her immediately, not merely in fancy, but alive, all of her—as she was in reality. He was already ascending the shallow steps of the verandah, stepping on the whole of his foot so as not to make a noise, when he suddenly remembered what he was always forgetting, the most painful part of his relations with her, namely her son, with his questioning and, as it seemed to Vronsky, inimical look.

That boy was a more frequent hindrance to their relations than anyone else. When he was present neither Vronsky nor Anna allowed themselves to speak about anything they could not have mentioned to every one or even to hint at things the boy would not have understood. They had not arranged this, but it had come about of itself. They would have considered it unworthy of themselves to deceive that child. In his presence they talked as acquaintances. Yet despite this caution Vronsky often noticed the child's attentive and perplexed gaze fixed upon him and a strange timidity toward him.

Anna was quite alone, sitting on the verandah. She wore a white dress trimmed with wide embroidery, and as she sat in a corner of the verandah behind some plants, did not hear Vronsky coming. Bowing her curly head she pressed her forehead against a cold watering-can that stood on the balustrade, and both her beautiful hands, with the rings he knew so well, were holding the can. Vronsky stopped, gazing at her with rapture. But just as he was going to step toward her, she felt his nearness, pushed away the can, and turned her hot face toward him.

'What is the matter? Aren't you well?' he said in French as he came up to her. He wished to run toward her, but remembering that there might be others near, blushed, as he always did when he felt that he had reason to fear and to be circumspect.

'No, I am quite well,' she said, rising and firmly pressing his out-stretched hand. 'I am alone and was expecting Serezha. He went for a walk; he will return this way.'

But though she tried to be calm her lips trembled.

'Forgive me for coming, but I could not let the day pass without see-ing you,' he continued in French.

'Why "forgive"? I am so glad!'

'But you are ill or in trouble,' he continued without releasing her hand, but bending over it. 'What were you thinking about?'

'Shall I tell him or not?' she thought, looking at his calm, caressing eyes. 'He is so happy, so full of his races, that he won't understand it properly, won't understand all the importance of the event for us.'

'I see that something has happened. How can I be a moment at peace knowing that you have some sorrow which I am not sharing? Tell me, for heaven's sake!' repeated he entreatingly.

'I am pregnant,' she said softly and slowly.

She did not move her eyes from his face, watching to see how he would take it. He grew pale, tried to say something, but stopped, dropped her hand, and bowed his head. 'Yes, he understands its full significance,' she thought, and gratefully pressed his hand.

But she was mistaken in thinking that he understood the importance of the news as she, a woman, understood it. He felt that the crisis he had hoped for had now come, that concealment from the husband was no longer possible, and that somehow or other the unnatural situation must be quickly ended. But, besides this, her physical agitation commu-nicated itself to him. He gave her a look full of emotion, humbly kissed her hand, rose, and began silently pacing up and down the verandah.

'Yes,' he said, resolutely approaching her. 'Neither you nor I looked on our union as an amusement, and now our fate is sealed. We must end'—he went on—'this falsehood in which we are living.'

'End it? How are we to end it, Alexis?' she said softly.

She was quiet now and her face shone with a tender smile.

'By your leaving your husband and our uniting our lives.'

'But how, Alexis, teach me how?' she said with pathetic irony at the inevitability of her position. 'Is there any escape from such a position? Am I not my husband's wife?'

'There is a way out of every position. One has to take a decision,' he said. 'Anything would be better than the condition in which you are living. Don't I see how you suffer from everything—Society, your son, and your husband?'

'What would you have me do?' she asked. She who had so feared that he might take her pregnancy too lightly now felt vexed that he deduced therefrom the necessity of doing something.

'Tell him everything, leave him.'

'Very well; suppose I do so!' she said. 'Do you know what the result will be? I will tell it you all in advance,' and an evil light came into her eyes which a minute before had been so tender. '"Ah, you love another and have entered into a guilty union with him?"' (mimicking her husband, she laid just such a stress on the word *guilty* as Karenin himself would have done). 'In short, he will tell me clearly and precisely in his official manner that he cannot let me go, but will take what measures he can to prevent a scandal. And he will do what he says, quietly and accurately. That is what will happen. He is not a man, but a machine, and a cruel machine when angry,' she added.

'But, Anna,' said Vronsky persuasively and gently, trying to pacify her, 'he must be told, all the same, and afterwards our action will be guided by his attitude.'

'What then, run away?'

'And why not run away? I think it is impossible to continue in this way. And not on my account,—I see that you suffer.'

'Yes, run away, and for me to live as your mistress,' she said maliciously, 'and ruin my ... everything.'

She was going to say 'son' but could not utter the word. When she thought about her son and his future relations with the mother who had left his father, she was so terrified at what she had done that she tried to comfort herself with false arguments and words in order that everything should remain as before and that she might forget the dreadful question of what would happen to her son.

'I beg you, I entreat you,' said she suddenly in quite an altered tone, sincerely and tenderly, taking him by the hand, 'never to speak to me about that!'

'But, Anna ... I don't understand ...' said he.

'I know,' she interrupted him, 'how hard it is for your honest nature to lie and I pity you. I often think how you have ruined your life because of me.'

'I was just thinking the same,' he said; 'wondering how you could sacrifice everything for my sake. I cannot forgive myself for your unhappiness.'

'I unhappy?' she said, drawing near to him and gazing at him with a smile of rapturous love. 'I unhappy? No, this is my happiness ...'

But she heard the voice of her son approaching, and glancing quickly round the verandah she rose hurriedly. Her eyes kindled with the light Vronsky knew so well, and with a rapid motion she seized his head, gave him a long look, lifted her face with parted smiling lips, quickly kissed his mouth and both eyes, and then pushed him away. She was about to go but he held her back.

'When?' he whispered, gazing rapturously at her.

'To-night at one,' she whispered, and with her quick light step went to meet her son.

Vronsky looked at his watch and hurried away.

15

When Vronsky looked at his watch on the Karenins' verandah he was so agitated and so preoccupied that he saw the hands and face of the watch without realizing the time. He went to the high road, stepping carefully over the mud, and made his way to his *calèche*. He was so full of his feeling for Anna that he did not consider what o'clock it was or whether he still had time to call on Bryansky. He approached his coachman, who was dozing on the box, and told him to drive to Bryansky's. Only after going some five miles did he recollect himself sufficiently to look at his watch and to realize that it was already half-past five, and that he was late. He could be in time for his own race, but, if he called on Bryansky first, he could only just manage it, and the whole Court would already be at the racecourse. That was not the correct thing to do. But he had promised Bryansky to call and therefore he decided to go on, telling the coachman not to spare the horses.

He saw Bryansky, stayed with him five minutes, and drove back at a gallop. This quick drive soothed him. All that was depressing in his relations with Anna, the indefiniteness that remained after their conversation, escaped from his mind. He now thought with enjoyment and agitation of the race, and that he would be there in time.

When he reached his quarters he found no one there—they had all gone to the races and his valet was waiting at the gate. While he was changing his things, the valet told him that the second race had already

begun and that many gentlemen had been to inquire for him, and a lad
had run over twice from the stables.

Having changed without hurrying (he never hurried or lost his self-
control), Vronsky ordered the coachman to drive him to the stables.
Probably the second race was just taking place, for as he entered the
stables he heard the bell ring. On his way he met Makhotin's white-
legged chestnut Gladiator, which in a blue-bordered orange covering,
with his ears looking enormous in their blue-trimmed cloth, was being
led to the course.

In her open box Frou-Frou stood ready saddled. They were just going
to lead her out.

'I am not late?'

'All right! all right!' answered the Englishman. 'Don't upset yourself.'

Vronsky once again glanced at the beautiful fascinating shape of the
mare, whose whole body was trembling, and tearing himself with difficulty from this sight he left the shed. He came towards the pavilions at
the very best time to avoid attracting anyone's attention. The two-verst
race was nearly over, and all eyes were fixed on an officer of the horse-
guards in front and on the winning-post. Vronsky joined the crowd
unnoticed, almost at the moment that the bell rang to announce the end
of the race, and the tall officer of the horse-guards all bespattered with
mud, who had come in first, was bending down in his saddle, loosen-
ing the reins of his grey gelding, which was dark with perspiration and
panting heavily.

When the winners were called up to the pavilion to receive their
prizes and every one was looking that way, Vronsky's elder brother,
Alexander, a colonel with shoulder knots, of medium height, as sturdy
as Alexis but handsomer and ruddier, with a red nose and a drunken
though open countenance, came up to him.

'Did you get my note?' he asked. 'One can never find you.'

Alexander Vronsky, despite the loose and, in particular, drunken life
for which he was noted, was quite a courtier.

While speaking to his brother of a matter very unpleasant to him
he, knowing that many eyes might be fixed on them, wore a smiling
expression, as if he were joking with him.

'I received it, but really do not understand what *you* are worrying
about,' replied Alexis.

'I am worrying because people have just remarked to me that you
were not here and that you were seen in Peterhof last Monday.'

'There are things which should be discussed only by those who are
directly interested. I beg you not to interfere, that is all.'

Alexander smiled gaily. 'I only wanted to deliver Mother's letter. Answer her, and don't upset yourself before the race. Good luck!' he added smiling and went away.

But just then another friendly greeting stopped Vronsky.

'Won't you recognize your friends? How do you do, *mon cher*?' said Oblonsky, shining here, amid all this Petersburg brilliancy, no less than he shone in Moscow, with his rosy face and glistening, well-brushed whiskers. 'I came yesterday and am very glad that I shall witness your triumph. When can we meet?'

'Come to the mess-room to-morrow,' said Vronsky, and apologetically pressing the sleeve of Oblonsky's overcoat, he went to the centre of the racecourse where the horses were already being led out for the steeplechase.

To the right the slender and beautiful Frou-Frou was being led up and down. Not far from her they were taking the horse-cloth off the big-eared Gladiator. The large, beautiful, perfectly regular shape of the horse, with his wonderful hind-quarters and his exceptionally short pasterns just above his hoofs, involuntarily arrested Vronsky's attention.

The riders were summoned to the pavilion to draw their numbers and places. With serious, stern, and in many cases pale faces, seventeen officers assembled at the pavilion and drew their numbers. Vronsky got number seven. The order was given: 'Mount!'

Vronsky glanced round at his rivals for the last time. The only one he did not see was Makhotin on his Gladiator.

'Don't hurry,' said Cord to Vronsky, 'and remember one thing: do not hold back or urge on your horse at an obstacle. Let her have her way. Lead if you can, but do not despair till the last moment if you are behind.'

The mare had not time to stir before Vronsky with a powerful and agile movement put his foot in the notched steel stirrup and seated himself lightly but firmly on the creaking leather of the saddle. Having got his right foot also in its stirrup he straightened out the double reins between his practised fingers.

They were approaching the starting-post. Some of the riders were in front, some behind, when Vronsky suddenly heard a horse galloping through the mud behind him, and Makhotin on his white-legged, large-eared Gladiator went past him. Makhotin smiled, showing his long teeth, but Vronsky looked at him angrily, vexed with him for galloping past and so exciting Frou-Frou. She broke into a canter, gave two leaps, and, angry at the tightened rein, changed back into a jerky trot, jolting her rider.

16

Seventeen officers in all had entered for the steeplechase. Three times the riders drew up in line, but each time some one's horse made a false start and they had to line up again. But at last, at the fourth try, the race began.

The excited and over-nervous Frou-Frou lost in the first moment, and several horses started ahead of her, but before reaching the brook Vronsky, who with all his strength was holding back the mare that was tugging at the reins, had easily passed three riders, and ahead of him there was only Makhotin's chestnut Gladiator.

After crossing the brook Vronsky had the mare quite under control. The big barrier was right in front of the Imperial Pavilion. The Emperor, the whole Court, and crowds of people were all looking at them—at him and at Makhotin, who was a full length ahead of him when they approached the Devil (as the solid barrier was called). Vronsky saw nothing except the ears and neck of his mare, the ground racing toward him, and Gladiator's hind-quarters and white legs rapidly striding before him, and keeping always the same distance ahead. Gladiator rose without touching anything, swished his short tail, and disappeared from Vronsky's sight.

Just then the boards of the barrier flashed close before Vronsky's eyes. Without the least change in her action his mare rose under him; the boards disappeared, only behind him there was a knock. Excited by the fact that Gladiator was in front, the mare had risen at the barrier a little too soon and had struck it with a hind hoof. But her pace did not change, and Vronsky, hit in the face by a lump of mud, realized that he was again at the same distance behind Gladiator.

At the very moment that Vronsky thought it time to pass Makhotin, Frou-Frou, understanding what was in his mind, without any urging, considerably increased her speed and began to draw nearer to Makhotin on the side where it was most advantageous to pass him—the side of the rope. Makhotin would not let her pass that side. Vronsky had just time to think of coming up on the outside, when Frou-Frou changed her legs and started to do so. Vronsky, not to lose ground, gave the mare her head and passed Makhotin.

The next two obstacles, a ditch and a fence, were easily passed, but Vronsky heard Gladiator galloping and snorting closer. He urged on his mare and felt with joy that she easily increased her speed.

Vronsky now was confident of success. His excitement and joy, and his tenderness for Frou-Frou, grew stronger and stronger.

There remained the most difficult obstacle; if he crossed it ahead of the others, he would come in first. The mare knew what was wanted, and, as he expected, she increased her speed, took off exactly at the right moment, and gave a leap the force of which carried her far across the ditch. Then without effort and without changing her legs Frou-Frou continued her gallop.

'Oh, my beauty!' he thought of Frou-Frou, as he listened to what was happening behind. 'He is over it!' he thought, as he heard Gladiator again galloping behind him. There remained one last water jump, only a yard and a half wide. Vronsky felt the mare was using her last reserve of strength but knew it was more than enough for the remaining five hundred yards. She leapt the ditch as if she did not notice it, seeming to fly across it like a bird. But at that very moment Vronsky, to his horror, made the unpardonable mistake of dropping back in his saddle and pulling up her head. Before he could realize this, the white legs of the gelding flashed close by him and Makhotin passed at a rapid gallop. Vronsky was touching the ground with one foot. He scarcely had time to withdraw the foot before Frou-Frou fell on her side, and snorting heavily and with her delicate damp neck making vain efforts to rise, began struggling on the ground at his feet, like a wounded, fluttering bird. Not understanding what had happened, Vronsky pulled at the reins. The mare again began to struggle like a fish, causing the flaps of the saddle to creak; she got her front legs free, but unable to lift her hind-quarters, struggled and immediately again fell on her side. He kicked her with his heel in the belly and again pulled at the reins. But she did not move and, nuzzling the ground, only looked at her master with eloquent eyes.

'Ah, ah, ah!' groaned Vronsky, seizing his head. 'Ah! what have I done?' he exclaimed. 'The race lost! And the fault mine—shameful and unpardonable. And this dear, unfortunate mare ruined! Ah! what have I done!'

Onlookers, a doctor, an attendant, and officers of his regiment ran toward him. To his regret he felt that he was himself sound and unhurt. The mare had broken her back, and it was decided to shoot her. Vronsky was unable to reply to questions or to speak to anyone. He turned away and, without picking up the cap that had fallen from his head, left the racecourse without knowing where he was going. He felt miserable. For the first time in his life he experienced the worst kind of misfortune—one that was irretrievable, and caused by his own fault.

The memory of that steeplechase long remained the most painful and distressing memory of his life.

17

Externally Karenin's relations with his wife remained as before. The
only difference was that he was even more occupied than before. As in
former years, at the beginning of the spring he went abroad to recuper-
ate his health, which was upset each year by the winter's work. And as
usual he returned in July and at once with increased energy took up his
customary work. And as usual his wife had moved to the country house
while he remained in Petersburg.

Since their conversation on the night of the Princess Tverskaya's
party he had never spoken to Anna of his suspicions and jealousy, and
that habitual tone of his which seemed to mock at some one was exactly
suited to his present relations with her. He was rather colder toward her.
He appeared only to be slightly dissatisfied with her for that first night's
talk which she had evaded. In his behaviour to her there was a shade of
vexation, but nothing more. But he had become particularly cold toward
his son, and treated him in the same bantering manner as he did his
wife. 'Ah, young man!' was the way in which he addressed him.

The country house the Karenins regularly occupied in summer was
in Peterhof, and generally the Countess Lydia Ivanovna also lived near
by and was in constant touch with Anna. That year the Countess Lydia
Ivanovna refused to live in Peterhof, did not once come to see Anna,
and hinted to Karenin the undesirability of Anna's intimacy with Betsy
and Vronsky. Karenin stopped her severely, expressing the opinion that
his wife was above suspicion, and from that time began to avoid the
Countess. He did not wish to see, and did not see, that many people in
Society already looked askance at Anna; yet at the bottom of his soul,
without admitting it to himself or having any proofs or even suspicions
of it, he nevertheless knew certainly that he was a wronged husband,
and was therefore profoundly unhappy.

Since his return from abroad Karenin had been twice at the country
house. Once he dined there, and the other time he spent an evening with
some visitors, but he had not once stayed the night, as he used to do in
former years.

The day of the races was a very busy one for Karenin; but in the
morning when he made his plans for the day he decided that immediately
after an early dinner he would go to see his wife at the country house,
and from there to the races, at which the whole Court would be present
and where he ought to appear.

Having with the mental control habitual to him considered these

matters concerning his wife, he did not allow his thoughts to run on
further about her.

He had a very busy morning. Then he received a visit from his doctor, a celebrated Petersburg physician who was on friendly terms with
Karenin. He had not expected him and was surprised to see him, and yet
more surprised that the doctor questioned him very particularly about
his state of health, sounding his chest and tapping and feeling his liver.
Karenin did not know that his friend Lydia Ivanovna, having noticed
that he was not in good health that summer, had asked the doctor to go
and see his patient.

The doctor was very dissatisfied with Karenin's state of health. He
found him insufficiently nourished and his liver much enlarged, and
that the waters had had no effect at all. He prescribed as much physical
exercise and as little mental strain as possible, and above all no worries
of any kind—that is, he advised what was for Karenin as impossible as
not to breathe, and he went away leaving Karenin with a disagreeable
consciousness that something was wrong with him which could not be
remedied.

After the doctor, Karenin had to finish his everyday business with
his private secretary, Slyudin, and had also to drive to see an important
personage on a grave and serious matter. He only managed to get back
at five, his dinner-time, and having dined with Slyudin, he invited the
latter to drive with him to his country house and to go to the races with
him. Without acknowledging it to himself, Karenin now looked out for
opportunities of having a third person present at his interviews with
his wife.

18

Anna was upstairs when she heard the wheels of a carriage grating on
the gravel at the entrance.

'It is too early for Betsy,' she thought, and glancing out of the window
she saw the carriage, and sticking out of it a black hat and Karenin's
familiar ears. 'How unfortunate! Can he mean to stay the night?' thought
she, and so awful and horrible appeared to her the consequences that
might result therefrom that, without a moment's hesitation, she went
out to meet him with a bright beaming face; and feeling within herself
the presence of the already familiar spirit of lies and deceit, she gave
herself up to it at once.

'Ah, how nice this is!' she said, giving her husband her hand and smilingly greeting Slyudin as a member of the household. 'You are staying the night, I hope?' were the first words prompted by the spirit of lies. 'And now we shall go together. Only it is a pity that I promised to go with Betsy. She will be coming for me.'

Karenin made a grimace at the mention of Betsy's name.

'Oh, I will not separate the inseparables,' he said in his usual facetious tone. 'I will go with Slyudin.'

'There is no hurry,' said Anna. 'Would you like some tea?'

She rang.

'Tea, please, and tell Serezha that his father is here. Well, how is your health? You have not been here before; look how pretty my verandah is,' she went on, turning now to her husband, now to Slyudin.

She spoke very simply and naturally, but too much and too fast. She felt this herself, especially as by the inquisitive way Slyudin looked at her she noticed that he seemed to be watching her.

Slyudin immediately went out on to the verandah, and she sat down by her husband.

'You are not looking quite well,' she said.

'No,' he replied, 'the doctor came to see me this morning and robbed me of an hour. I feel that some friend of mine must have sent him: my health is so precious ...'

'Yes, but what did he say?'

She questioned him about his health and his work, persuading him to take a rest and to move out to her in the country.

She said all this lightly, rapidly, and with peculiarly sparkling eyes; but Karenin did not now attach any importance to this tone of hers. He only heard her words, and gave them only their direct meaning. And he answered simply, though jokingly. In all this conversation nothing particular passed, but never afterwards could Anna recall this short scene without being tormented by shame.

Serezha came in, preceded by his governess.

'Ah, young man! He has grown. He is really getting quite a man. How do you do, young man?'

And he held out his hand to the frightened boy.

Serezha, who had always been timid with his father, now that the latter addressed him as 'young man', shrank from him. He looked round at his mother, as if asking for protection. Karenin meanwhile talked to the governess with his hand on his son's shoulder, and Serezha felt so extremely uncomfortable that Anna saw he was about to cry.

Anna, who had blushed when the boy came in, saw how distressed he was, and, rising, lifted Karenin's hand off her son's shoulder, kissed the boy, led him out on to the verandah, and returned at once.

'Well, it's time we were going,' she said, glancing at her watch. 'I wonder Betsy has not come ...'

'Yes,' said Karenin, and interlacing his hands he cracked his fingers. 'I also came to bring you some money. I expect you want it?'

'No, I don't. ... Yes, I do,' she replied without looking at him, and blushing to the roots of her hair. 'But I suppose you will call here after the races.'

'Oh, yes!' answered Karenin. 'And here is the ornament of Peterhof, the Princess Tverskaya,' he added, glancing out of the window at an approaching carriage of English build with a small body placed very high. Well then, we will start too.'

The Princess Tverskaya did not get out, only her footman in his black hat, cape, and gaiters jumped down at the front door.

'I am going, good-bye!' said Anna, and giving her son a kiss she went up to Karenin who kissed her hand.

'Well then, *au revoir!* You will come back for tea, that is right!' she said, and went out beaming and gay. But as soon as she ceased to see him she became conscious of the place on her hand his lips had touched and shuddered with disgust.

19

When Karenin appeared at the racecourse Anna was already sitting beside Betsy in the Grand Stand: the stand where all the highest Society was assembled. From afar she already felt the approach of her husband, and involuntarily watched him amid the surging crowd through which he was moving. She knew by the way he looked at the Ladies' Stand that he was trying to find her, but she purposely disregarded him.

'Alexis Alexandrovich!' the Princess Betsy called to him, 'I am sure you don't see your wife; here she is!'

He smiled his usual cold smile.

'There is so much splendour here that my eyes are dazzled,' he replied, and approached the stand. He smiled at Anna as a husband should smile when meeting his wife whom he has seen shortly before, and greeted the Princess and other acquaintances. At the foot of the stand stood a General Aide-de-Camp respected by Karenin, and noted for his intelligence and education. With him Karenin entered into conversation.

When the four-verst steeplechase was beginning Anna leaned forward, and did not take her eyes off Vronsky while he went up to his horse and mounted it, and at the same time she heard her husband's repulsive, unceasing voice. She was tormented by anxiety for Vronsky, but suffered even more from what seemed to her the incessant flow of her husband's familiar shrill voice.

'Princess, a bet!' came the voice of Oblonsky from below, addressing Betsy. 'Whom are you backing?'

'Anna and I are betting on Kuzovlev,' replied Betsy.

'And I on Vronsky. A pair of gloves?'

'All right.'

'What a fine scene, is it not?'

Karenin was silent while others were speaking near him. He was not interested in races and therefore did not watch the riders. His gaze rested on Anna.

Her face was pale and stern. She evidently saw nothing and nobody, with one exception. Her hand convulsively grasped her fan, and she did not breathe. He looked at her face, trying not to read what was so plainly written on it, but against his will he read in it with horror that which he did not want to know.

The first fall excited every one, but Karenin saw clearly by Anna's pale, triumphant face that he whom she was watching had not fallen. When after Makhotin and Vronsky had jumped the big barrier the officer following them fell on his head and swooned, a murmur of horror passed through the whole crowd; but Karenin saw that Anna did not even notice the fall and with difficulty understood what those around her were talking about. He looked at her more and more often, and more intently. Anna, though fully engrossed by the sight of the galloping Vronsky, became aware of the cold eyes of her husband bent upon her from one side.

She glanced for an instant at him with a look of inquiry, and, slightly frowning, turned away and then did not once look at him again.

The steeplechase was unlucky: more than half of the seventeen officers were thrown and hurt. By the end of the race every one was disturbed, and the Emperor was displeased.

Every one was loudly expressing disapproval and every one was feeling the horror of it, so that when Vronsky fell and Anna gave a loud exclamation, there was nothing remarkable about it. But afterwards a change came over Anna's face which was positively improper.

Karenin approached Anna and politely offered her his arm. 'Come, if you like,' he said in French; but Anna did not notice her husband. She raised her glasses and looked toward the spot where Vronsky had fallen; but it was so far off, and so many people had crowded there, that it was impossible to distinguish anything. An officer galloped up and reported something to the Emperor. Anna bent forward to listen.

'Stiva! Stiva!' she called to her brother.

But he did not hear her. She now saw an officer running to the Grand Stand from the place where Vronsky had fallen. Betsy waved her handkerchief to him. The officer brought the news that the rider was unhurt but that the horse had broken its back.

On hearing this Anna quickly sat down and hid her face behind her fan. Karenin saw that she was crying, and that she was unable to keep back either her tears or the sobs that made her bosom heave. He stepped forward so as to screen her, giving her time to recover.

'For the second time I offer you my arm,' he said after a while, turning toward her. Anna looked at him and did not know what to say. The Princess Betsy came to her aid.

'No, Alexis Alexandrovich,' she put in, 'I brought Anna here and I have promised to take her back again.'

'Excuse me, Princess,' he said, smiling politely but looking her firmly in the eyes, 'but I see that Anna is not very well, and I wish her to come with me.'

Anna looked round with alarm, rose obediently and put her hand on her husband's arm.

'I will send to him and find out, and will let you know,' Betsy whispered to her.

On leaving the stand Karenin as usual spoke to people he met, and Anna as usual had to reply and make conversation: but she was beside herself and walked as in a dream, holding her husband's arm.

In silence she took her place in her husband's carriage, and in silence they drove out of the crowd of vehicles. In spite of all he had seen, Karenin would still not allow himself to think of his wife's real position. He only saw the external sights. He saw that she had behaved with impropriety and he considered it his duty to tell her so.

'I must tell you that you behaved improperly to-day,' he said.

'How did I behave improperly?' she said aloud, quickly turning her head and looking him straight in the eyes with a determined air beneath which she had difficulty in hiding the fright she felt.

'The despair you were unable to conceal when one of the riders fell. Your conduct was improper and I do not wish it to occur again.'

What he knew was so terrible that he was now prepared to believe anything.

'Perhaps I am mistaken,' said he. 'In that case I beg your pardon.'

'No, you were not mistaken,' she said slowly, looking despairingly into his cold face. 'You were not mistaken. I was, and cannot help being, in despair. I listen to you but I am thinking of him. I love him, I am his mistress. I cannot endure you. I am afraid of you, and I hate you. ... Do what you like to me.'

And throwing herself back into the corner of the carriage she burst into sobs, hiding her face in her hands. Karenin did not move, and did not change the direction in which he was looking, but his face suddenly assumed the solemn immobility of the dead, and that expression did not alter till they reached the house. As they were driving up to it, he turned his face to her still with the same expression and said:

'Yes! But I demand that the external conditions of propriety shall be observed till'—his voice trembled—'till I take measures to safeguard my honour and inform you of them.'

He alighted first and helped her out. In the presence of the servants he pressed her hand, re-entered the carriage, and drove off toward Petersburg.

After he had gone the Princess Betsy's footman brought Anna a note.

'I sent to Alexis to inquire about his health. He writes that he is safe and sound, but in despair.'

'Then he will come,' thought she. 'What a good thing it is that I spoke out.'

She looked at the clock. She had three hours still to wait.

20

As always happens where people congregate, the usual crystallization, if we may so call it, of Society took place in the little German watering-place to which the Shcherbatskys had come, assigning to each person a definite and fixed position. Each new-comer on his arrival at the watering-place immediately settled into his natural position.

Prince Shcherbatsky with his wife and daughter, by the premises they occupied, by their name, and by the people they were acquainted with, at once crystallized into their definite and preordained place.

They made various acquaintances but the people with whom they necessarily associated most were a Moscow lady, Mary Evgenyevna Rtishcheva, and her daughter, whom Kitty found unpleasant because her illness was due to the same cause as Kitty's—a love affair; and a

Moscow Colonel, whom Kitty had known from childhood. When all this had become firmly established, Kitty began to feel very dull, especially as her father had gone to Carlsbad and she was left alone with her mother. She was not interested in the people she knew, for she felt that nothing new would come from them. Her chief private interest at the watering-place consisted in observing those whom she did not know and making conjectures about them.

Among these people she was specially interested in a young Russian girl who had come to the watering-place with an invalid Russian lady, Madame Stahl, as every one called her. Madame Stahl belonged to the highest Society, but she was so ill that she could not walk, and only on fine days occasionally appeared on the promenade in a bath-chair. But—not so much from illness as from pride, as the Princess Shcherbatskaya explained—Madame Stahl was not acquainted with any of the Russians there. The Russian girl looked after Madame Stahl, and also, as Kitty noticed, became intimate with all those who were seriously ill and waited on them in the most natural way. This Russian girl, Kitty decided, was not related to Madame Stahl, but neither was she a paid companion. Madame Stahl called her by the diminutive 'Varenka', and others called her Mademoiselle Varenka. But besides the fact that it interested Kitty to observe the relations of this girl with Madame Stahl and with others, she experienced an inexplicable attraction toward this Mlle Varenka, and felt, when the girl's eyes met hers, that the feeling was mutual.

Mlle Varenka seemed always occupied with something and therefore it seemed that no side issue could interest her. By this contrast to herself Kitty was specially attracted. She felt that in her and in her way of life could be found a model of what she herself was painfully seeking: interest in life, the worth of life—outside the social relations of girls to men, which now seemed disgusting to Kitty, who regarded them as shameful exhibitions of goods awaiting a buyer. The more Kitty observed her, the more she was convinced that this girl really was the perfect being she imagined her to be, and the more she wished to make her acquaintance.

Soon after the Shcherbatskys' arrival, two new persons who provoked everybody's disapproval began to appear of a morning at the Well. They were a very tall, round-shouldered man with black eyes, and enormous hands, who wore an old overcoat too short for him, and a slightly pockmarked, sweet-faced woman, badly and tastelessly dressed. The Princess, having found out from the visitors' list that they were Nicholas Levin and Mary Nikolavna, explained to Kitty what a bad man this Levin was, and because the man was Constantine's brother, these two people appeared very disagreeable to Kitty.

21

It was a dull day, it rained the whole morning, and the patients with their umbrellas crowded the covered gallery.

Kitty was walking with her mother and the Moscow Colonel. They kept to one side of the gallery, trying to avoid Levin, who was walking on the other side.

They were just turning to go back, when they suddenly heard Levin was shouting, and the doctor was also excited. A crowd collected about them. The Princess and Kitty withdrew hurriedly, but the Colonel joined the crowd to find out what the noise was all about.

In a few minutes he overtook Kitty and her mother.

'What was the matter?' asked the Princess.

'It's shameful and scandalous,' replied the Colonel. 'The tall gentleman has been quarrelling with the doctor and insulting him, because he is dissatisfied with the doctor's treatment. He shook his stick at him! It's simply shameful!'

'Ah, how unpleasant!' said the Princess. 'But how did it all end?'

'Luckily that Mlle Varenka knew what to do before anyone else. She took that fellow by the arm and led him away.'

Kitty begged her mother more than ever to allow her to make Varenka's acquaintance, and, much as the Princess disliked appearing to take the first step toward getting acquainted with Madame Stahl, she herself approached Varenka when her daughter had gone to the Well.

'Allow me to introduce myself,' said the Princess with her dignified smile. 'My daughter has fallen in love with you. Perhaps you don't know me. I ...'

'It is more than mutual, Princess,' replied Varenka hurriedly.

'What a good action you performed yesterday for our unfortunate fellow-countryman!' said the Princess.

Varenka blushed. 'I don't think I did anything,' she said.

'Oh, yes, you saved that Levin from unpleasantness.'

'Well, you see, his companion called me and I tried to soothe him; he is very ill and I am used to looking after invalids of that kind.'

'Oh, yes, I have heard that you live in Mentone with your aunt, I think, Madame Stahl. I knew her sister-in-law.'

'No, she is not my aunt. I call her Mama, but I am not related to her. She adopted me,' answered Varenka, and blushed again.

This was said so simply, and the frank and open expression of her face was so amiable, that the Princess understood what made Kitty so fond of this Varenka.

'Well, and what about that Levin?'

'He is leaving,' answered Varenka.

Just then Kitty returned from the Well.

'There, Kitty, your great wish to make acquaintance with Mlle ...'

'Varenka,' prompted Varenka with a smile.

Kitty blushed with joy, long and silently pressing her new friend's hand, which lay passively in hers. But though her hand did not return the pressure, Mlle Varenka's face shone with a soft and pleased, though rather sad, smile, which disclosed her large but splendid teeth.

'I have long wished it myself,' she said.

But at that very moment she had to leave her new friends because two little Russian girls, the children of one of the invalids, ran up to her.

'Varenka, Mama wants you!' they shouted.

And Varenka went with them.

The particulars the Princess Shcherbatskaya learnt about Varenka's past and about her relations with Madame Stahl, and about Madame Stahl herself, were the following:

Madame Stahl had always been a sickly and ecstatic woman. When her first baby was born, she being already divorced from her immoral husband, it died at once; and her relations, knowing how susceptible she was and fearing that this news might kill her, changed her dead child for one who had been born that night in the same house in Petersburg, the daughter of a *chef* at a palace. That child was Varenka. Madame Stahl learnt afterwards that Varenka was not her daughter, but continued to bring her up, the more readily because it happened that very soon Varenka had no relations left.

Madame Stahl had lived continuously abroad in the South for more than ten years, hardly ever leaving her bed. Some people said that she had made for herself a position in Society by her pose as a philanthropic and highly religious woman; others said that she really was the highly moral being, living only to do good, that she seemed to be. Varenka always lived with her abroad.

Having learnt all these particulars, the Princess saw nothing to object to in a friendship between her daughter and Varenka, and having heard that Varenka sang very well, invited her to come and sing to them one evening. Kitty noticed that Varenka did not wish to sing. However, she came in the evening and brought her music. The Princess had also invited Mary Evgenyevna with her daughter and the Colonel.

Varenka did not seem at all abashed by the fact that strangers were present, and she went straight up to the piano. Kitty, who played well, accompanied her.

'You have an exceptional talent,' said the Princess, after Varenka had sung her first song excellently.

'See,' said the Colonel, looking out of the window, 'what an audience has assembled to hear you.' Underneath the window a considerable crowd really had collected.

'I am very glad it gives you pleasure,' said Varenka simply.

Kitty looked at her friend with pride. She was enraptured by her singing, her voice, her face, and above all by her manner,—by the fact that Varenka evidently attached no importance to her own singing and was quite indifferent to the praise she got.

'If it were I,' thought Kitty, 'how proud I should feel! How glad I should be to see that crowd under the windows! But she is quite indifferent. She only wished not to refuse, and to give Mama pleasure. What is it in her? What gives her this power to disregard everything and to be so quietly independent? How I should like to know this, and to learn it from her!' thought Kitty, gazing into the calm face. The Princess asked Varenka to sing again.

The next piece in the music book was an Italian song. Kitty played the prelude and looked round at Varenka.

'Let us skip this one,' said Varenka, blushing.

Kitty anxiously and inquiringly fixed her eyes on Varenka's face. 'Well then, another one,' she said, hurriedly turning over the pages.

'No,' answered Varenka, putting her hand on the music and smiling. 'No, let us sing that one.' And she sang the piece just as calmly, coldly, and well as the previous ones.

When she had finished everybody again thanked her and went to drink tea. But Kitty and Varenka went out into the little garden belonging to the house.

'Am I not right, you have some memory attached to that song?' asked Kitty. 'Don't tell me about it,' she added hurriedly, 'only say if I am right!'

'Why not? I will tell you,' said Varenka simply. 'Yes, there is a memory attached to it and it was painful once. I loved a man and used to sing that song to him. I loved him and he loved me; but his mother would not have it, and he married another. You did not think that I too have had a romance?' she said, and on her handsome face there flickered for an instant a spark of the fire which, Kitty felt, had once lighted up her whole being.

'I—not think it? Why, if I were a man I could not have loved anyone else after knowing you. But I can't understand how, to satisfy his mother, he could forget you and make you unhappy. He must be quite heartless.'

'Oh no. He is a very good man, and I am not unhappy,' she added, and went toward the house.

'How good you are, how good!' exclaimed Kitty, stopping her and kissing her. 'If only I could be a little bit like you!'

'Why should you be like anyone? You're very good as you are,' said Varenka, smiling her gentle, weary smile.

'But tell me … is it possible that you are not offended at the thought that a man despised your love? That he did not wish …?'

'But he did not despise it; I believe that he loved me, but he was an obedient son …'

'Yes, but if it had not been his mother's doing, but his own?' said Kitty, her face, burning with a blush of shame, betraying her.

'Then he would have behaved badly and I should not regret him,' replied Varenka, conscious that they were now speaking about Kitty.

'But the humiliation?' said Kitty.

'Where is the humiliation? You did not do anything wrong?'

'Worse than wrong, shameful.'

Varenka shook her head and put her hand on Kitty's.

'Shameful in what respect?' she said. 'You could not have told a man who was himself indifferent to you that you loved him?'

'Of course not; I never said a single word, but he knew it. No, no; there are such things as looks and ways of behaving. If I live to be a hundred I shall never forget it.'

'What does it matter? I don't understand. The question is, do you love him now or not?' said Varenka.

'I hate him: and I cannot forgive myself.'

'Dear me, if every one were as sensitive as you are!' said Varenka. 'There is no girl who has not gone through the same sort of thing. And it is all so unimportant.'

'Then what is important?' asked Kitty, looking into her face with surprised curiosity. But at that moment they heard the Princess's voice from the window:

'Kitty, it is getting chilly! Either take a shawl or come in.'

'Yes, I really must be going!' said Varenka, rising. She went in, collected her music, and having said good-night to everybody, prepared to go.

'Allow me to see you home,' said the Colonel.

Kitty noticed that Varenka had difficulty in suppressing a smile at the idea that she needed anyone to see her home.

'Oh no, I always go out alone and nothing ever happens to me,' she said. And kissing Kitty again, she went out with vigorous steps with her music under her arm, and disappeared in the semi-darkness of the summer night, carrying with her the secret of what was important, and to what she owed her enviable tranquillity and dignity.

22

Kitty also became acquainted with Madame Stahl, and this acquaintanceship, together with Varenka's friendship, not only had a great influence on Kitty, but comforted her in her sorrow. It was revealed to her that besides that instinctive life she had lived hitherto there was also a spiritual life. That life was revealed by religion, but a religion that had nothing in common with that which Kitty had known since her childhood. This was a lofty, mystical religion connected with a series of beautiful thoughts and feelings, which it was not only possible to believe because one was told to, but even to love.

Kitty did not learn all this from words. Madame Stahl spoke with her as with a dear child and only once mentioned that love and faith alone can bring relief in all human sorrows and that no sorrows are too trivial for Christ's compassion. Then she immediately changed the subject.

But however lofty may have been Madame Stahl's character, and however elevated and tender her words, Kitty could not help noticing some perplexing traits in her. She noticed that Madame Stahl, when inquiring about Kitty's relatives, smiled contemptuously, which did not accord with Christian kindness. And once, when Kitty met a Roman Catholic priest at the house, she observed that Madame Stahl carefully hid her face behind the lampshade and smiled in a peculiar manner. Trifling as these things were they disturbed Kitty, and she felt doubts about Madame Stahl. But Varenka, lonely, without relatives or friends, with her sad disillusionment, wishing for nothing and regretting nothing, personified that perfection of which Kitty only allowed herself to dream. In Varenka she saw that it was only necessary to forget oneself and to love others in order to be at peace, happy, and lovely. And such a person Kitty wished to be. Having now clearly understood what was *most important*, Kitty was not content merely to delight in it, but immediately with her whole soul devoted herself to this newly-revealed life.

At first the Princess only noticed that Kitty not only imitated

Varenka's activities, but involuntarily copied her manner of walking, speaking, and blinking her eyes. But afterwards the Princess also noticed that a serious spiritual change was taking place in her daughter.

She saw that in the evening Kitty read the Gospels in French (given her by Madame Stahl)—which she had not done before—that she avoided her Society acquaintances and made up to the invalids who were under Varenka's protection, and especially to the family of Petrov, a poor, sick artist. Kitty evidently prided herself on fulfilling the duties of a sister-of-mercy in that family. This was all very well, and the Princess had nothing against it, especially as Petrov's wife was quite a well-bred woman.

'It seems a long time since Anna Pavlovna was here,' said the Princess once, speaking of Mrs Petrova. 'I invited her and she did not seem pleased.'

'I did not notice anything, Mama,' said Kitty, flushing up.

'Is it long since you went to see them?'

'We are all arranging to go for a drive up the mountains to-morrow,' replied Kitty.

'Well, go if you like,' said the Princess, looking intently into her daughter's confused face and trying to guess the cause.

That same day Varenka came to dinner, and said that Anna Pavlovna had changed her mind about going to the mountains.

The Princess noticed that Kitty blushed again.

'Kitty, have you not had some unpleasantness with the Petrovs?' the Princess asked when they were again alone together. 'Why has she stopped sending the children here and coming herself?'

Kitty replied that nothing had passed between them and that she did not at all understand why Anna Pavlovna seemed dissatisfied with her. Kitty spoke the truth: she did not know why Anna Pavlovna had changed toward her, but she guessed it. She guessed it to be one of those things which one knows and yet cannot say even to oneself—so dreadful and shameful would it be to make a mistake.

Again and again she went over in memory all the relations she had had with that family. She remembered the naïve pleasure expressed in Anna Pavlovna's round, good-natured face whenever they met; remembered their secret consultations about the patient, and their plots to draw him away from his work which the doctor had forbidden and to take him for walks, and the attachment to her felt by the youngest boy, who called her 'my Kitty', and did not want to go to bed without her. How good it had all been! Then she recalled Petrov's timid look, full of emotion, with which he gazed at her, and the strange feeling of compassion and awkwardness, followed by a consciousness of her own benevolence, that she had experienced. How good it had all been! But all that had been at first. Now for some days past Anna Pavlovna met Kitty with affected amiability and constantly watched her husband and her.

'Yes,' she remembered, 'there was something unnatural in Anna Pavlovna, quite unlike her usual kindness, when the day before yesterday she said crossly:

'"There, he has been waiting for you and would not drink his coffee without you, though he was growing dreadfully weak."

'Yes, and perhaps my giving him his plaid may also have been unpleasant to her. It was such a simple thing, but he took it so awkwardly, and thanked me so much that I myself felt awkward. And then that portrait of me, which he did so well! And above all—that look, confused and tender. ... Yes, yes, it is so!' Kitty said to herself quite horrified; and then, 'No, it is impossible, it must not be! He is so pathetic.'

23

Quite toward the end of the season Prince Shcherbatsky, who from Carlsbad had gone on to Baden and Kissingen, returned to his family looking thinner but in the brightest of spirits. His spirits were still better when he saw Kitty completely recovered. The news of her friendship with Madame Stahl and Varenka, and the information the Princess gave him of the change she had observed in Kitty, disturbed him and aroused in him his usual feelings of jealousy toward anything that drew his daughter away from him and of fear lest she might escape from his influence into regions inaccessible to him.

The day after his arrival the Prince, attired in a long overcoat, went out in the brightest of spirits to the Spring with his daughter.

In the gallery they met Varenka walking hurriedly toward them with an elegant little red bag in her hand.

'See! Papa has come!' said Kitty to her.

Simply and naturally, as she did everything, Varenka made a movement between a bow and a curtsy and immediately began talking to the Prince just as she talked to everybody, easily and naturally.

'Of course I know you, I've heard all about you,' the Prince said to her with a smile, by which Kitty saw with joy that her father liked Varenka. 'Where are you hurrying so to?'

'Mama is here,' said she, turning to Kitty. 'She did not sleep all night and the doctor advised her to go out. I am taking her her work.'

Kitty saw that he would have liked to make fun of Varenka, but was unable to do so because he liked her.

'Well, let us see all your friends,' he added, 'including Madame Stahl, if she will condescend to recognize me.'

'Oh, do you know her, Papa?' asked Kitty, alarmed by an ironical twinkle in the Prince's eyes when he mentioned Madame Stahl.

'I knew her husband and her too, slightly, before she joined the Pietists.'

'What are Pietists, Papa?' asked Kitty, frightened by the fact that what she valued so highly in Madame Stahl had a name.

'I don't know very well myself. I only know that she thanks God for everything, including all misfortunes, ... and thanks God for her husband's death. ... Who is that? What a pitiful face,' he said, noticing an invalid of medium height who sat on a bench in a brown coat and white trousers which fell into strange folds over his emaciated legs. The man raised his straw hat above his thin curly hair, uncovering a tall forehead with an unhealthy redness where the hat had pressed it.

'It is Petrov, an artist,' Kitty replied, blushing. 'And that is his wife,' she added, indicating Anna Pavlovna.

'Poor man, what a nice face he has!' said the Prince. 'Why did you not go up to him? He looked as if he wished to say something to you.'

'Well, come back then,' said Kitty, turning resolutely. 'How are you to-day?' she asked Petrov.

Petrov rose with the aid of a stick and looked timidly at the Prince.

'This is my daughter,' said the Prince; 'allow me to introduce myself.'

The artist bowed and smiled.

'We were expecting you yesterday, Princess,' he said to Kitty.

'I meant to come, but Varenka told me that Anna Pavlovna sent word that you were not going.'

'Not going?' said Petrov, flushing and immediately beginning to cough and looking round for his wife. 'Annetta, Annetta!' he said loudly, and the veins in his white neck protruded like thick cords.

Anna Pavlovna drew near.

'How is it you sent word to the Princess that we were not going?' he said in an irritable whisper, his voice failing him.

'Good morning, Princess,' said Anna Pavlovna with a forced smile, quite unlike her former way of greeting Kitty. 'I am very pleased to make your acquaintance,' she went on, turning to the Prince.

'How is it you sent to tell the Princess we were not going?' the painter whispered hoarsely and still more angrily.

'Oh, dear me! I thought we were not going,' said his wife.

'How so? When …' He was interrupted by a fit of coughing.

The Prince raised his hat and went away with his daughter.

'Oh, oh!' he sighed deeply. 'What poor things!'

'And there's Madame Stahl,' said Kitty, pointing to a bath-chair on which, under a sunshade, lay something supported by pillows, wrapped up in grey and pale-blue. Behind her was a sullen-looking, robust German workman who pushed her bath-chair. Several patients lingered near by, gazing at this lady as at something out of the common.

The Prince approached her, and Kitty immediately noticed in his eyes that ironical spark which so disturbed her.

'I do not know whether you will remember me, but I must recall myself to you in order to thank you for your kindness to my daughter,' he said, raising his hat and not putting it on again.

'Prince Alexander Shcherbatsky,' said Madame Stahl, lifting toward him her heavenly eyes, in which Kitty detected displeasure. 'I am very pleased. I have grown very fond of your daughter.'

'Your health is still not good?'

'No, but I am accustomed to it,' said Madame Stahl. 'God sends a cross and gives the strength to bear it. … On that side!' she said irritably to Varenka, who was not wrapping the plaid round her feet the right way.

'To do good, probably,' said the Prince, whose eyes were laughing.

'That is not for us to judge,' said Madame Stahl, detecting a something hardly perceptible on the Prince's face.

'Ah!' exclaimed the Prince, seeing the Moscow Colonel standing near by, and with a bow to Madame Stahl he moved away.

'That is our aristocracy, Prince!' remarked the Colonel wishing to appear sarcastic. He had a pique against Madame Stahl because she did not wish to be acquainted with him.

'Did you know her before her illness, Prince? I mean before she was laid up? I hear she has not been up for ten years.'

'She does not get up, because her legs are too short. She has a very bad figure …'

'Papa, impossible!' exclaimed Kitty.

'Evil tongues say so, my love. But your Varenka does get it,' he added. 'Oh, those invalid ladies!'

'Oh no, Papa,' Kitty objected warmly. 'Varenka adores her. And besides, she does so much good! Ask anyone you like!'

'Perhaps,' he said, pressing her arm with his elbow. 'But it is better to do good so that no one knows anything about it.'

Kitty was silent; she felt that the divine image of Madame Stahl which she had carried in her bosom for a whole month had irrevocably vanished. There remained only a short-legged woman who was always lying down because she had a bad figure, and who tormented poor unresisting Varenka for not tucking her plaid the right way. And by no efforts of imagination could the former Madame Stahl be recalled.

On returning from the Spring with Kitty, the Prince, who had invited the Colonel, Mary Evgenyevna, and Varenka to come and take coffee, had a table and chairs brought out into the garden under a chestnut tree and breakfast laid there. The landlord and the servants brightened up under his influence. Beneath the trembling shadow-circles of the leaves, around a table covered with a white cloth and set out with coffee-pot, bread, butter, cheese, and cold game, sat the Princess in a cap with lilac ribbons, handing out cups of coffee and sandwiches. At the other end sat the Prince, making a substantial meal and talking loudly and merrily. He spread out his purchases before him: carved caskets, spillikins, and paper-knives of all kinds, of which he had bought quantities at all the different watering-places, and he gave them away to everybody, including the maid, and the landlord, with whom he joked in his funny broken German, assuring him that not the waters had cured Kitty but his excellent food, especially his plum soup. The Princess laughed at her husband for his Russian ways, but was livelier and brighter than she had ever been during her stay at the watering-place. The Colonel smiled, as he always did at the Prince's jokes. The good-natured Mary Evgenyevna shook with laughter at everything the amusing Prince said, and even Varenka, in a way new to Kitty, succumbed to the feeble but infectious laughter inspired by the Prince's jokes.

All this cheered Kitty up, but she could not help being troubled. She could not solve the problem unconsciously set her by her father's jocular view of her friends and of the life she had begun to love so much. To this problem was added the change in her relations with the Petrovs, which had been so clearly and unpleasantly demonstrated that morning. Kitty could not be merry.

'Kitty, why are you so glum?' the Prince asked her.

'I'm all right.'

'Where are you off to? Stay a little longer,' he said, turning to Varenka.

'I must get home,' said Varenka; she took leave and went into the house for her hat.

Kitty followed her. Even Varenka seemed different now.

'Oh dear, I have not laughed so much for a long time!' said Varenka. 'What a dear your papa is!'

Kitty remained silent.

'When shall we meet?' asked Varenka.

'Mama was going to call on the Petrovs. Will you be there?' asked Kitty, trying to sound Varenka.

'I will,' answered Varenka. 'They are preparing to leave, so I have promised to help them pack.'

'Then I'll come too.'

'No, why should you?'

'Why not?' asked Kitty with wide-open eyes. 'No, wait a bit, tell me why you do not wish me to be often at the Petrovs'? You don't, do you? Why?'

'There is nothing special to tell, only Petrov used to want to leave sooner but now does not want to go,' said Varenka smiling.

'Well, go on,' Kitty hurried her, looking at her with a frown.

'Well, I don't know why, but Anna Pavlovna says he does not want to go, because you are here. They quarrelled about you. And you know how excitable such invalids are.'

Kitty frowned yet more, and remained silent, and only Varenka spoke, trying to soften and soothe Kitty.

'So it is better for you not to go. ... Don't be hurt ...'

'It serves me right, it serves me right!' Kitty began hurriedly.

'Why—serves you right? I don't understand,' she said.

'It serves me right because it was all pretence, all invented and not heartfelt. What business had I with a stranger? So it comes about that I am the cause of a quarrel, and have been doing what nobody asked me to do. Because it is all pretence, pretence and pretence! ...'

'But what motive had you for pretending?' said Varenka softly.

'To appear better than others to myself and to God—to deceive everybody. Let me be bad, but at any rate not false, not a humbug!'

'But who is a "humbug"?' asked Varenka reproachfully. 'You speak as if ...'

But Kitty was in one of her fits of passion. She would not let Varenka finish.

'I am not talking about you. You are perfection. Yes, yes, you are all perfection; but how can I help it if I am bad? So let me be what I am, but not pretend. What is Anna Pavlovna to me? ... And it's all not the thing, not the thing!'

'But what is not the thing?' said Varenka, quite perplexed.

'It's all not the thing. I can't live except by my own heart, but you live by principles. I have loved you quite simply, but you, I expect, only in order to save me, to teach me.'

'You are unjust,' said Varenka.

'But I am not talking about others, only about myself.'

'Kitty!' came her mother's voice, 'come here and show Papa your corals.'

Kitty took from the table a little box which held the corals, and with a proud look, without having made it up with her friend, went to where her mother was.

'What's the matter? Why are you so red?' asked both her mother and father together.

'Nothing,' she said. 'I'll come back in a minute,' and ran away.

'She is still here,' thought Kitty and stopped at the door.

Varenka, with her hat on, sat at the table. She looked up.

'Varenka, forgive me, forgive me!' whispered Kitty, coming close to her. 'I don't remember what I said. I ...'

'Really, I did not wish to distress you,' said Varenka with a smile.

Peace was made. But with her father's return the world in which she had been living completely changed for Kitty. She felt the oppressiveness of that world of sorrow, sickness and death in which she was living. The efforts she had been making to love it, now seemed tormenting, and she longed to get away quickly to the fresh air, back to Russia, to Ergushevo, where as she knew from a letter her sister Dolly had moved with the children.

But her affection for Varenka was not weakened. When taking leave of her, Kitty tried to persuade her to come and stay with them in Russia.

'I will come when you are married,' said Varenka.

'I shall never marry.'

'Well, then, I shall never come.'

'Then I will marry for that purpose only. Mind now, don't forget your promise!' said Kitty.

Kitty returned to Russia quite cured! She was not as careless and light-hearted as before, but she was at peace. Her old Moscow sorrows were no more than a memory.

PART THREE

1

Sergius Ivanich Koznyshev, wishing to take a rest from mental work, went to stay with his brother in the country instead of going abroad as usual. Constantine Levin was very pleased, especially as he no longer expected his brother Nicholas to come that summer. But in spite of his affection and respect for Koznyshev, Constantine did not feel at ease with him in the country especially during the summer. While Levin was always busy with the farm and the long summer days were too short for doing all that had to be done, Koznyshev was resting. But even though he was resting from mental labours and was not writing, he was so used to mental activity that he liked expressing his thoughts in an elegant, concise style, and liked having a listener. His most usual and natural listener was his brother; and therefore, despite their friendly relations, Constantine felt uncomfortable at leaving him alone. Koznyshev loved to lie basking in the sunshine, talking lazily.

But it wearied Constantine to sit listening to him, particularly because he knew that during his absence the manure was being carted into the field, and it was impossible to guess where they would throw it if he were not there to see. The ploughshares too would not be screwed up properly, or taken out; and then he would be told that these ploughs were a silly invention and so on.

At the beginning of June Agatha Mikhaylovna happened to slip and sprained her wrist. A talkative young medical man who had only just qualified and been appointed doctor for the Zemstvo district arrived, examined the hand, and enjoyed a talk with the celebrated Sergius Ivanich Koznyshev. He told him all the gossip of the district to show off his enlightened views and complained of the unsatisfactory conditions prevailing there. Koznyshev listened attentively, asked questions, and, enlivened by the presence of a new listener, became quite chatty, made some pointed and weighty remarks respectfully appreciated by the young doctor, and reached that state of animation his brother so well knew, which generally followed a brilliant and lively conversation. After the doctor's departure Koznyshev felt inclined to go to the river with his fishing-rod. He was fond of angling, and seemed proud of being able to like such a stupid occupation. Constantine offered to give his brother a lift in his trap.

When they reached the meadow Levin stopped. At the roots of the thick grass the morning dew still lingered, and Koznyshev, afraid of wetting his feet, asked his brother to drive him across the meadow to the willow clump near which perch could be caught. Though Constantine was loath to crush his grass, he drove across the meadow.

Though he had caught nothing, Koznyshev did not feel bored and seemed in the best of spirits. Levin saw that he had been roused by his conversation with the doctor and wanted to have a talk. Levin, on the contrary, was impatient to get home in order to give orders about hiring the mowers on the morrow, and to decide about the hay harvest, which greatly occupied his mind.

'Well, let's go,' said he.

'Where's the hurry? Let's sit here a little. Though nothing bites, it's pleasant; hunting and similar sports are good because they bring one in touch with nature.'

Constantine was silent and without replying to his brother began reflecting on a totally different and personal matter.

Koznyshev wound up his last line, untied the horse, and they started on their homeward way.

The personal matter that occupied Levin was this. The year before, when visiting a field that was being mown, he had lost his temper with his steward, and to calm himself had used a remedy of his own—he took a scythe from one of the peasants and himself began mowing.

He liked this work so much that he went mowing several times: he mowed all the meadow in front of his house, and when spring came he planned to devote several whole days to mowing with the peasants. Since his brother's arrival, however, he was in doubt whether to go mowing or not. He did not feel comfortable at the thought of leaving his brother alone all day long, and he also feared that Koznyshev might laugh at him. But while walking over the meadow he recalled the impression mowing had made on him, and almost made up his mind to do it.

'I need physical exercise; without it my character gets quite spoilt,' thought he, and determined to go and mow, however uncomfortable his brother and the peasants might make him feel.

In the evening Constantine went to the office and gave orders about the work, sending round to the villages to tell the mowers to come next day to the Kalina meadow, the largest and finest he had.

'And please send my scythe to Titus to be sharpened, and have it taken to the meadow to-morrow: I may go mowing myself,' he said, trying to overcome his confusion.

The steward smiled and said, 'All right, sir.'

That evening, at tea, Levin said to his brother:

'The weather looks settled; to-morrow we begin mowing.'

'I like that work very much,' said Koznyshev.

'I like it awfully too. I have mown with the peasants now and then, and to-morrow I want to mow all day.'

Koznyshev looked up at his brother in surprise.

'It is splendid physical exercise, but you will hardly be able to hold out,' remarked Koznyshev, without the least sarcasm.

'I have tried it. At first it seems hard, but one gets drawn into it. I don't think I shall lag behind ...'

'Dear me! But tell me, how do the peasants take it? I expect they laugh at their crank of a master?'

'No, I don't think so; but it is such pleasant work, and at the same time so hard, that one has no time for thinking.'

Next morning Constantine got up earlier than usual, but giving instructions about the farming delayed him, and when he came to the meadow each man was already mowing his second swath.

Levin dismounted and, tethering his horse by the roadside, went up to Titus, who fetched another scythe from behind a bush and gave it to Levin.

'It's ready, master! Like a razor, it will mow of itself,' said Titus, taking off his cap and smiling as he handed the scythe.

Levin took it and began to put himself in position. The peasants, perspiring and merry, who had finished their swaths came out on to the road one after another, and laughingly exchanged greetings with their master. They all looked at him, but no one made any remark.

Titus made room for Levin, and Levin followed him. By the roadside the grass was short and tough, and Levin, who had not done any mowing for a long time and was confused by so many eyes upon him mowed badly for the first ten minutes, though he swung his scythe with much vigour. They came to softer grass, and Levin followed Titus and tried to mow as well as possible.

As Levin was aware, Titus had been mowing this swath with special rapidity, probably to put his master to the test, and it chanced to be a very long one. The next swaths were easier, but still Levin had to work with all his might to keep even with the peasants. He thought of nothing and desired nothing, except not to lag behind and to do his work as well as possible. Suddenly he was conscious of a pleasant coolness on his hot perspiring shoulders, without knowing what it was or whence it came. He glanced up at the sky whilst whetting his scythe. A dark cloud was hanging low overhead, and large drops of rain were falling.

He finished a swath and was about to start another when Titus paused and looked at the sun.

'Breakfast-time, master,' said Titus.

'Is it time? Well, then, breakfast!'

Levin handed his scythe to Titus and with the peasants, who were going to fetch the bread that lay with their coats, went across the swaths of the long mown portion of the meadow, slightly sprinkled with rain. Only then he remembered that he had not been right about the weather and that the rain was wetting the hay.

'The hay will be spoilt,' said he.

'It won't hurt, master. "Mow in the rain, rake when it's fine!"'

Levin untied his horse and rode home to his coffee.

2

After breakfast Levin got placed between a humorous old man who invited him to be his neighbour and a young peasant who had only got married last autumn and was now out for his first summer's mowing. The old man went along holding himself erect, moving with regular, long steps, turning out his toes, and with a precise and even motion the sharp scythe whizzed through the juicy grass.

Levin did not notice how time passed. Had he been asked how long he had been mowing, he would have answered 'half an hour', although it was nearly noon. As they were about to begin another swath the old man drew Levin's attention to the little boys and girls approaching from all sides along the road and through the long grass, hardly visible above it, carrying jugs of kvas stoppered with rags, and bundles of bread which strained their little arms.

'Come, master! It's dinner-time,' said he with decision. All the mowers on reaching the river went across the swaths to where their coats lay, and where the children who had brought their dinners sat waiting for them. The men who had driven from a distance gathered in the shadow of their carts; those who lived nearer sheltered under the willow growth, on which they hung grass.

Levin sat down beside them; he did not want to go away.

All the peasants' restraint in the presence of the master had vanished.

'Come, master, have some of my dinner,' said the old man, kneeling in front of his bowl.

The bread and water was so nice that Levin gave up all intention of going home to lunch. He shared the old man's meal and got into conversation with him about his domestic affairs, taking a lively interest in them and telling him about his own, giving him all the particulars which would interest the old peasant. When the old man got up and, having said grace, lay down beneath the willows with an armful of grass under his head, Levin did the same. He at once fell asleep, waking only when the sun touched the opposite side of the willows and reached him.

When he was fully awake Levin began to calculate how much had been done and how much could still be done that day.

'What do you think—could we manage to get Mashkin Heights mown to-day?' he asked the old man.

'Well, God willing, we might! The sun is not very high though. Perhaps—if the lads could have a little vodka!'

At half-time, when they sat down again and those who smoked were lighting their pipes, the old man informed the young fellows that if they mowed the Mashkin Heights there would be vodka.

And young and old vied with each other at mowing. But in spite of their haste they did not spoil the grass, and the swaths fell just as evenly and exactly as before.

Levin was again mowing between the old man and the lad. The old man, who had put on his sheep-skin jacket, was still as jolly, witty, and easy in his movements as before.

Mashkin Heights were mown, and the peasants, having completed their last swaths, put on their coats and went home in high spirits. Levin, having regretfully taken leave of them, mounted and rode home.

Koznyshev had long had his dinner, and was in his room drinking iced water with lemon, while looking over the papers and magazines just arrived by post, when Levin rushed in, his tangled hair clinging to his moist brow, his shirt saturated back and front and dark with perspiration, and cried out joyfully:

'We have finished the whole of the meadow! How delightful it is! You would not believe what enjoyment it was! And how have you spent the day?'

'Quite well. But have you really been mowing all day? You must be as hungry as a wolf. Kuzma has everything ready for you.'

'No, I don't want to eat; I have had something there. But I'll go and wash.'

'Yes, yes, go; and I will come presently.' Koznyshev shook his head as he looked at his brother. 'Go, go, and be quick!' he added with a smile, as, gathering together his books, he prepared to go too. He also felt suddenly quite cheerful and did not wish to part from his brother.

Five minutes later the brothers met again in the dining-room. Though Levin had imagined that he was not hungry, and sat down to table only not to offend Kuzma, yet when he began eating he thought everything delicious. Koznyshev smiled as he looked at him.

'Oh, yes, there's a letter for you,' said he.

The letter was from Oblonsky. Levin read it aloud. Oblonsky wrote from Petersburg: 'I have had a letter from Dolly. She is in Ergushevo, and everything is out of gear there. Please go and see her and help her with your advice—you know all about everything. She is quite alone, poor thing; my mother-in-law is still abroad.'

'That's splendid! I will certainly go and see her,' said Levin. 'Or shall we both go?'

'I shall be very glad,' replied Koznyshev, still smiling. The sight of his younger brother had a distinctly cheering influence on him. 'I see that on the whole you are well satisfied with your day.'

'Very well indeed! We finished the meadow. And I chummed up with such a fine old man! You can't imagine what a charming fellow he is.'

'Well, then, you are satisfied with your day, and so am I.'

Levin rose, stretching himself and smiling. Koznyshev smiled too.

'Shall we go for a stroll together?' he said, not wishing to part from his brother, who seemed to be exhaling freshness and vigour. 'Come along! We could call in at the office if you want to.'

'Oh, dear me!' exclaimed Levin, so loudly that he scared Koznyshev.

'What's the matter?'

'How's Agatha Mikhaylovna's arm?' asked Levin, slapping his head. 'I had forgotten all about it.'

'Much better.'

'Well, I'll run and see her, all the same. You won't have got your hat before I am back.'

And his heels clattered swiftly down the stairs.

3

Oblonsky had gone to Petersburg to fulfil a very necessary duty—which to officials seems most natural and familiar, though to laymen it is incomprehensible—that of reminding the Ministry of his existence, without the performance of which rite continuance in Government service is impossible. Having taken away with him all the money there was in the house, he contrived while attending to duty to pass his time very pleasantly, going to races and visiting at country houses. Meanwhile, to curtail expenses, Dolly and her children moved to Ergushevo, the estate which had formed part of her dowry, the very place where in spring the forest had been sold.

The first days in the country were very trying for Dolly. The day after her arrival it poured with rain and in the night the rain came through into the passage and nursery, so that the children's beds had to be carried into the drawing-room. There was no scullery-maid. Of the nine cows some, according to the dairymaids, were about to calve, others had calved for the first time, some were too old, and the rest were difficult to milk, so there was no butter and scarcely enough milk even for the children. There were no eggs. It was impossible to get a chicken, and they were obliged to boil and roast tough old purple-coloured roosters. No peasant women could be got to scrub the floors: they were all out planting potatoes. It was impossible to go for a drive because one of the horses was restive and would not run in harness. There was no place for bathing, the river banks being all trampled over by the cattle and exposed to the road; it was not even possible to walk in the garden because the fence was broken and the peasants' cattle could get in, and the herd included a terrible bull that was given to bellowing. There was nowhere to hang dresses, because what few wardrobes there were would not shut, or else opened of themselves when anyone passed by. There was no mangle in the laundry, not even an ironing board, and no large pots or pans.

The position seemed irremediable; but Matrena Filimonovna consoled her mistress, assuring her that everything would 'shape itself' (this phrase was her own, and Matthew had learnt it from her), and she went to work deliberately and without excitement.

She at once made friends with the steward's wife, and on the very day of the removal drank tea with her and with the steward beneath the laburnums, discussing arrangements. A club was soon established beneath the laburnums, consisting of Matrena Filimonovna, the steward's wife, the village elder, and the office clerk; and by means of this club the troubles began gradually to subside, so that in a week's time everything had really 'shaped itself'. The roof was mended, a scullery-maid—a relative of the elder's—was engaged, hens were bought, the cows gave enough milk, the garden was fenced in, a mangle was made by the carpenter, hooks were put into the wardrobes, which no longer opened at their own sweet will; an ironing board covered with coarse cloth lay across the arm of a chair and a chest of drawers in the maid's room, and the smell of hot irons soon pervaded the room.

Even a bathing-house was constructed out of straw-plaited screens. Lily started bathing, and at least part of Dolly's expectations were fulfilled, if not that of a quiet, at least that of a comfortable, country life. But these cares and anxieties were the only kind of happiness possible for Dolly. Had it not been for them she would have been left to her thoughts about the husband who did not love her. Besides, her children were already beginning to repay her care by affording her small joys. These joys were so trifling as to be as imperceptible as grains of gold among the sand, and in moments of depression she saw nothing but the sand; yet there were brighter moments when she felt nothing but joy, saw nothing but the gold.

At the end of May, when the house was more or less in order, Dolly received from her husband an answer to her letter of complaint. He wrote asking her to forgive his not having seen to everything, and saying that he would come as soon as possible. That possibility, however, had not been fulfilled, and up to the beginning of June Dolly was still living without him in the country.

4

Surrounded by her children, all freshly bathed and with heads still damp, Dolly with a kerchief tied round her own head was nearing home when the coachman said:

'There's a gentleman coming—I think it's the Pokrovsk squire.'

Dolly leant forward and was pleased to see the familiar figure of Levin, who in a grey hat and coat was walking toward them. She was always glad to see him, but on this day was more pleased than ever because he would now see her in all her glory. No one could understand the dignity of her position better than Levin. On seeing her he found himself confronted by just such a picture of family life as his fancy painted.

'You are like a hen with her chickens, Darya Alexandrovna!'

'Oh, I'm so glad!' said she, holding out her hand.

'You're glad, yet you never sent me word. My brother is staying with me. It was from Stephen I heard, at last, that you were here.'

'From Stephen?' asked Dolly in a surprised tone.

'Yes, he wrote that you had moved here, and he thought I might be of some use to you,' replied Levin, and having said this grew confused because he imagined that Dolly might not like to accept the help of a stranger in matters that ought to be attended to by her husband. It was for his quick perception and delicacy of feeling that Dolly liked him.

'Of course I understood that this only meant you wanted to see me, and was very pleased. I can well imagine how strange everything here must seem to you, used as you are to managing a town house; and if you require anything I am quite at your disposal.'

'Oh no!' said Dolly. 'At first it was inconvenient, but now everything is quite comfortable, thanks to my old nurse,' she said, indicating the nurse, who, aware that she was being mentioned, looked at Levin with a bright and friendly smile.

'Won't you sit down, sir? We'll move closer together,' she said.

'No, I will walk. Children, who will race the horses with me?'

Here in the country among the children, and in the company of Dolly whom he found very congenial, Levin's spirits rose to that childlike merriment Dolly liked so much in him. He ran about with the children, taught them gymnastics, and talked to Dolly about his rural occupations.

After dinner, left alone with him on the verandah, Dolly alluded to Kitty.

'Do you know Kitty is coming here to spend the summer with me?'

'Really?' said he, flushing up, passionately longing and yet dreading to hear every particular concerning Kitty. He feared that the peace of mind he had acquired with so much effort might be destroyed.

'Kitty writes that she wishes for nothing so much as seclusion and quiet,' said Dolly after a pause in the conversation.

'And her health! Is she better?' asked Levin anxiously.

'Yes, thank God! she has quite recovered. I never believed that she had lung trouble.'

'Oh I am so glad!' said Levin, and Dolly thought she saw something pathetic and helpless in his face as he said it, and then silently looked at her.

'Tell me, Constantine Dmitrich,' said Dolly with her kind though slightly ironical smile, 'why are you angry with Kitty?'

'I? ... I am not angry,' said Levin.

'Yes, you are. Why did you not call either on us or on them when you were in Moscow?'

'Darya Alexandrovna,' said he, blushing, 'I am surprised that one so kind as you are should not feel what the reason was. How is it that you have no pity for me, knowing as you do ...'

'What do I know?'

'You know I proposed and was rejected,' muttered Levin.

'Why did you think I knew?'

'Because everybody knows it.'

'In that, at any rate, you are mistaken; I did not know it, though I had my suspicions.'

'Well, anyhow you know it now.'

'All I knew was that something had happened that tormented her dreadfully, and she asked me never to speak about it. And since she had not told me, she won't have told anybody. ... Well, what did happen to you? Tell me.'

'I have told you what happened.'

'When was it?'

'When I last visited you.'

'Do you know,' said Dolly, 'I am terribly, terribly sorry for her! You are suffering only through pride ... but for her, poor child, I am terribly, terribly sorry. Now I understand everything. When you proposed to Kitty she was just in that state when it was impossible for her to give an answer: she was undecided—undecided between you and Vronsky; she saw him every day, you she had not seen for a long time. I admit that had she been older ... I, for instance, could not have been undecided in her place. To me he was always repulsive, and so he has proved in the end.'

'Darya Alexandrovna,' he replied drily, 'I value your confidence in me, but think you are mistaken. Whether I am right or wrong, that pride which you so despise makes any thought of your sister impossible for me—do you understand me?—perfectly impossible.'

'I will only add just this: you understand that I am speaking about my sister, whom I love as much as my own children. I do not say she loves you; I only wished to tell you that her refusal proves nothing.'

'I don't know!' said Levin, jumping up. 'If you know how you hurt me! It is just as if you had lost a child, and they kept on telling you: "Now he would have been so and so, and might be living and you rejoicing in him, but he is dead, dead, dead ...!"'

'How funny you are!' said Dolly, regarding Levin's agitation with a sad smile. 'Then you won't come to see us while Kitty is here?'

'No, I won't. Of course I will not avoid her, but whenever I can I will try to save her the unpleasantness of meeting me.'

'All right then! Let it be as if nothing had been said about it. Stay a little longer.'

5

In the middle of July the Elder from the village belonging to Levin's sister (which lay fifteen miles from Pokrovsk) came to see Levin and report on business matters and on the hay-harvest.

From the Elder's vague replies to Levin's questions as to how much hay the largest meadow had yielded, from his haste to apportion the hay without waiting for permission, and from the general tone of the peasant, Levin knew that there was something not quite square about the apportionment, and decided to go and investigate the matter himself.

Levin arrived at his sister's village at noon and left his horse with a friendly old peasant, the husband of his brother's nurse. Wishing to hear particulars of the hay-harvest from this old man, Levin went to speak to him in his apiary. Parmenich, a loquacious, handsome old man, welcomed Levin joyfully, showed him over his homestead, and told him all about the swarming of his bees that year; but to Levin's questions about the hay-harvest he gave vague and reluctant answers. This still further confirmed Levin's suspicions. He went to inspect the hay, examined the stacks, and saw that there could not be fifty cartloads in each. To put the peasant to the proof Levin ordered the carts on which the hay was being moved to be fetched, and one of the stacks to be carried to the barn. There were only thirty-two loads in the stack. In spite of the Elder's explanations that the hay had been loose, but had settled down in the stacks, and his swearing that all had been done in a 'godly way', Levin insisted that the hay had been apportioned without his order and that he would not accept the stacks as containing fifty loads each. After lengthy disputes it was settled that the peasants themselves should take those eleven stacks, counting them as fifty loads each, and that the owner's share should be measured afresh. These disputes and the apportioning of the haycocks went on till late in the evening. When the last of the hay had been apportioned, Levin entrusted the rest of the supervision to the steward and he went back down the high road toward the village. A slight breeze was blowing and all looked grey and dull.

'What's that? Who can it be coming?' thought he, hearing the tinkling of bells. At a distance of forty paces along the road on which he was walking he saw a coach with four horses abreast and luggage on top approaching him.

Levin, without wondering who might be inside, glanced in at the window absent-mindedly.

In one corner an elderly woman was dozing; and close to the window sat a young girl who was holding the ribbons of her white night-cap with both hands.

At the very moment when this vision was about to disappear, her candid eyes fell on him. She recognized him and joyful surprise lit up her face. He could not be mistaken. There were no other eyes in the world like them. In the whole world there was only one being able to unite in itself the universe and the meaning of life for him. It was Kitty. He guessed that she was on her way from the station to her sister's house at Ergushevo.

'Oh,' said he to himself. 'I love *her*!'

6

None but those who knew Karenin most intimately knew that this apparently cold and sober-minded man had one weakness, quite inconsistent with the general trend of his character. Karenin could not with equanimity hear or see a child or a woman weeping.

When Anna on their way home from the races announced to him what her relations with Vronsky were and immediately hid her face in her hands and began crying, Karenin, despite his indignation with her, was as usual overcome by that mental perturbation. Being aware of this and of the fact that any expression he could at that moment find for his feelings would be incompatible with the situation, he tried to conceal all signs of life within himself and neither moved nor looked at her. That was the cause of the strange deathlike look on his face which had so struck Anna. When they reached home he helped her out of the carriage and took leave of her with his usual courtesy; he said he would let her know his decision next day.

His wife's words, confirming as they did his worst suspicions, had given Karenin a cruel pain in his heart. This pain was rendered more acute by physical pity for her, evoked by her tears. But when alone in the carriage, to his surprise and joy he felt completely relieved of that pity and of the suspicions and jealousy that had lately so tormented him. He felt like a man who has just had a tooth drawn which has been hurting him a long time.

What would happen to her and to her son, toward whom his feelings had changed as they had toward her, no longer occupied his mind. The one thing that pre-occupied him was the question of how he could best divest himself of the mud with which she in her fall had bespattered him: of how to do it in the way which would be most decent, most convenient for him, and consequently fairest, and how he should continue his active, honest, and useful career.

'It is a misfortune that may befall anyone and it has befallen me. The only question is, how best to face the situation. A duel is unthinkable and no one expects it of me. My aim is to safeguard my reputation, which I need for the uninterrupted pursuit of my career.' His official pursuits, which had always appeared essential to Karenin, now assumed even greater importance.

Having rejected the idea of a duel, Karenin turned his thoughts to divorce, the next expedient of which some of the wronged husbands he remembered had availed themselves. Going over all the cases of divorce he knew—there were very many, and in the highest Society, with which he was well acquainted—Karenin could not recall one in which the purpose of the divorce was the one he had in view; that is, a divorce in which the guilty wife would be simply cast off. He knew that in their complex conditions of life it would not be possible to obtain those coarse proofs of a wife's infidelity which the law demanded. The chief object of his life, the settling of conditions with the least possible amount of disturbance, could not be furthered by divorce. Besides, in Karenin's soul, despite the complete and contemptuous indifference he thought he felt for his wife, there was one feeling left with regard to her: an objection to her being in a position to unite unhindered with Vronsky, so making her crime advantageous to her. The very thought of it irritated him to such an extent that he groaned with inner pain.

'Besides a formal divorce, it would be possible to just separate,' he resumed when he had grown calm again; but this measure would have all the inconvenience of a divorce-scandal, and would throw his wife into Vronsky's arms just in the same way. 'No, it is impossible, impossible!' he said aloud, wrapping the rug round his legs, 'I cannot be unhappy, but she and he must not be happy.'

Karenin came to the conclusion that there was only one course to be followed: to keep her with him, hiding from the world what had happened, and taking all necessary steps to put a stop to her love-affair, and above all (though he did not confess this to himself) to punish her. In confirmation of this decision, after it had already been reached, another powerful argument occurred to Karenin. 'It is only by this course that I can conform with religion,' said he to himself. 'It is the only way that makes it possible for me not to disown my guilty wife and to give her a chance of repenting, and even, painful as it will be, to devote part of my powers to her redemption.'

Proceeding to consider further details, Karenin could not even see why his relations with his wife should not remain almost the same as before. He could of course never again revive his respect for her; but there was no occasion for him to spoil his own life and to suffer just because she had proved a bad and unfaithful wife.

By the time he reached Petersburg Karenin had not only resolved to keep to his decision, but had mentally composed a letter to his wife. On entering the hall of his house he glanced at the letters and papers which had been sent from the Ministry and ordered them to be brought into his study.

'Tell him to unharness; and no one is to be admitted,' he said in answer to the hall-porter's inquiry, accentuating with a certain pleasure the word *admitted*. It was a sign that he was in good spirits.

He paced twice up and down his study and then halted at the gigantic writing-table, on which his valet had already lit six candles. Cracking his fingers, he sat down and arranged his writing materials. With his elbow on the table and his head bent to one side he sat and thought for a minute, and then wrote without an instant's pause. He did not begin by addressing her, and wrote in French.

'During our last conversation I expressed my intention of communicating my decision with reference to the subject of that conversation. Having carefully and fully considered everything, I now write to fulfil my promise. My decision is as follows: Whatever your actions may have been, I do not consider myself justified in severing the bonds with which a Higher Power has united us. A family must not be broken up through the caprice, perversity, or even crime, of one of the married couple, and our life must go on as heretofore. This is unavoidable for my sake, for yours, and for that of our son. I am perfectly convinced that you have repented, and are repenting, of the action which has led to this letter, and will completely co-operate with me to eradicate the cause of our discord and to forget the past. If not, you can yourself foresee what awaits you and your son. I hope to talk all this over with you in more detail at a personal interview. As the summer season is drawing to a close, I would ask you to return to Petersburg as soon as possible, and not later than Tuesday. All necessary preparations shall be made for your return. I beg you to note that I attach importance to this request of mine.

A. KARENIN.

'P.S.—I enclose some money, which you may need for your expenses.'

He read the letter over and was satisfied with it, especially with having remembered to enclose the money; there was not a single cruel word or threat in it, yet it was not yielding in tone. Above all it provided a golden bridge for her to return by. Having folded the letter, smoothed it out with a massive ivory paper-knife, and put it and the money in an envelope—with the pleasure that the use of his well-arranged writing appliances always caused him—he rang.

'Give this to the messenger, and tell him to take it to Anna Arkadyevna, to-morrow,' he said, and got up.

'Yes, your Excellency! Shall tea be served in the study?'

Karenin assented, and, toying with his paper-knife, went to his arm-chair, beside which a lamp was burning. Above the arm-chair hung a beautifully-painted portrait of Anna by a celebrated artist. To Karenin the splendidly-painted black lace on the head, the black hair, and the beautiful white hand with many rings on the third finger, suggested something intolerably bold and provocative. After looking at the portrait for about a minute he shuddered and his lips trembled and made a sound like 'brr' as he turned way. He sat down hurriedly and opened his book.

At eleven o'clock he went to bed, and when as he lay there he remembered what had occurred with his wife, it no longer appeared to him in such gloomy colours.

7

Though Anna had angrily and obstinately contradicted Vronsky when he said that her position was an impossible one, in the depths of her soul she felt that the situation was a false one and wished with all her heart to put an end to it. On her way back from the races, in a moment of excitement—in spite of the pain it caused her—she had told her husband everything. After he left her, she told herself that she was glad she had told him, that now everything would be definite—at any rate, the falsehood and deception would no longer exist. She thought it quite certain that her position would be cleared up for good. Her new position might be a bad one but it would be definite, and there would be no vagueness or falsehood. She saw Vronsky that same evening, but did not tell him what had passed between her and her husband, though he would have to be told before her position could be settled.

When she woke up in the morning the first thing that came into her mind was what she had said to her husband, and it now appeared so terrible that she could not understand how she had been able to utter such strange and coarse words and could not imagine what result they would have. But the words had been spoken and Karenin had gone away without saying anything.

'I saw Vronsky and did not tell him. Why did I not tell him?'

And in answer to this question a hot blush of shame spread all over her face. She knew what had stopped her, knew she had been ashamed. The situation which the night before had appeared to be clearing up now seemed quite hopeless. She dreaded the disgrace, which she had not considered before. She felt as if the words she had used to her husband, which she kept repeating in imagination, had been said by her to every one and that every one had heard them.

She had not the courage to look into the eyes of the people she lived with. She could not make up her mind to call her maid, and still less to go down and face her son and his governess.

The maid, who had long been listening at the door, at last came in of her own accord. Anna looked inquiringly into her eyes and blushed with alarm. The maid begged pardon and said she thought she had heard the bell.

She brought a dress and a note. The note was from Betsy, who reminded her that she (Betsy) was that day expecting Lisa Merkalova and the Baroness Stolz, with their admirers Kaluzhsky and old Stremov, to a game of croquet.

'Do come, if only to study manners and customs. I expect you,' she wrote in conclusion.

Anna read the note and sighed deeply.

'I don't want anything, anything at all,' she said to Annushka, who was moving the bottles and brushes on the dressing-table. 'I will get dressed and come down at once. I want nothing, nothing at all.'

Annushka went out, but Anna did not get dressed. She remained in the same position with head and arms drooping. Every now and then her whole body shuddered as she tried to make some movement or to say something, and then became rigid again. 'Oh, my God! My God!' she kept repeating, but neither the word *God* or *my* had any meaning for her. She was not only disturbed, but was beginning to be afraid of a new mental condition such as she had never before experienced. Sometimes she could not tell what she feared and what she desired. Whether she feared and desired what had been, or what would be, and what it was she desired she did not know.

'Coffee is ready, and Ma'm'selle and Serezha are waiting,' said Annushka, coming in again and finding Anna in the same position.

The thought of her son at once took Anna out of the hopeless condition she had been in. She remembered that partly sincere but greatly exaggerated rôle of a mother living for her son which she had assumed during the last five years; and felt with joy that in the position in which she found herself she had still one stay, independent of her relations with her husband and Vronsky. That stay was her son. Whatever position she might accept she could not give up her son. She had an aim in life and must act so as to ensure her position toward her son, while they had not yet taken him from her. She must take him away. That was the only thing to do at present. She must be calm and escape from this terrible situation.

The thought of decided action concerned with her son—of going away somewhere with him—made her feel calmer.

She dressed quickly and with determined steps entered the drawing-room, where Serezha and his governess were waiting breakfast for her as usual.

His governess, looking exceptionally stern, began to give a long and detailed account of his misconduct, but Anna did not listen to her. She was wondering whether to take her also or not.

'No, I won't,' she decided. 'I will go alone with my son.'

'Yes, that was very wrong,' said Anna, and putting her hand on his shoulder she looked at him not with a severe but with a timid expression which confused and gladdened the boy. She kissed him.

'Leave him to me,' she said to the astonished governess, and holding his hand she sat down at the breakfast table.

'Serezha,' she said as soon as the governess had gone away, 'it was wrong, but you won't do it again? ... You love me?'

She felt the tears coming into her eyes.

'As if I could help loving him,' she said to herself, looking into his frightened and yet happy face. 'And is it possible that he would take sides with his father to torment me?' The tears were already streaming down her cheeks, and in order to hide them she jumped up abruptly and went out on to the verandah.

After the thunderstorms of the last few days the weather had grown clear and cold.

She shivered with cold, and with the terror that seized her with new power out in the open air.

'Go to Mariette,' she said to Serezha, who had come out after her; and she began pacing up and down the straw matting of the verandah.

'Is it possible that they could not forgive me or understand that it could not have been otherwise?' she asked herself and again she felt that duality in her soul.

'No, no, I must not think,' she said to herself; 'I must get ready to go. Where? To Moscow? Yes, by the evening train, with Annushka and Serezha, and with only the most necessary things. But first I must write to both of them.'

She quickly went to her sitting-room where Annushka drew her attention to the noise of approaching carriage wheels. Anna looked out and saw Karenin's messenger in the porch ringing the bell.

'Go and see what it is,' she said, and, calmly prepared for anything, sat down in an easy-chair and folded her hands on her knees. A footman brought her a thick envelope addressed in her husband's handwriting.

'The messenger has been told to wait for an answer,' he said.

'All right,' she replied, and as soon as he had gone she tore open the envelope with trembling fingers.

A packet of new still unfolded notes in a paper band fell out. She unfolded the letter and read the end first: 'All necessary preparations shall be made for your return. I beg you to note that I attach importance to this request of mine,' she read. Having glanced through it, she went back and read it again from the beginning. When she had finished she felt cold, and knew that a more dreadful misfortune had befallen her than she had ever expected.

She had that morning repented of having told her husband and wished it were possible to unsay her words; and here was a letter treating her words as unsaid and giving her what she had desired; but now the letter appeared more terrible than anything she could have imagined.

'He's in the right, he's in the right!' she muttered; 'of course he always is in the right, he is a Christian, he is magnanimous! Yes, a mean, horrid man! And no one but I understands or will understand it, and I cannot explain it. They say he's a religious, moral, honest, and wise man, but they do not see what I have seen. They do not know how for eight years he has been smothering my life, smothering everything that was alive in me, that he never once thought I was a live woman, in need of love. They do not know how at every step he hurt me and remained self-satisfied.

'"You can yourself foresee what awaits you and your son!"—she repeated the words of the letter. 'That is a threat that he will take my son from me, and probably their stupid laws will permit it. But don't I know why he said it? He does not believe in my love for my son or he despises it. He knows that I will not give up my son, that I cannot give him up, that without my son I cannot live even with the man I love,—that if I forsook my son I should act like a horrid disreputable woman. He knows that and knows that I have not the power to do it.'

She sat down at her writing-table, but instead of writing she folded her arms on the table and put her head on them, and sobbed without restraint, like a punished child.

The approaching step of the footman recalled her to herself, and hiding her face from him she pretended to be writing.

'The messenger is asking for the answer,' he said.

'The answer? Yes, let him wait: I will ring,' said Anna.

'What can I write?' she thought. 'What can I decide alone?' She seized the first pretext for action that occurred to her to divert her thoughts from herself. 'I must see Alexis,' as she called Vronsky in her thoughts. 'He alone can tell me what to do. I shall go to Betsy's and perhaps shall meet him there,' quite forgetting that the evening before when she had told him she was not going to the Princess Tverskaya's, he had replied that in that case he would not go either. She wrote to her husband:

'I have received your letter.—A.,' rang, and gave the note to the footman.

8

Anna arrived at the Princess Tverskaya's house before the other visitors.

Just as she arrived Vronsky's footman also came up. He stopped at the door, took off his cap, and let her pass. Anna saw him, and only then remembered that the evening before Vronsky had said that he was not coming. Probably he had sent a note to say so.

She heard in front of her the bell that announced her arrival, and the Princess Tverskaya's footman was already standing half-turned toward her at an open door, waiting for her to enter the inner rooms.

When she met Betsy coming toward her in a white costume that struck Anna by its elegance, Anna smiled at her as usual.

There must have been something unusual about Anna's look, for Betsy noticed it at once.

'I have slept badly,' answered Anna, gazing at the footman, who she guessed was bringing Vronsky's note.

'How glad I am that you have come!' said Betsy. 'I am tired, and am going to have a cup of tea before they arrive. We can have a heart-to-heart talk over our tea,' she added in English.

'Yes, especially as I cannot stay long. I must go to the old Countess Vrede—I promised to, ages ago,' said Anna, to whom falsehood—so alien to her by nature—had now become so simple and natural in Society that it even gave her pleasure. Her only reason for saying it was that since Vronsky was not coming she must secure her freedom and try to see him in some other way.

'No, I won't let you go on any account,' said Betsy, fixing her eyes intently on Anna. 'I should be really hurt, if I were not so fond of you. Please bring us tea in the little drawing-room,' she said to the footman as she took the note from him and read it.

'Alexis has failed us,' she said in French. 'He writes that he cannot come.' She spoke in a natural and matter-of-fact tone, as if it never entered her head that Vronsky had any other interest for Anna than as a croquet player. But Anna saw by her bright intelligent look that she partly understood Anna's position and was devising something. They were in a small sitting-room.

'But I must write to Alexis.' Betsy sat down at the table, wrote a few words, and put the paper in an envelope. 'I am writing to ask him to come to dinner; I have one lady too many. See if I have made it pressing enough! Excuse me! I must leave you for a minute; please close the envelope and send it,' she said from the doorway; 'I have some orders to give.'

Without thinking for an instant Anna sat down at the table with Betsy's note, and without reading it added at the bottom: 'I must see you. Come to Vrede's garden. I shall be there at six.' She closed it, and Betsy returning sent it off in her presence.

Over their tea, which was brought them in the cool little drawing-room, the two women really had before the arrival of the visitors the cosy chat the Princess Tverskaya had promised Anna. Then recalling what awaited her when alone at home if she took no decision she took her leave and went away.

9

Vronsky was particularly fortunate in that he had a code of rules which clearly defined what should and should not be done. This code categorically determined that though the card-sharper must be paid, the tailor need not be; that one may not lie to a man, but might to a woman; that one must not deceive anyone, except a husband; that one must not forgive an insult but may insult others, and so on. These rules might be irrational and bad but they were absolute, and in complying with them Vronsky felt at ease and could carry his head high. Only quite lately, in reference to his relations to Anna, had he begun to feel that his code did not quite meet all circumstances.

Only yesterday she had told him that she was pregnant, and he felt that this news and what she expected of him called for something that was not fully defined by his code of rules. He was taken by surprise.

'When I told her to leave her husband, that meant that she should unite herself with me. Am I ready for that? How can I take her away now when I have no money? No doubt I could arrange that ... but how could I go away with her while I am in the army? Having proposed it, I must be ready to carry it out—that is to say I must find the money and leave the army.'

He pondered. The question of whether to leave or not to leave the army led him to another private matter. Ambition was the old motive of his childhood and youth, one which he did not acknowledge even to himself, but which was so strong a passion that it now struggled against his love. But two years ago he had made a bad blunder. He had refused a post that was offered him, hoping that this refusal would enhance his value, but it turned out that he had been too bold and he was passed over. Having then perforce to assume the rôle of an independent character, he played it very adroitly and cleverly, as though he had no grudge against anyone, did not feel himself at all offended, and only wished to be left in peace to enjoy himself. In reality he had begun to feel dissatisfied about the time that he went to Moscow the year before.

He felt that the rôle of the independent man, who could have anything but wanted nothing, was beginning to pall, and that many people were beginning to think he could never do anything more than be an honest, good-natured fellow. His intrigue with Anna Karenina, which had caused such a sensation and attracted so much notice in Society, by investing him with fresh glamour had for a while quieted the worm of ambition that gnawed him, but a week ago that worm had reawakened with fresh vigour.

A playmate of his childhood, and his fellow-pupil at the Cadet Corps, Serpukhovskoy, who belonged to the same social circle, and had been his rival in the classroom, at gymnastics, in mischief, and in ambitious dreams, had just returned from Central Asia, where he had gained two steps in official rank and had won a distinction rarely awarded to so young a General.

He was expecting an appointment that might have an influence on State affairs; while Vronsky, though independent and brilliant and beloved by an enchanting woman, remained only a Cavalry Captain and was allowed to be as independent as he pleased. 'Of course I am not jealous and could not be jealous of Serpukhovskoy, but his promotion shows me that if one bides one's time the career of such a man as myself may be very quickly made. Three years ago he and I were in the same position. If I retire I burn my boats. By remaining in the service I lose nothing. She herself said that she did not want to change her position; and I, having her love, cannot envy Serpukhovskoy.' He shaved, had a cold bath, dressed, and went out.

10

Demin the C.O. occupied a large country house, and the whole party were gathered together on the roomy verandah. In the grounds, what first met Vronsky's eyes were the soldier-singers in their white linen uniforms, standing beside a cask of vodka, then the jolly, healthy figure of the C.O. surrounded by his officers. Having come out on the top step of the verandah, he was gesticulating and above the noise of the band was loudly giving orders to some soldiers who were standing somewhat apart. After returning to the table, the Commander again came forward with a glass of champagne in his hand and announced a toast: 'To the health of our comrade, the gallant General, Prince Serpukhovskoy! Hurrah!'

Following the Commander, champagne glass in hand, Serpukhovskoy came down smiling.

Vronsky had not seen Serpukhovskoy for three years. He had matured and had grown whiskers, but still had just as good a figure, and was just as striking—not so much for his good looks as for the delicacy and nobility of his face and bearing. One change Vronsky noticed in him was that quiet and permanent radiance which comes upon the faces of people who have succeeded and feel assured that everybody recognizes their success.

As he was descending the steps Serpukhovskoy noticed Vronsky. A smile of joy lit up his face. He jerked his head backwards and raised his glass, welcoming Vronsky.

'Ah, here he is!' exclaimed the Commander, 'and Yashvin told me that you were in one of your dismal moods.'

Serpukhovskoy stepped up to Vronsky.

'Well, I am glad!' he said, taking him apart and pressing his hand.

'You look after him,' shouted the Commander to Yashvin, and went out to the soldiers.

'Vronsky, will you eat something, or have a drink?' said Yashvin. 'Hey! Bring the Count something to eat! Here, drink this!'

The carousing at the house of the C.O. continued long.

They drank a great deal. Serpukhovskoy was lifted and tossed by the officers. Then the C.O. was tossed. Then it quieted down for a moment. Serpukhovskoy went to the dressing-room to wash his hands, and found Vronsky there. Vronsky had taken off his coat and was washing his hairy red neck under the washstand tap, rubbing it and his head with his hands. When he had finished his ablutions Vronsky sat down beside Serpukhovskoy on a little sofa in the dressing-room.

'I used to hear all about you from my wife,' said Serpukhovskoy. 'I am glad you saw a good deal of her.'

'She is friends with Varya, and they are the only women in Petersburg whom it is a pleasure for me to meet,' said Vronsky with a smile.

'The only ones?' asked Serpukhovskoy, smiling.

'Yes, and I used to hear about you, but not only from your wife,' said Vronsky, checking the hint by a serious look. 'I am very glad of your success but not at all surprised.'

Serpukhovskoy smiled. Vronsky's opinion of him evidently gave him pleasure and he saw no reason to hide it.

'I am ambitious, it is my weakness, and I acknowledge it. Of course I may be making a mistake, but I believe I have some capacity for the career I have adopted, and that in my hands power of any kind, if I ever possess it, will be used in a better way than in the hands of many whom I know,' said he with the radiant consciousness of success. 'Therefore the nearer I am to getting it the more pleased I am.'

'It may be so for you, but not for every one. I used to think the same, yet here I am living and find that it is not worth while living for that alone,' said Vronsky.

'There you are! There you are!' said Serpukhovskoy, laughing. 'I had begun by saying that I used to hear about you, and your refusal. ... Of course I approved of it. But there is a way of doing a thing, and I think that, though your action was good in itself, you did not do it the right way.'

'What is done is done, and you know that I never go back on what I have done. Besides, I am quite all right.'

'All right for a time! But you will not remain satisfied for long. I should not say that to your brother. He is a dear child, just like this host of ours: but that would not satisfy you.'

'I do not say that it would.'

'And that is not all: men like you are wanted by Russia. Russia needs an influential Party of independent men like you and me.'

'But why—' Vronsky named several influential men, 'why are not they independent men?'

'Only because they have not, or had not by birth, an independent position—had no name, were not born as near the sun as we were. You and I have one great advantage: we cannot be bought so easily. And such men are more needed than ever.'

Vronsky listened attentively, but it was not so much the meaning of Serpukhovskoy's words that interested him as his outlook on these questions, for Serpukhovskoy was already dreaming of a struggle with the powers-that-be and already had sympathies and antipathies in that sphere. Vronsky realized, too, how powerful Serpukhovskoy might become. And, ashamed as he was of the fact, he felt jealous.

'All the same I lack the most necessary thing,' he replied. 'I lack the wish for power. I had it once, but it is gone.'

'Pardon me, that is not true,' said Serpukhovskoy with a smile.

'Yes, it is true … at present—to be quite frank,' added Vronsky.

'Yes, it is true at present—that is another matter, but the present will not last for ever.'

'Perhaps,' said Vronsky.

'You say "perhaps",' continued Serpukhovskoy as if he had guessed Vronsky's thoughts; 'but I say, *certainly*. That is why I wanted to see you. I only ask you to give me *carte blanche*. I am not patronizing you. … I hope our friendship is above that sort of thing! Yes,' he said with a smile, 'give me *carte blanche*, leave the regiment, and I will draw you on imperceptibly.'

'But try to understand that I do want nothing except that everything should remain as it is,' said Vronsky.

Serpukhovskoy rose and said, as he stood before Vronsky, 'You say, "that all should remain as it is"! I know what you mean, but hear me! We are both of the same age; it may be that in number you have known more women than I have,' the smile of Serpukhovskoy's face and his gesture showed that Vronsky need have no fear, and that he would touch the tender spot gently and carefully. 'But I am married, and believe me, women are the chief stumbling-block in a man's career. It is difficult to love a woman and do anything else. To achieve it and to love in comfort and unhampered, the only way is to marry! How am I to put to you what I think?' and Serpukhovskoy, who was fond of similes, went on: 'Yes, if you had to carry a load and use your hands at the same time, it would be possible only if the load were strapped on your back: and that is marriage. I found that out when I married. I suddenly had my hands free. But if you drag that load without marriage, your hands are so full that you can do nothing else.'

'You have never loved,' said Vronsky softly, with his eyes looking straight before him and with Anna in his thoughts.

A footman entered and brought Vronsky a note.

'Your man brought this from the Princess Tverskaya.'

Vronsky opened the note and his face flushed. 'My head has begun aching,' he said. 'I shall go home.'

'Well, then, good-bye! Do you give me *carte blanche*?'

'We'll talk it over another time. I will look you up in Petersburg.'

11

It was already past five, and in order not to be late and not to use his own horses, which were known to everybody, Vronsky took Yashvin's hired carriage and told the coachman to drive as fast as possible. The old four-seated hired vehicle was very roomy; he sat down in a corner, put his legs on the opposite seat. A vague memory of Serpukhovskoy's friendship for him, and the flattering thought that the latter considered him a necessary man, and above all the anticipation of the coming meeting, merged into one general feeling of joyful vitality. This feeling was so strong that he could not help smiling.

'I want nothing, nothing but that happiness,' he thought, his mind full of Anna as he had last seen her.

'And the longer it continues the more I love her! And here is the garden of Vrede's country house. Where is she? Where? Why? Why has she given me an appointment here, in a letter from Betsy?' he thought; but there was no longer any time for thinking. Before reaching the avenue he ordered the coachman to stop, opened the carriage door, jumped out while the carriage was still moving, and went up the avenue leading to the house. There was no one in the avenue, but turning to the right he saw her. Her face was veiled, but his joyous glance took in that special manner of walking peculiar to her alone: and immediately a thrill passed like an electric current though his body. On reaching him she clasped his hand firmly.

'You are not angry that I told you to come? It was absolutely necessary for me to see you,' she said.

'I angry? But how did you get here?'

'Never mind!' she said, putting her hand on his arm. 'Come, I must speak to you.'

'What is it? What?' he asked, pressing her hand against his side with his elbow and trying to read her face.

She took a few steps in silence to gather courage, and then suddenly stopped.

'I did not tell you last night,' she began, breathing quickly and heavily, 'that on my way back with Alexis Alexandrovich I told him everything … said I could not be his wife, and … I told him all.'

He listened, involuntarily leaning forward with his whole body as if trying to ease her burden. But as soon as she had spoken he straightened himself and his face assumed a proud and stern expression.

'Yes, yes, that is better! A thousand times better! I understand how hard it must have been for you,' he said, but she was not listening to his words—only trying to read his thoughts from his face. She could not guess that it expressed the first idea that had entered Vronsky's mind: the thought of an inevitable duel; therefore she explained that momentary look of severity in another way. She had hoped that the meeting might bring about a change in her position and save her. But the news had not the effect on him that she had desired: he only looked as if he had been offended by something.

'It was not at all hard for me—it all came about of itself,' she said, irritably. 'And here …' she pulled her husband's note from under her glove.

'Who's that coming?' said Vronsky, pointing to two ladies who were coming toward them. 'They may know us!' and he moved quickly in the direction of a sidewalk, drawing her along with him.

'Oh, I don't care!' she said. Her lips trembled and her eyes seemed to him to be looking at him with strange malevolence from under the veil. 'As I was saying, that's not the point! I cannot doubt that, but see what he writes to me. Read—' she stopped again.

After he had read the letter he looked up at her.

'You see what a man he is!' she said in a trembling voice. 'He …'

'Forgive, me, but I am glad of it!' Vronsky interrupted. 'For God's sake hear me out!' he added, with an air of entreaty that she would let him explain his words. 'I am glad because I know that it is quite impossible for things to remain as they are, as he imagines.'

'Why impossible?' said Anna, forcing back her tears and clearly no longer attaching any importance to what he would say.

'It cannot continue. I hope that you will now leave him. I hope …' he became confused and blushed, 'that you will allow me to arrange, and to think out a life for ourselves. To-morrow …' he began, but she did not let him finish.

'And my son?' she exclaimed. 'You see what he writes? I must leave him, and I cannot do that and do not want to.'

'But for heaven's sake, which is better? To leave your son, or to continue in this degrading situation?'

'Degrading for whom?'

'For everybody, and especially for you.'

'You call it degrading! Try to understand that since I loved you everything has changed for me. There is only one single thing in the world for me: your love! If I have it, I feel so high and firm that nothing can be degrading for me. I am proud of my position because ... proud of ...' She could not say what she was proud of. Tears of shame and despair choked her. She stopped and burst into sobs. For the first time in his life he felt ready to cry. He could not explain what it was that had so moved him; he was sorry for her and felt that he could not help her, because he knew that he was the cause of her trouble, that he had done wrong.

'Would divorce be impossible?' he asked weakly. She silently shook her head. 'Would it not be possible to take your son away with you and go away all the same?'

'Yes, but all that depends on him. Now I go back to him,' she said drily. 'On Tuesday I shall go back to Petersburg and everything will be decided. Yes,' she said, 'but don't let us talk about it.'

Anna's carriage, which she had sent away and ordered to return to the gate of the Vrede Garden, drove up. Anna took leave of Vronsky and went home.

12

On Monday the usual meeting of the Committee of the Second of July took place. Karenin entered the Council room, greeted the members and the president as usual, and took his seat, his hand lying ready on the papers before him. As he listened to the general reports his face wore a most innocent and artless look. When they had been heard, Karenin in his quiet thin voice informed the meeting that he wished to bring to their notice some considerations of his own on the question of the settlement of the native races, and the attention of the meeting turned to him. Karenin cleared his throat and began to explain his considerations. When he came to the Fundamental and Organic Law his opponent jumped up and began to raise objections. Stremov, stung to the quick, began justifying himself, and the meeting became quite a stormy one. But Karenin triumphed and his motion was carried. Karenin's success was even greater than he had expected.

When he woke on the Tuesday morning he recalled with pleasure his victory of the previous day, and could not help smiling, even while wishing to appear indifferent, when the secretary, with a desire to flatter him, reported the rumours that had reached him concerning what had happened at the meeting.

Busy with the secretary, Karenin quite forgot that it was the day fixed for Anna's return, and was surprised and unpleasantly startled when the footman came in to inform him of her arrival. But he did not come out to meet her. She was told that he was busy with his secretary. She went to her boudoir, where she set to work sorting her things, expecting that he would come in to see her. But an hour passed and he did not come. She went down into the dining-room on a plea of giving orders and purposely spoke in a loud voice, thinking that he would come; but although she heard him go out of the study door to take leave of the secretary, he did not come to her. She knew that according to his habit he would soon go away to his work and she wished to see him first.

She passed through the ballroom to his study and resolutely went in. When she entered he was sitting in his official uniform evidently ready to start, with his elbows on a little table, looking wearily in front of him. She saw him before he saw her and knew that he was thinking about her.

When he saw her he was about to rise, but changed his mind as his face flushed—a thing Anna had never seen it do before. However, he quickly rose and came up, took her hand, and asked her to sit down.

'I am very glad you have come,' he said, sitting down beside her. He evidently wished to say something, but faltered. Several times he tried to speak, but stopped. Although while preparing for this interview she had been teaching herself to despise and blame him, she did not know what to say, and pitied him.

'Is Serezha well?' he asked; and without waiting for a reply he added, 'I am not dining at home to-day and must be going at once.'

'Alexis Alexandrovich!' she said, studying his face and without dropping her eyes under his gaze fixed on her hair, 'I am a guilty woman and a bad one, but I am what I was before, as I then told you. I have come to tell you now I cannot make any change.'

'I am not questioning you about it,' he replied suddenly in a firm tone and looking with hatred straight into her eyes. 'I had expected it.' Under the influence of anger he had regained perfect self-possession. 'But I repeat again what I then told you and subsequently wrote,' he went on in a shrill thin voice, 'I repeat that I will not know it; I ignore it as long as it is not known to the rest of the world, as long as my name is not dishonoured. Therefore I warn you that our relations must remain what they have been, and that if you let yourself be *compromised* I shall be obliged to take measures to safeguard my honour.'

'Alexis Alexandrovich, what do you want of me?'

'What I want, is not to meet that person here, and for you to behave in such a way that neither Society nor the servants shall be able to accuse you,—for you not to see that man. I think that is not much to ask! And in return you will enjoy all the advantages of a wife without fulfilling her duties. That is all I have to say! Now I must be going. ... And I shan't be back to dinner.' He rose and went toward the door. Anna too rose. He stopped and let her pass first.

13

Kitty Shcherbatskaya was not more than twenty miles away, and Levin wanted to meet her, yet could not. Having seen Kitty he knew that he had not ceased to love her, yet he could not go to the Oblonskys' house while she was there. That he had proposed and she had refused him had put an impossible barrier between them.

'I cannot ask her to be my wife just because she cannot be the wife of the man she wanted,' he said to himself, and this thought rendered him cold and hostile toward her.

'I shall not have the strength to speak to her without reproach or to look at her without ill will, and she will only hate me all the more—as it is only right she should! Besides, how can I go there now after what Darya Alexandrovna told me? Can I help betraying what she told me? And I should come magnanimously to forgive her, to show mercy to her! I—stand before her in the rôle of one who forgives her and honours her with his love! Why did Darya Alexandrovna tell me this? I might have met her accidentally and then all would have come naturally, but now it is impossible!'

Dolly sent to him to ask for a side-saddle for Kitty.

'I have been told,' she wrote, 'that you have a side-saddle. I hope you will bring it yourself.'

That was more than he could stand. 'How can an intelligent woman with any delicacy so humiliate a sister?' He wrote ten notes and tore them all up, sending the saddle at last without any reply. To say that he would come was impossible, because he could not come; to say that something prevented him from coming, or that he was leaving home, was still worse. He sent the saddle without an answer, conscious of doing something shameful; and next day, putting the management of the estate into the hands of the steward, he went away to a distant district to visit his friend Sviyazhsky, who had splendid shooting, an occupation which served him as the best solace in all his troubles.

Sviyazhsky was Marshal of the Nobility in his district. He was five years older than Levin and had long been married. His young sister-in-law, Nastya, whom Levin thought very pleasant, lived with them. He knew that both Sviyazhsky and his wife wanted to see her married to him, Levin. He knew this as certainly as all so-called eligible young men know these things, though he could never have said so to anyone; and he also knew that although he wanted to marry, and although this girl, to all appearance very fascinating, ought to make a splendid wife, he could as soon fly as marry her, even had he not been in love with Kitty. And this knowledge spoilt the pleasure which he hoped his visit to Sviyazhsky would give him.

Levin had thought of this when he received Sviyazhsky's invitation, but in spite of it he made up his mind that this idea of Sviyazhsky's intentions was only an unfounded conjecture of his and that he would go. Besides, at the bottom of his heart he wanted to put himself to the test and again to estimate his feelings for the girl. Sviyazhsky's home life was extremely pleasant, he lived with his wife in such a way that it gave everybody pleasure to see the friendly relationship in which they passed their childless life, and had so arranged that his wife did nothing and could do nothing except share her husband's efforts to spend their time as pleasantly and merrily as possible.

Sviyazhsky was not only very intelligent but also a very well-educated man, who carried his education with extreme modesty. There was no subject with which he was not acquainted, but he only exhibited his knowledge when forced to do so. Sviyazhsky was an honest, kind-hearted, and clever man, always joyfully and actively engaged on work highly prized by all around, and certainly a man who could never consciously do anything bad.

The shooting did not prove as good as Levin had expected. The marsh had dried up and there were hardly any snipe. He went about all day and only brought back three, but on the other hand he brought back, as he always did after a day's shooting, a splendid appetite, good spirits, and the stimulated mental condition which in his case always accompanied physical exertion.

In the evening at tea a very interesting conversation sprang up, just as Levin had expected, in the company of two landlords who had come about some guardianship business.

'My farming is very simple, thank heaven!' said Michael Petrovich.

'My farming is to have money ready for the autumn taxes. The peasants come along, and say, "Be a father to us! Help us!" Well, of course they are all our own people, our neighbours: one pities them, and lends them what they want, enough to pay the one-third then due, and one agrees for so much work from each family. But it is true there are some dishonest ones among them.'

Levin, who had long been acquainted with these patriarchal methods, exchanged a glance with Sviyazhsky, and, interrupting Michael Petrovich, addressed the other landowner.

'How then, in your opinion, should one carry on at present?'

'Why, carry on the way Michael Petrovich does: either pay the peasants in kind, or rent it to them! But the wealth of the community as a whole is ruined by such methods. Where my land used to yield ninefold under serfdom with good management, it only now yields threefold when the labourers are paid in kind. Russia has been ruined by the emancipation of the peasants.'

Much of what the landowner said subsequently, to prove that Russia was ruined by the Emancipation, even appeared to Levin to be very true, new, and undeniable. The landowner was evidently expressing thoughts to which he had been led by the conditions of his life: thoughts which he had hatched in his rural solitude and considered from every side.

'The fact of the matter is, you see, that progress can only be achieved by authority,' he said. 'We landlords under serfdom applied improved methods of agriculture—all by our authority, and the peasants at first resisted and afterwards copied us. Now that serfdom has been abolished and the power taken out of our hands, our agriculture where it has been brought to a high level must descend to a savage and primitive condition.'

'But why? You can carry it on with hired labour,' said Sviyazhsky.

'Hired labourers don't want to work well with good tools. Our labourers understand one thing only: to get drunk like swine, and when drunk to spoil everything you put into their hands. They'll water the horses at the wrong time, tear good harness, change a wheel with an iron tyre for one without, or drop a bolt into the threshing machine in order to break it. They hate to see anything that is beyond them. That is why the level of agriculture has gone down.' And he began to develop his plan of emancipation, which might have prevented this dislocation.

But it did not interest Levin, and, as soon as the landowner had finished, Levin returned to the first proposition, and continued the conversation with him, trying to prove to him that all our difficulties arise from the fact that we do not wish to understand the characteristics and habits of our labourers; but the landowner insisted that the Russian peasant was a pig and loved piggishness, and that, to lead him out of the pigsty, power was needed, but there was no such power.

'Why do you think,' asked Levin, trying to bring him back to the question, 'that we could not establish some relation with labour which would make it remunerative?'

'It will never be done with Russians! We have no power!' answered the landowner.

'What new conditions could be discovered?' said Sviyazhsky. 'Every possible relation to the power of labour has been defined and investigated. The remnant of barbarism, the primitive commune with its reciprocal bonds, falls to pieces of itself when serfdom is abolished, and there is nothing left but free labour; its forms are defined and ready and we must accept them.'

'But the rest of Europe is not satisfied with that system.'

'No, it is dissatisfied and it is seeking new methods. It will probably find them.'

'All I wish to say is,' said Levin, 'why should we not seek them for ourselves?'

'Because it would be just the same as inventing new methods of building a railway. They are invented and ready.'

'But if they don't suit us? If they are stupid?' said Levin.

'The question is at present occupying the best brains in Europe. I am, of course, not a professor of Sociology, but it interests me, and really if it interests you, you had better study the matter.'

Left alone in the room assigned to him, it was long before Levin could sleep: the landowner's arguments required consideration. He involuntarily remembered all that the man had said, and corrected in imagination the answers he himself had given.

'I ought to have said to him: "You say that our farming is not a success because the peasants hate all improvements and that these should be introduced by force; and if farming did not pay at all without these improvements, you would be right. But it succeeds where and only where the labourers act in conformity with their habits. Your and our common dissatisfaction with farming shows that we, and not the peasants, are at fault. We have long pushed on in our own way—the European way—without considering the nature of the labour force available. Let us consider the labourer not as an abstract labour force but as a Russian peasant with his own instincts, and let us arrange our farming accordingly. Imagine!" I ought to have said to him, "that you have found means to interest the labourers in the results of their work, and have found improvements which they must recognize as such—then, without impoverishing the soil, you will get double and treble the crops you get now. Divide equally and give half the produce to labour, and the share left for you will be larger, and the labour force will receive more. And to do this we must lower the level of cultivation and give the peasants an interest in its success. How this can be done is a question of details, but it is certainly possible.'"

This thought strongly excited Levin. He lay awake half the night considering the details necessary for carrying his thought into effect. He had not meant to leave next day, but now decided to go away early in the morning. Above all he had to get away immediately to propose his new plan to the peasants before the winter corn was sown, so that the work might be done on the new conditions. He decided completely to reverse his former methods of farming.

14

The carrying out of Levin's plans presented many difficulties, but he struggled with all his might to attain, if not all he desired, at any rate a possibility of believing without self-deception that the thing was worth doing. One of the chief difficulties was that the farming was actually going on and it was impossible to stop it all and start afresh; so that the machine had to be altered while it was working.

When, on the evening of his return, he informed the steward that he, like the peasants, should participate as a shareholder would in the farming, the steward only put on a look of great depression and expressed no definite opinion, but at once began to speak of the necessity of carting the last sheaves of rye next day and of starting the second ploughing; so that Levin felt that it was not the time for his plans to be considered.

When speaking of the matter to the peasants and offering them land on the new conditions, Levin again met with the same difficulty; they too were so fully occupied with the labour of the day that they had no time to consider the advantages and disadvantages of the venture.

At first Levin thought of letting the whole of his farm as it stood to the peasants, to the labourers, and to his steward, on the new co-partnership lines, but he very soon saw that this was impossible and decided to divide up the different parts. The cattle-yard, the fruit and vegetable gardens, the meadows and the corn-fields, divided into several parts, should come under different sections. The naïve Ivan, the cowman, who, it seemed to Levin, best understood the plan, formed an *artel* consisting chiefly of his own family, and became partner in the dairy section. The far field that had lain fallow for eight years was, with the aid of the intelligent carpenter Theodore Rezunov, taken up by six peasants' families on the new co-operative lines, and the peasant Shuraev rented the vegetable gardens on similar terms. The rest remained as before; but these three sections were the beginning of a new order and fully occupied Levin.

It is true that the dairy farm did not as yet go on any better than before, and Ivan strongly opposed heating the cow-sheds and making butter from fresh cream, maintaining that cows required less food when kept in the cold and that butter made from sour cream went further; and that he expected his wages to be paid as before, not being at all interested to know that they were not wages but an advance on account of profits.

It was true that Theodore Rezunov's group did not plough the corn land twice with the English plough as they had agreed to do, pleading lack of time. It was true that the peasants of that group, though they had agreed to farm the land on the new conditions, did not speak of it as co-operatively held land, but as land held for payment in kind; and that the members of that group and Rezunov himself said to Levin: 'If you would only accept money for the land it would be less trouble for you, and we should feel freer.' Moreover, these peasants, on all sorts of pretexts, kept putting off the building of the cattle-sheds and granary they had agreed to put up on his land, and dragged the matter on till winter.

It was true that Shuraev had taken steps to sublet the kitchen garden in small lots to the other peasants; he evidently quite misunderstood, and apparently intentionally misunderstood, the conditions on which the land was let to him.

But in spite of this, Levin thought matters were getting on, and that by keeping strict accounts and insisting on having his way he would eventually be able to prove to the peasants the advantage of these new arrangements.

These affairs added to the rest of the farming which remained on his hands, and the indoor work on his book, so filled Levin's whole summer that he hardly ever made time to go out shooting. At the end of August he heard from a servant who brought back the side-saddle that the Oblonskys had gone back to Moscow. He felt that by not having answered Dolly Oblonskaya's letter (a rudeness he could not remember without blushing) he had burned his boats and could never visit there again. He had treated the Sviyazhskys just as badly, having left their house without saying good-bye. But neither would he ever visit them again. That made no difference to him now. The rearrangement of his farming interested him more than anything had ever done in his life. He read books on political economy and socialistic books on the same subject, but, as he had expected, he found nothing in them related to what Levin, and all the Russian peasants and landowners with their millions of hands and acres, should do to make them as productive as possible for the general welfare.

He knew what he wanted. He saw that Russia had splendid soil and splendid labourers, and that in some cases the labourers and land produced much: but that in the majority of cases, when capital was expended in the European way, they produced little, and that this happened simply because the labourers are only willing to work and work well, in the way natural to them, and that their opposition was not accidental but permanent, being rooted in the spirit of the people. This he wanted to prove theoretically in his book and practically by his farming.

15

By the end of September the timber for the buildings to be erected on the land let to the peasant-group was carted, the butter was all sold and the profits divided. Everything on the estate was going well practically, at least Levin thought so. But rain set in, making it impossible to get in what remained of the corn and potatoes, stopped all the work, and even prevented the delivery of the wheat. The mud made the roads impassable: two mills had been carried away by floods, and the weather was getting worse and worse.

On the thirtieth of September the sun showed itself in the morning, and, in hopes of fine weather, Levin gave orders that the grain was to be got ready for carting and sent the steward to the merchant to collect the money for the wheat.

Having got through all this business, soaked by the streams of water that had run in at the neck of his leather coat and at the top of his high boots, but in the most buoyant and animated spirits, he returned home in the evening. The weather grew still worse and the frozen sleet beat the whole body of his drenched horse so painfully that it shook its head and ears and went sideways. But Levin under his hood felt peculiarly elated. His conversation with the peasants of the outlying village showed that they were beginning to get used to the new conditions. An old innkeeper, into whose house he had gone to dry himself, evidently approved of Levin's plan and had offered to join a group to buy cattle.

'I need only push on steadily toward my aim and I shall achieve it,' he thought, 'and it is worth working and striving for. It is not a personal affair of my own but one of public welfare. The whole system of farming, and above all the position of the people, must be completely altered: instead of poverty—wealth and satisfaction for all; instead of hostility—concord and a bond of common interest. In a word—a revolution bloodless but immense; first in our own small district, then throughout the province, throughout Russia, and the whole world—for a good thought must be fruitful. Yes, it is an aim worth working for!'

With such thoughts Levin reached home when it was already dark.

The steward, having been to the merchant, had returned bringing an instalment of the money for the wheat. An arrangement had been made with the innkeeper, and the steward, while away, had learnt that the corn had nowhere been got in, so that Levin's hundred and sixty stacks still in the fields were a trifle compared to what others were losing.

Having dined, Levin as usual sat down in his easy-chair with a book. To-day the importance of his work presented itself to him with especial clearness, and whole paragraphs of their own accord shaped themselves in his mind, expressing the gist of his thoughts. 'I must write that down,' thought he. But he had no time to write his thoughts down, for the labourers' foremen had come, and Levin went into the hall to speak to them.

After arranging about the next day's work by seeing the peasants who had come on business, Levin went to his study and sat down to his work. Laska lay down under the table, and Agatha Mikhaylovna with her knitting sat down in her usual place.

Having written for some time, Levin suddenly with particular vividness remembered Kitty, her refusal, and their last meeting. He rose and began to pace up and down the room.

'What is the use of fretting?' said Agatha Mikhaylovna. 'Why do you always sit at home? Have you not done enough for the peasants as it is! Why, they are saying, "Your master will get a reward from the Tsar for it!" And it is strange: why should you bother about the peasants?'

'I am not bothering about them: I am doing it for myself.'

Agatha Mikhaylovna knew all the details of Levin's farming plans. But this time she quite misunderstood what he said.

'Of course one must think of one's soul before everything else,' she remarked with a sigh.

'I am not speaking about that,' he said. 'I mean that I am doing it for my own profit. My gains are bigger when the peasants work better. You yourself say that Ivan looks after the cattle better now.'

'I only say,' answered Agatha Mikhaylovna, evidently not speaking at random but with strict sequence of thought, 'you must marry, that is all!'

Her mention of the very thing he was just thinking about grieved and hurt him. He frowned, and without replying again sat down to his work. Only occasionally, in the stillness, he listened to the clicking of her needles and, remembering what he did not wish to remember, made a wry face.

At nine o'clock he heard the sound of a bell and the heavy lurching of a carriage through the mud.

'There now! Visitors have come to you,' said Agatha Mikhaylovna, rising and going toward the door. 'Now you won't feel dull.'

16

Half-way to the front door Levin heard a familiar sound of coughing in the hall, but the noise of his own footsteps prevented his hearing it clearly and he hoped he was mistaken. Then he saw the whole of his brother's long, bony, familiar figure, and it seemed that there could be no mistake that this tall man, who was taking off his overcoat and coughing, was his brother Nicholas.

Levin was fond of his brother, but to be with him was always a torment. Under the sway of the thoughts that had come to him and of Agatha Mikhaylovna's reminders, he was in an unsettled and confused state of mind and instead of a cheerful, healthy stranger who, he hoped, would have diverted him from his mental perplexity, he had to meet his brother.

Angry with himself for this bad feeling Levin ran into the hall; and as soon as he had a near view of his brother this feeling of disappointment vanished and was replaced by pity. Dreadful as his emaciation and illness had previously made Nicholas, he was now still thinner and weaker. He was a mere skeleton covered with skin.

He stood in the hall jerking his long, thin neck, drawing a scarf from it, and smiling in a strangely piteous manner. When he saw this meek, submissive smile, Levin felt his throat contract convulsively.

'There! I *have* come to see you,' said Nicholas in a hollow voice, without taking his eyes for an instant from his brother's face. 'I have long wanted to, but did not feel well. Now I am much better,' and he wiped his beard with the thin palms of his hands.

'Yes, yes!' answered Levin. He was still more terrified when, kissing his brother's face, his lips felt the dryness of the skin and he saw his large strangely brilliant eyes close at hand.

Nicholas said that he had now come chiefly to touch his native soil, in order like the heroes of old to gather strength from it for the work that lay before him. Levin took him to his room.

Nicholas dressed carefully, a thing he never used to do, brushed his thin, straight hair and went smiling upstairs.

He was in a most affectionate and cheerful mood, such as Levin remembered his often being in as a child: and he even mentioned Sergius Ivanich without irritation. When he met Agatha Mikhaylovna he joked with her and questioned her about the other old servants.

'Well, I will spend a month or two with you and then I will go to Moscow. D'you know, I am entering the Civil Service. I will now arrange my life quite differently,' he continued. 'You know, I have got rid of that woman?'

'Mary Nikolavna? Why, what for?'

'Oh, she was a horrid woman! She has caused me a lot of unpleasantness,' but he did not explain that he had turned Mary Nikolavna away because she made his tea too weak, and chiefly because she waited on him as on an invalid.

'Besides, I want to alter my life completely. Of course, like everybody else, I have done stupid things but health is the great thing, and my health, thank God, has improved.'

Levin listened, trying but unable to think of what to say. Nicholas probably felt the same; he began questioning his brother about his affairs, and Levin was glad to talk about himself because he could do so without any pretence. He told Nicholas of his plans and activities.

Nicholas listened but evidently was not interested.

At present the same thought filled both their minds and dominated all else: Nicholas's illness and approaching death. But neither of them dared speak of it, and not having expressed the one thing that occupied their thoughts, whatever they said rang false. Never before had Levin felt so glad when an evening was over and it was time to go to bed. Never had he been so unnatural and artificial as he was that day. He wished to weep over his dear, dying brother, but had to listen and keep up a conversation about how Nicholas was going to live.

The house being damp, and only his bedroom heated, Levin put his brother to sleep behind a partition in that room.

Nicholas went to bed but, whether he slept or not, kept tossing and coughing like a sick man and, when unable to clear his throat, muttering some complaint. Levin long lay awake listening to him. His thoughts were very various, but they all led up to death.

'I am working, I want to do something, and I had forgotten that it will all end in Death!'

He sat on his bed in the dark. But the more mental effort he made the clearer he saw that it was undoubtedly so: that he had really forgotten and overlooked one little circumstance in life—that Death would come and end everything, so that it was useless to begin anything, and that there was no help for it. Yes, it was terrible, but true.

'But I am still alive: what am I to do now? What am I to do?' he said despairingly. He lit a candle and got up carefully.

'Kha, kha! Oh, the devil! What are you fidgeting for? Why don't you sleep?' his brother's voice called to him.

'Oh, I don't know, just sleeplessness.'

Levin put out the candle, but was long unable to sleep. Just when the question of how to live had become a little clearer to him, a new insoluble problem presented itself—Death.

17

Levin had long ago noticed that after people have made one uncomfortable by their pliancy and submissiveness they soon become unbearably exacting and aggressive. He felt that this would happen with his brother. And really Nicholas's meekness did not last long. The very next morning he grew irritable and cavilled at everything his brother said, touching his most sensitive spots.

Levin felt guilty but could do nothing. He felt that if they both spoke without dissimulation and straight from the heart, they would only look into one another's eyes and Constantine would say nothing but, 'You will die! You will die!' and Nicholas would only say in reply: 'I know I shall die and I am afraid, afraid, afraid!' But that would make life impossible; therefore Constantine tried to do what all his life he had tried and never known how to do: he tried to say something different from what he thought; and he felt all the time that it sounded false and that his brother detected him and grew irritable.

On the third day of his stay Nicholas challenged his brother to explain his plans to him once more, and not only found fault with them but purposely confused them with communism.

'But I tell you that the two things have nothing in common! Communists deny the justice of property, capital, or inheritance, while I do not deny that main stimulus but want only to regulate labour.'

'That is it. You have taken other people's idea, dropped all that gave it force, and wish to make one believe that it is something new,' said Nicholas, angrily jerking his neck.

'Why do you muddle it? I never was a communist.'

'But I have been, and now I think it is premature but reasonable, and that is has a future as Christianity had in the first centuries.'

'I only think that the force of labour must be dealt with in a scientifically experimental manner. It must be studied ...'

'But that is quite unnecessary! That force finds its own form of activity in accord with its degree of development. There used to be slaves everywhere, then villeins; and we have labour paid in kind, and leaseholders, and hired labour: so what are you looking for?'

At these words Levin suddenly grew warm, for at the bottom of his heart he felt that it was true—true that he wished to balance between communism and the existing forms of life, and that this was hardly possible.

'I am seeking for a way of making labour profitable for me and for the labourers,' he answered hotly. 'I want to establish ...'

'You do not want to establish anything. You simply want to be original, as you always have done, and to show that you are not just exploiting the peasants, but have ideas!'

'You think so? Well, then, leave me alone!' said Levin.

'I will, and high time too! And I am sorry I came!'

However much Levin tried afterwards to pacify his brother, Nicholas would not listen to it, but said that it was much better for them to part. And Levin saw that life had become simply intolerable for his brother.

Only just before he left Nicholas kissed Constantine, and suddenly said with a strange and serious look at his brother, 'Do not think too badly of me, Kostya!' and his voice trembled.

These were the only sincere words that had passed between them. Levin understood that they were meant to say, 'You see that I am in a bad way, and perhaps we shall not meet again.' He understood this, and tears trembled in his eyes, but he did not know what to answer.

PART FOUR

1

The Karenins, husband and wife, continued to live in the same house and to meet daily, but they were wholly estranged. Karenin made it a rule to see his wife every day, so as not to give the servants any grounds for making conjectures, but he avoided dining at home. Vronsky never came to the Karenins' house, but Anna met him elsewhere and her husband knew it.

The situation was a torment to all three, and not one of them could have stood it for a single day but for the hope that the whole matter was only a temporary, though painful, trial. Karenin expected the passion to pass, as everything passes; all would be forgotten and his name not dishonoured. Anna, for whom among the three it was most painful, bore it because she felt sure that very soon everything would be settled. She had not the least idea what would settle it, but was quite certain that it would now come very soon. Submitting to her judgment, Vronsky too expected something, not dependent on him, to clear up all these difficulties.

In the middle of the winter he spent a very dull week. He had been chosen to act as guide to a foreign Prince, and was obliged to show him the sights of Petersburg. Vronsky had a distinguished appearance, possessed the art of carrying himself with respectful dignity, and was in the habit of associating with people of that class. But the task seemed a hard one to him. The Prince did not want to miss seeing anything about which he might be questioned at home and he also wanted to enjoy as many Russian amusements as possible; and Vronsky was obliged to accompany him in both cases.

On returning home Vronsky found a note from Anna awaiting him. She wrote, 'I am ill and unhappy. I cannot go out, neither can I go on any longer without seeing you. Come this evening; Alexis Alexandrovich is going to the Council and will remain there till ten.' After wondering for a moment at the strangeness of her asking him straight out to come to her house in spite of her husband's injunctions, he decided to go.

He had that winter been promoted to the rank of colonel, had left the regiment, and was living alone. Immediately after lunch he lay down on the sofa and fell asleep. He woke up in the dark trembling with fear, and hurriedly lit a candle. 'What horrors I dreamt! Yes, yes, the peasant, the bear-hunt beater—I think he was small and dirty with a tangled beard—was stooping down and doing something or other, and suddenly began to say strange words in French. That is all there was in that dream,' he thought. 'But why did it seem so terrible?' He vividly recalled the peasant and the incomprehensible words that the man had uttered, and a shudder of terror ran down his back. 'What nonsense!' he thought, glancing at his watch. It was already half-past eight.

He rang for his valet, dressed hurriedly, and went out worried only by the fact that he was late. As he drove up to the Karenins' porch he again glanced at his watch and saw that it was ten minutes to nine. A high narrow brougham with a pair of grey horses stood before the front door. Vronsky got out of his sledge. The door opened and the hall-porter with a rug over his arm called to the coachman. Vronsky, though not in the habit of noticing details, noticed the look of surprise on the man's face. In the doorway he nearly knocked up against Karenin. The gaslight lit up Karenin's worn, bloodless face beneath the black hat, and his white tie showing from beneath the beaver collar of his overcoat. His dull, expressionless eyes were fixed on Vronsky's face. Vronsky bowed, and Karenin lifted his hand to his hat, and went out. Vronsky saw him get into the carriage without looking round, take the rug and a pair of opera-glasses through the carriage window; then he disappeared in the darkness. Vronsky entered the hall. His brows were knit and his eyes shone with a proud, angry light.

'You met him?' she asked when they sat down at a table under the lamp. 'That is your punishment for being late.'

'Yes, but how did it happen? He had to be at the Council!'

'He had been and had come back, and afterwards went somewhere else. But never mind: don't speak about it. Where have you been? With the Prince all the time?'

She knew all the details of his life. He wished to say that he had been up all night and had fallen asleep, but seeing her excited and happy face he felt ashamed. So he said that he had to go and report the Prince's departure.

'But now that is all over? He has gone?'

'Yes, thank heaven! That is all over. You would hardly believe how intolerable it was.'

'Why? Is it not the kind of life all you young men lead?' she said, frowning; and taking up her crochet-work from the table began disentangling the hook without looking at Vronsky.

'I have long since abandoned that kind of life,' he said, wondering at the change in her face and trying to penetrate its meaning.

She held her work in her hands, without crocheting, gazing at him with a strange, glittering, unfriendly look.

'Lisa called on me this morning; they still visit me in spite of the Countess Lydia Ivanovna,' she said, 'and she told me about your Athenian party. How disgusting!'

'I was only going to say that …'

She interrupted him.

'It was Thérèse, whom you knew before?'

'I was going to say …'

'How horrid you men are! How is it that you can forget that a woman cannot forget these things?' she said, getting more and more heated and thereby betraying the cause of her irritation. 'Especially a woman who cannot know your life. What do I know? What did I know? Only what you tell me. And what proof have I that you tell me the truth?'

'Anna, you hurt me. Don't you believe me? Have I not told you that I have not a thought that I would hide from you?'

'Yes, yes!' she said, evidently trying to drive away her jealous thoughts. 'But if you only knew how hard it is for me! I believe you, I do believe you. … Well, what were you going to say?'

But he could not at once remember what he had wished to say. These fits of jealousy which had lately begun to repeat themselves more and more frequently, horrified him and, however much he tried to hide the fact, they made him feel colder toward her, although he knew that the jealousy was caused by love for him. How often he had told himself that to be loved by her was happiness! and now that she loved him as only a woman can for whom love outweighs all else that is good in life, he was much further from happiness than when he had followed her from Moscow. Then he thought himself unhappy, but happiness was all in the future; now he felt that the best happiness was already in the past.

'Well, what were you going to tell me about the Prince? I have driven away the demon,' she added. They spoke of jealousy as 'the demon'. 'Yes, what had you begun telling me about the Prince? What was it you found so hard to bear?'

'Oh, it was intolerable!' he said, trying to pick up the lost thread of what he had in his mind. 'He does not improve on nearer acquaintance. If I am to describe him, he is a finely-bred animal, like those that get prizes at cattle-shows, and nothing more,' he concluded.

She turned away from him. 'Well, and what happened? Where did you meet Alexis Alexandrovich?' she suddenly asked, her voice ringing unnaturally.

'I knocked up against him in the doorway.'

'And he bowed like this to you?' She drew up her face, half closed her eyes and quickly changed the expression of her face, folding her hands; and Vronsky saw at once upon her beautiful face the very look with which Karenin had bowed to him. He smiled, and she laughed merrily, a delightful laughter, one of her special charms.

'But still, don't let us talk about him. Tell me what you have been doing? What is that illness of yours? What does the doctor say? I expect it is not illness at all, but only your condition. When is it to be?'

The mocking light in her eyes faded, but a smile of a different kind—the knowledge of something unknown to him, and gentle sadness—replaced the former expression of her face.

'Soon, soon. If you only knew how hard it is on me! What would I not give to be able to love you freely and boldly! I should not be tortured, I would not torment you with my jealousy. ... It will happen soon, but not in the way you think.' And at the thought of how it was going to happen she felt so sorry for herself that the tears came into her eyes and she could not continue. She laid her hand, sparkling with rings and the whiteness of the skin, on his sleeve.

'I do not understand,' he said, though he did understand.

'You were asking when? Soon, and I shall not survive it. Don't interrupt,' she said hurriedly. 'I shall die, and I am very glad that I shall die: I shall find deliverance and deliver you.'

The tears ran down her cheeks; he stooped over her hand and began kissing it, trying to hide the emotion which he knew to be groundless but could not master.

'That is right, that is better,' she said, firmly pressing his hand. 'This is all, all that remains to us.'

He recovered and lifted his head.

'What rubbish, what senseless rubbish you are talking!'

'No, it is not! It is true. I have had a dream.'

'A dream?' Vronsky instantly remembered his dream.

'Yes, a dream,' she said. 'I dreamed it a long time ago. I thought I had run into my bedroom, that I had to fetch or find out something there: you know how it happens in dreams,' and her eyes dilated with horror. 'And in the bedroom there was a peasant with a rough beard, small and dreadful. I wanted to run away, but he stooped over a sack and was fumbling about in it ...'

She showed how he fumbled in the sack. Her face was full of horror.

And Vronsky, remembering his dream, felt the same horror filling his soul.

'He fumbles about and mutters French words, so quickly, so quickly, and with a burr, you know: "*Il faut le battre, le fer: le broyer, le pétrir …*"[1] And in my horror I tried to wake, but I woke still in a dream and began asking myself what it could mean; and Korney says to me: "You will die in childbed, in childbed, ma'am …" Then I woke.'

'What nonsense, what nonsense!' said Vronsky, but he felt that there was no conviction in his voice.

'Well, don't let us talk about it. Ring the bell, I will order tea. But wait, it won't be long and I …'

But suddenly she stopped. The expression of her face changed instantaneously. The horror and agitation were replaced by an expression of quiet, serious, and blissful attention. He could not understand the meaning of this change. She had felt a new life quickening within her.

2

Karenin after meeting Vronsky in his own porch went on as had been his intention to the Italian Opera. He sat through the first two acts and saw everybody that it was necessary for him to see. On his return home he carefully looked at the coat-stand, and noticing that no military coat hung there he went to his study as usual; contrary to his habit, however, he did not go to bed but walked up and down the room till three in the morning. The feeling of anger with his wife, who would not observe the rules of propriety and fulfil the only condition he had insisted on, that is, that she should not see her lover in his house, gave him no rest. He was obliged to punish her and carry out his threat: to divorce her and take away her son. He knew the difficulties connected with such a step: but he had said he would do it and was now obliged to do it.

He did not sleep at all, and his wrath, increasing in a kind of gigantic progression, had reached its utmost limits by the morning.

He dressed in haste, and went to her room as soon as he knew that she was up.

Anna, who thought that she knew her husband so well, was struck by his appearance when he entered her boudoir and without saying 'Good morning!' went straight to her writing-table, took up her keys, and opened the drawer.

---

[1] It must be beaten, the iron: pound it, knead it.

'What do you want?' she exclaimed.

'Your lover's letters.'

'They are not there,' she said, closing the drawer; but this action proved to him that he had guessed rightly, and rudely pushing away her hand he quickly drew out a letter-case in which he knew that she kept her most important papers. She wished to snatch away the letter-case, but he thrust her aside.

'Sit down: I must speak to you,' he said, taking the letter-case under his arm. Astonished and abashed, she silently looked at him.

'I told you that I would not allow you to see your lover here.'

'I wanted to see him in order ...'

She paused, unable to invent a reason.

'I do not go into particulars of why a woman wants to see her lover.'

'I have not seen this new trait of cruelty in you before.'

'You call it cruelty when a husband gives his wife complete freedom while he affords her honourable shelter, on the one condition that she should observe the laws of propriety. Is that cruelty?'

'It is worse than cruelty, it is—baseness, if you want to know!' Anna exclaimed in a burst of anger, and rose to go.

'No!' he shouted in his squeaky voice, which now rose to a higher note than usual; and seizing her so tightly by the wrists with his large fingers that the bracelet he pressed left red marks, he forced her back into her seat.

'Baseness? Since you wish to use that word—it is baseness to abandon a husband and a son for a lover and to go on eating the husband's bread!'

Her head dropped. She felt all the justice of his words and only said softly:

'You cannot describe my position as being worse than I know it to be; but why do you tell me all this?'

'Why do I tell you? Why!' he went on just as angrily, 'that you should know that as you have not fulfilled my wish that propriety should be observed, I shall take steps to put an end to this situation.'

'Soon, very soon, it will come to an end of itself!' she muttered, and at the thought of the nearness of death, which she now desired, tears again filled her eyes.

'I have come to tell you that I am going to Moscow to-morrow and shall not return to this house again, and that you will hear my decision through the lawyer whom I shall employ in the divorce suit. My son will stay with my sister,' said Karenin, making an effort to remember what he had wanted to say about his son.

'You want Serezha in order to hurt me,' she said. 'You do not care for him. ... Leave me Serezha!'

'Yes, I have even lost my affection for my son, because he is connected with my repulsion for you. But all the same I shall take him away. Good-bye!'

And he was about to go, but now she stopped him.

'Alexis Alexandrovich! Leave me Serezha!' she whispered again. 'That is all I have to say: leave me Serezha till my ... I shall soon be confined, leave him!'

Karenin flushed, and pulling away his hand left the room.

3

Karenin had gained a brilliant victory at the Committee Meeting of the seventeenth of August; but the consequence of that victory undermined his power. The new committee for investigating the conditions of the subject-races from every point of view had been formed and sent to its field of action with unusual promptitude and energy, stirred up by Karenin. Three months later the committee sent in its report. And the solutions arrived at were in accord with Karenin's opinions. But Stremov, who had been touched to the quick at the last meeting, made use of tactics for which Karenin was not prepared. Stremov suddenly changed over to Karenin's side, bringing several other members in his train, and not only warmly supported the measures advocated by Karenin, but proposed other more extreme measures of the same nature. These measures, going beyond Karenin's original idea, were accepted, and then Stremov's tactics became manifest. The measures, carried to extremes, proved so stupid that persons in office, public opinion, and the Press, all at the same moment fell upon them, expressing indignation at the measures themselves, and at Karenin, their acknowledged originator. Stremov stood aside, pretending to have blindly followed Karenin's plans and to be himself indignant now at what had been done, thus undermining Karenin. But, in spite of failing health and family troubles, Karenin did not give in. There was a split in the Committee. Karenin's position, partly in consequence of this and partly from the contempt that fell on him as a result of his wife's infidelity, became very shaky. In these circumstances he took an important resolution. He announced, to the surprise of the Committee, that he would ask to be allowed to go and investigate the matter himself, and having received permission he started for the distant Provinces.

On his way Karenin stopped three days in Moscow. On the day after his arrival he went to call on the Governor-General. At the crossing of Gazetny Street, he suddenly heard some one calling out his name in such a loud and cheerful voice that he could not help looking round. On the pavement at the corner of the street, in a short fashionable overcoat and a small fashionable hat, his teeth gleaming between his smiling red lips, young, gay, and beaming, stood Oblonsky, determinedly and insistently shouting and demanding that Karenin should stop. He was holding with one hand the window of a carriage (from which the head of a lady in a velvet bonnet and two little children's heads were leaning out) and was smilingly beckoning with his other hand to his brother-in-law. The lady too with a kind smile waved her hand to Karenin. The lady with the children was Dolly.

Karenin did not wish to see anyone in Moscow, and certainly not his wife's brother. He raised his hat and was going on, but Oblonsky told the coachman to stop and ran across the snow.

'What a shame not to have sent word! Been here long? And I went into Dusseaux's Hotel yesterday and saw "Karenin" on the board, and it never entered my head that it could be you!' said Oblonsky, thrusting his head in at the carriage window, 'else I should have looked you up. I am glad to see you!' and he kicked his feet together to knock off the snow. 'What a shame not to send word!'

'I could not find time: I am very busy,' Karenin answered drily.

'Come and speak to my wife; she is so anxious to see you.'

Karenin unfolded the rug he had wrapped round his legs, which were so sensitive to the cold, got out of the carriage, and making his way through the snow approached Dolly.

'What is the matter, Alexis Alexandrovich? Why do you avoid us in this way?' Dolly smilingly asked.

'I was exceedingly busy! Very pleased to see you,' he said in a tone that expressed clearly that he was very sorry. 'How are you?'

'And how is my dear Anna?'

Karenin muttered something and was about to go, when Oblonsky stopped him.

'D'you know what we'll do to-morrow? Dolly, ask him to come and dine with us! We shall invite Koznyshev and Pestsov, so as to let him taste the Moscow intellectuals.'

'Yes, do come!' said Dolly. 'We shall expect you at five or six, just as you like. But how is my dear Anna? It is so long ...'

'She is well,' replied Karenin, frowning. 'I shall be very pleased,' and he went back to his carriage.

'I shall call to-morrow!' shouted Oblonsky to him.

Karenin got into his carriage and sat far back, so as neither to see nor to be seen.

'Queer chap!' said Oblonsky to his wife, and after glancing at his watch waved his hand in front of his face as a sign of endearment to his wife and children, and walked jauntily away along the pavement.

4

The next day was Sunday. Oblonsky went to the market, and himself selected the fish and asparagus for dinner; and at noon he was already at Dusseaux's Hotel, where he had to call on three people who, fortunately for him, had all put up at the same place. These were: Levin, who had only just returned from abroad; a newly-appointed superior official who was making a tour of inspection in Moscow; and Karenin, his brother-in-law, whom he wanted to secure for dinner.

Oblonsky liked a good dinner, but liked still more giving a dinner-party: not a big affair, but one select in food, drink, and guests. With the programme for that day's dinner he was very satisfied; as for the guests, there would be Kitty and Levin, and, in order that they should not be too conspicuous, a girl cousin and young Shcherbatsky; here the *pièce de résistance* was to consist of Sergius Ivanich Koznyshev: a Muscovite and a philosopher, and Alexis Alexandrovich Karenin: a Petersburger and a practical politician. Besides these he meant to ask the well-known crank and enthusiast Pestsov, a Liberal and a great talker, a musician and historian, and the dearest of fifty-year-old boys, who would serve as sauce or condiment to Koznyshev and Karenin; while he himself, Oblonsky, would stir them all up and set them by the ears.

The second instalment of the forest money had been paid and was not yet all spent. Dolly had been very nice and kind of late, and the thought of his dinner-party pleased Oblonsky in every respect. He was in very high spirits. Just two circumstances were not quite satisfactory. From the fact that when he had met Karenin in the street the previous day the latter had treated him with cold stiffness, and had not called or even informed them of his arrival—from this, added to the rumour about Anna and Vronsky that had reached him, Oblonsky concluded that all was not as it should be between the husband and wife.

This was one of the unpleasant things, while the other was the fact that his new superior, like all new superiors, had the reputation of being a dreadful man who got up at six in the morning, worked like a horse, and expected his subordinates to do the same. On the previous day Oblonsky had appeared on Service business in uniform; the new superior was very pleasant and chatted with him as with an old acquaintance; therefore Oblonsky now considered it his duty to call on him in a morning coat. The thought that the new superior might not take this in good part was the second unpleasant circumstance, but Oblonsky felt instinctively that everything would 'turn out' splendidly.

Levin was standing in the middle of the room beside a peasant from Tver, measuring a fresh bearskin with a yard measure, when Oblonsky entered.

'Ah! Killed it?' cried Oblonsky. 'Fine thing! A she-bear? How d'you do, Arkhip?'

He shook hands with the peasant and sat down without taking off his overcoat or hat.

'Do take your things off and stay,' said Levin, removing the hat.

'No, I have no time. I've only come in for a moment,' replied Oblonsky, throwing open his coat.

'Don't go yet!' said Levin, trying to detain him. 'When shall we meet again? I am leaving to-morrow.'

'Well, I'm a good one! Why, I came on purpose … You must come and dine with us to-day. Your brother is coming, and my brother-in-law, Karenin.'

'Is he here?' asked Levin.

'Then you will come?'

'Yes, of course.'

'Well, then, at five, and in morning dress!' And Oblonsky got up and went downstairs to call on the new superior. His instinct had not deceived him; the dreadful new superior turned out to be a most affable man. Oblonsky had lunch with him and sat talking so long that it was going on for four when he arrived at Karenin's.

5

Karenin, after returning from church, spent the rest of the morning in the hotel. That day he had to interview a deputation from a subject-race, which was in Moscow at that time, and give them instructions, and to write to the lawyer as he had promised. The interview, though the deputation had been summoned on his initiative, was an affair that presented many difficulties and even dangers, and Karenin was very glad that it chanced to be in Moscow when he was there. Karenin had a prolonged tussle with them, and wrote out for them a programme which they were not to overstep, and having dismissed them he wrote a letter regarding this deputation. In this matter his chief helper was the Countess Lydia Ivanovna, who was a specialist in deputations. No one else could so well pilot a deputation or give it a good start.

Oblonsky was disputing with Karenin's servant, and insisting that he should be announced.

'No matter!' thought Karenin, 'it is even better so. I will tell him about my position with regard to his sister at once, and will explain why I cannot dine at his house.'

'Ask the gentleman in!' he said in a loud voice, collecting his papers and placing them inside a blotter.

'There, you see, you were lying to me! He is at home!' came the voice of Oblonsky in answer to the man who had been trying to stop him, as he entered the room, taking off his overcoat as he came. 'I'm awfully glad I have found you in! Well, I hope ...' began Oblonsky, cheerfully.

'I can't come,' Karenin, who was standing, said coldly, without offering his visitor a seat.

Oblonsky opened his clear and shining eyes wide.

'Why can't you? What do you mean?' he demanded, quite taken aback. 'Oh no, you have promised and we are reckoning on you.'

'I must tell you that I can't come because I am about to take proceedings to divorce your sister, my wife. I was obliged to ...'

But before Karenin could finish what he was about to say, Oblonsky did something quite unexpected. He uttered an exclamation of dismay and sat down in an easy-chair.

'Dear me, Alexis Alexandrovich! What are you talking about?' he cried, a look of pain appearing on his face.

'It is true.'

'Forgive me, but I can't—I can't believe it ... There must be some misunderstanding!' said Oblonsky.

'Ah, if it were only a misunderstanding! ...'

'Wait a moment—I understand,' Oblonsky interrupted him. 'But of course ... Only this: one should not be in a hurry.'

'I was not in a hurry,' replied Karenin, coldly. 'In a case like this it was impossible to consult anyone. I have quite made up my mind.'

'But it is awful!' said Oblonsky, sighing deeply. 'One thing I would do, Alexis Alexandrovich, if I were you—I entreat you to do it! You have not yet commenced proceedings, as I understand? Well, before doing so, see my wife and talk it over with her! She cares for Anna as for a sister, she is fond of you, and she is a wonderful woman. You will come and see her?'

'I hardly know. The reason I did not call on you is that I think our relationship must be altered.'

'Why? I don't see it. Allow me to believe that beside our family relationship, you share at least to some extent the friendly feeling I have always had for you ... and sincere respect,' added Oblonsky, pressing the other's hand. 'Even if your worst suspicions proved correct, I see no reason why our relations should change. But do, now do come and see my wife!'

'Ah, we look at the matter differently,' said Karenin, coldly.

'But why won't you come? Supposing you came to dinner to-day? My wife expects you. Do come, and above all, do talk it over with her. She is a wonderful woman. For heaven's sake—I implore you on my bended knees!'

'If you wish it so much, I will come,' said Karenin with a sigh.

Oblonsky looked at his watch.

'Dear me, it is getting on for five! ... Well, then, do please come to dinner! You have no idea how grieved I and my wife will be if you don't.'

Karenin parted from his brother-in-law in a very different manner to that in which he had met him.

'I have promised, and I will come,' he answered in a dejected tone.

'Believe me, I appreciate it and hope that you will not repent it,' Oblonsky replied, smiling. 'Five o'clock, and morning dress, if you please!' he sang out, returning to the door.

6

It was past five, and some of the visitors had already arrived, when the master of the house came home. He entered together with Sergius Ivanich Koznyshev and Pestsov, who had met on the doorstep. These two were the chief representatives of the Moscow intellectuals, as Oblonsky called them. Both were men respected for their characters and abilities. They respected one another, but in almost everything they were completely and hopelessly at variance, not because they belonged to different schools of thought but just because they belonged to one camp and in that camp each of them had his own shade. And as there is nothing less amenable to agreement than disagreement on semi-abstract themes, they not only disagreed in their opinions but had long been accustomed without anger to ridicule each other's incorrigible delusions.

They were entering when Oblonsky overtook them, and were talking about the weather. Prince Alexander Dmitrich Shcherbatsky, and young Shcherbatsky, Turovtsyn, Kitty, and Karenin were already in the drawing-room.

Oblonsky noticed at once that, without him, things were going badly in the drawing-room. His wife in her gala dress, a grey silk, evidently worried about her husband who had not returned, had not managed in his absence to mix the guests properly. The good-natured Turovtsyn clearly felt quite out of it. The old Prince sat silent, his shining eyes looking askance at Karenin, and Oblonsky saw that he had already prepared some remark wherewith to polish off that dignitary of State. Kitty kept looking toward the door, gathering courage not to blush when Constantine Levin should enter. Young Shcherbatsky, who had not been introduced to Karenin tried to look as if this did not make him feel at all awkward. Karenin himself, as the Petersburg way is when one dines with ladies, was in evening dress with a white tie, and Oblonsky saw by his face that he had come only to keep his promise, and by being in that company was fulfilling an unpleasant duty. He was the chief cause of the iciness which had frozen all the visitors till Oblonsky's arrival.

On entering the drawing-room Oblonsky made his excuses, explaining that he had been kept by the particular Prince who was his usual scapegoat whenever he was late or absent, and in a moment he had reintroduced everybody, and having brought Karenin and Koznyshev together, he started them off on the subject of the Russification of Poland, and they immediately caught on, Pestsov joining them. Having patted Turovtsyn on the shoulder, he whispered something funny in his ear, and got him to sit down next to Dolly and the old Prince. Then he told Kitty that she was looking very nice, and introduced young Shcherbatsky to Karenin. In a moment he had kneaded all that Society dough in such a way that the drawing-room was in first-rate form, and was filled with animated voices. Only Constantine Levin had not arrived. However, that was all for the best, for Oblonsky, on looking in at the dining-room, saw to his horror that the port-wine and sherry were from Depret and not from Levé, and having given orders to send the coachman as quickly as possible to Levé he turned to go back to the drawing-room.

But he met Levin at the door.

'I am not late?'

'As if you ever could help being late!' said Oblonsky taking his hand.

'Are there many people here? Whom have you got?' asked Levin.

'All our own people. Kitty is here. Come, I will introduce you to Karenin.'

Oblonsky, in spite of being Liberal, knew that to be acquainted with Karenin could not but be an honour, and therefore treated his best friends to that honour. But at that moment Constantine Levin was not in a state fully to appreciate the pleasure of such an acquaintance. He had not seen Kitty since the memorable evening when he had met Vronsky, excepting for that one moment when he had caught sight of her on the high road. In the depths of his soul he had felt sure that he should meet her that evening, but to maintain his freedom of thought he had tried to assure himself that he did not know it. Now, when he heard that she was here, he was suddenly filled with such joy and at the same time with such fear, that it took away his breath and he could not utter what he wished to say. With despairing determination he entered the drawing-room and saw her.

She was not as she had been before nor as he had seen her in the carriage. She was quite different.

She was frightened, shy, shamefaced, and therefore even more charming. She saw him as soon as he entered. She was filled with joy, and that joy made her feel so confused that for a moment when, as he was approaching the hostess, he again glanced at her, Kitty herself, he, and Dolly all thought she would not be able to control herself but would burst into tears. She blushed again, and quite rigid, with only her lips quivering slightly, sat waiting for him. He came up, bowed, and silently held out his hand. Had it not been for the light quivering of her lips and the moisture that made her eyes brighter, her smile would have appeared almost calm when she said:

'What a long time it is since we saw one another!' while with a desperate resolve her cold hand pressed his.

Oblonsky took his arm and led him up to Karenin.

'Very pleased to meet you again,' said Karenin coldly, as he shook hands with Levin.

'Are you acquainted?' asked Oblonsky with surprise.

'We spent three hours together in a railway carriage,' said Levin with a smile.

'Dear me! If you please,' said Oblonsky, motioning them toward the dining-room.

The men went to the side-table in the dining-room, on which stood bottles with six kinds of vodka and plates with as many sorts of cheese with and without silver cheese-knives, caviar, herrings, different kinds of tinned delicacies, and slices of French rolls.

'Have you really been doing gymnastics again?' Oblonsky asked Levin, feeling his bulging biceps. 'Here's a real Samson!'

'I expect great strength is needed for bear-hunting,' said Karenin, who had the vaguest notions about sport.

Levin smiled.

'None at all. On the contrary a child can kill a bear,' he said, making room, with a slight bow, for the ladies who were coming up to the side-table with the hostess.

'You have killed a bear, I hear?' said Kitty. 'Have you any bears near your estate?' she added, turning her lovely little head toward him and smiling. There was a prayer for forgiveness, and trust in him, and a caress—a tender, timid caress, and a promise, and hope, and love for him in which he could not but believe and which suffocated him with joy.

'No, we went to the Tver Province. On my return journey I met your brother-in-law, or rather your brother-in-law's brother-in-law, on the train,' he said smiling. 'It was a funny meeting.'

And gaily and amusingly he told how after not sleeping all night he, in his sheep-skin coat, had rushed into Karenin's compartment.

'The guard judged me by my clothes and wished to turn me out, but I began to use long words and … you too,' he went on, turning to Karenin, 'judging me by my peasant coat were going to turn me out, but afterwards you took my part, for which I am very grateful.'

'The rights of passengers to a choice of seats are very ill-defined,' said Karenin, wiping the tips of his fingers on his handkerchief.

'I noticed that you were not quite sure what to make of me,' said Levin with a good-natured smile, 'so I hastened to start an intellectual conversation, to expiate my sheep-skin.'

Koznyshev, while continuing his conversation with the hostess, listened with one ear to his brother, turning his eyes toward him, and thought, 'What has happened to him to-day? He behaves like a conqueror.' Levin knew that she was listening to his words and liked hearing him, and that was the only thing he cared about. Not only in that room but in the whole world there existed for him nothing but Kitty and himself; and he had now acquired a great significance and importance. He felt himself at a height that made him giddy.

Quite casually, without looking at them, Oblonsky placed Levin and Kitty side by side.

The dinner was as good as the dinner service, a thing of which Oblonsky was a connoisseur. Two footmen and Matthew, wearing white ties, manipulated the food and the wines unostentatiously, quietly, and quickly. The dinner was a success on the material side, and no less so on the non-material side. The conversation, sometimes general and sometimes *tête-à-tête*, never ceased, and toward the end became so animated that the men left the table without ceasing to talk, and even Karenin was infected.

Everybody took part in the general conversation except Kitty and Levin. They were carrying on their own separate conversation, and it was not even a conversation but a kind of mystic intercourse, which every moment bound them closer and closer and created in both a feeling of joyful fear before the unknown upon which they were entering.

'How pleasantly Turovtsyn laughs!' said Levin, looking with pleasure at his moist eyes and shaking body.

'Have you known him long?' asked Kitty.

'Who does not know him?'

'I can see you think he is a bad man.'

'Not bad, but a mere cipher.'

'He is not. Change your opinion quickly,' said Kitty. 'I too did not think much of him, but he is … he is a dear fellow and wonderfully kind-hearted. Last winter Dolly's children all had scarlet fever and he happened to call. And fancy!' she went on in a whisper, 'he was so sorry for her that he stopped and helped her to nurse the children. Really, he stayed three weeks.

'I am telling Constantine Dmitrich about Turovtsyn and the scarlet fever,' she said, leaning over toward her sister.

'Yes? it was wonderful! he is splendid!' said Dolly, looking toward Turovtsyn who felt that he was being talked about, and giving him a gentle smile.

Levin looked at Turovtsyn again and wondered how it was he had failed to realize what a charming man he was.

'I am sorry, very sorry. I shall never again think ill of anyone!' he said merrily; expressing what he sincerely felt at the moment.

7

When they rose from table and the ladies had left the room, Pestsov did not follow them but turned to Karenin and began to state that the chief cause of inequality between husband and wife, in his opinion, lay in the fact that the infidelity of a wife and that of a husband were unequally punished both by law and by public opinion.

'I imagine that the cause of the prevailing opinion lies in the very nature of things,' Karenin said, and was about to go to the drawing-room but Turovtsyn quite unexpectedly addressed him.

'Have you heard about Pryachnikov?' said Turovtsyn, animated by the champagne he had drunk. And with a kindly smile on his moist and rosy lips, he went on addressing himself chiefly to Karenin, the principal guest.

'Vasya Pryachnikov, as I was told to-day, has fought a duel with Kvitsky and killed him.'

As one always seems to knock a sore place, so that day Oblonsky felt that unfortunately the conversation kept striking Karenin's sore place. He made an attempt to draw his brother-in-law away, but Karenin himself asked with interest:

'What did Pryachnikov fight about?'

'His wife. He behaved like a brick! Challenged the other and killed him!'

'Oh!' said Karenin indifferently, and raising his eyebrows he went to the drawing-room.

'I am so glad you came,' said Dolly with a frightened smile, as she met him in the sitting-room through which he had to pass: 'I must speak with you. Let us sit down here.'

Karenin, with the same look of indifference, produced by his raised eyebrows, sat down beside her and feigned a smile.

'Yes,' he said, 'especially as I wished to ask you to excuse me for having to go away at once. I am leaving Moscow to-morrow.'

Dolly was firmly convinced of Anna's innocence, and felt herself growing pale and her lips trembling from anger with this cold, unfeeling man who so calmly intended to ruin her innocent friend.

'Alexis Alexandrovich,' she said, looking into his eyes with desperate determination. 'I have no right to ... but I love Anna like a sister, and respect her; and I beg, I implore you to tell me what has happened between you; what do you accuse her of?'

Alexis Alexandrovich winced, and bowed his head.

'I expect your husband has told you the reasons which make me consider it necessary to change my former relations with Anna Arkadyevna,' he said without looking in her eyes, discontentedly eyeing Shcherbatsky who was passing through the sitting-room.

'I don't, I don't believe it, I cannot believe it!' Dolly said.

'One can't disbelieve facts, Darya Alexandrovna,' said he, emphasizing the word *facts*.

'But what has she done?' asked Darya Alexandrovna.

'She has despised her duties and betrayed her husband. That is what she has done,' he said.

'No, no, it can't be! No, for God's sake! ... you are mistaken,' said Dolly, raising her hands to her temples and closing her eyes.

'It is difficult to make a mistake when a wife herself announces to her husband that eight years of married life and a son have all been an error, and that she wants to begin life from the beginning again,' he said crossly, sniffing.

'Anna and—vice ... I cannot combine them, I cannot believe it!'

'Darya Alexandrovna,' he said, now looking straight at Dolly's kind, excited face and feeling his tongue involuntarily loosened. 'I would give much for the possibility of doubting. While I doubted, I had hope; but now there is no hope left and all the same I doubt everything so much that I hate my son, and sometimes believe he is not my son. I am very unhappy.'

There was no need for him to say this. Dolly had understood it as soon as he looked her in the face. She felt sorry for him, and her faith in her friend's innocence was shaken.

'Oh, it is terrible, terrible! But can it be true that you have decided on a divorce?'

'I have decided. That is just what is so terrible in this kind of grief, that you can't do as in losses or deaths—just bear your cross, but here you must act,' he said, as if guessing her thoughts. 'You must come out of the degrading position in which you are placed.'

'No, this is too awful. She will be ruined.'

'What can I do?' said Karenin. The recollection of his wife's last delinquency irritated him so much that he again became as cold as he had been at the beginning of the conversation. 'I am very grateful for your sympathy, but it is time for me to go,' he said rising.

'No, wait a bit! You should not ruin her. You must forgive.'

'I cannot forgive; I don't wish to and don't think it would be right. I am not a cruel man, I have never hated anyone, but I hate her with the whole strength of my soul and I cannot even forgive her, because I hate her so much for all the wrong she has done me!' he said with tears of anger choking him.

'Love those that hate you ...' whispered Dolly shamefacedly.

'Love them that hate you, but you can't love them whom you hate. Forgive me for having upset you!' And having got himself under control, Karenin quietly rose, said good-bye and went away.

8

When everybody was leaving the table Levin wanted to follow Kitty into the drawing-room but was afraid she would not like it because it would make his attentions to her too obvious. So he stopped with the group of men, taking part in their conversation. But without looking through the open door at Kitty he was conscious of her movements, her looks, and the place in the drawing-room where she sat. He was not at all interested in what he himself said, still less in what they were saying. He now knew the one thing that was important. And that one thing was at first there in the drawing-room, but afterwards began moving and paused in the doorway. Without looking round he felt a pair of eyes and a smile directed toward him, and he could not help turning. She stood in the doorway with Shcherbatsky and was looking at him.

'I thought you were going to the piano,' he said, moving toward her. 'That is what I miss in the country—music.'

'No, we were only coming to call you away. Thank you for coming,' she said, rewarding him with a smile as with a gift. 'What is the use of arguing? No one ever convinces another.'

'Yes, you are quite right,' said Levin, 'for the most part, people argue so warmly only because they cannot make out what it is that their opponent wants to prove.'

She wrinkled her forehead, trying to understand. But as soon as he began to explain she understood.

'I see: one must find out what one's opponent is contending for, what he likes, and then one can ...'

She had completely grasped and found the right expression for his badly-expressed thought. Levin smiled joyfully.

Shcherbatsky left them, and Kitty went up to a table prepared for cards, sat down, took a piece of chalk, and began drawing concentric circles on the new green cloth of the table. Her eyes shone with a soft light. Submitting to her mood, Levin felt in his whole being an ever-increasing stress of joy.

'I have long wished to ask you something!'

He looked straight into her kind though frightened eyes.

'Please do.'

'There,' he said, and wrote the following letters,—W, y, a: i, c, n, b; d, y, m, t, o, n? These letters stood for: When you answered: it can not be; did you mean then or never? It was quite unlikely that she would be able to make out this complicated sentence; but he looked at her with an expression as if his life depended on her understanding what those letters meant.

She glanced seriously at him and then, leaning her frowning forehead on her hand, began reading.

'I have understood,' she said with a blush.

'What word is this?' he asked pointing to the 'n'.

'That word is never,' she said, 'but it is not true.'

He quickly rubbed out what he had written, handed her the chalk.

She wrote: T, I, c, n, a, o: 'Then I could not answer otherwise.'

He looked at her questioningly, and timidly.

'And n … And now?' he said.

'Well, then, read this. I will tell you what I wish, what I very much wish!' and she wrote these initial letters: T, y, m, f, a, f, w, h. This meant: 'That you might forgive and forget what happened.'

He seized the chalk with nervous, trembling fingers, broke it, and wrote the initial letters of the following: 'I have nothing to forget or forgive, I never ceased to love you.'

She looked at him with a smile that remained fixed on her lips.

'I understand,' she whispered.

He sat down and wrote out a long sentence. She understood it all, and without asking if she was right, took the chalk, and wrote the answer at once.

For a long time he could not make out what she meant and he often looked up in her eyes. He was dazed with happiness. He could not find the words she meant at all; but in her beautiful eyes, radiant with joy, he saw all that he wanted to know. And he wrote down three letters. But before he had finished writing she read it under his hand, finished the sentence herself and wrote the answer: 'Yes.'

'Playing "secretary"?' said the old Prince approaching them. 'Come now, we must be going, if you mean to come to the theatre.'

Levin rose and accompanied Kitty to the door.

Everything had been said in that conversation. She had said that she loved him, and would tell her father and mother, and he had said that he would call in the morning.

9

The streets were still empty. Levin went to the Shcherbatskys' house. The front door was locked, everybody was still sleeping. He went back to his room in the hotel and ordered coffee. Levin tried to drink a little coffee, and put a piece of roll into his mouth, but his mouth could do nothing with it. He took the piece out of his mouth, put on his overcoat and went out to walk about again. It was past nine when he reached the Shcherbatskys' porch a second time. The inmates of the house were only just up, and the cook was going out to buy provisions. It would be necessary to live through another two hours at least.

All that night and morning Levin had lived quite unconsciously, and felt quite outside the conditions of material existence. He was sure that he could fly upwards or knock down the corner of a house, were it necessary. He spent the rest of the time walking about the street, looking at his watch, and gazing around.

After a long round, through the Gazetny Street and the Kislovka, he returned to the hotel, put his watch in front of him, and sat down waiting. The hand reached twelve. Levin went out into the porch. The *izvoshchiks* evidently knew all about it. With joyful faces they surrounded Levin, disputing among themselves, and offering him their services. Trying not to offend the others, he hired one and told him to drive to the Shcherbatskys'.

The Shcherbatskys' hall-porter certainly knew everything. That was evident from the smile in his eyes and the tone in which he said:

'It's long since you were here last, Constantine Dmitrich!'

Glancing into his kind old eyes, Levin felt something new even in his happiness.

'Are they up?'

'Come in, sir! Won't you leave it here?' he said, when Levin turned back for his cap. That meant something.

'Whom shall I announce you to?' asked the footman.

The footman was young, of the new-fashioned kind, and a dandy, but a very kind and good fellow, and he too understood it all.

'The Prince ... The Princess ... The young lady ...' said Levin.

He heard the rustle of a dress outside the door, and the joyful terror of the nearness of his happiness seized him. He heard the sound of very, very rapid light steps on the parquet floor, and his joy, his life, his own self, the best in himself, that which he had sought and yearned for so long, advanced very, very rapidly toward him. She did not walk but was borne toward him by some invisible force.

He saw nothing but her clear, true eyes, frightened by the same joy of love which filled his own heart. Those eyes beamed nearer to him, dazzling him with their glow of love. She stopped so close that she touched him. Her arms rose and her hands dropped on his shoulders. He put his arms round her and pressed his lips to her mouth that was waiting for his kiss.

She too had not slept all night and had waited for him the whole morning.

'Come to Mama!' she said, taking him by the hand. For some time he could not say anything, not so much because he feared that words might spoil the loftiness of his feelings, as because every time he wished to speak he felt that, instead of words, tears of joy would come. He took her hand and kissed it.

'Can it be true?' he said at last in a smothered voice. 'Dear, I cannot believe that you love me.'

She smiled at the word 'dear', and at the timid look he gave her.

'Yes!' she said significantly and slowly. 'I am so happy!'

Without letting go of his hand, she entered the drawing-room. The Princess, on seeing them, breathed quickly and immediately burst into tears, then she at once laughed and ran up to them with energy such as Levin never expected from her, and putting her arms round his head kissed him and wetted his cheeks with her tears.

'I am so glad! Love her. I am so glad ... Kitty!'

'Well, you've settled it quickly!' said the old Prince, trying to be indifferent; but Levin noticed that his eyes were moist when he addressed him. 'I have long, I have always wished it!' said the old Prince, taking Levin's hand and drawing him nearer.

He embraced Kitty, kissed her face, her hand, then her face again, and made the sign of the cross over her.

And Levin was seized with a new feeling of affection for this man who had been strange to him before, when he saw how Kitty long and tenderly kissed his fleshy hand.

The Princess was the first to bring all their thoughts and feelings back to the practical side of life, and for the first moments this seemed strange and even painful to them all.

'When is it to be? There is the betrothal, and cards must be sent out. And when is the wedding to be? What do you think, Alexander?'

'Here he is,' said the old Prince, pointing to Levin. 'He is the principal person concerned.'

'When?' said Levin, blushing. 'To-morrow! If you ask me—the betrothal to-day and the wedding to-morrow!'

'What an idea!' said the mother with a pleased smile at his haste. 'And the trousseau?'

'Well, you see, I don't know at all; I only expressed my wish,' he said, to excuse himself.

'Then we will decide. We can have the betrothal, and send out the cards at once. That will be all right.'

The Princess went up to her husband, kissed him and was about to go away, but he stopped her, embraced her, and tenderly, like a young lover, kissed her several times, with a smile. When they had gone Levin came up to his betrothed and took her hand. He had now mastered himself and was able to speak, and there was much he had to say to her; but what he said was not at all what he had intended.

'How well I knew it would happen! I never dared hope, yet in my soul I was always certain,' said he. 'I believe it was predestined.'

'And I,' she said. 'Even when …' she stopped, and again went on, her truthful eyes looking into his face resolutely, 'even when I drove my happiness from me I always loved you only, but I was carried away. I must ask you: can you forget it?'

'Perhaps it was all for the best. You have much to forgive me. I must tell you. … You will not reject me …'

Their conversation was interrupted; the servants entered with their congratulations. Afterwards relatives arrived, and that beatific tumult began which did not cease until the day after the wedding. All that time Levin felt uncomfortable and bored, but the stress of his joy went on increasing. All that time he felt that many things he did not know were expected of him, but he did all he was told, and it all gave him joy. He had thought that his courtship would be quite unlike any other, that the ordinary conditions of courtship would spoil his peculiar happiness; but he ended by doing what others do, and his happiness was thereby only increased, becoming more and more peculiar to him, unlike anyone else's was or is.

10

Involuntarily reviewing the impressions left on his mind by the conversations at dinner and after, Karenin returned to his solitary room. Of all that had been said the words of the silly good-natured Turovtsyn had sunk deepest into his mind—'*He acted like a brick, challenged the other man, and killed him.*' Evidently everybody had agreed with that, though they were too polite to say so. 'However, that point is settled and not worth thinking about,' said Karenin to himself; and with nothing in his mind but his impending journey and his work of inspection, he ordered tea, sat down at a table, took up a time-table, and began planning his journey.

'Two telegrams,' said the valet, entering.

Karenin took the telegrams and opened them. The first contained the news that Stremov had obtained the very appointment Karenin had been hoping for. He threw down the telegram and flushed. Rising, he began to pace the room. He was vexed, not so much at having missed that post himself as at the incomprehensible and surprising fact that they did not realize how much less suitable than anyone else was that voluble windbag, Stremov.

He opened the second telegram. It was from his wife, and *Anna*, written in blue pencil, was the first word he saw. '*I am dying. I beg and entreat you, come! I shall die easier for your forgiveness*,' he read. His first thought was that beyond doubt it was only falsehood and cunning. He re-read the telegram, and was suddenly struck by the direct meaning of the words. 'Supposing it is true?' he said to himself. 'If it is true, and at the approach to death she is sincerely repentant, and I, believing it to be false, refuse to come? It would not only be cruel and everybody would condemn me, but it would be stupid on my part.'

'Peter! I am returning to Petersburg,' he told the valet.

If the news of her illness were false, he would go away again saying nothing; but if she were really ill and dying, and wished to see him before her death, he would, should he find her still living, forgive her and should he arrive too late he would perform his last duty to her.

While on his way he did not again think about what he should do.

With the sense of fatigue and want of cleanliness resulting from a night spent in a railway carriage, Karenin drove through the fog of a Petersburg morning, along the deserted Nevsky, looking straight before him and not thinking of what awaited him. He dared not think of it, because when he imagined what would happen he could not drive from his mind the thought that her death would at once dissolve all the difficulties of the situation. He tried to stifle the thought of what lay before him and of what he dared not desire and yet could not help desiring. The carriage stopped at the porch. A carriage, with a coachman asleep on the box, and an *izvoshchik* were standing at the entrance.

The door was opened by the hall-porter.

'How is your mistress?'

'Safely delivered yesterday.'

Karenin halted and turned pale. Now he clearly realized how much he had desired her death.

'And her health?'

Korney, wearing his morning apron, came running downstairs.

'Very bad,' he said. 'There was a consultation yesterday and the doctor is here now.'

'Take my things,' said Karenin, somewhat relieved by the news that there was still some hope of her dying.

'Who is here?'

'The doctor, the midwife, and Count Vronsky.'

Karenin passed on to the inner apartments.

There was no one in the drawing-room, but the midwife, with lilac ribbons in her cap, came out of Anna's boudoir. She approached Karenin, took him by the hand and led him toward the bedroom.

'Thank God you have come! She talks only about you and nothing but you,' said she.

Karenin entered the boudoir. Beside the table, sitting with his side toward the back of a low chair, was Vronsky, his hands covering his face, weeping. At the sound of the doctor's voice he jumped up, uncovered his face, and saw Karenin. But at the sight of her husband he was filled with such confusion that he again sat down, drawing his head down between his shoulders as if trying to become invisible. Then, making an effort, he rose and said:

'She is dying. The doctors say there is no hope. I am entirely in your hands ... but allow me to remain here, please! ...'

Karenin went toward the door without heeding what Vronsky was saying. Anna's voice came from the bedroom. It sounded cheerful and animated, and its articulation was extremely distinct. Karenin entered and went up to the bed.

She appeared not only fresh and well but in the best of spirits. She spoke rapidly, in a ringing voice with extraordinarily accurate intonations, full of feeling.

'Because Alexis ... I am speaking of Alexis Alexandrovich—how strange and terrible that they are both called Alexis, is it not?—Alexis would not have refused me. I should have forgotten and he would have forgiven. ... But why does he not come?'

'Anna Arkadyevna, he has come! Here he is,' said the midwife, trying to draw Anna's attention to Alexis Alexandrovich.

'Oh, what nonsense!' Anna went on, taking no notice of her husband. 'But let me have her, let me have my little girl! He has not come yet. You say he won't forgive me, because you don't know him. No one knew him, only I, and even for me it has become hard. One must know his eyes. Serezha's are just the same—'

Suddenly she recoiled, became silent and frightened, and put her arms before her face as if in expectation of a blow; she had seen her husband.

'No, no!' she began again. 'I am not afraid of him. I am afraid of death. Alexis, come here! I have not long to live, I shall soon become feverish and then I shall no longer understand anything. Now I understand everything and see everything!'

Over Karenin's drawn face came a look of suffering; he took her hand and was about to say something, but could not speak. His lower jaw trembled; he struggled with his agitation, every now and then glancing at her. And every time he did so he saw her eyes looking at him with such tender and ecstatic emotion as he had never before seen in them.

'Wait a bit—you don't know ... Wait, wait! ...' she paused as if to collect her thoughts. 'Yes,' she continued, 'yes, yes, yes! This is what I wished to say. Don't be surprised at me; I am still the same. ... But there is another in me as well, and I am afraid of her. She fell in love with that other one, and I wished to hate you but could not forget her who was before. That other is not I. Now I am the real one, all of me. I am dying now, I know I am; ask him. Even now I feel it. ... I only want one thing: forgive me, forgive me completely! I am dreadfully bad, but ... No, you cannot forgive me! I know that I cannot be forgiven. No, no, go! You are too good!' With one hot hand she held his, while with the other she pushed him away.

The perturbation in Karenin's soul reached a point where he gave up struggling against it. Suddenly a joyous feeling of forgiveness and love for his enemies filled his soul. He knelt with his head resting on her bent arm, which burnt through its sleeve like fire, and sobbed like a child. She put her arm round his bald head, moved closer to him, and looked up with an expression of proud defiance.

'Here he is; I knew! Now good-bye to all! ... They have come again, why don't they go away? ... Oh, take these furs off me!'

The doctor moved her arms and carefully drew the bedclothes over her shoulders. She meekly lay down on her back and gazed with radiant eyes straight before her.

'Remember that the only thing I want is your forgiveness, I wish for nothing else. ... Why does he not come in!' she cried, calling to Vronsky. 'Come, come! Give him your hand.'

Vronsky came to her bedside and, on seeing Anna, again hid his face in his hands.

'Uncover your face! Look at him! He is a saint,' said she. 'Uncover yes, uncover your face!' she went on angrily. 'Alexis Alexandrovich, uncover his face! I want to see him.'

Karenin took Vronsky's hands and moved them away from his face, terrible with its look of suffering and shame.

'Give him your hand. Forgive him ...'

Karenin held out his hand, without restraining the tears that were falling.

'Thank God, thank God!' she cried. 'Now everything is ready.'

The doctor and his colleagues said it was puerperal fever, which in ninety-nine cases out of a hundred ended fatally. All day she was feverish, delirious, and unconscious. At midnight she lay insensible, with hardly any pulse.

The end was expected every moment.

Vronsky went away, but came again in the morning to inquire. Karenin met him in the ante-room and said: 'Remain here: she may ask for you,' and himself showed him into Anna's boudoir. Toward morning she had become excited and animated, and her thoughts and words flowed rapidly; but again this state lapsed into unconsciousness. On the third day she was just the same, and the doctors gave some hope. That day Karenin went out to the boudoir where Vronsky sat, and having locked the door took a seat opposite him.

'Alexis Alexandrovich,' said Vronsky, feeling that an explanation was coming. 'I am unable to think, unable to understand. However painful it may be to you, believe me it is still more terrible for me.'

He was about to rise, but Karenin took him by the hand and said:

'I beg you to hear me; it is necessary. I must explain to you my feelings, those that have guided me and will guide me in future, so that you may not misunderstand me. You know that I resolved on a divorce and I confess that I was haunted by a desire for vengeance. On receiving the telegram I came here with the same feelings—more than that, I wished for her death. But ...' He stopped and reflected whether he should reveal his feelings or not. 'But I saw her and forgave her. And the joy of forgiving has revealed my duty to me.'

Tears filled his eyes, and their clear calm expression struck Vronsky.

'That is my position. You may make me the laughing-stock of the world,—I will not forsake her and will never utter a word of reproach to you,' continued Karenin. 'My duty is clearly defined: I must and will remain with her. If she wishes to see you I will let you know; but now I think it will be best for you to leave.'

11

After his conversation with Karenin Vronsky went out on to the Karenins' porch and then stopped, recalling with difficulty where he was and where he ought to go. He felt ashamed, humiliated, guilty, and deprived of the possibility of cleansing himself from his degradation. He felt himself knocked quite out of the rut along which he had hitherto trodden so proudly and so lightly. All the apparently solid habits and rules of his life suddenly seemed false and inapplicable. The deceived husband—who up till now had appeared a pitiful creature, an accidental and rather ridiculous obstacle to his happiness—suddenly recalled by her and raised to a pedestal that inspired the utmost respect, that husband in his lofty elevation turned out to be, not only not cruel, false, or absurd, but kind, simple, and dignified. Vronsky could not help being conscious of this. They had suddenly exchanged rôles. Vronsky felt Karenin's greatness and his own humiliation, Karenin's rightness and his own wrongdoing. He felt that the husband in his sorrow was magnanimous, while he himself was mean and trivial in his deceptions. But the consciousness of his degradation toward the man whom he had unjustly despised accounted for but a small portion of his grief. During her illness he had learnt to know her thoroughly, had seen into her very soul; and it seemed to him that he had never loved her before. And just now, when he knew her and loved her in the right way, he had been humiliated before her and had lost her for ever, leaving her nothing but the ridiculous, shameful figure he had cut when Karenin was pulling his hands from before his shame-suffused face.

Returning home after the three sleepless nights, Vronsky did not undress but lay down prone on a sofa, with his head on his folded arms. His head was heavy. Fancies, memories, and most strange thoughts followed one another with extreme rapidity and clearness.

'Sleep, sleep,' he kept repeating to himself. But with his eyes closed he could see yet more distinctly Anna's face. 'All that is ended and never will be again, and she wishes to efface it from her memory. I can't live without it. Then how can we be reconciled?' said he aloud, and went on unconsciously repeating those words. Following each other with great rapidity, his happiest moments rose in his fancy; and with them his recent humiliation.

He still lay trying to fall asleep, though he had lost all hope of succeeding, and kept repeating in a whisper random words connected with disjointed thoughts, in order to prevent other images from rising. He listened and heard repeated in a strange mad whisper the words, 'Unable to value, unable to enjoy ...'

'What is this? Am I going mad?' he asked himself. 'Perhaps! What else makes people go mad? What makes them shoot themselves?' he replied to his own thought, 'No, I must sleep!' But his eyes would not remain closed without effort. He jumped up and sat down. 'That's at an end for me,' he thought, 'I must think over what I must do, what is left me.' His thoughts glided quickly over his life unconnected with his passion for Anna.

'Ambition? Serpukhovskoy? Society? The Court?' he could not dwell on any of these things. He rose from the sofa, took off his coat, loosened the strap, and, baring his shaggy chest to breathe more freely, walked across the room. 'That's how one goes mad,' he said again, 'and how one shoots oneself so as not to be ashamed,' he concluded slowly. Going up to a door he closed it, then with fixed gaze and tightly clenched teeth, approached the table, took up his revolver, examined it, turned it to a loaded chamber, and pondered. For a minute or two he stood motionless with bowed head, a strained expression of effort on his face, holding the revolver in his hand. 'Of course!' he said to himself, as if led to a definite conclusion by a logical, continued, and clear line of reasoning. In reality that convinced 'Of course!' was merely the outcome of the repetition of a round of fancies and recollections similar to those he had already gone over dozens of times in the last hour. They were the same memories of happiness lost for ever, the same thoughts of the senselessness of all that life had in store for him, and the same consciousness of his humiliation. And they followed in the same rotation. 'Of course!' he said again when thought returned a third time to that point in the enchanted circle of memories and ideas; and placing the revolver against the left side of his chest, with a strong movement of his whole hand as if to clench the fist, he pulled the trigger.

The servant was so upset when he saw his master lying on the floor, that he left him to bleed to death and ran away to get help. In an hour's time Varya arrived, and with the assistance of three doctors whom she had summoned from every quarter, and who all arrived at the same time, she got the wounded man to bed, and then stayed in the house to nurse him.

12

The mistake Karenin had made when, preparing to see his wife, he had not considered the possibility either of her repentance being real or of her recovery, faced him in all its significance two months after his return from Moscow. He forgave his wife and pitied her for her sufferings and remorse. He forgave Vronsky and pitied him, especially when reports of Vronsky's desperate action reached him. He pitied his son too, more than he had done before, and reproached himself for not having paid more attention to him. But for the newborn little girl he had a peculiar sentiment, not of pity alone but even of tenderness. At first commiseration alone drew his attention to the delicate infant, not his daughter, who had been neglected during her mother's illness and would certainly have died then had it not been for his solicitude; and he himself hardly knew how he grew fond of her. Several times a day he went to the nursery, and remained there so long that the nurses, who had been shy in his presence, became quite used to him. At such moments Karenin felt quite calm and at peace with himself, seeing nothing exceptional in his position.

But as time went on he saw more and more clearly that, however natural his position might appear to him at the time, he would not be allowed to remain in it. He felt that everybody looked at him with questioning surprise without understanding him, expecting something from him; and especially he was aware of the insecurity and artificiality of his relation to his wife.

When the softened mood caused by the nearness of death had passed, Karenin began to notice that Anna feared him, was oppressed by his presence, and avoided looking him straight in the eyes.

At the end of February Anna's newborn daughter, also named Anna, happened to fall ill. Karenin had been in the nursery that morning, and having given orders to send for the doctor, had gone to the Department. Toward four o'clock, having finished his work, he returned home. On entering the ante-room he saw there a handsome footman in gold-braided livery with a bearskin cape, holding a cloak lined with white fur.

'Who is here?' asked Karenin.

'Princess Elizabeth Federovna Tverskaya,' answered the footman.

The presence of Princess Tverskaya and the memories associated with her, coupled with the fact that he had never liked her, was unpleasant to Karenin, and he went straight to the nursery. In the front nursery Serezha, lying with his chest on the table and his legs on a chair, was drawing something and chattering merrily. An English nursery governess, who since Anna's illness had replaced the French governess with the boy, sat doing some crochet-work. She hurriedly rose, curtseyed, and nudged Serezha.

Karenin passed his hand over his son's hair, answered the governess's inquiry about Anna's health, and asked what the doctor had said about baby.

'The doctor says there is no danger and has ordered baths, sir.'

'But she is still suffering,' remarked Karenin, listening to the crying child in the next room.

'I think the nurse is unsuitable, sir,' said the Englishwoman.

'Why do you think so?' he asked, stopping short.

'The nurse has no milk, sir.'

Karenin reflected a moment and then entered the other room. The little girl lay with her head thrown back, wriggling in the wet-nurse's arms, and would neither take the breast nor cease screaming, despite the hushing of two nurses who were bending over her.

'Still no better?' asked Karenin.

'Very restless,' said the head-nurse in a whisper.

'Miss Edwards says that perhaps the nurse has no milk,' he said.

'I think so too, Alexis Alexandrovich.'

'Then why did you not say so?'

'Whom could I speak to? Anna Arkadyevna is still ill ...' said the old nurse in a dissatisfied tone, and in her simple words Karenin thought he noticed a hint at his position.

'The doctor must be asked to examine the nurse,' said Karenin.

The healthy-looking wet-nurse, evidently afraid of being dismissed, muttered something to herself as she covered her well-developed breast, and smiled contemptuously at the idea of her not having sufficient milk. In that smile also Karenin thought he saw himself and his position ridiculed.

When the child was pacified and laid in her deep cot, and the nurse after smoothing the little pillow went away, Karenin rose, and on tiptoe approached the infant. For a moment he stood silent, regarding the child with a weary expression; but suddenly a smile lit up his face, and he quietly left the room.

He rang the bell in the dining-room and told the servant to send for the doctor once more. He was vexed with his wife for not troubling about the charming baby, felt disinclined to go in and see her while in that frame of mind, and also disinclined to meet the Princess Betsy; but his wife might think it strange if he did not come in as usual, and so he mastered himself and went to her bedroom. Stepping on the soft carpet, as he approached the door he involuntarily overheard a conversation which he had no wish to hear.

'If he had not been going away I should understand your refusal and his too. But your husband must be above that,' Betsy was saying.

'It is not for my husband's sake but for my own that I don't wish it. Don't talk about it,' answered Anna in an excited voice.

'Yes, but you can't but wish to say good-bye to a man who tried to shoot himself for your sake ...'

'It's just for that reason that I don't wish it.'

Karenin, with a frightened and guilty face, stopped short and thought of returning unnoticed; but coming to the conclusion that this would be undignified he turned, coughed, and went toward the bedroom door. The voices were silent and he entered.

Anna, in a grey dressing-gown, with her black hair cropped short but already growing again like a thick brush over her round head, sat on a couch. As usual when she saw her husband all her animation vanished from her face; she bowed her head and glanced uneasily at Betsy. Betsy, dressed in the very latest fashion, was sitting beside Anna. She met Karenin with an ironical smile.

'Ah!' she exclaimed. 'I am so glad you are at home. I have not seen you since Anna's illness. I have heard everything. Yes, you are a wonderful husband!' she said with a significant and affable expression.

Karenin bowed coldly, and kissing his wife's hand asked about her health.

'I think I am better,' she said, avoiding his eyes.

'But your face looks feverish,' said he, emphasizing the word *feverish*.

'We have been talking too much,' said Betsy. 'I know it was selfish of me and I am going.'

She rose, but Anna, suddenly blushing, quickly seized her hand.

'No, please stay! I must tell you ... you, I mean,' and she turned toward her husband, the colour spreading over her neck and forehead. 'I don't wish to hide anything from you.'

Karenin cracked his fingers and bowed his head.

'Betsy says Count Vronsky wanted to come and say good-bye before leaving for Tashkent.' She was not looking at her husband, and evidently was in a hurry to get through what she meant to say at any cost. 'I said I could not receive him.'

'You said, my love, that it would depend on Alexis Alexandrovich,' Betsy corrected her.

'Oh no! I can't receive him, and it would lead ...' She stopped suddenly and glanced inquiringly at her husband, who was not looking at her. 'In a word, I don't wish ...'

Karenin drew nearer and was going to take her hand.

Her first impulse was to draw away her hand from his moist one with the thick swelling veins, that was seeking hers; but with evident effort she pressed it.

'I am very grateful for your confidence, but ...' He stopped and looked at the Princess.

'Well, good-bye, my precious!' said Betsy, rising again. She kissed Anna and went out. Karenin followed her.

'Alexis Alexandrovich! I know you to be a really high-minded man,' said Betsy. 'I am only an outsider, but am so fond of her and respect you so much that I will take the liberty of advising you. Receive him! Alexis Vronsky is honour personified, and besides he is leaving for Tashkent.'

'Thanks for your sympathy and advice, Princess! But the question whom my wife will and whom she will not receive she will decide for herself.'

He said this from force of habit, with a dignified raising of his eyebrows, but immediately remembered that whatever he might say there could be no question of dignity in his position, and saw the confirmation of this in the suppressed cruel and ironical smile with which Betsy glanced at him when he had spoken.

Karenin took leave of Betsy when they reached the dining-room and returned to his wife. She was lying down, but on hearing his step she quickly sat up in her former place and glanced at him with apprehension. He saw that she had been crying.

'I am very grateful to you for your confidence,' he repeated. 'And I am very grateful for your decision. I too think that, as he is going away, there is no need whatever for Count Vronsky to come here. However ...'

'But I have already said so! Then why repeat it?' Anna suddenly interrupted him, with an irritation she could not repress. 'No need whatever,' she thought, 'for a man to come and take leave of a woman he loves, for whose sake he wanted to die and has ruined himself, a woman who cannot live without him! No need whatever!' And she pressed her lips together and lowered her glistening eyes, looking at his hands with their swollen veins, which he was slowly rubbing together.

'Let us say no more about it,' she added more calmly.

'I left it to you to decide the matter, and am very glad to see ...' began Karenin.

'That my wish coincides with yours,' she rapidly completed his sentence, exasperated by the slowness with which he spoke, and knowing beforehand what he would say.

'I have just sent for the doctor,' said he.

'I am quite well—why should I need the doctor?'

'Yes, but the little one keeps screaming, and they say the nurse has not enough milk.'

'Then why would you not let me nurse her, when I entreated you to? She is a child anyhow' (he understood what she meant by that *anyhow*) 'and they will kill her.' She rang, and ordered the baby to be brought. 'I asked to be allowed to nurse her, and I wasn't; and now I am blamed.'

'I don't blame ...'

'Yes, you are blaming me! Oh God, why did I not die?' and she began to sob. 'Forgive me, I am upset! I am unjust,' she went on, controlling herself. 'But go ...'

'No, it can't go on like that,' he told himself after leaving her; never before had the impossibility of his position appeared so evident.

13

Before Betsy had passed out of the dining-room Oblonsky met her in the doorway.

'Ah, Princess! What a pleasure to meet you,' he began.

'We meet only for a moment, as I am just going,' said Betsy, smiling and putting on her glove.

'Wait a little, Princess.'

'You are not worth it,' said Betsy, smiling.

'Yes, I am well worth it, because I not only settle my own, but other people's family affairs,' said he with a significant glance.

'Oh, I am very glad!' said Betsy, at once understanding that he referred to Anna. She returned to the dining-room with him and they stood together in a corner. 'He will kill her,' said Betsy in a significant whisper. 'The whole town is talking of it,' she said. 'It is an impossible situation. She is fading away, fading away! He does not understand that she is one of those women who cannot play with their feelings. One of two things must happen: either he must take her away, acting energetically—or he must divorce her. But all this is stifling her.'

'Yes, yes ... exactly!' said Oblonsky, sighing. 'I have come because of that—I mean, not entirely because of it. ... I have been made Chamberlain, and had to tender my thanks. But the chief thing is to get this affair settled.'

'Well then, may God help you,' said Betsy.

Having seen her down to the hall and kissed her hand, Oblonsky went to his sister's room. He found her in tears.

Though he was overflowing with high spirits Oblonsky immediately fell into a sympathetic and romantic mood suited to hers, inquired after her health and asked how she had spent the morning.

'Very, very badly. This afternoon and morning and all other days, past and future,' she replied.

'I think you give way to melancholy. You should rouse yourself, and look life straight in the face. I know it is hard, but ...'

'I have heard it said that women love men for their very faults,' Anna began suddenly, 'but I hate him for his virtues. I cannot live with him. Try and realize it: even his looks have a physical effect on me and drive me beside myself. I cannot live with him! What am I to do? I was unhappy and thought it impossible to be more so; but I could never have imagined such a terrible position as I am now in. Will you believe it? Knowing that he is a kind and generous man—that I am not worth his little finger—nevertheless I hate him! I hate him for his generosity. And there is nothing left for me but ...'

'You are ill and excited,' said he. 'Believe me, you are greatly exaggerating the case. There is nothing so very terrible about it.'

Oblonsky smiled. His soft comforting words and smiles had a soothing and calming effect, and Anna soon felt this.

'No, Stiva,' said she. 'I am lost, quite lost! And even worse than lost. I am not lost yet; I cannot say "all is finished": on the contrary, I feel that all is not yet finished ... and it will end in some dreadful manner.'

'Oh no! There is no situation from which there is no escape.'

'I have been thinking and thinking. Only one ...'

Again he understood from her frightened face that she considered death to be the only escape, and did not let her finish.

'Not at all!' he replied. 'Listen. You can't see your position as I can. Let me tell you my frank opinion. Can you go on living with your husband? Do you wish it? Does he wish it?'

'I don't know at all.'

'But you yourself say you cannot endure him?'

'You can't understand. I feel that I am flying headlong over some precipice but must not even try to save myself. And I can't.'

'Never mind, we'll spread out something to catch you. I understand that you cannot take it upon yourself to express your wishes and feelings.'

'I have no wishes at all ... except that everything were at an end.'

'And he sees that and knows it. Do you think it weighs on him less than on you? You suffer and he suffers; what can come of that? While a divorce would solve the whole problem,' said Oblonsky not without difficulty expressing his main idea, and looking at her significantly.

She replied only by shaking her cropped head; but by the expression of her face, suddenly illuminated with its old beauty, he saw that the only reason she did not wish for this solution was because it seemed to her an impossible happiness.

'I am dreadfully sorry for you both! How happy I should be if I could arrange it,' continued Oblonsky, now smiling more boldly. 'Don't, don't say a word! I shall go to him.'

Anna looked at him with dreamy, shining eyes, but said nothing.

14

Oblonsky, with the same rather solemn expression with which he was wont to take the chair at Council meetings, entered Karenin's study. Karenin, with his arms crossed behind him, was pacing up and down, meditating on the very subject that his wife and Oblonsky had been discussing.

'I am not disturbing you?' asked Oblonsky, experiencing at the sight of his brother-in-law a feeling of embarrassment quite unusual with him.

'No. Do you want anything?' Karenin answered reluctantly.

'Yes. I wished ... I must have ... I must have a talk with you about my sister and your mutual position,' said Oblonsky, struggling with his unwonted timidity.

Karenin smiled sadly, looked at his brother-in-law, and without replying went to the table and took from it an unfinished letter which he handed to him.

'I think about that subject incessantly, and this is what I have begun to write, as I think I can put it better in writing, and my presence is distasteful to her,' he said, holding out the letter.

Oblonsky took the letter, looked with perplexed amazement at the dull eyes fixed on him, and began reading:

'I see that my presence is distasteful to you. Hard as it was for me to assure myself of this, I see that it is so, and there is no help for it. I do not blame you, and God is my witness that when I saw you ill, I resolved with my whole soul to forget everything that had come between us and to begin a new life. I do not repent and never shall repent of what I did, as my only desire was for your welfare, the welfare of your soul; but now I see that I have not succeeded. Tell me yourself what would give you real happiness and peace of mind! I submit myself entirely to your wishes and sense of justice.'

Oblonsky returned the letter not knowing what to say.

'That is what I wanted to tell her,' said Karenin as he turned away.

'Yes, yes!' said Oblonsky, tears choking him and preventing his reply. 'Yes, yes, I understand you,' he brought out at last.

'I must know what she wants,' said Karenin.

'I am afraid she does not understand her position herself. She is no judge of it,' replied Oblonsky, growing more composed. 'She is crushed, literally crushed by your generosity. If she reads this letter she will not have the strength to say anything—she will only hang her head lower than ever.'

'Yes, but under these circumstances how is an explanation to be arrived at? ... How am I to find out what she wishes?'

'If you will permit me to express my opinion, I think it is for you to say what you think should be done in order to put an end to this state of affairs.'

'Then you think that an end should be put to it?' Karenin interrupted him. 'But how? I don't see any possible way out.'

'There is a way out of every situation,' said Oblonsky with the same soothing, tender smile with which he had addressed Anna. 'She would never say so, but there is one way out, one thing she might wish! It would be, to terminate your relations and everything that reminds her of them.'

'Divorce!' Karenin interrupted with disgust.

'Yes, divorce, I think. Yes, divorce,' Oblonsky answered, reddening. 'That would be the most reasonable way, from every point of view, with a couple placed as you are.'

Karenin sighed heavily and closed his eyes.

'The only question is, on what conditions you will agree to a divorce. She does not want anything, does not ask for anything, but leaves all to your generosity.'

'O God, O God! How have I deserved this?' thought Karenin, recalling the particulars of a divorce suit in which the husband took all the blame on himself; and with the same ashamed gesture with which Vronsky had covered his face, he hid his own in his hands.

'You are upset. I quite understand. But if you consider ...'

'Yes, yes!' he cried in a shrill voice. 'I will take the disgrace, and even give up my son ... but ... However, do as you like!' and turning away so that his brother-in-law should not see his face, he sat down on a chair by the window. It was very bitter, and he felt ashamed; yet mixed with the bitterness and the shame he felt a sense of joy and emotion at the greatness of his own humility.

Oblonsky was touched. He remained silent for a while.

'Alexis Alexandrovich! Believe me, she will esteem your generosity,' said he. 'But evidently it was God's will,' he added, and having said it felt how silly it was.

Karenin would have answered, but could not for his tears.

When he left his brother-in-law's room Oblonsky was touched, but this feeling did not spoil his contentment at having successfully arranged the matter, for he was certain that Alexis Alexandrovich would not go back on his word.

15

Although Vronsky's wound had missed the heart it was dangerous, and for several days he lay between life and death. When he was first able to talk again his brother's wife Varya was alone with him.

'Varya!' he said looking sternly at her, 'it went off accidentally! Never speak of it, please, and tell everybody else that.'

Without saying a word Varya bent over him and looked in his face with a joyful smile. His eyes were clear and no longer feverish, but their expression was stern.

'Well, thank God!' she exclaimed.

'I am not delirious. ... Please arrange so that no one shall say that I shot myself on purpose.'

'But no one does say so. Only I hope you will not go letting it off accidentally any more,' said she with an inquiring smile.

'I expect I shan't, but it would have been better ...' and he smiled gloomily.

Despite these words and that smile, which greatly perturbed Varya, when the inflammation left him and he became convalescent, he felt that he had rid himself entirely of one part of his grief. By his action he seemed to have washed off the shame and degradation he had previously felt. Now he could think quietly about Karenin, fully realizing his generosity without being humiliated thereby. He found he could look people in the face once more, and he was able to live in accord with his former habits. The one thing he could not tear out of his heart, although he continually struggled against it, was a regret bordering on despair at having lost Anna for ever.

Serpukhovskoy thought out a post for him in Tashkent and Vronsky accepted without the least hesitation. But the nearer the hour for his departure approached the harder seemed the sacrifice he was making to what he considered his duty. 'Only to see her once more, and then to bury myself, to die!' he thought, as he was making a round of farewell calls, and he expressed this thought to Betsy. It was with this message that Betsy went to Anna, and she brought him an answer in the negative.

'So much the better,' thought Vronsky. 'It would have been a weakness—would have taken away all the strength I have left.'

Next day Betsy herself came and announced that she had received, through Oblonsky, the definite news that Karenin consented to a divorce and that therefore Vronsky might see Anna. Without so much as taking the trouble of seeing Betsy to the door, or of asking when he could see Anna and where her husband was, Vronsky, in spite of all his resolutions, at once went to the Karenins'. Without seeing anyone he ran up the stairs and entered her room. Without thinking, or considering whether they were alone or not, he embraced her and covered her face, hands, and neck with kisses.

Anna had prepared herself for this meeting and had thought about what she would say to him; but she had no time to say any of it, seized by his passion. She wished to calm him and herself, but it was too late. His passion communicated itself to her. Her lip trembled so that for a long time she could not speak.

'Yes, you have taken possession of me and I am yours,' she brought out at last, pressing his hands to her bosom.

'It had to be!' said he. 'As long as we live it will have to be. Now I am sure of it.'

'It is true,' she said, growing paler and paler, putting her arms about his head. 'Still, there is something terrible in this, after what has been.'

'It will pass, it will all pass, and we shall be so happy! If our love could be stronger, there being something terrible in it would make it so,' he said, raising his head with a smile that showed his fine teeth.

She could not help smiling in answer, not to his words but to his enamoured eyes. She took his hand and stroked with it her cold cheek and cropped hair.

'I don't know you with this short hair! You have improved so, you little boy!—But how pale you are!'

'Yes, I feel very weak,' she said and her lip trembled again.

'We shall go to Italy and you will soon get well,' said he.

'Is it possible that we shall be like husband and wife, alone, a family, you and I?' she said, looking closely into his eyes.

'I am only surprised that it could ever have been otherwise.'

'Stiva says *he* will agree to anything, but I cannot accept *his* generosity,' she said dreamily, gazing past Vronsky's face. 'I don't want a divorce. Nothing matters to me now. Only I don't know what to decide about Serezha.'

He was quite unable to understand how she could, at the moment of their first reunion, think about her son and divorce.

'Don't talk and don't think about it,' he said, playing with her hand and trying to draw her attention to himself; but she continued to gaze past him.

'Oh, why did I not die? It would have been best!' she said, the tears streaming noiselessly down her cheeks; but unwilling to pain him, she tried to smile.

To refuse the flattering offer of a post at Tashkent, which was a dangerous one, would have seemed disgraceful and impossible according to Vronsky's former views. But now without a moment's hesitation he did refuse it and, observing that his superiors frowned upon his action, at once resigned his commission. A month later Karenin and his son were left alone in the house, and Anna went abroad with Vronsky—having resolutely refused a divorce.

PART FIVE

1

The Princess Shcherbatskaya at first considered it out of the question to have the wedding before Lent, to which there remained but five weeks, but could not help agreeing with Levin that to put it off until after the Fast might involve waiting too long, for Prince Shcherbatsky's old aunt was very ill and likely to die soon, and then the family would be in mourning and the wedding would have to be considerably deferred. Consequently, having decided to divide her daughter's trousseau into two parts, a lesser and a larger, the Princess eventually consented to have the wedding before Lent. She decided that she would have the smaller part of the trousseau got ready at once, and would send on the larger part later. This plan would be all the more convenient because the young couple intended immediately after the wedding to go to the country, where the larger part of the trousseau would not be required.

Levin continued in the same condition of delirium as before, imagining that he and his joy were the chief or only purpose of all existence, and that he need not now think or bother about anything, as other people would see to everything for him. His brother Sergius Ivanich, Oblonsky, and the Princess directed his actions. He quite agreed to every proposal. His brother borrowed money for him, the Princess advised him to return to the country after the wedding, and Oblonsky suggested going abroad. When he told Kitty of Oblonsky's advice that they should go abroad, he was quite surprised at her opposition to it and to find that she had definite ideas of her own about their future life. She knew that in the country Levin had work of which he was fond. As he saw, she not only did not understand that work but did not wish to understand it. This, however, did not prevent her considering it very important, and besides, she knew their home would be in the country, and she wanted to go to where her home would be. This decided expression of her wish surprised Levin, but, as it was quite immaterial to him, he at once begged Oblonsky to go to the house in the country and arrange everything there according to his own good taste.

2

On his wedding-day Levin, according to custom, did not see his bride, and dined at his hotel with three bachelors who happened to drop in; Sergius Ivanich, Katavasov, an old fellow-student at the university and now a professor of Natural Science, whom Levin had chanced to meet in the street and induced to come, and Chirikov, his best man, a Moscow magistrate, and a bear-hunting comrade of Levin's. The dinner was a very merry one. Sergius Ivanich was in the best of spirits and was tickled by Katavasov's originality. Katavasov, feeling that his originality was observed and appreciated, showed it off. Chirikov gaily and good-naturedly backed up every one else.

'There now!' said Katavasov with a drawl, a habit he had fallen into when lecturing. 'What a talented fellow our friend Constantine Dmitrich used to be! I am speaking of one who is not with us, because he is no more. In those days he loved science. When he left the university he had human interests; but now half his talents are bent on self-deception, and the other half toward justification of that deception.'

'How delighted I shall be when I hear of your falling in love!' said Levin. 'Pray invite me to your wedding!'

'I am in love already.'

'Yes, with a mollusc! Do you know,' said Levin, turning to his brother, 'Katavasov is writing a work on nutriment and ...'

'Oh, don't confuse matters! What does it matter what I write about? The fact is, I really do love molluscs.'

'But they would not prevent you loving a wife!'

'They would not, but the wife would.'

'Why?'

'Oh, you'll soon find out! Now you like farming, sport. ... Well, you just wait and see! Your wife won't allow it.'

Levin smiled. The idea that his wife would not allow it seemed so agreeable that he was prepared to forgo the pleasure of ever setting eyes on a bear again.

'I am ready to swear I can't find in my soul a trace of regret for my freedom,' said Levin, with a smile.

'Very bad! A hopeless case!' said Katavasov. 'Well, let us drink to his recovery, or let us wish that at least a hundredth part of his dreams come true. Even that will be such joy as was never seen on earth!'

Soon after dinner the visitors left to get ready for the wedding.

3

More than twenty carriages had already been ranged along the street by the mounted police. A police officer, unmindful of the frost, stood at the entrance to the church, looking brilliant in his blue uniform. More carriages kept driving up, and now ladies with flowers in their hair got out, holding up their trains; or men appeared who doffed their military caps or black hats as they entered the church. Every time the door creaked every one turned round, expecting to see the bride and bridegroom enter. But the door had opened more than ten times and each time it turned out to be a guest who had been detained and now joined the crowd on the right, or a spectator who had managed to deceive or soften the heart of the police officer and who joined the throng of strangers on the left; and both relatives and spectators had passed through every phase of anticipation.

At first they expected the bride and bridegroom to enter at any moment, and attached no importance to the delay. Then they turned more and more often toward the door, wondering whether anything had happened. At length the delay became awkward, and the friends and relatives tried to look as if they were not thinking about the bride and bridegroom but were absorbed in their conversations. At last one of the ladies looked at her watch and said, 'Well, this is strange!' and then all the guests became restless and expressed their surprise and dissatisfaction aloud. The best man went to find out what had occurred.

All this while Kitty, long since ready in her white dress, long veil, and crown of orange blossoms, stood with the Princess Lvova who was to accompany her, at a window of the ball-room at the Shcherbatskys', for the last half-hour vainly expecting her best man to come and announce that the bridegroom had reached the church.

Levin meanwhile, in trousers but without coat or waistcoat, was pacing up and down his room, perpetually putting his head out at the door and glancing up the corridor. But in the corridor there was nobody, and in despair he returned and addressed Oblonsky, who was quietly smoking.

'Was ever a man in such a terribly idiotic position?' he demanded.

'Yes, it is stupid,' Oblonsky concurred with a soothing smile. 'But don't worry, it will be here in a minute.'

'Oh, how can I help it?' said Levin with suppressed fury. 'And these idiotic open waistcoats—it's impossible!' He glanced at his crumpled shirt-front. 'And suppose the things have already gone to the station!' he exclaimed in despair.

'Then you'll have to wear mine.'

'I ought to have done that long ago.'

'It is better not to look ridiculous. Wait! It will all "shape itself"!'

The fact of the matter was that when Levin told his old servant Kuzma to get his things ready, Kuzma had duly brought his dress coat, waistcoat and what else he considered necessary. He had not thought of leaving out a clean shirt, and having been told to pack everything and send it to the Shcherbatskys', whence they were to start that evening, he had done so and had left out only the dress suit. The shirt Levin had been wearing since the morning was crumpled and quite unfit to wear with the fashionable low-cut waistcoat. They sent for one of Oblonsky's, but it was much too wide and too short. They were obliged to send to the Shcherbatskys' after all, and the things had to be unpacked. Meantime in the church every one was waiting for the bridegroom; while he was pacing up and down like a caged beast, looking despairingly along the corridor.

At last Kuzma, quite out of breath, rushed in with the shirt.

'Only just in time—they were hoisting the trunk into the cart,' he gasped.

Three minutes later Levin, not looking at the clock to avoid upsetting himself still more, ran as fast as he could down the corridor.

4

Levin met his bride at the door and entered the church with her. Oblonsky told his wife the reason for the delay, and the guests smiled and whispered to one another. Levin saw no one and nothing; he did not take his eyes off his bride.

He looked at her hair dressed high beneath the long veil and white flowers, at the high frill that covered her long neck at the sides and showed it in front in a particularly maidenly way, and at her strikingly slender waist. He thought she was prettier than ever: not that those flowers, the veil, or the dress ordered from Paris enhanced her beauty in any way, but because, despite all the carefully-planned richness of her attire, the look on her sweet face and lips was still that look of innocent truthfulness.

'I thought you meant to run away,' she said, smiling at him.

'It was such a stupid thing that happened! I am ashamed to tell it,' he said with a blush, and was obliged to turn round to the approaching Sergius Ivanich.

'Nice story that, about your shirt!' said Sergius Ivanich with a smile and shake of the head.

The priest and deacon came forward to the lectern that stood near the entrance doors. The priest turned to Levin and said something that Levin did not hear.

'Take the bride's hand and lead her,' said the best man.

For a long time Levin could not be made to understand that he with his right hand, without changing his position, must take her by her right hand. When at last he had taken her hand properly, the priest went a few steps in front of them and halted at the lectern. The crowd of friends and relatives, their voices buzzing and the ladies' trains rustling, moved after them. Some one stooped down to arrange the bride's veil. The church became so quiet that the drops of wax were heard falling from the candles.

The old priest, with his sacerdotal headgear and his locks of grey hair, glistening like silver, combed back behind his ears, drew his small old hands out from beneath his vestments of heavy silver cloth with a large gold cross on the back, and lit two wax candles decorated with flowers, and holding them askew in his left hand so that the wax kept slowly dripping, turned to the young couple. He looked wearily and sadly at the bride and bridegroom, sighed, and disengaging his right hand from the vestments, held it up in blessing over the bridegroom, and then over the bride; only in his manner when he placed his fingers on Kitty's bowed head there was a shade of tenderness. Then he gave them the candles, took the censer, and slowly stepped away from them.

'Is it really true?' thought Levin, and glanced round at his bride. All the worry about his shirt, his lateness, suddenly vanished from his mind and he felt happy though scared.

The handsome, tall senior deacon in a silver cloth alb, his curled hair parted down the middle, came briskly forward lifting his stole with a practised movement of two fingers, and stopped opposite the priest.

'Bless us, Lord!' slowly succeeding one another, and vibratingly resonant, came the solemn tones.

'Eternal God who joinest them that were separate,' the priest read in his mild sing-song voice, 'and hast ordained for them an indissoluble union in love; Thou who didst bless Isaac and Rebecca and hast kept Thy promise to their heirs, bless these Thy servants, Constantine and Catherine, and lead them on the path of righteousness! Most merciful God, Lover of Man, we praise Thee! Glory be to the Father, and to the Son, and to the Holy Ghost, now and hereafter and for ever and ever!'

'Amen!' from the invisible choir, floated through the air.

'"Joinest them that were separate"—what a depth of meaning is in those words, and how well they fit in with what I am feeling at this moment!' thought Levin. 'Does she feel the same?'

Looking round he met her eyes. From the expression in them he concluded that she understood them as he did; but this was not so. She was not even listening to the words of the ceremony so deep was the one feeling that filled her soul and became ever stronger and stronger. It was a feeling of joy at the fruition of what had been for the last month and a half going on in her soul, of that which for those six weeks had gladdened and tortured her. On the day when, in the ball-room of the house in Arbat Street, she in her brown dress had gone up to him and silently plighted herself to him, on that day and in that hour a complete rupture seemed to have taken place within her soul between her former life and this other new and entirely unknown life—although in fact the old life still went on. She could not think of or desire anything but life with this man; but, as that life had not yet begun, there was only anticipation, fear, and joy at something new and unknown; and now at any moment the anticipation and uncertainty, and the remorse at repudiating her former life, would all come to an end and something new would begin.

Again turning to the reading-desk the priest with some difficulty picked up Kitty's little ring, and asking Levin for his hand put the ring on the tip of his finger. 'The servant of God, Constantine, is betrothed to the servant of God, Catherine,' and having put a big ring on Kitty's slender, rosy finger, the priest repeated the same words.

'Thou hast from the beginning created them male and female,' read the priest when they had exchanged rings. 'Through Thee the wife is knit to the husband for a helpmeet and to procreate the human race. Therefore, O God our Lord ... look down upon Thy servant Constantine and Thy servant Catherine and strengthen them in their union with faith and concord in truth and love ...'

When the first part of the ceremony was over, a verger spread out a piece of pink silk cloth in front of the lectern. The choir began singing a psalm and the priest, turning round, motioned the couple to the piece of pink silk. Often as they had heard the saying that the one who stepped first on the mat would be head of the household, neither Levin nor Kitty could think of that as they took those few steps, nor did they hear the loud remarks and disputes of those who maintained that he was first, and of others who said that they did it both together.

After the usual questions of whether they wished to be married and whether they had promised themselves to others, and their answers, which sounded strange to themselves, the second part of the service began. Kitty listened to the words of the prayer, trying to comprehend their meaning but unable to do so. Triumph and radiant joy filled her heart more and more as the ceremony proceeded, and made it impossible for her to be attentive.

A smile of joy, which involuntarily communicated itself to all who regarded her, shone on her radiant face.

'Put it quite on!' came the words of advice when the priest had put crowns on their heads and Shcherbatsky, his hand in its three-buttoned glove trembling, held the crown high above Kitty's head.

'Put it on,' she whispered, smiling.

Levin glanced round at her, was struck by the joyous radiance of her face, and was involuntarily infected by her feeling. He felt bright and joyous as she did.

With light hearts they heard the Epistle read and the roll of the senior deacon's voice in the last verse. They drank the warm wine and water from the shallow cup, and their spirits rose still higher when the priest, throwing back his vestments, took their hands in his and led them round the lectern. The spark of joy that was glowing in Kitty's heart seemed to have spread to every one in the church. Levin fancied that the priest and deacon wanted to smile just as he did.

Having lifted the crowns from their heads, the priest read the last prayer and congratulated the married couple. Levin glanced at Kitty and thought he had never seen her so enchanting with the new light of happiness irradiating her face. He wished to speak to her, but did not know whether it was all over yet. The priest helped him out of the difficulty, saying softly, with a smile on his kindly mouth, 'Kiss your wife; and you, kiss your husband!' He took the candles from their hands.

Levin kissed her carefully on her smiling lips, offered his arm, and with a feeling of strange closeness led her out of the church. He could not believe it was all true, and only realized it when their surprised and timid glances met and he felt that they were already one.

After supper that same night the young couple left for the country.

5

Vronsky and Anna had already been travelling together in Europe for three months. They had visited Venice, Rome, and Naples, and had only just reached a small Italian town where they meant to make a longer stay.

The handsome head-waiter recognized the Russian Count who

occupied the best rooms in the hotel. He respectfully bowed, and said that the courier had been, and that the business of renting the palazzo was settled. The steward was ready to sign the contract.

'Ah, I am very glad,' said Vronsky. After an absent-minded glance at the man who was standing there watching him, he was about to go in.

'This gentleman is a Russian and was asking about you,' said the head-waiter.

With a mixture of vexation at the impossibility of evading his acquaintances anywhere and of desire to find something to distract the monotony of his life, Vronsky looked round again at the man, who had first moved away and then halted; and at the same moment the eyes of both brightened.

'Golenishchev!'

'Vronsky!'

It was really Golenishchev, his fellow-student in the Corps des Pages. In the Corps Golenishchev had been a Liberal, had left the Corps a civilian, and had never served. The two friends had separated and had met but once since then.

'How pleased I am to see you!' said Vronsky.

'I heard the name of Vronsky but I did not know which Vronsky. I am very, very pleased.'

'Come in! Well, and what are you doing?'

'Oh, I have been here over a year. I am working.'

'Ah!' said Vronsky in an interested tone. 'Well, come in.

'You know Madame Karenina? We are travelling together. I am now going to her,' he said in French, attentively watching Golenishchev's expression.

'Ah? I did not know,' Golenishchev replied in a tone of indifference, though he was quite aware of it. 'Been here long?' he added.

'I? ... Three days,' answered Vronsky, still attentively scrutinizing his friend's face, understanding the meaning of the other's look and the change of subject. He said to himself, 'I can introduce him to Anna, as he sees the matter rightly.'

During the three months he had spent abroad with Anna, Vronsky when coming across new people had always asked himself how the new person would be likely to regard his relations with Anna, and in most cases he had found that the men he met understood it in the 'right' way. As well-bred persons do with regard to all complicated and unanswerable problems, they conducted themselves properly, avoiding insinuations and inconvenient questions.

Vronsky at once guessed that Golenishchev was one of that sort, and therefore doubly pleased to have met him; and Golenishchev behaved to Anna, when he had been introduced, as well as Vronsky could have wished.

He had never met Anna before and was struck by her beauty, and still more by the simplicity with which she accepted her position. She blushed when Vronsky showed Golenishchev in, and the childlike flush that suffused her open and handsome face pleased him exceedingly. But what pleased him most was that at once, and apparently intentionally to prevent any possibility of misapprehension in the stranger's mind, she called Vronsky simply Alexis, and said that they were about to move into a palazzo. This straightforward and simple attitude toward her own position pleased Golenishchev.

'I say, the weather is glorious: let us go and have another look at it,' said Vronsky to Anna.

'I should like to very much. I'll just go and put on my hat.' She gave him a smile and went out with rapid steps.

The two friends looked at each other, and in both faces appeared an embarrassed expression, as if Golenishchev—who obviously admired her—tried but failed to hit on the right thing to say about her; and as if Vronsky both feared and wished that he should succeed.

'Well, and so you have settled down here?' said Vronsky. 'You are still busy at the same thing?' he went on, recollecting that he had heard the other was writing something.

'Yes, I am writing the second part of *Two Principles*,' said Golenishchev, flushing with pleasure at the question. 'To be quite exact, I mean, I am not yet writing, but am collecting the materials. The book will be much fuller and will deal with almost all the questions. We in Russia are slow to realize that we are the inheritors of Byzantium,' and he began a long and heated explanation.

When Anna returned with her hat and mantle on, and stood beside him toying with her sunshade with quick motions of her beautiful hand, Vronsky with a feeling of relief turned from Golenishchev's eyes which were fixed on him plaintively. With renewed love he glanced at his charming companion, so full of vitality and joy. With an effort Golenishchev recollected himself, but he was at first dejected and morose. Anna, however, who at that time was amiably disposed to every one, soon revived him by her simple and cheerful behaviour. After trying several topics of conversation she led him on to the subject of art, about which he talked very well, and listened to him with attention. They walked to the house they had taken and looked over it.

'I am very pleased about one thing,' said Anna to Golenishchev when they had returned to the hotel. 'Alexis will have a nice studio. You must certainly have that room, Alexis,' she added, having understood that Golenishchev was to be on an intimate footing with them and that there was no need to pretend in his presence.

'Do you paint?' inquired Golenishchev, turning to Vronsky.

'Yes, I went in for it long ago, and now have begun a little,' answered Vronsky with a blush.

'He is very talented,' said Anna with a pleased smile. 'Of course I am no judge, but people who do know say so.'

6

During this, the first period of her freedom and rapid recovery, Anna was unpardonably happy and full of the joy of life. The memory of her husband's grief did not poison her happiness. On the one hand this memory was too terrible to dwell upon, and on the other hand her husband's misfortune had meant for her too great a joy for repentance to be possible. The recollection of all that had happened to her since her illness now seemed a delirious dream from which she had wakened abroad and alone with Vronsky.

One comforting reflection about her conduct had come to her in the first moment of the rupture, and when she now remembered the past she also recalled that reflection. 'I was the inevitable cause of unhappiness to him,' she thought, 'but I don't wish to profit by his calamity. I too am suffering and must suffer: I am losing what I most cherished—my good name and my son. I have done wrong, and therefore do not ask for happiness and do not want a divorce. I must go on suffering from the degradation and by the separation from my son.' But sincerely as Anna desired to suffer, she was not suffering. She was not conscious of degradation. The parting from her son, whom she loved, did not trouble her at first either. The little girl, his child, was so sweet, and Anna had grown so attached to her since she was the only child left to her, that she rarely thought of her son.

The desire to live, enhanced by her recovery, was so powerful, and the conditions of her life were so novel and pleasant, that Anna felt unpardonably happy. The better she knew Vronsky the more she loved him. She loved him both for his own sake and for his love of her. To possess him entirely was a continual joy to her. His nearness was always pleasant. All the traits of character, with which she became better and better acquainted, seemed inexpressibly delightful. In all he said, thought, or did, she saw something peculiarly noble and exalted. She herself was frightened at the rapture with which he inspired her; she sought, but could not find, anything in him that was not beautiful. There was nothing she now feared more—though she had no reason to do so—than the loss of his love. But she could not help being grateful to him for his treatment of her, and showing him how much she valued it. He had sacrificed his ambitions for her and never showed the least regret. He was even more lovingly respectful to her than before, and the thought that she must never be allowed to feel the awkwardness of her situation never left his mind for a moment. He seemed to be only occupied in anticipating her every wish. She could not help appreciating this, although his strained attentiveness, the atmosphere of solicitude with which he surrounded her, became burdensome at times.

Vronsky meanwhile, in spite of the complete fulfilment of what he had so long desired, was not completely happy. When first he united his life with hers and donned civilian clothes, he felt the delight of freedom in general, such as he had not before known, and also the freedom of love—he was contented then, but not for long. Soon he felt boredom rising in his soul. Involuntarily he began to snatch at every passing caprice, mistaking it for a desire and a purpose. As a hungry animal seizes every object it meets, hoping to find food in it, so Vronsky unconsciously seized now on politics, now on new books, now on pictures.

As in his youth he had shown aptitude for art, and not knowing how to spend his money had begun to collect engravings, he now settled down to painting and began to work at it, putting into it the surplus stock of desire which demanded satisfaction.

He had a talent for understanding art and for imitating it with accuracy and good taste, and he imagined that he possessed the real power an artist needs. He liked the graceful and effective French School of painting best, and in that style began painting a portrait of Anna dressed as an Italian, and he, as well as every one else who saw it, considered the portrait a great success.

7

The neglected old palazzo, when they had moved into it, by its very appearance kept alive in Vronsky the pleasant delusion that he was not so much a Russian landowner and equerry without a post as an enlightened connoisseur and art patron, and withal a modest artist himself, who had renounced the world, his connections and ambitions, for the sake of the woman he loved.

The rôle Vronsky had chosen was quite successful; and having through Golenishchev made the acquaintance of several interesting persons, he felt tranquil for a time. He painted studies from nature under the direction of an Italian professor, and studied Italian life in the Middle Ages which had at that time become so fascinating to him that he even began to wear his hat and throw his cloak across his shoulder in a mediæval manner which was very becoming to him.

'Here we live and know nothing,' said Vronsky one morning to Golenishchev, who had come to see him. 'Have you seen Mikhaylov's picture?' and he passed his visitor a Russian newspaper that had just arrived, and pointed to an article on a Russian artist who was living in that town, and had just finished a picture long talked of. The article reproached the Government and the Academy for leaving a remarkable artist without encouragement or help.

'I have,' answered Golenishchev.

'What is the subject of his picture?' asked Anna.

'Christ before Pilate. Christ is pictured as a Jew with all the realism of the New School.'

'And is it true that this Mikhaylov is so poor?' inquired Vronsky, thinking that he ought to help this artist regardless of whether his picture was good or bad.

'Hardly. He is a wonderful portrait-painter. But it seems he does not want to paint any more portraits, so it is possible he may be in want. I say that ...'

'Couldn't one ask him to paint Anna Arkadyevna's portrait?' said Vronsky.

'Why mine?' said Anna. 'After the one you painted I want no other. Better have one of Annie' (as she called her little girl). 'There she is!' she added, looking from the window at the beautiful Italian nurse who had taken the baby into the garden, and then immediately glancing round at Vronsky. The beautiful nurse, whose head Vronsky was painting for his picture, was the only and secret sorrow of Anna's life. Vronsky painted her, admired her beauty and her 'mediævalness', and Anna dared not confess to herself that she was afraid of being jealous of the nurse; so she treated the woman with special kindness.

Vronsky too looked out of the window and into Anna's eyes, and at once turned to Golenishchev saying:

'Do you know this Mikhaylov?'

'I have met him. But he is a crank. He is the son of a head footman,

I think, and has had no education. When he entered the Academy and won a reputation for himself he, not being stupid, wanted to get some education. So he resorted to what seemed to him to be the wellspring of education—the magazines. You see, formerly a man who wished to get an education—a Frenchman, let us say—'

'Do you know what we'll do?' cried Anna, who had been furtively exchanging looks with Vronsky and knew that the latter was not at all interested in the education of the artist but was only concerned to help him by giving him a commission for a portrait. 'Let us go and see him.'

Golenishchev pulled himself up and unwillingly agreed, but as the artist lived in a distant part of the town they decided to hire a carriage.

An hour later Anna, seated beside Golenishchev with Vronsky facing them, drove to a new ugly house in a distant quarter of the town. Having learnt from the house-porter's wife who came out to meet them that Mikhaylov allowed visitors into his studio, but was at that moment at his lodgings a few steps away, they sent her with their cards to beg permission to see his pictures.

8

Mikhaylov had been angry with his wife because she had not managed to pacify the landlady, who clamoured for the rent.

'Then you shouldn't get into arrears! It's not my fault! If I had any money ...'

'Shut up, for heaven's sake!' cried Mikhaylov with tears in his voice, stopping his ears with his hands as he went into his workroom behind a partition, and having opened a portfolio he at once set to work with particular ardour at an unfinished drawing.

He never worked with such ardour or so successfully as when things were going badly with him, and especially after a quarrel with his wife. He was sketching the figure of a man in a fit of anger. He had sketched him before, but had been dissatisfied with the result. 'No, the other one was better. ... Where is it?' He went back to his wife, and frowning, without looking at her, asked his eldest little girl where the paper was that he had given them. The paper with the drawing that he had thrown away was found, but it was dirty now and spotted with candle grease. Nevertheless, he took it, put it on his table, and, stepping backward and screwing up his eyes, began examining it. Suddenly he smiled and flung up his arms joyfully.

'That's it! That's it!' he said, and taking up his pencil he began drawing rapidly. A grease spot had given the figure a new pose.

He copied that new pose, and, suddenly remembering the energetic pose and prominent chin of a shopman from whom he had bought cigars, he gave the figure that man's face and chin. He laughed with joy, for the inanimate, unnatural figure had become alive, and was just the thing. He was carefully finishing the drawing when the cards were brought to him.

'Directly! Directly!'

He went out to his wife. 'Come, Sasha, don't be angry,' he said, smiling timidly and tenderly. 'You were wrong and so was I. I'll settle it all!'

Having made it up with his wife he put on an olive-green overcoat with a velvet collar, and a hat, and went to the studio. His successful drawing was already forgotten. Now he was pleased and excited by the visit to his studio of these grand Russians.

With rapid steps he approached the door of his studio, and in spite of his excitement was struck by the soft light on Anna's figure as she stood in the shadow of the porch listening to something Golenishchev was vehemently saying, and at the same time evidently wishing to look at the approaching artist. The visitors, already disenchanted by Golenishchev's account of the artist, were still further disillusioned by his appearance. Of medium height, thick-set and with a loose gait, Mikhaylov in his brown hat, olive-green overcoat and narrow trousers (at a time when wide ones had long since come into fashion), and his commonplace broad face, expressing a combination of timidity and a desire to be dignified, created an unpleasant impression.

'Come in, please!' he said, trying to put on an air of indifference, as he entered the hall and took a key to unlock the door.

On entering his studio the artist again cast a glance at his visitors. Of Golenishchev he thought, 'That one is a Russian who lives here.' Mikhaylov did not remember his name or where he had seen him or what they had talked about; he remembered only his face, one of the faces he had mentally put aside with the enormous class of falsely important faces, faces lacking expression. Vronsky and Anna, according to Mikhaylov's conception, were in all probability distinguished wealthy Russians, who like all these wealthy Russians comprehended nothing of art but pretended to be amateurs and critics. But in spite of all this, as he turned over his studies, pulled up the blinds, and withdrew the sheet from his picture, he felt very excited—all the more so because, though he regarded distinguished and wealthy Russians as mostly beasts and fools, Vronsky and especially Anna pleased him.

'There!' he said, stepping aside with his loose gait, and pointing to the picture. 'This is *Pilate's Admonition*—Matthew, chapter 27,' he went on, conscious that his lips were beginning to tremble with excitement; and he stepped behind the visitors.

The silence grew too unbearable, though it had not lasted more than a minute. To break it and to appear calm, he made an effort and addressed Golenishchev.

'I think I have had the pleasure of meeting you?' he said, glancing uneasily now at Anna and now at Vronsky, in order not to lose any detail of their expressions.

'Of course! We first met at Rossi's,' began Golenishchev glibly, turning away from the picture to the artist without the slightest regret. Noticing, however, that Mikhaylov was waiting to hear his criticism of the picture, he said:

'Your picture has progressed very much since I last saw it, and now, as then, I am specially struck by the figure of Pilate. One can so well understand that man, a kind, first-rate fellow, but an official to his very backbone, who does not know what he is doing ...'

The whole of Mikhaylov's mobile face suddenly lighted up. His eyes brightened. He wanted to speak but was too agitated, and pretended to cough instead. Little as he valued Golenishchev's capacity to understand art, unimportant as was his remark about the truth of Pilate's official expression, Mikhaylov was delighted with it. His opinion of that figure was the same. He took a liking to Golenishchev because of that remark, and his depression changed suddenly into delight and he was unable to speak. Vronsky and Anna were talking in the hushed voice in which people generally talk at picture exhibitions. Mikhaylov thought that on them too the picture had created an impression, and went up to them.

'How wonderful Christ's expression is!' said Anna. That expression pleased her more than all else she saw, and she felt that it was the centre of the picture, and that therefore praise of it would be agreeable to the artist. 'One sees he is sorry for Pilate.'

Mikhaylov's face shone with ecstasy.

'Yes, and how well that figure is done, and what an atmosphere there is!' said Golenishchev, showing evidently by this remark that he did not approve of the content and idea of the figure.

'Yes, it is wonderfully masterly! How those figures in the background stand out! That is technique,' said Vronsky, addressing Golenishchev and alluding to a conversation they had had about Vronsky's despair of attaining technical mastery.

Anna and Vronsky crossed the room to look at another picture.

'Oh, how charming! How charming! Wonderful! Charming!' he and Anna began both at once.

'What is it they like so much?' wondered Mikhaylov. He had forgotten all about that picture, painted three years before.

'That's nothing—only an old study,' he said.

'How good!' remarked Golenishchev, evidently sincerely impressed by the charm of the picture.

Their delight in his picture aroused in Mikhaylov his former excitement, but he feared and disliked their idle interest in his past work, and therefore, though their praises gave him pleasure, he tried to draw his visitors' attention to a third picture.

But Vronsky inquired whether this picture was for sale. To Mikhaylov, in his excitement over their visit, this mention of money matters was very disagreeable.

'It is put out for sale,' he replied, frowning darkly.

Mikhaylov sold Vronsky the picture and consented to paint Anna's portrait. After the fifth sitting the portrait struck every one not only by its likeness but also by its beauty. It was strange that Mikhaylov had been able to discover that special beauty. 'One needed to know and love her as I love her, to find just that sweetest spiritual expression of hers,' thought Vronsky, though he himself had only learnt to know that 'sweetest spiritual expression' through the portrait.

In another man's house, and particularly in Vronsky's palazzo, Mikhaylov was unpleasantly deferential, as if fearful of intimacy with persons whom he did not respect. He addressed Vronsky as 'Your Excellency', and never stayed to dinner, though Anna and Vronsky both invited him, and he never came except for a sitting. Anna was even kinder to him and was grateful for her portrait. Vronsky was more than polite to him, and was evidently interested in the artist's opinion of his (Vronsky's) picture. Golenishchev never missed an opportunity to instil into Mikhaylov a true understanding of art. But the latter remained equally cold toward them all. Anna felt by his look that he liked looking at her, but he avoided conversation with her. When Vronsky talked about his art Mikhaylov remained stubbornly silent, and as stubbornly silent when they showed him Vronsky's picture; and he was evidently oppressed by Golenishchev's discourses, to which he made no rejoinder.

Altogether, they were glad when the sittings were over, the beautiful portrait was theirs, and his visits ceased.

Meanwhile Mikhaylov, though Anna's portrait had much engrossed him, was even better pleased than they when the sittings were over and he was no longer obliged to listen to Golenishchev's disquisitions on art and was able to forget Vronsky's paintings. He knew it was not possible to forbid Vronsky to trifle with art, knew that he and all the dilettanti had a perfect right to paint what they liked—but to him it was unpleasant. When he saw Vronsky's pictures he was amused, vexed, sorry, and hurt.

Vronsky's interest in art and the Middle Ages did not last long. He had sufficient taste for art to be unable to finish his picture. He ceased painting it because he was dimly conscious that its defects, little noticeable at first, would become striking if he went on. With characteristic firmness he left off painting, without explanation or excuse.

But without that occupation his life and Anna's—who was surprised at his disenchantment—appeared very dull in the Italian town. A change was necessary. So they decided to return to Russia and live in the country. In Petersburg Vronsky planned to separate his property from his brother's, and Anna to see her son. The summer they intended to spend on Vronsky's large family estate.

9

Levin had been married three months. He was happy, but in quite a different way from what he had expected. At every step he met disillusionments in his old fancies and new and unexpected enchantments. He was happy, but having embarked on family life he saw at every step that it was not at all what he had anticipated.

As a bachelor seeing the married life of others—their petty cares, their disputes, their jealousies—he used mentally to smile contemptuously. And now, behold! his life with his wife was all made up of those petty trifles which he had formerly so despised. Levin saw that the arrangement of all those trifles was not at all so easy as he had formerly supposed. Like all men, he forgot that she too must work; and was surprised how she, the poetic, charming Kitty, could, during the very first weeks and even in the first days of married life, think, remember, and fuss about table-cloths, furniture, spare-room mattresses, a tray, the cook, the dinner, and so forth, and was repeatedly pained by her petty cares. But he saw that this was necessary to her, and, loving her, though he could not understand what it was all about, and laughed at her worries, he could not help admiring them. He saw the old cook smile admiringly and listen to her inexperienced and impossible orders; saw that Agatha Mikhaylovna shook her head thoughtfully and kindly at her young mistress's arrangements in the storeroom; saw that Kitty was peculiarly charming when she came, half laughing and half crying, to report that her maid, Masha, was used to considering her merely as a young lady in her mother's house, and that therefore no one would obey her. It struck him as very charming, but strange, and he thought it would have been better without all that. He did not realize the feeling of change that she was experiencing after her life at home.

Kitty's absorption in these trifles, quite contrary to Levin's early ideal of lofty happiness, was one of his disappointments; yet that sweet absorption, the meaning of which he could not understand but which he could not help liking, was also one of his new enchantments. Another disenchantment and new enchantment was afforded by their quarrels. Levin had never thought it possible that between him and his wife there could ever be any but tender, respectful, and loving relations; and yet from the very beginning they had quarrelled. This first quarrel arose because Levin had ridden over to see his new farm and returned half an hour late, having attempted a short cut home and lost his way. He rode home thinking only of her, of her love and of his happiness, and the nearer he came the warmer grew his tenderness for her. He ran into the room with the same feelings as, and even stronger ones than, those with which he had gone to the Shcherbatskys' house to propose—and to his astonishment was met with such a dismal look as he had never seen on her face before. He tried to kiss her but she pushed him away.

Directly she opened her mouth, words of reproach, senseless jealousy, and everything else that had been torturing her during the half-hour she had sat motionless waiting at the window, burst from her. Then it was that he first clearly understood what he did not realize when leading her out of church after the wedding: that she was not only very close to him but that he could not now tell where she ended and he began. He understood this by a tormenting sensation of cleavage which he experienced at that moment. For an instant he was offended, but immediately knew he could not be offended with her because she was himself.

Never again did he feel this so strongly as this first time, and for a long time he could not recover his balance. His natural feelings prompted him to justify himself and prove that she was in the wrong; but to prove her in the wrong would mean widening the breach which was the cause of all the trouble. All he could do was to try to soothe the ache and endure it, and this he did.

They made it up. Having realized that she was in the wrong, though she did not acknowledge it, she became more tender to him, and they enjoyed a new and doubled happiness in their love. But this did not prevent such collisions recurring quite frequently, and on very unexpected and trivial provocation. When one of them was in good spirits and the other was not, peace was not broken; but if both chanced to be out of sorts, collisions resulted from causes so trifling as to be incomprehensible. Often afterwards they could not remember what they had quarrelled about. However, when both were in good spirits their happiness was doubled—and yet the early days of their married life were very trying.

All that time they were conscious of peculiar strain, as if the chain that bound them were being pulled first one way and then the other. Altogether, the honeymoon—the first month of their marriage, from which Levin had expected so much—was not delightful, but remained in both their recollections as the most oppressive and humiliating time of their lives. Only in the third month of their married life, after returning from Moscow where they had spent a month, did their life begin to run more smoothly.

After Moscow they were glad of the solitude. He was in his study and sat at the table writing. She sat with her embroidery on that same old leather-covered sofa which had stood in the study through his father's and grandfather's times. As he sat thinking and writing he was all the while blissfully conscious of her presence.

He went on with his work with a feeling that the centre of gravity of his attention had shifted, and that he consequently saw the matter differently and with greater clearness. Formerly this work had been his salvation from life. He used to feel that without it life would be too dismal, and now he needed it in order that his life should not be too monotonously bright.

While he was writing his thoughts, she glanced with a feeling of proprietorship, strange to herself, at the nape of his red neck. 'Though it's a pity to interrupt him at his work (but he'll have time enough) I must see his face. Will he feel that I am looking at him! I want him to turn ... I want it! Well!' and she opened her eyes wider, trying thereby to increase the force of her look.

'Yes, they divert all the sap, they produce a false glamour,' he muttered, pausing, and feeling that she was looking at him he turned round smiling.

'Well?' he asked with a smile, and rose.

'Nothing, I only wanted to make you turn round,' said she, gazing at him and trying to discover whether he was vexed at the interruption.

'I say, how delightful it is for us to be alone together! For me, I mean ...' he said, coming toward her with a beaming smile of happiness.

'It is delightful for me too! I shan't go anywhere, especially not to Moscow.'

'And what were you thinking about?'

'I? ... I was thinking. ... No, no! Go and write, don't let me distract you,' she said, puckering her lips. 'And I must cut out these little holes, you see!'

Taking up her scissors she began cutting.

'Come, tell me what it was,' he said, sitting down beside her and watching the circular movement of her tiny scissors.

'Oh, what was I thinking about? About Moscow, and about the nape of your neck.'

'Why should such happiness come just to me? It's not natural. It is too beautiful!' he said, kissing her hand.

'To me the more beautiful it is the more natural it seems.'

'Your hair comes to a point behind,' he said, carefully turning her head round.

'A point? Yes, so it does. There! But enough! We are engaged on serious matters!'

But their serious matters did not get on, and they jumped apart guiltily when Kuzma came to say that tea was served.

'Be quick and come,' she said as she left the study, 'or else I shall read all the letters without you. And after that let's have a duet.'

10

When Levin came upstairs his wife was sitting beside the new silver samovar with a new tea-service before her, reading a letter from Dolly, with whom she kept up a regular and active correspondence. She had made old Agatha Mikhaylovna sit at a little table with a cup of tea she had poured out for her.

'You see, your lady has made me sit with her,' said Agatha Mikhaylovna, glancing with a friendly smile at Kitty.

In these words of Agatha Mikhaylovna's Levin read the conclusion of the drama which had lately been enacted between Agatha Mikhaylovna and Kitty. He perceived that despite Agatha Mikhaylovna's grief at the advent of the new mistress who had taken the reins of management into her own hands, Kitty had conquered and had made the old woman love her.

'There! I've read your letter,' said Kitty, handing him a badly-written letter. 'It is from that woman, I think—your brother's ... No, I have not read it ...'

But Levin did not listen. He blushed as he took Mary Nikolavna's letter. This was the second letter he had received from the woman who had been his brother's mistress. In the first she wrote that his brother had sent her away for no fault of hers, adding with touching naïveté that, though she was again in want she did not ask anything, but wrote because she was crushed by the thought that Nicholas Dmitrich would perish without her, his health being so bad. She begged Levin to keep watch over his brother. This time she wrote differently: she had found Nicholas Dmitrich and had gone with him to a provincial town where he had obtained a post in the Civil Service. But he had quarrelled with his chief, and they had started again for Moscow, when he fell so ill on the way that it was hardly likely he would ever get up again. She wrote: 'He keeps on thinking of you; besides, there is no money left.'

'Read it. ... Dolly writes about you,' Kitty began with a smile, but paused suddenly, noticing the changed expression on her husband's face. 'What's the matter? What is it?'

'She writes that my brother Nicholas is on his deathbed. I am going.'

Kitty's look changed. Thoughts of Dolly had quite vanished.

'I shall go too, may I?'

'Kitty! What do you mean?' he said reproachfully. 'I am going because my brother is dying,' said Levin, 'but why should you ...?'

'Why? For the same reason as you.'

'It is impossible,' he replied sternly.

Agatha Mikhaylovna, seeing that a quarrel was imminent, softly put down her cup and went out. Kitty did not even notice her. The tone in which her husband had said these words hurt her, especially as he evidently disbelieved what she had said.

'And I say that if you go I shall go with you!' she said angrily. 'Why is it impossible? Why do you say it is impossible?'

'Because it means going goodness knows where, and by what roads! to what inns! You would be in my way,' said Levin, endeavouring to keep cool.

'Not at all! I shan't want anything, and where you can go I can.'

'Well, if only because that woman is there, with whom you cannot associate ...'

'I don't know and don't want to know anything about who and what is there. I know that my husband's brother is dying, that my husband is going to him, and that I am going with my husband in order ...'

'Kitty, don't be angry! But just think, this matter is so important—it hurts me to think that you are mixing up with it your weakness, your dislike of remaining alone. Well, if you feel dull alone—well, go to Moscow!'

'There, you see! You *always* attribute bad and vile motives to me,' she began, with tears of anger and resentment. 'I am all right, not weak, nor anything. ... I feel that it's my duty to be with my husband when he is in trouble, but you wish to hurt me on purpose, you purposely don't want to understand me!'

'No, this is awful ... being a sort of slave!' exclaimed Levin, unable to restrain his annoyance any longer, but immediately conscious that he had dealt a blow to himself.

'Then why did you marry? You might have been free! Why, since you are repenting?' she said and ran into the drawing-room.

When he came in after her, she was sobbing. He began speaking, trying to find words not so much to dissuade as to pacify her. But she did not listen and did not agree to anything he said. He stooped and took her resisting hand; he kissed her hand, her hair, and again her hand, but she remained silent. But when he took her face in his hands and said 'Kitty!' she suddenly recovered, cried a little, and then they made it up.

It was settled that they would start together the next day.

11

The hotel in the provincial town where Nicholas Levin was lying ill was one of those with the best intentions of cleanliness, comfort and even elegance, but which, owing to the people who use them, very soon degenerate into mere dirty pothouses with pretensions to modern improvements, these very pretensions making them worse than the old-fashioned inns which were simply dirty.

After the inquiry as to what priced rooms they desired, it turned out that there was not a single good room vacant: there was just one dirty room to be had, but they were promised that an adjoining one would be free by the evening. Vexed with his wife because his expectations were being realized—namely, that, at the moment of arrival when his heart was seized with agitation at the thought of his brother's condition, he was obliged to consider her instead of running to him at once—Levin led her to the room.

'Go, go!' she said with a timid, guilty look at him. He went out silently, and at the very door came upon Mary Nikolavna, who had heard of his arrival but had not dared to enter. She was just the same as he had seen her in Moscow—only somewhat stouter.

'Well? How is he? What is it?'

'Very bad! Does not get up. He was expecting you all the time. He … you … are with your wife?'

For a moment he did not understand the cause of her confusion, but she immediately explained it.

'I will go … I will go to the kitchen,' she brought out. 'He will be pleased. He heard, and he knows and remembers her abroad.'

Levin understood that she referred to his wife, and did not know what to say.

'Come along, come!' he said.

He had not expected what he saw and felt when he reached his brother's side. In the dirty little room with a painted dado spotted with spittle, behind the thin partition-wall of which could be heard the sound of voices, in stuffy, smelly, foul air, on a bed drawn away from the wall, lay a body covered with a blanket. One arm of that body lay outside the blanket, and the enormous hand, like a rake, seemed to be attached in some incomprehensible way to a long thin spindle that was quite straight from the end to the middle. The head lay on its side on the pillow. Levin could see the moist thin hair on the temples and the drawn transparent-looking forehead.

'Impossible that this terrible body can be my brother Nicholas,' he thought. But he drew nearer, saw the face, and doubt was no longer possible. In spite of the dreadful change on the face, Levin had only to glance at those living eyes raised toward him, to notice the slight move-ment of the mouth beneath the moustache, in order to understand the dreadful truth that this dead body was his living brother.

When Constantine took him by the hand, Nicholas smiled. The smile was very faint, hardly perceptible, and in spite of it the stern expression of the eyes did not change.

'You did not expect to find me like this?' he said, speaking with difficulty.

'Yes … no …' said Levin, confusing his words. 'How is it you did not let me know sooner, I mean at the time of my marriage? I inquired for you everywhere.'

His brother made no reply but only gazed fixedly at him. Levin told his brother that his wife had come with him. Nicholas seemed pleased at this, but said he was afraid the condition he was in might frighten her. A silence followed. Suddenly Nicholas moved and began to talk. He found fault with the doctor, and regretted that he could not have a celebrated

Moscow doctor; so Levin understood that he was still hoping.

Taking advantage of the first moment of silence, Levin got up, wishing to free himself if only for a few minutes from his painful sensations, and said he would fetch his wife.

'All right, and I will have the place cleaned up a bit. It is dirty here, and it smells, I should think. Masha! Tidy up,' said the invalid with an effort. 'And when you have finished, go away,' he added, with a questioning look at his brother.

Levin did not reply. He went out and stopped in the corridor. He had said he would bring his wife, but now, analysing the impressions he was experiencing, he made up his mind that he would on the contrary try to dissuade her from entering the sick-room. 'Why should she too be tortured as I am?' he reflected.

'Well, how is he? Kitty asked with a frightened look.

'Oh, it's awful! Awful! Why did you come?' said Levin.

Kitty was silent a moment, looking timidly and pitifully at her husband; then she took hold of his elbow with both hands.

'Kostya, take me to him! It will be easier for us to bear it together! Just take me there and then go away,' she began. 'Try and realize that for me to see you and not to see him is much more painful. There I can perhaps be of use to him and you. Please let me!' she entreated.

He was obliged to yield, and he returned with Kitty to his brother.

Stepping lightly and glancing repeatedly at her husband, showing him a brave face full of sympathy, she entered the sick-room, and, with noiseless steps she advanced toward the bedside, went round so that he need not turn his head, and at once grasping his enormous skeleton hand with her fresh young one, pressed it, and with that sympathetic, quiet animation which gives no offence.

'It was in Soden we met, but we were not acquainted,' she said. 'You little thought I should one day be your sister?'

'You would not have known me again?' he asked, with a smile that had lit up his face at her entrance.

'Oh yes, I should! What a good thing it is that you did send us word! Not a day passed without Kostya's thinking and being anxious about you. I'm afraid you are not quite comfortable here,' she said, turning away from his penetrating glance and looking round the room. 'We shall have to ask the landlord for another room, and see that we are nearer to each other,' she said to her husband.

12

Levin could not look at his brother calmly and could not be either natural or tranquil in his presence. When he entered the sick-room his eyes and his attention became clouded without his being conscious of it, and he did not see or distinguish the various details of his brother's condition. He smelt the terribly foul air, saw the dirt and disorder, the agonizing posture of the body, and heard the groans; but he felt there was no help for it. He was convinced beyond doubt that nothing could be done to prolong that life or to alleviate those sufferings. But Kitty felt and acted quite differently. When she saw the invalid she pitied him, and that pity produced in her a need for action, for finding out all the particulars of his condition, and a desire to help him. Those very details, the thought of which alone filled her husband with horror, at once arrested her attention. She made the maid she had brought with her help Mary Nikolavna sweep, dust, and wash; and herself washed and scrubbed some articles and spread something under the blanket. At her command things were brought in and taken out of the sick-room.

When Levin opened the door, on his return from the doctor's whither Kitty had sent him, he found the invalid arranged in bed and everything around him quite altered. Instead of the foul smell there was an odour of vinegar and of scent, which Kitty—pouting her lips and puffing out her rosy cheeks—was blowing through a little glass tube. There was no trace of dust left about; there was a mat beside the bed; on the table medicine bottles and a bottle of water were neatly placed, also a pile of folded linen which would be required later, and Kitty's embroidery. On another table by the bedside were a glass of some refreshing drink and some powders. The invalid himself, washed and with his hair brushed, lay between clean sheets in a clean shirt, its white collar round his abnormally thin neck, gazing with a new look of hope at Kitty and not taking his eyes off her.

The doctor whom Levin had fetched was not the one who had hitherto attended Nicholas, with whom the patient was dissatisfied. The new doctor took out a stethoscope and sounded him, shook his head, prescribed some medicine and gave extremely precise instructions about giving the medicine and about diet. When the doctor had gone the patient said something to his brother of which Levin caught only the last words: 'your Kate'; but by the look he gave her Levin saw that his brother was praising her. He asked 'Kate', as he called her, to come nearer.

'I feel much better,' he said. 'Had I been with you I should have recovered long ago. How pleasant!'

He took her hand and drew it toward his lips, but as if fearful that this might be disagreeable to her he changed his mind, let her hand drop, and merely stroked it.

'Now turn me over on the left side and go to bed,' he murmured.

No one heard what he said, but Kitty understood him. She understood because her mind incessantly watched for his needs.

'On the other side,' she said to her husband, 'he always sleeps on the other side. Turn him over; I cannot do it. Can you?' she said, addressing Mary Nikolavna.

'I am afraid to,' answered Mary Nikolavna.

Dreadful as it seemed to Levin to put his arms round that terrible body, to grasp those parts under the blanket which he did not wish to remember, yet submitting to his wife, with that determined expression which she knew, he thrust his arms under the blanket, and despite his great strength was struck by the strange heaviness of those emaciated limbs. While he was turning him, with the enormous lean arm about his neck, Kitty quickly and unostentatiously turned and beat the pillow, and arranged the invalid's head and the hair that again clung to the temples. The patient retained his brother's hand in his and kissed it. Levin, trembling, choking with sobs and unable to utter a word, left the room.

When Levin returned to their two rooms for the night he sat with hanging head not knowing what to do. Not only could he not think of supper, of getting ready for the night, of considering what they were to do; he could not even talk to his wife: he was ashamed to. Kitty, on the contrary, was more active than usual and even more animated. She ordered supper to be brought, unpacked their things herself, helped to make the beds, and did not forget to sprinkle insect powder on them.

It seemed to Levin that it would be inexcusable to eat, sleep, or even to talk, and he felt that his every movement was improper. She, however, sorted combs and brushes, and did it all in such a way that there was nothing offensive about it.

'I am very glad I have persuaded him to receive Extreme Unction to-morrow,' she said as she sat in her dressing-jacket before her folding-glass and combed her soft fragrant hair with a small comb. 'I have never been present, but Mama told me that there are prayers for the restoration of health …'

'Do you really think he can recover?' he asked.

'I asked the doctor. He says he can't live more than three days. But how can they know? Still, I am very glad I persuaded him,' she said, turning her eyes toward her husband. 'Everything is possible,' she added with the peculiar and rather cunning expression which always appeared on her face when she spoke of religious matters.

'Yes, you see that woman Mary Nikolavna could not arrange all that,' said Levin. 'I ... I must confess I am very glad you came. You are purity itself, and ...' He took her hand and did not kiss it (to do so with death so near seemed to him unbecoming), but only pressed it, looking guiltily into her brightening eyes.

'No,' she said, 'she did not know how to. ... Luckily I learnt a good deal in Soden.'

'Can there have been such sick people there?'

'Oh, worse.'

'It is so terrible to me that I cannot help seeing him as he was when young. ... You would not believe what a charming lad he was, and I did not understand him then.'

'I quite believe it, quite. I feel that we *should have been* friends, he and I ...' she said, and, frightened at her own words, she glanced at her husband, and tears filled her eyes.

'Yes, *would have been*,' he said sadly. 'He is really one of those of whom it is said, they are not for this world.'

'However, we have hard days before us—let us go to bed,' said Kitty with a glance at her tiny watch.

13

Next day the patient received Communion and Extreme Unction. During the ceremony he prayed fervently. In his large eyes, fixed upon an icon which had been placed on a little table covered with a coloured cloth, was a look of such passionate entreaty and hope that Levin was frightened at seeing it. During the sacrament Levin did that which, agnostic though he was, he had done a thousand times before. He said, addressing himself to God, 'If Thou dost exist, heal this man (such things have often happened), and Thou wilt save both him and me!'

After receiving Extreme Unction the invalid suddenly felt better. He did not cough once for a whole hour, smiled, kissed Kitty's hand, thanking her with tears in his eyes, and said he felt well, had no pain, but had an appetite and felt stronger. He even sat up when they brought him some soup, and asked for a cutlet too. Hopeless as his case was, obvious as it was that he could not recover, Levin and Kitty were for that hour both in the same state of excitement, happy yet timid and fearful of being mistaken.

But this illusion did not last long. The invalid fell quietly asleep, but awoke half an hour later with a fit of coughing, and immediately every hope fled from those around him and from himself.

Nicholas told them to give him a bottle of iodine covered with perforated paper for inhaling. Levin handed it to him, and at once a look of passionate hope was fixed on his brother, demanding from him a confirmation of the doctor's words to the effect that inhaling iodine worked miracles.

'Kitty is not here?' he asked hoarsely, glancing round when Levin had reluctantly confirmed the doctor's statement.

'No? Then I can tell you ... It's for her sake I went through that comedy—she is such a dear! But you and I cannot deceive ourselves like that! Now, in this I do believe,' he said, clutching the bottle with his bony hand and beginning to inhale from it.

Between seven and eight o'clock that evening Levin and his wife were drinking tea in their room when Mary Nikolavna rushed in breathless. 'He is dying!' she whispered.

Both ran to his room. He was sitting up with his long back bent, leaning his elbows on the bed and hanging his head.

'What do you feel?' asked Levin in a whisper, after a pause.

'I feel I am departing,' uttered Nicholas with an effort, but very distinctly, as if he were pressing the words out of his body. He did not lift his head but only turned up his eyes, failing to reach his brother's face. 'Kate, go away,' he added.

Mary Nikolavna approached.

'You had better lie down, you would feel easier,' she said.

'I'll soon be lying,' he said softly. 'Dead!' he added cynically and angrily. 'Well, lay me down if you like.'

Levin laid his brother on his back, sat down beside him, and holding his breath gazed at his face. The dying man lay with closed eyes, but at intervals the muscles of his forehead worked as if he were thinking deeply and intently. Levin involuntarily meditated upon what was taking place within his brother at that moment.

Mary Nikolavna felt his feet. 'Growing cold,' she whispered.

For a long, a very long, time as it seemed to Levin the invalid lay motionless, but he still lived and at long intervals sighed. Levin sat leaning over Nicholas, waiting for the end. But the end did not come. The door opened and Kitty appeared. Levin rose to stop her, but at that moment he heard the dying man move.

'Don't go,' said Nicholas, and stretched out his hand. Levin gave him his hand, signing angrily with the other to his wife.

Day began to dawn, but the sick man's condition remained the same. Levin gently disengaged his hand, and without looking at his brother went to his own room and fell asleep. When he woke, instead of the news he expected, that his brother was dead, he heard that his former condition had returned. He again sat up, coughed, ate and talked, no longer of death, expressed hopes of recovery, and was even more irritable and depressed than before. No one, neither his brother nor Kitty, could comfort him. He was angry with every one, said disagreeable things, blamed everybody for his sufferings, and demanded that they should fetch a celebrated doctor from Moscow. To all questions of how he felt, he gave the same answer, with an angry and reproachful look: 'I am suffering terribly, intolerably!'

Levin, who had long wished to reconcile his brothers, even if only at the moment of death, had written to Sergius Ivanich, and having received his answer read it to Nicholas. Sergius Ivanich wrote that he could not come personally, but, in touching words, asked his brother's pardon. The invalid made no comment.

'What am I to write to him?' asked Levin. 'I hope you are not angry with him?'

'No, not at all,' answered Nicholas, vexed at the question. 'Tell him to send me a doctor.'

Another three days of torture went by. The sick man was still in the same condition. Every one who saw him now desired his death. Only the invalid himself did not show that desire, but on the contrary was angry because the doctor had not been fetched, and he continued taking medicine and talking of life. Only at rare moments, when opium made him forget his incessant sufferings for a moment, did he sometimes when half asleep express what was stronger in his soul than in any of the others': 'Oh, if only it were over!'

On the tenth day after their arrival in that town Kitty fell ill. She had a headache, was sick, and could not leave her bed all the morning.

The doctor explained her illness as the result of fatigue and agitation, and ordered mental tranquillity.

After dinner, however, Kitty got up and went as usual to the sick man, taking her embroidery. Nicholas looked at her sternly when she entered, and smiled contemptuously when she said she had been ill. That day he continually blew his nose and moaned piteously.

Toward night the patient could no longer raise his hands, and only gazed straight before him without changing the attentive concentrated expression of his eyes. Even when his brother or Kitty bent over him so that he could see them, he did not look at them. Kitty sent for the priest to read the prayers for the dying. While the priest read, the dying man showed no sign of life: his eyes were closed. Levin, Kitty, and Mary Nikolavna stood by the bedside. The prayers were not yet ended when the dying man stretched himself, sighed and opened his eyes. A moment later his face brightened, a smile appeared under the moustache, and the women who had gathered round him began zealously to lay out the body.

The sight of his brother and the proximity of death renewed in Levin's soul that feeling of horror at the inscrutability, nearness, and inevitability of death which had seized him on that autumn evening when his brother had arrived in the country. That feeling was now stronger even than before; he felt even less able than before to understand the meaning of death, and its inevitability appeared yet more terrible to him; but now, thanks to his wife's presence, that feeling did not drive him to despair; in spite of death, he felt the necessity of living and loving. He felt that love had saved him from despair, and that love under the menace of despair grew still stronger and purer.

Scarcely had the unexplained mystery of death been enacted before his eyes when another mystery just as inexplicable presented itself, calling to love and life. The doctor confirmed their supposition about Kitty. Her illness was pregnancy.

14

From the moment that Karenin understood from his conversations with Betsy and Oblonsky that all that was asked of him was that he should leave his wife in peace and not trouble her with his presence and that his wife herself wished this, he felt so lost that he could decide nothing for himself, did not know what he now wanted, and having placed himself in the hands of those who with so much pleasure busied themselves with his affairs, he consented to everything. Only after Anna had left his house, and the English governess sent to ask him whether she was to dine with him or alone, did he for the first time clearly understand his position, and he was horror-struck at it.

He could not at all reconcile his recent forgiveness, his emotion and love for his sick wife and for another man's baby, with the fact that he was now left alone, disgraced, ridiculed, not wanted by anyone and despised by all.

The first two days after his wife's departure Karenin received petitioners, and his private secretary, attended Committee Meetings, and went to the dining-room to dinner as usual. When answering questions as to what should be done with Anna's rooms and belongings, he made the greatest efforts to seem like a man by whom what had taken place had not been unforeseen, and who did not consider it extraordinary.

Karenin realized that he could not any longer maintain an appearance of firmness and calm. He ordered the carriage that was waiting, to be unharnessed, said that he would receive no one, and did not appear at dinner.

His despair was heightened by the consciousness that he was quite alone in his sorrow. Not only was there not a soul in Petersburg to whom he could express what he felt, who would pity him, not as a high official, not as a member of a society, but simply as a suffering human being—but nowhere at all had he any such friends.

Karenin had forgotten the Countess Lydia Ivanovna, but she had not forgotten him. At that most painful time of lonely despair she came to his house and entered his study unannounced. She found him in the posture in which he had long sat, resting his head on his hands.

'I've forced my way in,' she said as she entered with hurried steps, breathing heavily from her rapid movement and from excitement. 'I have heard everything. Alexis Alexandrovich, my dear friend!' she continued, firmly clasping his hand in both hers and gazing with her beautiful dreamy eyes into his.

Karenin rose frowning, and disengaging his hand moved a chair toward her.

'If you please, Countess!—I do not receive because I am ill,' he said, and his lips trembled.

'My dear friend!' repeated the Countess with her eyes fixed on him; Karenin felt that she was sorry for him and ready to cry. He was moved, and seizing her plump hand began kissing it.

'My dear friend!' she repeated in a voice broken by emotion, 'you must not give way to sorrow. Your sorrow is great, but you will find consolation.'

'I am broken, I am stricken! I am no longer a man!' said Karenin, releasing her hand but continuing to gaze into her tearful eyes. 'My position is terrible because I cannot find support anywhere, cannot find it even in myself.'

'You will find support; do not seek it in me, though I want you to believe in my friendship,' she replied with a sigh. 'Love is the only support, that love which He has bequeathed us! His yoke is easy,' she went on with that ecstatic look he knew so well. 'He will support you and help you!'

Though it was evident that she was touched by her own lofty sentiments, and though her words proceeded from that new, ecstatic, mystic
influence which had lately spread through Petersburg and which Karenin
had considered superfluous, it was pleasant to him to hear them now.

'I am weak—I am done for! I did not foresee it, and don't understand
it now! It is not the loss of what no longer exists, it is not that,' continued
Karenin. 'I don't regret that, but I cannot help feeling ashamed before
others. That is wrong, but I can't help it, I can't.'

'It is not you who have performed that great act of forgiveness which
fills me and everybody else with rapture, but He that dwells within your
heart,' said the Countess, turning up her eyes ecstatically, 'and therefore
you must not be ashamed of your action.'

Karenin frowned, and bending his hands backward began cracking
his fingers.

'One must know all the details,' he said in a high-pitched voice.
'Human strength has its limits, Countess, and I have reached the limits
of mine. All day long I have had to take domestic decisions resulting
from' (he emphasized the word *resulting*) 'my new solitary position. The
servants, the governess, the bills … At dinner … yesterday, I very nearly
left the table. I could not bear the way my son looked at me. He did
not ask me the meaning of it all, but he wanted to ask, and I could not
endure his look. He was afraid of looking at me.'

'I understand, dear friend,' said the Countess Lydia Ivanovna. 'I
understand it all. Not in me will you find help and consolation, though
I have come to help you if I can. If I could take all those trivial humiliating cares off your shoulders? … I see that a woman's word, a woman's
direction, is wanted. Will you entrust it to me?'

Karenin silently and gratefully pressed her hand.

'We will look after Serezha together. I am not good in practical matters, still I will undertake it—I will be your housekeeper. Do not thank
me. I am not doing it of myself …'

'I cannot help thanking you!'

'But, my dear friend, do not give away to that feeling you were
speaking about—of being ashamed of that which is the utmost height
of Christianity! "He that humbleth himself shall be exalted," and you
must not thank me! You must thank Him, and ask Him for help. In
Him alone you will find peace, comfort, salvation, and love!' And raising
her eyes to Heaven she began to pray, as Karenin understood from her
silence.

'I am very, very grateful to you, both for your actions and your words,'
said he when she had finished praying.

The Countess Lydia Ivanovna once more pressed both the hands of her friend.

'Now I am going to act,' she said, smiling and wiping the traces of tears from her face. 'I am going to see Serezha. Only in extreme cases will I apply to you,' and she rose and went out.

The Countess went to Serezha's part of the house and there, watering the frightened boy's cheeks with her tears, told him that his father was a saint and that his mother was dead.

The Countess kept her word. She really took upon herself the care of arranging and managing Karenin's household, but she had not exaggerated when she said she was not good at practical matters. None of her directions could be carried out without alteration, and the alterations were made by Karenin's valet, Korney, who now imperceptibly directed the whole household. Quietly and tactfully, while helping his master dress, he would inform him of anything that was necessary. But nevertheless Lydia Ivanovna's help was in the highest degree effective, for it gave Karenin the moral support of the consciousness of her affection and respect.

15

The Countess Lydia Ivanovna when quite a young and ecstatic girl was married to a rich, aristocratic, very good-natured, and most jovial profligate. About two months after their marriage her husband left her, and only answered her ecstatic assurances of tenderness with ridicule and even with animosity—which those who knew the Count's good-nature, and who saw no fault in the ecstatic Lydia, were quite unable to explain. Since then, though not divorced, they lived apart; and when the husband did meet his wife he always treated her with an unchanging venomous irony which seemed inexplicable.

The Countess Lydia had long ago ceased to be in love with her husband, but since then had never ceased to be in love with somebody else. But from the time she took Karenin under her special protection after his misfortune—from the time she exerted herself in his house, labouring for his welfare—she felt that she now truly loved only Karenin. Analysing that feeling, and comparing it with her previous loves, she saw clearly that she loved Karenin for himself, for his lofty, misunderstood soul, for the high-pitched tone of his voice with the long-drawn inflections which she thought charming, for his weary eyes, for his character, and for his soft hands with their swollen veins. She was not only glad to meet him, but searched his face for signs of the impression she created on him. She blushed with excitement when he entered the room, and could not repress a smile of delight when he said something agreeable to her.

For some days the Countess Lydia Ivanovna had been greatly excited. She had heard that Anna and Vronsky were in Petersburg. It was necessary to save Karenin from meeting her, necessary even to save him from the painful knowledge that that dreadful woman was in the same town as him, and that he might come across her at any moment.

Lydia Ivanovna found out through a young adjutant, a comrade of Vronsky's, who hoped through her influence to obtain a concession; he told her that they had finished their affairs and were leaving Petersburg next day. Lydia Ivanovna was beginning to breathe freely again, when next morning she received a note and with horror recognized the handwriting. It was Anna Karenina's.

It was some time before the Countess Lydia Ivanovna could sit down to read the letter. Her agitation brought on a fit of asthma, to which she was subject. When she grew calmer, she read the following:

'MADAME LA COMTESSE!—The Christian feelings which fill your heart encourage me to what I feel to be the unpardonable boldness of writing to you. I am unhappy at being parted from my son. I entreat you to permit me to see him once before my departure. Forgive me for reminding you of myself. I address myself to you, instead of to Alexis Alexandrovich, only because I do not wish to give pain to that high-minded man by reminding him of myself. Knowing your friendship for him, I feel that you will understand me. Will you send Serezha to me or shall I come to the house at an appointed time, or will you let me know when and where I can meet him away from home? I do not anticipate a refusal, knowing the magnanimity of the person on whom the decision depends. You cannot imagine the yearning I have to see him, and therefore cannot imagine the gratitude which your help will awaken in me.—ANNA.'

Everything in that letter irritated the Countess Lydia Ivanovna: its matter, the hint contained in the word 'magnanimity', and especially what seemed to her its free and easy tone.

'Say there will be no answer,' said the Countess Lydia Ivanovna, and at once opened her blotter and wrote to Karenin that she hoped to meet him after the Birthday Reception at the Palace.

'I must talk over an important and sad matter with you, at my house, where I will have your special tea ready. It is necessary. He sends a cross, but He also sends strength to bear it,' she added, to prepare him somewhat.

When Karenin entered the Countess Lydia Ivanovna's snug little boudoir, which was full of old china and had its walls covered with portraits, the hostess was not yet there.

Upon a round table covered with a cloth stood a Chinese tea-service and a silver kettle over a spirit lamp. Karenin glanced absent-mindedly at the numberless familiar portraits decorating the boudoir, and sitting down by the table opened a New Testament that was on it. The rustle of the Countess's silk dress roused him.

After a few words of preparation the Countess, breathing heavily and blushing, handed him the letter she had received.

When he had read the letter Karenin was silent for a long time.

'I don't consider that I have a right to refuse,' he said timidly, raising his eyes.

'My dear friend, you see no evil in anyone!'

'On the contrary, I see that everything is evil. But is it right … I have quite forgiven her, and therefore cannot refuse her what her love for her son demands.'

'But have we the right to act thus toward the soul of that angel? He thinks she is dead. What will he think?'

'I had not thought of that,' said Karenin.

The Countess covered her face with her hands and remained silent.

'If you ask my advice,' she said, when her prayer was ended and she uncovered her face, 'I do not advise you to do it! What can it lead to? Renewed pain for yourself, and pain for the child! If there is anything human left in her, she herself should not desire it. No, I advise you not to allow it, and with your permission I will write to her.'

Karenin agreed, and the Countess Lydia Ivanovna wrote:

'MADAME!—To remind your son of you might lead to his asking questions which it would be impossible to answer without implanting in his soul a spirit of condemnation for what should be holy to him, and therefore I beg you to take your husband's refusal in the spirit of Christian love. I pray the Almighty to be merciful to you.—COUNTESS LYDIA.'

This letter achieved the secret purpose which the Countess hid even from herself. It wounded Anna to the depths of her soul.

16

'Well, Kapitonich?' said Serezha, as on the day before his birthday he returned rosy and bright from a walk, and gave his overcoat to the tall old hall-porter, who looked smilingly down from his height at the little fellow. 'Well, has anything been brought?'

'Well, sir,' said the porter, shaking his head and whispering, 'there is something from the Countess.'

Serezha knew at once that the hall-porter was speaking of a birthday present for him from the Countess Lydia Ivanovna.

'You don't say so? Where is it?'

'Korney has taken it in to your papa.'

'A book?'

'No, just a thing. Go, go! Vasily Lukich is calling you,' said the hall-porter, hearing the approaching step of the tutor.

'Vasily Lukich, one moment!' said Serezha with that bright and affectionate smile which always overcame the conscientious tutor.

Serezha was in too high spirits, too happy not to share with his friend the hall-porter another family joy about which he had heard from Lydia Ivanovna's niece, whom he met walking in the Summer Gardens. This joy appeared to him particularly important because it coincided with his own happiness that a present had been brought.

'Do you know, Papa has received the Order of Alexander Nevsky?'

'Of course I do! People have already been calling to congratulate him.'

'Well, and is he pleased?'

'How can he help being pleased at the Tsar's favour? It shows he's deserved it,' replied the hall-porter sternly and seriously. 'Go along!'

On entering the schoolroom, instead of sitting down to his lessons, Serezha told his tutor of his guess that the parcel that had been brought must be a railway train.

'What do you think?' he asked.

But Vasily Lukich only thought that Serezha must prepare his grammar lesson, as his teacher was coming at two.

After the teacher's lesson Serezha had a lesson from his father. Before his father came Serezha sat at the table playing with a pocket-knife and thinking. Among his favourite occupations was keeping a look out for his mother when he went out walking. He did not believe in death in general, and especially not in *her* death, despite what Lydia Ivanovna had told him and his father had confirmed, and therefore even after he had been told she was dead, he went on looking for her when on his walks. He imagined that every well-developed and graceful woman with dark hair was his mother. At the sight of any such woman a feeling of such tenderness awoke in his heart that he grew breathless and tears came to his eyes. He expected that at any moment she would approach and lift her veil. Then he would see her whole face, she would smile, embrace him. To-day Serezha was more than ever conscious of a flow of love for his mother in his heart, and now as he sat waiting for his father looking before him with shining eyes and thinking about her.

Vasily Lukich roused him. 'Your papa is coming!'

Serezha jumped up, approached his father, kissed his hand, and looked at him attentively, trying to find some sign of his joy at receiving the Order of Alexander Nevsky.

'Have you had a nice walk?' asked Karenin, as he sat down in his arm-chair, drew toward him an Old Testament and opened it.

'Yes, Papa, it was very amusing,' answered Serezha, sitting down sideways on his chair and beginning to rock it, which was forbidden. 'I met Nadenka' (Nadenka was Lydia Ivanovna's niece, who was being educated at her aunt's house). 'She told me you had received another Order, a new one. Are you glad, Papa?'

'First of all, don't rock your chair,' said Karenin. 'Secondly, it's not the reward but the work that is precious. I wish you understood that. You see, if you take pains and learn in order to get a reward, the work will seem hard; but when you love your work, you will find your reward in that.'

Serezha's eyes, which had been shining with affection and joy, grew dull and drooped under his father's gaze. It was the same long-familiar tone in which his father always addressed him, and to which Serezha had already learnt to adapt himself.

'You understand me, I hope,' said the father.

'Yes, Papa,' answered the boy.

17

When Vronsky and Anna reached Petersburg they put up at one of the best hotels: Vronsky separately on the first floor, and Anna with the baby, the nurse, and a maid, upstairs in a large suite.

On the day they arrived Vronsky went to see his brother. There he met his mother, who had come from Moscow on business. His mother and his sister-in-law received him just as usual, asked him about his trip abroad and spoke of mutual acquaintances, but did not say a single word about his union with Anna. His brother, however, having come to see him next morning, asked about her, and Alexis Vronsky told him frankly that he regarded his union with her as a marriage, that he hoped to arrange a divorce for her, and would then marry her, and that meanwhile he considered her his wife, just like any other wife, and he asked his brother to say so to their mother and to his own wife.

The elder brother, who had always respected his younger brother's opinions, was not sure whether he was right or wrong, until the world had decided the point; but for his own part he had nothing against it and went up with Alexis to see Anna.

In his brother's presence Vronsky spoke to Anna merely as to a close acquaintance, as he always did in the presence of a third party; but it was assumed that his brother knew of their relations, and they spoke of Anna's going to Vronsky's estate.

Despite all his experience of the world, Vronsky, in the new position in which he found himself, was making a terrible mistake. He had some sort of vague notion that public opinion had changed and it was possible they would be received in Society. 'Of course they will not receive her at Court, but intimate friends can and should see things the right way,' he thought.

But he very soon noticed that though the great world was open to him personally, it was closed to Anna.

One of the first Society ladies he met was his cousin Betsy.

'At last!' she exclaimed joyfully. 'And Anna? I am so glad! Where are you staying? And the divorce? Is it all arranged?'

He noticed that Betsy's delight cooled down when she learnt that Anna had not yet been divorced.

'They will throw stones at me, I know,' she said, 'but I shall come and see Anna. Yes, I will certainly come. You are not staying here long?'

And really she came to see Anna that same day; but her manner was very different from what it had formerly been. She was evidently proud of her boldness and wished Anna to appreciate the fidelity of her friendship. She did not stay more than ten minutes, chattering Society gossip, and as she was leaving said:

'You have not told me when you will be divorced? Of course I have kicked over the traces, but others, strait-laced people, will give you the cold shoulder until you get married. So you are leaving on Friday? I am sorry we shan't see one another again!'

From Betsy's tone Vronsky might have realized what he had to expect from Society, but he made another attempt with his relations. He knew that his mother, who had been so delighted with Anna when she first made her acquaintance, was now merciless toward her for having caused the ruin of her son's career. But he placed great hopes on Varya, his brother's wife. She, he thought, would simply and resolutely go and see Anna and receive her at her own house.

The day after his arrival Vronsky called on her, and having found her alone, expressed his wish.

'You know how fond I am of you, Alexis,' she replied when she had heard him out, 'and how ready I am to do anything for you; but please understand that I *cannot* do it! I have daughters growing up, and I must move in Society, for my husband's sake. Alexis, don't be angry with me! Please understand that it is not my fault,' said Varya, looking at him with a timid smile.

'I am not angry with you,' he said just as gloomily, 'but I am doubly pained. I am pained too because this weakens our friendship. You understand that for me too there can be no other course!'

With those words he left her.

Vronsky understood that it was vain to make any further attempts and that they would have to spend those few days in Petersburg avoiding contact with their former world in order not to lay themselves open to unpleasantness and insults.

The stay in Petersburg seemed to him still more trying because he noticed all the time in Anna a new and to him incomprehensible mood. At one moment she appeared to be in love with him, and at the next would turn cold, irritable, and impenetrable. Something tormented her and she hid it from him, appearing not to notice the insults that were poisoning his life, and which should have been still more painful to her with her acuteness of perception.

18

One of Anna's reasons for returning to Russia was to see her son. From the day she left Italy the thought of that meeting did not cease to agitate her. The nearer they came to Petersburg the greater its joy and importance appeared. She did not ask herself how she should contrive it. It seemed to her natural and simple that she should see her son when she was in the same town with him. But on reaching Petersburg her present social position presented itself clearly to her, and she realized that it would be difficult to arrange the meeting.

Having heard about Karenin's intimate friendship with the Countess

Lydia Ivanovna, Anna resolved to write her a letter, which cost her much effort, and in which she intentionally mentioned that permission to see her son must depend on her husband's magnanimity. She knew that if that letter were shown to him he, continuing his magnanimous rôle, would not refuse her request.

The commissionaire who delivered her letter brought back the most cruel and unexpected reply: that there would be no answer! Anna felt herself humiliated and wounded, but she saw that the Countess Lydia Ivanovna was right from her own point of view. Her grief was the more poignant because she had to bear it alone. She could not share it with Vronsky and did not wish to. She knew he would never be able to appreciate the depth of her anguish, and that his coldness if the matter were mentioned would make her hate him and therefore she hid from him everything concerning her son.

Having spent all that day at the hotel considering how she might see her son, she resolved to write to her husband. She had already composed the letter when she received Lydia Ivanovna's reply. The Countess's silence had made her feel humble, but the letter and what she read between its lines so irritated her, its malevolence seemed so revolting when compared with her passionate and legitimate love for her son, that she became indignant with others and ceased to blame herself. There and then she resolved that next day, Serezha's birthday, she would go straight to her husband's house, and would bribe the servants or deceive them, but would at any cost see her son. She drove to a toyshop, and purchased a lot of toys.

Next morning Anna went alone, and at eight o'clock got out of the hired carriage and rang the bell at the front door of the house which used to be her home.

'Go and see what it is. It's some lady,' said Kapitonich, who was not yet dressed, and in overcoat and galoshes peeped from the window at the veiled lady standing close to the door. His assistant, a lad whom Anna did not know, had hardly opened the door when she entered, and taking a three-rouble note from her muff hastily thrust it into his hand.

'Serezha ... Sergey Alexeyich!' she said, and walked on. After examining the note the porter's assistant stopped her at the inner glass door.

'Whom do you want?' he asked.

She did not hear his words, and made no reply.

Noticing the stranger's confusion, Kapitonich himself came out, admitted her, and inquired what she wanted.

'I come from Prince Skorodumov to see Sergey Alexeyich.'

'He is not up yet,' said the hall-porter, carefully scrutinizing her face.

Anna had not foreseen at all that the totally unaltered appearance of the hall of the house where she had lived for nine years would so deeply affect her. One memory after another, both joyful and painful, rose in her mind, and for a moment she forgot why she had come.

'Would you like to wait?' said Kapitonich, helping her off with her cloak.

Having done so he glanced again at her face and, recognizing her, silently bowed low.

'Come in, your Excellency,' he said.

She wished to speak, but her voice refused to utter a sound; with a look of guilty entreaty at the old man she went with light steps up the stairs. Bending forward and catching the steps with his galoshes, Kapitonich ran after her, trying to overtake her.

'The tutor may be there and not yet dressed. I will announce you.'

Anna continued to ascend the familiar steps without understanding what the old man was saying.

'This way, please! To the left! He has been moved to the old sitting-room now,' said the hall-porter, panting. 'Allow me! Please wait a little, your Excellency. I'll just look in,' he said, having overtaken her. He opened a big door and vanished behind it. 'He's only just woken up,' said the porter when he came out again.

Just as he spoke Anna recognized her son by the sound of the yawn and pictured him vividly before her.

'Let me in, let me in!' she cried, and entered at the big door. To the right of the door stood a bed on which sat the boy, his nightshirt unbuttoned, bending his little body backward, stretching himself and finishing his yawn.

'Serezha!' she whispered, drawing nearer with inaudible steps. 'Serezha, my dear little boy!' she uttered, catching her breath.

'Mama!' he muttered, leaning against her and enveloping her in that sweet scent of sleepiness and warmth which only children possess, and began rubbing himself against her neck and shoulder.

'I knew!' he said, opening his eyes. 'To-day is my birthday. I knew you would come! I'll get up directly …'

Anna watched him with greedy eyes. She noticed how he had grown and changed during her absence. She recognized and yet did not quite recognize his bare legs, now so big, which he had freed from the blanket, and his cheeks, now grown thinner, and the short locks of hair at the back of his head, where she had so often kissed him. She touched it all, and could not speak: tears were choking her.

'What are you crying about, Mama?' he asked, now quite awake.

'Mama, what are you crying about?' he exclaimed in a fretful voice.

'I won't cry. … I am crying for joy! It is so long since I saw you. I won't, I won't,' she said, swallowing her tears and turning away. 'But it's time for you to get dressed,' she said after a pause when she had recovered; and without releasing his hands she sat down by his bed on a chair on which his clothes were lying ready.

'Mama! Dearest, darling!' he shouted, again throwing himself upon her, and embracing her.

'You don't want that,' he said, taking off her bonnet; and on seeing her without it, he began kissing her again as though he had only just seen her.

'Well, and what did you think about me? You did not think I was dead?'

'I never believed it!'

'You didn't believe it, my darling?'

'I knew! I knew!' he cried, and seizing her hand he pressed her palm to his mouth, covering it with kisses.

Vasily Lukich, who had not at first understood who the lady was, having realized from what he heard that she was the mother who had left her husband, hesitated whether to go in or not, or whether to tell Karenin. Having at last concluded that his duty was to get Serezha up at the appointed time, he dressed, went up to the door, and opened it.

But the caresses of the mother and son, the sound of their voices and what they were saying, made him change his mind.

He shook his head, sighed, and closed the door again. 'I will wait another ten minutes,' he said to himself, wiping away his tears.

Meanwhile among the servants there was great commotion. They all knew that the mistress had come, that Kapitonich had admitted her, and that she was now in the nursery. But the master always went to the nursery before nine, and they all understood that a meeting between him and his wife must be prevented. Korney, the valet, went down into the hall-porter's room to inquire who had let her in, and hearing that it was Kapitonich who had done so, he reprimanded the old man. The hall-porter remaining obstinately silent, he turned to the nurse who had just entered. 'Now, judge for yourself, Mary Efimovna,' he said to her. 'He's let her in without telling anybody; and Alexis Alexandrovich will be ready in a minute and will go to the nursery.'

'Dear! Dear! What a business!' said the nurse. 'You must detain him somehow, Korney Vasilich—the master, I mean! And I'll run and get her out of the way. What a business!'

When the nurse entered, Serezha was just telling his mother how he and Nadenka fell down together when ice-hilling, and turned three somersaults. She was listening to the sound of his voice, saw his face and the play of his features, felt his hands, but did not understand what he was saying. She must go away, must leave him—that was all she thought and felt.

'Madam, dear!' the nurse began, coming up to Anna and kissing her hands and shoulders. 'What joy God has sent our little one on his birthday! And you have not changed at all.'

'Oh, nurse dear, I did not know you were in the house,' said Anna, rousing herself for a moment.

'I don't live here; I live with my daughter, and have only come to wish him many happy returns, Anna Arkadyevna, dear!'

Suddenly the nurse burst into tears and again began to kiss Anna's hand. Serezha, with bright eyes and beaming smile, holding his mother with one hand and his nurse with the other, jumped with his bare feet on to the carpet. The tenderness of his beloved nurse for his mother sent him into raptures.

'Mama! She often comes to see me, and when she comes ...' he began, but stopped, noticing that his nurse was whispering something in his mother's ear, and that a look of fear and of something like shame, that did not at all suit her face, appeared there.

She came up to him and said, 'My darling!'

She could not say *good-bye*, but the expression of her face said it and he understood. 'Darling, darling Kutik!' she said, calling him by the pet name she used when he was quite little, 'you won't forget me? You ...' but she could say no more.

Serezha pressed against her in silence and then whispered:

'Don't go—he is not coming yet!'

His mother moved him away from her, to see whether he really believed what he was saying; and in the frightened look on his face she saw not only that he was speaking about his father, but that he was, as it were, asking her what he ought to think of him.

'Serezha, my darling!' she said, 'love him! He is better and kinder than I am, and I am to blame toward him. When you are grown up you will be able to judge.'

'There is nobody better than you! ...' he cried out in desperation through his tears, and seizing her by her shoulders he hugged her with all his might, his arms trembling with the effort.

'Darling little one!' said Anna, and began to cry in the same weak and childlike way as he.

At that moment the door opened and Vasily Lukich entered.

Steps were heard approaching the other door, and the nurse said in a frightened whisper, 'Coming! …' and handed Anna her bonnet.

Serezha sank down on his bed and began to sob, hiding his face in his hands. Anna moved the hands away, kissed him again on his wet face, and went rapidly out. Karenin was advancing toward her. When he saw her, he stopped and bowed his head.

Despite what she had just said,—that he was better and kinder than she was—after casting at him a rapid glance which took in his whole figure to the minutest detail, she was seized by a feeling of loathing and anger toward him and of jealousy for her son. She swiftly let down her veil and with quickened steps almost ran out of the room.

19

Greatly as Anna had desired to see her son, and long as she had thought of and prepared herself for the interview, she had not at all expected that it would affect her so powerfully. On returning to her lonely suite in the hotel she could not for a long time understand why she was there.

The French maid, whom she had brought from abroad, came and asked whether she would not dress. She looked at her in astonishment and replied, 'Later.' A waiter offered her coffee. 'Later,' she said.

The Italian nurse, having smartened up the baby girl, came in and held her out to Anna. The plump, well-nourished baby, as usual when she saw her mother, turned her little hands palms downward and, smiling with her toothless mouth, began waving them as a fish moves its fins, making the starched folds of her embroidered frock rustle. It was impossible not to smile, not to kiss the little thing. Anna did all these things. She took her in her arms, dandled her, and kissed her fresh cheek and bare elbows; but, at the sight of this child, she realized still more clearly that what she felt for her could not even be called love in comparison with her feeling for Serezha. Everything about this baby was sweet, but for some reason she did not grip the heart. Upon the first child, though by an unloved man, all Anna's unsatisfied capacity for loving was lavished; but the girl was born under most trying conditions and had not received a hundredth part of the care given to the first child. Besides, everything about the baby was still prospective, while Serezha was already an individual and a beloved one; thoughts and feelings struggling in his mind; he understood and loved and judged her, she thought, recalling his words and looks. And from him she was for ever sundered, not only physically but spiritually, and there was no remedy for it.

She returned the baby to its nurse, sent them away, and opened a locket with Serezha's portrait as a baby about the same age as the little girl. Rising, she took from the table an album in which were photographs of her son at different ages. She wanted to compare these likenesses and began drawing them out of the album. She took them all out but one, the last and best of the photographs. He was there in a white shirt, astride a chair, his brows frowning while his mouth smiled. This was his most characteristic and best expression. She caught hold of a corner of this photo several times but she could not get the picture out. There was no knife on the table, and she drew out the photo next to it (one, taken in Rome, of Vronsky with long hair and wearing a round hat), and with it pushed out her son's photo. 'Yes, there he is!' she said with a glance at Vronsky's likeness, and suddenly remembered that he was the cause of her present grief. She had not called him to mind all that morning; but now, having caught sight of that manly, noble face, so familiar and dear to her, she felt an unexpected flow of love toward him.

'But where is he? How can he leave me alone in my anguish?' she suddenly thought with a sense of reproach, forgetting that she herself had hidden from him all that concerned her son. She sent to ask him to come up to her at once. She awaited him, thinking with a sinking heart of the words in which she would tell him everything and of the expressions of his love which would comfort her. The servant returned with the reply that he had a visitor, but would come up at once, and wished to know whether he might bring with him Prince Yashvin, who had just arrived in Petersburg. 'So he won't come alone,' she thought, 'he won't come so that I can tell him everything, but will bring Yashvin ...' And suddenly a strange idea crossed her mind: what if he had ceased to love her?

Going over in her mind the events of the last few days, she thought she perceived in everything a confirmation of that dreadful thought: in the fact that he had not dined at home the day before, and that he had insisted on having separate apartments while in Petersburg, and that even now he was not coming alone, perhaps to avoid a tête-à-tête with her.

'But he must tell me. I must know it! If I know it, then I know what I shall do,' she told herself, powerless to imagine the position she would find herself in when she was convinced of his indifference. She rang for her maid, and going into the dressing-room paid more attention to her toilet than she had done all these days, as if, having ceased to love her, his love might be recalled by her wearing the dress and having her hair done in the style most becoming to her.

She heard the bell before she was ready. When she entered the drawing-room not his eyes but Yashvin's met hers. Vronsky was examining her son's photos, which she had forgotten on the table, and did not hurry to look at her.

'We are acquainted,' she said, placing her little hand in the enormous hand of the embarrassed Yashvin, whose confusion did not seem to accord with his huge figure and rough face. 'We have been acquainted since last year's races. ... Let me have them,' she added, with a rapid movement taking from Vronsky the photos he was looking at, and glancing at him impressively with glistening eyes.

After a short talk, noticing that Vronsky looked at the clock, Yashvin asked her whether she would be staying long in Petersburg, and straightening his immense body picked up his cap.

'Not long, I think,' she replied with embarrassment, glancing at Vronsky.

'Then we shall not meet again?' said Yashvin, rising; and then turning to Vronsky he asked, 'Where are you dining?'

'Come and dine with me,' said Anna resolutely, as if vexed with herself for her embarrassment, yet blushing as she always did when she revealed her position to a fresh person. 'Of all his regimental friends Alexis liked you best.'

'I shall be very pleased,' said Yashvin, with a smile which showed Vronsky that he liked Anna very much.

Yashvin bowed and went out. Vronsky remained behind.

'You are going too?' she asked.

'I am late as it is,' he answered. 'Go on! I shall catch you up in a minute!' he shouted to Yashvin.

She took his hand and looked fixedly at him, trying to think of something to say to prevent his leaving her.

'Wait—I have something to tell you,' she said, and raising his short hand she pressed it to her neck. 'Was it wrong of me to ask him to dinner?'

'You have done very well,' he replied, kissing her hand.

'Alexis, you have not changed toward me?' she asked. 'Alexis, I am in torment here! When are we going?'

'Soon, very soon! You would hardly believe how trying our life here is to me too,' he said, drawing away his hand.

20

When Vronsky returned Anna had not yet come home. He was told that, soon after he left, a lady came to see her and they went away together. Her departure without mentioning where she was going, her prolonged absence, and the fact that she had been away somewhere in the morning without telling him about it, added to her strangely excited look that morning, and the animosity with which in Yashvin's presence she had almost snatched her son's photographs out of his hands, made Vronsky reflect. He decided that it was necessary to have an explanation from her, and he waited for her in the drawing-room. But Anna did not return alone; she brought with her her old maiden aunt, Princess Oblonskaya. She it was who had been to see Anna that morning, and they had been shopping together. Anna seemed not to notice the worried look of inquiry on Vronsky's face, but chattered gaily about what she had been buying. He saw that something unusual was taking place within her: her eyes glittered with an expression of strained attention when her look rested on him, and in her speech and motions there was that nervous quickness and grace which, during the first period of their intimacy, had so captivated him, but which now troubled and alarmed him.

The table was laid for four. They were all assembled and about to enter the little dining-room, when Tushkevich arrived with a message for Anna from the Princess Betsy. The Princess asked to be excused for not coming to say good-bye; she was not well, but asked Anna to come and see her between half-past six and nine. Vronsky glanced at Anna when that definite time was mentioned, which showed that care had been taken to prevent her meeting anyone there; but Anna did not seem to observe it.

'I'm sorry that between half-past six and nine is just the time when I cannot come,' she replied with a faint smile.

'The Princess will be very sorry.'

'And I too.'

'I expect you are going to hear Patti?' asked Tushkevich.

'Patti? That's an idea! I would go if I could get a box.'

'I could get you one,' said Tushkevich.

'I should be very, very grateful if you would!' replied Anna. 'But won't you stay and dine with us?'

Vronsky slightly shrugged his shoulders. He could not in the least understand what Anna was after. Why had she brought the old Princess, why had she asked Tushkevich to stay to dinner, and, strangest of all, why was she sending him to get her a box for the opera? Was it conceivable that, in her position, she was going to the opera when Patti was to sing, and when her Society acquaintances would be present? He looked seriously at her, but she answered him with the same provocative glance of high spirits or desperation, the meaning of which he could not make out. At dinner Anna was aggressively merry, seeming to flirt with both Tushkevich and Yashvin. After dinner Tushkevich went to get a box and Yashvin to have a smoke. Vronsky went with Yashvin down to his own rooms, but after sitting with him a while, ran upstairs again. Anna was already dressed in a light silk dress cut low in front and trimmed with velvet—a dress she had had made in Paris; and on her head she wore some rich, white lace, which outlined her face and set off her brilliant beauty to great advantage.

'You are really going to the theatre?' said he, trying not to look at her.

'Why do you ask in such a frightened way?' she said, again offended because he did not look at her. 'Why should I not go?'

'Anna! For heaven's sake, what has come to you?' he said. 'You know it is out of the question for you to go.'

'Why? I am not going alone! The Princess Barbara has gone to dress, and is coming with me.'

He shrugged his shoulders with a bewildered and despairing look.

'But don't you know ...?' he began.

'I don't want to know!' she almost screamed. 'I don't! Do I repent of what I have done? No! No! No! If it had to begin again from the beginning I should do just the same. For us, for you and me, only one thing is important: whether we love each other. No other considerations exist. Why do we live here, separated and not seeing one another? Why can't I go? I love you, and it's all the same to me,' she said, while her eyes as she looked at him glittered with a light he could not understand, 'so long as you have not changed toward me! Why don't you look at me?'

He looked at her. He saw all the beauty of her face and of her dress, which suited her as her dresses always did. But now it was just this beauty and elegance that irritated him.

'My feelings cannot change, you know that; but I beg you not to go! I entreat you!' he said, speaking French with tender entreaty in his voice but with a cold look in his eyes.

She did not hear his words, but saw the coldness of his look, and replied irritably:

'And I beg you will explain why I should not go.'

'Because it might cause you ...' He became confused. For the first time he felt vexed and almost angry with Anna for her unwillingness to realize her position. 'But how can she fail to understand it? And what is happening to her?' he asked himself. He felt that his regard for her had diminished and his consciousness of her beauty increased simultaneously.

He went down frowning to his rooms, and taking a seat beside Yashvin, who sat with his long legs stretched out on a chair drinking brandy and seltzer, ordered the same for himself.

'Anna Arkadyevna sent me to say that she has gone to the theatre,' said a servant.

Yashvin emptied another glass of brandy into the sparkling water, drank it, and then rose, buttoning his coat.

'Well, let us go,' he said, smiling slightly under cover of his big moustache, and showing by that smile that he understood the cause of Vronsky's depression, but did not attach importance to it.

'I'm not going,' said Vronsky dismally.

'Well, I have got to, I promised. Then *au revoir*! But why not come to the stalls? Take Krasinsky's place,' Yashvin added as he went out.

'No, I have something to do.'

'With a wife one has trouble, but with one who is not a wife it's worse,' thought Yashvin as he left the hotel.

Vronsky entered the theatre at half-past eight. The act had just finished when he entered the auditorium, so before going to his brother's box he went up to the front row and paused beside Serpukhovskoy, who had noticed Vronsky afar off and welcomed him with a smile.

Vronsky had not yet seen Anna, he intentionally avoided looking her way; but from the direction in which people were looking he knew where she was. He glanced around unobtrusively, but did not look at her: prepared for the worst, he looked for Karenin. Luckily for him, Karenin was not in the theatre that evening.

'How little of the military man is left in you!' remarked Serpukhovskoy. 'You might be a diplomatist, an artist, or anything of that kind.'

'Yes, as soon as I returned home I put on a black coat,' Vronsky replied with a smile, slowly taking out his opera-glasses.

'Now in that, I confess, I envy you! I, when I come back from abroad and put this on again, regret my freedom,' he said, touching his shoulder-knot.

Serpukhovskoy had long ago ceased to trouble himself about Vronsky's career, but was as fond of him as ever and was particularly amiable to him now.

'A pity you were late for the first act!'

Vronsky, listening with one ear, levelled his glasses first at the lower tier and then at the boxes in the dress circle, taking them all in review. Anna was in the fifth box in the lower tier, some twenty paces from him. She sat in the front of the box and, slightly turning back, was saying something to Yashvin. The poise of her head on her fine broad shoulders reminded him precisely of how he had seen her at the ball in Moscow. But her beauty affected him very differently now. There was no longer anything mysterious in his feelings for her, and therefore though her beauty attracted him even more strongly, it also offended him. She was not looking his way, but he felt that she had already seen him.

When Vronsky directed his glasses that way again he noticed that the Princess Barbara was very red, and that she was laughing unnaturally and looking round incessantly at the next box, while Anna, tapping with her closed fan the red-velvet edge of the box, was gazing fixedly, somewhere else, not seeing, and evidently not wishing to see, what was taking place in the next box. Yashvin's face wore the expression it had when he was losing at cards. He was frowning and drawing the left side of his moustache further and further into his mouth, looking askance at the adjoining box.

In that box to the left were the Kartasovs. Vronsky knew them and knew that Anna had been acquainted with them. The wife, a thin little woman, was standing up in her box with her back to Anna, putting on an opera-cloak which her husband was holding for her. Her face looked pale and angry and she was speaking excitedly. Kartasov, a stout bald-headed man, kept glancing round at Anna while trying to pacify his wife. When the wife left the box the husband loitered behind, trying to catch Anna's eye and evidently wishing to bow to her. But Anna, with obvious intention, took no notice of him and, turning round, was saying something to Yashvin, whose cropped head was bent toward her. Kartasov went out without bowing and the box remained empty.

Vronsky could not make out what had taken place between the Kartasovs and Anna, but he saw that it was something humiliating for Anna. He realized that from what he had seen, and especially from Anna's face, who, he knew, was summoning her utmost strength to sustain the rôle she had undertaken. She fully succeeded in playing that rôle—of external tranquillity.

Knowing that something had happened, but not knowing just what, Vronsky felt painfully agitated, and, hoping to find out something, set out for his brother's box.

In the box was Vronsky's mother, the old Countess, with her iron-grey curls. Varya and the Princess Sorokina he met in the corridor outside.

Having conducted the Princess Sorokina back to Vronsky's mother, Varya held out her hand to her brother-in-law and at once began to talk of the matter that interested him.

'I consider it mean and disgusting, and Madame Kartasova had no right to do it! Madame Karenina ...' she began.

'But what is it? I don't know.'

'My husband told me. ... She insulted Madame Karenina. Her husband began conversing with her from his box, and Kartasova flew at him! It seems she said something insulting out loud, and then went out.'

'Count, your *maman* wants you,' said the Princess Sorokina, looking out of the box door.

'I have been expecting you all the time,' said his mother with a sarcastic smile. 'I never see anything of you.'

Her son saw that she could not repress a smile of satisfaction.

'Good evening, *Maman*! I was coming to you,' he replied coldly.

'Why don't you go *faire la cour à*[1] *Madame Karenine*?' she added, when the Princess Sorokina had stepped aside. '*Elle fait sensation. On oublie la Patti pour elle!*[2]

'*Maman*! I asked you not to speak to me about that subject,' he answered frowning.

'I am saying what every one says.'

Vronsky did not reply, and after a few words addressed to the Princess Sorokina he left the box. In the doorway he met his brother.

'Ah, Alexis!' said his brother. 'What a shame! That woman is a fool, that's all. ... I was just going to see her! Let's go together.'

Vronsky did not listen to him. He hurried downstairs feeling that he must do something, he knew not what. He was disturbed both by vexation with Anna for placing herself and him in this false position, and by pity for her sufferings. He descended to the stalls, went straight to Anna's box, and bowed to her.

'I think you got here late and missed the finest *aria*,' said Anna to him, with a mocking glance as it seemed to him.

'I am a poor judge,' he replied, looking severely at her.

'Like Prince Yashvin, who considers that Patti sings too loud,' she returned with a smile.

'Thank you!' she said, taking with her small gloved hand a programme Vronsky had picked up for her; and suddenly at that instant her beautiful face quivered.

---

[1] Pay court to.
[2] She is making a sensation. They are forgetting Patti because of her.

Noticing that during the next act her box remained empty, Vronsky left the theatre. He went to his hotel.

Anna had already returned. When Vronsky entered she was still dressed as she had been at the theatre. She was sitting in the first arm-chair by the wall, fixedly gazing before her. She glanced at him and immediately resumed her former posture.

'Anna!' he said.

'It's all your fault! Your fault!' she exclaimed with tears of despair and spite in her voice, and rose.

'But I asked, I entreated you not to go!—I knew it would be unpleasant for you!'

'Unpleasant!' she cried. 'It was awful! However long I may live I shall never forget it! She said it was a disgrace to sit near me.'

'The words of a silly woman,' he said. 'But why risk it? Why provoke? …'

'I hate your calmness! You should not have driven me to it. If you loved me …'

'Anna! Is it a question of my love? …'

'Yes! If you loved me as I love you, if you suffered the anguish I do …' she replied with a frightened glance at him.

He was sorry for her and yet vexed with her. He assured her of his love, because he saw that that alone could pacify her now, and did not reproach her with words, though he reproached her in his heart.

And those assurances of love, which to him appeared so trivial that he felt ashamed to utter them, she drank in, and gradually became calm. Next day, fully reconciled, they left for the country.

PART SIX

1

Dolly and her children were spending the summer with her sister Kitty at Pokrovsk. Oblonsky quite approved of this arrangement. He said he greatly regretted that his duties prevented his spending the summer with his family in the country; and he remained in Moscow, visiting the country occasionally for a day or two at a time. Beside the Oblonskys with all their children and their governess, the Levins had other visitors—the old Princess, who considered it her duty to watch over her inexperienced daughter *in that condition*; and also Varenka, Kitty's friend from abroad, who was keeping her promise to visit her friend now that she was married. All these were relations and friends of Kitty's, and, though Levin liked them, he regretted his own—the Levin—world and order of things, which was being submerged. Only one of his relatives, Sergius Ivanich, visited him that summer—and he was a man of the Koznyshev type and not a Levin.

In the Levin house, so long empty, there were now so many people that nearly every room was occupied, and Kitty, who conducted her household with great assiduity, had no little trouble to procure all the chickens, turkeys, and ducks which were required.

The whole family was assembled at dinner. Dolly's children, their governess, and Varenka were planning where they should hunt for mushrooms; Koznyshev, who by his intellect and learning commanded a respect almost amounting to veneration from all the visitors, surprised every one by joining in the conversation about mushrooms.

'You must take me too! I am very fond of looking for mushrooms,' he said with a glance at Varenka.

'Why, certainly! We shall be very pleased,' replied Varenka with a blush. Kitty and Dolly exchanged significant looks.

After dinner Koznyshev sat down by the drawing-room window, continuing his conversation with his brother over a cup of coffee and glancing now and then at the door through which the children, who were preparing to set out on the mushroom hunt, would enter. Levin sat down on the window-sill beside his brother.

Kitty stood near her husband, evidently waiting for the end of the conversation—which did not interest her—before speaking to him.

'In many ways you have changed since your marriage, and for the better,' said Koznyshev, smiling at Kitty and apparently not much interested in his conversation with his brother; 'but you have remained true to your passion for defending the most paradoxical views.'

'Kate, it is not good for you to be standing,' said her husband, with a meaning look, moving a chair toward her.

The children came running in. In advance of them all came Tanya, running toward Koznyshev, flourishing a basket and his hat.

'Varenka is waiting,' she said, carefully placing his hat on his head when she saw from his smile that she had permission to do so.

Varenka, who was wearing a yellow print dress and a white kerchief on her head, stood in the doorway.

'I'm coming, Mlle Varenka,' said Koznyshev, drinking up his coffee and pocketing his handkerchief and cigar-case.

'What a darling my Varenka is, eh?' Kitty said to her husband as soon as Koznyshev had risen. She said it so that the latter could hear, with an evident desire that he should do so. 'And how handsome, how nobly handsome! … Varenka!' she exclaimed. 'You will be in the wood by the mill? We will drive there.'

'You quite forget your condition, Kitty,' said the old Princess, hurrying in. 'You should not shout so.'

Varenka, hearing Kitty's voice and her mother reprimanding her, came up with her light step. The quickness of Varenka's movements, the colour suffusing her animated face, all showed that something unusual was taking place within her. Kitty had called Varenka only to give her a silent blessing for the important event which, according to Kitty, was to happen in the woods.

'Varenka, I shall be very happy if a certain thing comes to pass,' she whispered, kissing her.

'And are you coming with us?' Varenka, quite confused, asked Levin, pretending not to have heard what had been said to her.

'I will come, but only as far as the threshing-floor. I must look at the new waggons, and count them,' said Levin.

2

All the women of the household were assembled on the balcony. They always liked to sit there after dinner, but to-day they had special business there. To-day jam was being made there without the addition of water to the fruit. Kitty was introducing this new way, which had been employed in her old home; but Agatha Mikhaylovna, to whom this work had formerly been entrusted, and who considered that nothing that used to be done in the Levin house could be wrong, had, despite her directions, put water to the strawberry jam, declaring it to be indispensable. She had been detected doing this, and now the raspberry jam was being made in every one's presence, as Agatha Mikhaylovna had to be convinced that without water the jam could turn out well.

Agatha Mikhaylovna, with a flushed face and aggrieved expression, was shaking the preserving pan over the brazier with a circular movement, looking dismally at the raspberries and hoping with all her heart that they would set and not get cooked through.

'*A propos de* Varenka,' said Kitty in French, which they had been talking all the time so that Agatha Mikhaylovna should not understand them. 'Do you know, Mama, I am somehow expecting it to be settled to-day! How nice it would be!'

'Dear me! What a skilful matchmaker!' teased Dolly. 'How carefully and adroitly she brings them together!'

'Come, Mama! Tell me what you think about it?'

'What am I to think? He' (*he* meant Koznyshev) 'could have made the best match in Russia any time; now he is no longer so young, but all the same I am sure many would marry him even now ...'

And the three women meditated silently on the same subject. Kitty was the first to break the silence.

'There's one thing ... that old love-affair of Varenka's,' she said, 'I wished to tell Koznyshev somehow, to prepare him. Men, all of them, are terribly jealous of our pasts.'

'Not all,' said Dolly. 'You judge by your own husband. He is still tormented by the memory of Vronsky. Eh? Am I not right?'

'You are,' answered Kitty, her eyes smiling dreamily.

'How happily it turned out for you that Anna came,' said Dolly, 'and how unhappily for her! The exact reverse,' she added, struck by her thought. 'Then Anna was so happy and Kitty considered herself miserable. Now it's the exact reverse! I often think of her.'

'She's not worth thinking about! A horrid, disgusting woman without a heart,' said their mother, unable to forget that Kitty had not married Vronsky but Levin.

'What is the use of talking about that?' expostulated Kitty with vexation, listening to her husband coming up the balcony steps. 'I don't want to think about it.'

'About what don't you want to think?' he asked as he came up.

No one answered and he did not repeat the question.

'I am sorry I have intruded into your women's domain,' he said.

For an instant he felt that he shared Agatha Mikhaylovna's dissatisfaction that the jam was boiled without water, and with the alien Shcherbatsky influence. He smiled, however, and went up to Kitty.

'Well?' he asked.

'Quite all right,' replied Kitty with a smile. 'And your affairs?'

'The waggons'll hold three times as much as peasant carts. Shall we go and fetch the children? I have ordered the trap.'

'What? Are you going to take Kitty in the trap?' said her mother reproachfully.

'Only at a walking pace, Princess.'

'Well, then I'll go on foot! Walking is good for me,' and Kitty rose, went to her husband and took his arm.

'Well, Agatha Mikhaylovna, is the jam done?' asked Levin, smiling and wishing to cheer her up. 'Has it turned out well the new way?'

'I suppose. We'd have thought it overdone.'

'It's better so, Agatha Mikhaylovna: it won't ferment,' said Kitty, immediately seeing her husband's intention and addressing the old woman in the same spirit. 'On the other hand, your pickling is such that Mama says she never tasted anything like it!' she added, smiling and putting the old woman's kerchief straight.

Agatha Mikhaylovna looked crossly at Kitty.

'You need not comfort me, ma'am! I just look at you and *him*, and then I feel happy,' she said, and that disrespectful way of speaking of her master as *him* seemed touching to Kitty.

'Come with us and get mushrooms! You will show us the right places.'

Agatha Mikhaylovna smiled and shook her head, as much as to say: 'Though I should like to be cross with you, I can't do it.'

3

Kitty was glad of the opportunity of being alone with her husband, for she had noticed the shadow of pain that flitted over his face, which so vividly reflected all his emotions, when he came on the balcony, asked what they were talking about and received no reply.

He had already forgotten that momentarily unpleasant impression, and being alone with her experienced, now that the thought of her pregnancy never left him, a feeling still novel and joyful to him of pleasure, entirely free from sensuality, at the nearness of a beloved woman.

'You're sure you won't be tired? Lean more on me,' he said.

'No. I am so glad of a chance to be alone with you; and I own that, nice as it is to have them all, I miss our evenings alone together.'

'They were pleasant, but this is still better. ... Both are better,' he said, pressing her hand.

'Do you know what we were talking about when you came in?'

'About the jam?'

'Yes, about jam, and then ... about Sergius and Varenka. Did you notice? ... I want it so much,' she went on. 'What do you think about it?' and she looked into his face.

'I don't know what to think,' Levin replied with a smile. 'Sergius seems very strange to me in that regard. He is a peculiar, a wonderful man, but he is so used to living a purely spiritual life that he cannot reconcile himself to realities, and, after all, Varenka is a reality!'

Levin had become accustomed to express his thoughts boldly, without troubling to put them into precise phraseology; he knew that at such loving moments as the present his wife would understand what he meant from a mere hint, and she did understand him.

'Yes, but in her there is not so much of that reality as there is in me; I know he would never have loved me. She is all spirit.'

'Oh no! He is very fond of you, and it is always such a pleasure to me when my people are fond of you.'

'Yes, he is kind to me, but ...'

'But it's not like poor Nicholas. ... You would have loved one another,' said Levin, finishing her sentence for her. 'Why not speak of him?' he added. 'Sometimes I blame myself for not doing so; it will end by my forgetting him. Oh, what a dreadful, what a charming man he was! ... Yes, what were we talking about?' he concluded after a pause.

'You think he can't fall in love, then?' said Kitty.

'Not exactly that he can't fall in love,' Levin answered with a smile, 'but he has none of that weakness which is necessary ... I always envied him, and even now, when I am so happy, I still envy him.'

'You envy him because he can't fall in love?'

'I envy him because he is better than I am,' replied he, smiling. 'I am happy, but dissatisfied with myself ...'.

'How can you be dissatisfied if you are happy?'

'I mean ... How shall I put it? ... In my heart I wish for nothing more, except that you shouldn't stumble. Oh dear! How can you jump so!' he said, interrupting the conversation to rebuke her for making too quick a movement while stepping over a branch that lay across the path. 'But when I examine myself and compare myself with others, especially with my brother, I feel how bad I am.'

'In what way?' asked she, still smiling. 'What about your small holdings, your farming, and your book?'

'No. I feel it now more than ever—and it is your fault,' he answered, pressing her arm, 'that it's not the right thing. I do it, but it is superficial. If I could love all that work as I love you ... but of late I have been doing it like a task set me ...'

'Well then, what do you say to Papa?' asked Kitty. 'Is he bad too, because he does nothing for the common good?'

'He? Oh no! But one must have your father's simplicity, clearness, and kindness, and have I got all that? I don't act and I worry. It's you who have done it. Before you were there, and *that*,' he said with a glance at her figure, which she understood, 'I put all my strength into my work; but now I can't and I feel ashamed. I pretend ...'

'Then would you now like to change places with Sergius Ivanich?' asked Kitty. 'Would you prefer to do that public work, and love that given task as he does, and nothing more?'

'Of course not!' replied Levin. 'However, I am so happy that I don't understand anything. ... So you think he will propose to-day?' he added after a pause.

'I do, and I don't. But I want him to, awfully! Wait, we'll see. And here's the trap overtaking us,' said Levin.

'Aren't you tired, Kitty?' the Princess called out.

'Not at all.'

'If so you'd better get in, if the horses go at a walking pace.'

But it was not worth while to drive as they had nearly reached the place, and so they all went on foot.

4

Varenka with the white kerchief over her black hair, surrounded by the children and good-naturedly and cheerfully busy with them, and evidently excited by the possibility of an offer of marriage from a man she liked, looked very attractive. Koznyshev walked by her side and did not cease admiring her. Looking at her he remembered all the charming things he had heard her say, and all he knew of her that was good, and he grew more and more conscious that what he felt for her was something rare, something he had felt but once before, a long, long time ago, when he was very young. His sense of pleasure at her nearness went on increasing until it reached a point where, when placing in her basket an enormous wood mushroom with a thin stem and up-curling top, he looked into her eyes and, noting the flush of joyful and frightened agitation that suffused her face, he himself became embarrassed.

'If it is so, I must think it over and come to a decision, and not let myself be carried away by the impulse of the moment,' he told himself.

'Now I will go and gather mushrooms quite on my own account, or else my harvest will not be noticeable,' said he, and went away and penetrated deeper into the wood. When he had gone some forty paces he stepped behind a spindle bush with pink and red earring-shaped blossoms, and paused, knowing that he could no longer be seen. Around him everything was quiet. Only the hum of flies sounded continually high up in the birch trees beneath which he stood, and occasionally the children's voices reached him. Suddenly, from the skirts of the wood not far off, he heard Varenka's contralto voice calling to Grisha, and a smile of pleasure lit up his face. Conscious of that smile, Koznyshev shook his head disapprovingly at his own state and took out a cigar. Watching the sheet of smoke, he went on slowly, meditating on his condition of mind.

'Why not?' he thought. 'The one thing I can find against it is that when I lost Marie I told myself that I would remain true to her memory. That is the only thing I can say against my feeling. ... That is important,' thought Koznyshev, conscious nevertheless that this consideration could not have any importance for him personally, although in the eyes of others it might spoil his poetic rôle. 'But, apart from that, however much I searched I could find nothing to say against my feeling. If I had chosen by reason alone, I could find nothing better!'

He recalled the women and girls he had known, but try as he would he could not recall one who united in herself to such a degree all, literally all, the qualities which he, thinking the matter over in cold blood, would desire in a wife. She had all the charm and freshness of youth but was no longer a child, and if she loved him, loved him consciously as a woman ought to love. That was one favourable consideration. The second one was: she was not only far from worldly, but evidently felt a repulsion from the world, yet she knew the world and had all the ways of a woman of good Society, without which a life-companion would be unthinkable for him. The third was: her life was based on religious convictions. Even down to small details Koznyshev found in her all that he desired in a wife: she was poor and solitary, so that she would not bring into her husband's house a crowd of relations and their influence, as he saw Kitty doing. And this girl, uniting all these qualities, loved him. He was modest, but could not help being aware of this. And he loved her. One of the opposite arguments was his age. But he came of a long-lived race, he had not a single grey hair, no one thought he was forty, and what was the use of counting by years, when he felt as young at heart as he had been twenty years ago? Was it not youth that he was experiencing now, when coming out again on the other side of the wood he saw, in the bright slanting sunbeams, the graceful form of Varenka in her yellow dress and with a basket on her arm, stepping lightly past the trunk of an old birch. His heart leapt with joy. He felt that the matter was decided. Varenka, who had bent to pick a mushroom, rose buoyantly and glanced round. Throwing away his cigar Koznyshev went toward her with resolute steps.

On seeing Koznyshev approaching she did not move; yet everything told him that she felt his approach and was glad of it.

'Well, have you found anything?' she asked from beneath her white kerchief, turning her handsome face toward him, with a gentle smile.

'Not one,' said Koznyshev. 'And you?'

She did not reply, being busy with the children.

'There's another, near the branch,' she said. Varenka rose when Masha had picked the mushroom, breaking it into two white pieces. 'It reminds me of my childhood,' she added, moving away from the children with Koznyshev.

They went a few paces in silence. Varenka saw that he wanted to speak, and guessing the subject she grew faint with joy and fear. They had gone far enough not to be overheard, but he still had not begun. It would have been easier after a silence to say what they wished to say than after talking about mushrooms; yet against her will, and as if by accident, she said:

'So you have not found anything? But of course deep in the wood there are always fewer.'

Koznyshev sighed and did not speak. He was vexed that she had spoken about mushrooms. He wished to bring her back to her first remark about her childhood; but without wishing to, after a pause, he replied to her last words:

'I have only heard that the white boleti grow chiefly on the outskirts, but I can't even tell which are the white ones.'

A few more minutes passed; they had gone still further from the children and were quite alone. Varenka's heart beat so that she seemed to hear it, and she felt herself growing red and then pale and red again.

To be the wife of a man like Koznyshev after her difficult life with Madame Stahl seemed to her the height of bliss. Besides, she was almost sure she loved him, and now in a moment it must be decided. She was frightened: frightened of what he might or might not say.

'He must make his declaration now or never'; Koznyshev also felt this. Everything—Varenka's look, her blush, her downcast eyes—betrayed painful expectation. He saw it and was sorry for her. He even felt that to say nothing now would be to offend her. His mind went rapidly over all the arguments in favour of his decision. He repeated to himself the words with which he had intended to propose; but instead of those words some unexpected thought caused him to say:

'What difference is there between the white boleti and the birch-tree variety?'

Varenka's lips trembled with emotion when she replied:

'There is hardly any difference in the tops, but only in the stems.'

And as soon as those words were spoken, both he and she understood that all was over, and that what ought to have been said would not be said, and their excitement began to subside. Varenka felt pained and ashamed, but at the same time she experienced a sense of relief.

Koznyshev when he got home and went again over all his reasons, came to the conclusion that at first he had judged wrongly. He could not be unfaithful to Marie's memory.

'Gently, gently, children!' shouted Levin almost angrily, stepping in front of his wife to shield her, when the crowd of children came rushing at them with shrieks of delight.

Behind the children Koznyshev and Varenka came out of the wood. Kitty had no need to question Varenka: from the calm and rather shamefaced look on both faces she knew that her plan had not been realized.

'Well?' inquired her husband on their way home.

'Won't bite,' answered Kitty with a smile and manner of speaking like her father, which Levin often observed in her with pleasure.

5

During the children's tea the grown-ups sat on the balcony and talked as if nothing had happened, though they all, especially Koznyshev and Varenka, knew very well that something had happened which though negative was highly important. Every one talked with peculiar anima-tion about extraneous topics.

'Take my word for it, Alexander won't come,' said the old Princess.

They were expecting Oblonsky by the evening train, and the old

Prince had written that he would perhaps accompany him.

'And I know why,' continued the Princess. 'He says young married folk should be left to themselves for a while.'

'Yes, Papa has really abandoned us,' said Kitty.

'Only if he doesn't come I too shall say good-bye to you children,' said the Princess with a sorrowful sigh.

'Oh, what an idea, Mama!' rejoined both her daughters.

'Just consider him! Why, at present …' They did not know that pleasant as it was for her to stay with her daughter and necessary as she felt herself to be there, she suffered keenly, both on her own and on her husband's account, since they gave their last and favourite daughter in marriage and the family nest was left empty.

'What is it, Agatha Mikhaylovna?' Kitty asked suddenly when the old woman stopped in front of her with a look of mystery and importance.

'How about supper?'

'Oh, that's just right,' said Dolly. 'You go and give your orders, and I will hear Grisha his lesson. He hasn't done anything to-day.'

'That's a rebuke for me! No, Dolly! I will go,' said Levin who, vexed with Oblonsky for carelessly leaving the boy's mother to look after his lessons which she did not understand, had volunteered himself as tutor. He went off to find Grisha.

'I will see about supper,' Varenka said, and she rose to accompany Agatha Mikhaylovna.

'What a nice girl!' said the Princess.

'Not *nice*, Mama, but so charming that there is no one else like her!'

'So you are expecting Stephen Arkadyevich to-night?' asked Koznyshev, evidently disinclined to join in a conversation about Varenka.

In the midst of their conversation they heard the snorting of horses and the scraping of wheels on the gravel of the avenue.

Dolly had not had time to rise to go to meet her husband, before Levin had jumped out of the window of the room below, where he had been teaching Grisha, and had lifted the boy out too.

'It's Stiva!' called Levin from under the balcony. 'We have finished, Dolly, don't worry!' he added, running to meet the carriage.

'And some one with him. It must be Papa!' shouted Levin, who had stopped at the bend of the avenue. 'Kitty, don't come down those steep steps, go round!'

But Levin was mistaken. When he came nearer he saw, sitting beside Oblonsky, a stout handsome young man wearing a Scotch bonnet with long ribbons streaming behind. It was Vasenka Veslovsky, a second cousin of the Shcherbatskys. 'A most splendid fellow and a passionate sportsman,' as Oblonsky said when he introduced him.

Not at all dismayed by the disappointment he caused by appearing instead of the old Prince, Veslovsky gaily greeted Levin, reminding him that they had met before, and lifting Grisha he caught him up in to the vehicle over the pointer Oblonsky had brought with him.

Levin did not get in, but followed the *calèche*. He was rather vexed that the old Prince, whom he liked more and more the better he knew him, had not come, and vexed because this Vasenka Veslovsky, a quite superfluous stranger, had come. Veslovsky seemed to him still more alien and superfluous when they arrived at the porch and he saw him kissing Kitty's hand with a particularly tender and gallant air.

'We, your wife and I, are cousins and old acquaintances,' said Vasenka Veslovsky, giving Levin's hand a very, very hard squeeze.

'Well, is there any game?' asked Oblonsky of Levin, scarcely giving himself time to say a word of greeting to everybody. 'He and I have the cruellest intentions. ... How much refreshed you are looking, Dolly, dear!' he went on, kissing his wife's hand and holding it in his own while he patted it with the other hand.

Levin, who but a few moments before had been in the brightest of spirits, was now dissatisfied with everything.

'Whom was he kissing yesterday with those same lips?' he thought as he looked at Oblonsky caressing his wife. He looked at Dolly, and was not pleased with her either.

'Of course she does not believe in his love. Then why is she so pleased? Disgusting!' thought he.

He looked at the Princess, who a few moments before had seemed so nice, and did not like the way she welcomed that beribboned Vasenka, as if to her own house.

Even Koznyshev, who had also come out of the porch, displeased Levin by the feigned friendliness with which he greeted Oblonsky, whom, as Levin knew, he neither liked nor respected.

And Varenka too seemed disgusting because of the holy manner in which she made that gentleman's acquaintance, while all her thought was how to get married.

But most repugnant of all was Kitty, for the way she fell in with the gay tone of that gentleman, who appeared to consider his arrival in the country a regular festival for everybody, and particularly objectionable was the smile with which she responded to his smiles.

Talking noisily, they all went into the house, but as soon as all were seated Levin turned and left the room.

6

Levin did not return until they called him to supper. On the stairs stood Kitty and Agatha Mikhaylovna, deliberating what wines to serve.

'But why all this fuss? Serve the same as usual.'

'No, Stiva does not drink it. ... Kostya! Wait a moment—what's the matter with you?' said Kitty, hurrying after him, but, without waiting for her, he went away pitilessly with big strides to the dining-room, where he immediately joined in the general animated conversation which was kept going by Vasenka Veslovsky and Oblonsky.

'Well then, shall we go shooting to-morrow?' Oblonsky inquired.

'Yes! Do let's go!' cried Veslovsky, sitting sideways with one of his fat legs doubled under him.

'I shall be very pleased! And have you had any shooting this year?' Levin asked, gazing intently at this leg but with that pretended politeness of his which Kitty knew so well, and which suited him so ill.

'Dolly dear!' said Oblonsky, stepping across to her side of the long supper-table. 'Do you know, Veslovsky has been to see Anna? And he is going there again. You know it's only some seventy versts off. I shall certainly go over. Veslovsky, come here!'

Vasenka came over to the ladies, and took a seat beside Kitty.

'Oh, do tell me! How is she?' asked Dolly.

Levin remained at the other end of the table, and while not ceasing to talk with the Princess and Varenka, saw that Oblonsky, Dolly, Kitty, and Veslovsky were carrying on an animated and mysterious conversation. Moreover, he saw his wife had an expression of serious feeling as she gazed attentively at Vasenka's handsome face while he was vivaciously narrating something.

'It's very nice at their place,' Vasenka was saying, talking of Vronsky and Anna. 'Of course I do not take it upon myself to judge, but in their house one feels oneself to be in a family.'

'And will you go?' Oblonsky asked his wife.

'I have long wanted to go and certainly shall go,' replied Dolly. 'I shall go alone when you are away, and won't inconvenience anyone.'

'That's all right,' replied he; 'and you, Kitty?'

'I? Why should I go?' said Kitty, flushing deeply and glancing round at her husband.

'Are you acquainted with Anna Arkadyevna?' Veslovsky asked her.

'Yes,' said Kitty, with a still deeper blush, and she rose and went to her husband.

'So you are off shooting to-morrow?' she asked.

Levin's jealousy during those few minutes had gone far, especially after the blush that had suffused her face when speaking to Veslovsky. Now as he listened to her question he interpreted it in his own way. Strange as it seemed to him when he remembered it later, it now appeared clear to him that she asked whether he was going shooting, only because she wanted to know whether he would give that pleasure to Vasenka Veslovsky, with whom he fancied she was already in love.

'Yes, I am going,' he answered in an unnatural voice that was disagreeable to himself.

'No—wait a day, because Dolly has seen nothing of her husband. You could go the day after to-morrow,' said she.

Levin now interpreted her words thus: 'Do not part me from *him*. Your going does not matter to me, but do let me enjoy the society of this charming young man!'

'Oh, if you wish it we will stay at home to-morrow,' replied Levin with particular amiability.

Meanwhile Vasenka rose from the table after Kitty and followed her, smiling pleasantly.

Levin saw that smile. He grew pale and for a moment could hardly breathe. 'How dare he look like that at my wife!' he thought, boiling with rage.

'To-morrow then? Please let's go!' said Vasenka, sitting down and once more doubling his leg under him, as his habit was.

Levin's jealousy rose still higher. Already he fancied himself a deceived husband. ... But nevertheless he asked Vasenka in an amiable and hospitable manner about his shooting, his gun, his boots—and agreed to go shooting next day.

Happily for Levin the old Princess put a stop to his sufferings by herself getting up and advising Kitty to go to bed. But he did not escape a fresh pang. Taking leave of his hostess, Vasenka again wanted to kiss her hand; but Kitty, blushing, drew away her hand, and said with naïve rudeness:

'That's not customary in our house.'

In Levin's eyes Kitty was to blame for having laid herself open to such behaviour, and still more to blame for so awkwardly showing that it displeased her.

After the rest had separated for the night Levin sat frowning, in an easy-chair in his wife's bedroom, meeting her inquiries as to what was the matter with stubborn silence. But when at length she asked with a timid smile: 'Aren't you displeased about something connected with Veslovsky?' he gave vent to his feelings and told her everything.

He stood before her, his eyes glittering terribly under his frowning brows, and pressed his powerful arms to his breast, as if trying with all his might to restrain himself. The expression of his face would have been hard and even cruel, but for a look of suffering which touched her. His jaw trembled and his voice faltered.

'Understand that I am not jealous: that is a vile word! I cannot be jealous nor believe that ... I cannot say what I feel, but it is dreadful. ... I am not jealous, but I am offended and humiliated that anyone dares imagine—dares look at you with such eyes ...'

'What eyes? What can you be thinking of, since men do not exist for me? They don't! They don't! ... Well then, would you like me not to see anybody?'

For the first moment his jealousy had offended her: she was annoyed that the least relaxation, even the most innocent, was forbidden her; but now she would gladly have sacrificed anything to free him from the torments he was suffering.

'Try and understand the horror and absurdity of my position,' he continued in a despairing whisper. 'He is in my house, and strictly speaking he has done nothing improper except by his free and easy manner and doubling up his legs! He considers it to be in the best form, and therefore I have to be polite to him!'

'Come, Kostya, you are exaggerating!' remonstrated Kitty.

'The worst of it all is that you—are as you always are, and now when we are so specially happy—suddenly this good-for-nothing comes along ... Why am I abusing him? He does not concern me. But our happiness, mine and yours ... why ...?'

'Do you know, I see how it happened ...' Kitty began. 'I noticed your look while we were talking at supper.'

'Yes, yes!' said he in a frightened tone.

She told him what they had been talking about, and while she spoke she was breathless with excitement. Levin paused, and then after scrutinizing her pale, frightened features, suddenly clapped his hands to his head.

'Kate, I have been tormenting you! My darling, forgive me! It was madness! Kate, it is all my fault. How could I torture myself like that about such nonsense?'

'Oh no! I am sorry for you.'

'For me? Me? Because I am a madman! But why should I make you

wretched? It is dreadful to think that a mere stranger can destroy our
bliss!'

'Of course, and that is what offends me ...'

'Well then, I will keep him here all the summer on purpose. I will
lavish attentions on him,' said Levin, kissing her hands. 'You'll see!
To-morrow. ... Oh, but we are going out to-morrow.'

7

Next day, before the ladies were up, the vehicles—a cart and a small
trap—stood at the porch waiting for the sportsmen; and Laska was sitting in the cart beside the coachman, regarding the doorway whence
the sportsmen had not yet emerged, with excitement and with disapproval of the delay. The first to appear was Vasenka Veslovsky in new
boots reaching half-way up his fat thighs, his green blouse girdled with
a new cartridge-belt smelling of leather, and on his head the Scotch
bonnet with the ribbons. He carried a new English gun without a sling.
At length the door opened noisily and out bounded Krak, Oblonsky's
yellow spotted pointer, followed by Oblonsky himself with a gun in his
hand and a cigar in his mouth.

Oblonsky was wearing raw hide shoes, bands of linen wound round
his feet instead of socks, a pair of tattered trousers and a short coat. On
his head were the ruins of some sort of hat; but his gun was of a new
type and his game-bag and cartridge-belt, though much worn, were of
the best quality.

Vasenka had been ignorant that the stylishness of a real sportsman
consists in being dressed in rags but having one's shooting implements
of the very best quality. He realized it now that he saw Oblonsky and
resolved to follow his example next time.

'Well, and where is our host?' he inquired.

'He has a young wife,' answered Oblonsky, with a smile.

'Yes, and such a charming one.'

'He was ready dressed. I expect he has run back to her.'

Oblonsky was right in this surmise. Levin had run back to ask his wife
once more whether she had forgiven him his foolishness of the previous
day, and also to entreat her to take care of herself. Then he had to obtain
a repeated assurance that she was not angry with him for going away
for two days, and also to beg her to be sure next day to send a man on
horseback with a note—only a word or two—that he might know that
all was well with her.

'Sorry, gentlemen!' he said, running out on to the porch. 'Is the lunch put in? Why is the roan on the right? Well, never mind! Laska, be quiet! Go and lie down!'

'Let them out with the flock,' he said, turning to the herdsman who was waiting for orders about some young sheep.

Having left the cares of home and estate behind him, Levin experienced such a strong sense of the joy of life and anticipation, that he felt disinclined to talk. Besides, he experienced that feeling of concentrated excitement which every sportsman knows when approaching the scene of action. If his mind was occupied with anything now, it was only with questions, whether they would find anything in the Kolpensky marsh, how Laska would compare with Krak, and how he would shoot to-day.

Oblonsky shared these feelings and was likewise not talkative. Vasenka Veslovsky alone chattered incessantly and merrily. Now, as he listened to him, Levin felt ashamed of his injustice toward him the day before. Vasenka was really a good sort, simple, kind-hearted, and very jolly. Whether it was that Veslovsky's nature was congenial to him, or that, to expiate his sin of yesterday, he tried to see only what was good in him, Levin liked Veslovsky's company.

When they came to a small marsh Levin wished to drive past it, but Oblonsky, with the practised eye of a sportsman, noticed the place from the road.

'Oughtn't we to go there?' he asked, pointing to the marsh.

'Levin, do let us! How delightful!' begged Vasenka Veslovsky, and Levin could not but agree.

'There is not room for three: I'll wait here,' said Levin, hoping they would find nothing but peewits.

'No! Come along, Levin, let's go together,' said Veslovsky.

'Really, there's not room! Back, Laska! … Laska! …'

Levin remained with the trap and looked enviously at the sportsmen. They went over the whole marsh, but there was nothing there except waterfowl and some peewits, one of which Veslovsky killed.

'There, you see I was not grudging you the marsh!' said Levin. 'It only meant losing time.'

When they reached the second marsh, which was of considerable size and would take a good deal of time Levin tried to dissuade them from getting out. But again Veslovsky persuaded him, and again, the marsh being a narrow one, Levin as a hospitable host remained with the vehicles.

Krak immediately went toward the hummocks. Vasenka Veslovsky was the first to follow the dog. Before Oblonsky had time to approach, a snipe rose. Veslovsky missed it, and it flew over to an unmown meadow. The bird was left to Veslovsky, who killed it and went back to the vehicles.

'Now you go, and I will remain with the horses,' he said.

A sportsman's jealousy was beginning to torment Levin. He handed the reins to Veslovsky and went into the marsh.

Laska, who had long been whining plaintively, as if complaining of the injustice, rushed straight forward to a likely spot covered with hummocks and known to Levin, where Krak had not yet been. She described a circle in front of the hummocks, and began another, but suddenly shuddered and stopped dead.

'Come along, Stiva!' Levin shouted, feeling his heart beat more rapidly, and suddenly, as if some bar had been withdrawn from his strained sense of hearing, he lost the faculty of measuring distance, and was struck by sounds which reached him clearly but without any order. He heard Oblonsky's steps and took them for the distant tramp of horses; he heard the crumbling of a bit of hummock on which he stepped and which broke off, pulling out the grass by the roots, and he took it for the noise of a snipe on the wing; behind him he heard too a sound of splashing for which he could not account.

Picking his way, he approached the dog.

A snipe rose before the dog. Levin raised his gun, but just as he was taking aim the splashing sounded louder and nearer, mingled with Veslovsky's voice shouting strangely and loudly. Levin knew he was aiming behind the snipe, but fired, nevertheless.

After making sure he had missed, he turned and saw that the trap and horses were no longer on the road but in the marsh.

Veslovsky, wishing to watch the shooting, had driven into the marsh, where the horses had stuck fast.

Levin was vexed that he had been put off his shot, and that his horses had been led into the bog. He worked silently with the coachman to disengage the horses. But when heated with the work, and seeing Veslovsky pulling at the splashboard so strenuously and zealously that he actually wrenched it off, Levin reproached himself with being influenced by his sentiments of the previous day and with treating Veslovsky too coldly, and he tried to efface his unfriendliness by particular courtesy. When everything was in order and the vehicles had been brought back to the road, Levin gave orders for lunch to be served.

Vasenka, who had brightened up again, finished a second chicken. 'Now our misfortunes are ended and all will be well. But for my sin I must sit on the box. Don't you think so, eh? No, no, wait and see how I will drive you!' he said, keeping hold of the reins, in reply to Levin who wanted him to let the coachman drive. 'No, I must expiate my sin, and besides, it's delightful on the box.'

Levin was rather afraid Veslovsky would tire out the horses, especially the roan on the left, whom he did not know how to hold in; but he could not resist Veslovsky's high spirits, the songs he sang all the way while sitting on the box, the stories he told, and his representation of the English way of driving four-in-hand; and they were all in the best of spirits when they reached the Gvozdevo marsh.

8

Veslovsky drove so fast that they arrived at the marsh too soon, while it was still hot.

When they got to the object of their journey, Levin wished to rid himself of Vasenka and go about unhindered. Oblonsky evidently wanted the same thing, and on his face Levin noticed the preoccupation, which every true sportsman feels before the shooting begins, and also a little good-natured cunning, characteristic of him.

'Well, what shall we do …? It's a splendid marsh,' said Oblonsky.

'Well then, gentlemen,' said Levin with a somewhat gloomy expression, pulling up his boots and examining his percussion caps, 'you see that sedge? The marsh begins here, just in front of us: you can see, where it is greener? That's the best place. I once shot seventeen grouse there. …
We will separate, going different ways with the two dogs, and will meet again by the mill.'

'Well then, who goes to the left and who to the right?' asked Oblonsky. 'The space on the right is broader, so you two go there together, and I will keep to the left,' he added with affected indifference.

'Good! We'll make the best bag,' chimed in Vasenka.

Levin could not avoid agreeing, and they separated.

'Veslovsky, walk beside me—beside me!' he whispered with bated breath to his comrade, who was splashing in the water behind him.

'No, I don't want to hamper you. Don't trouble about me.'

But Levin recollected Kitty's parting words: 'Mind, and don't shoot one another!' Nearer and nearer came the dogs, keeping out of each other's way and each following its scent. Levin had barely time to turn, before he heard the cry of a snipe, then another, and a third, and about eight more rose one after the other.

Oblonsky got one just as it was preparing to begin its zigzag flight, and the bird fell like a small lump into the bog. Oblonsky quietly aimed at another which was flying low toward the sedges, and at the moment of the report that one too fell.

Levin was not so lucky: he fired at the first snipe too near, and missed; he followed it with his gun when it had already risen, but at that instant another rose just at his feet and diverted his attention, and he missed again.

While they were reloading another bird rose, and Veslovsky, who had finished reloading, fired two charges of small shot over the water. Oblonsky picked up his two snipe and looked with sparkling eyes at Levin.

'Well, now let's part,' he said, and holding his gun ready, he whistled to his dog and went off in one direction. Levin and Veslovsky went in the other.

Levin, if his first shots were unsuccessful, always became excited and annoyed, and shot badly all the rest of the day. So it was this time. There were a great many snipe. They kept rising before the dogs and at the very feet of the sportsmen, and Levin might have recovered himself; but the oftener he fired the more he disgraced himself before Veslovsky, who was puffing away merrily, in and out of range, never killing anything, but not in the least abashed thereby. Meanwhile from the opposite side of the marsh came not frequent but, as it seemed to Levin, significant reports from Oblonsky's gun.

Having traversed more than half the marsh, Levin and Veslovsky came to a spot where the peasants' meadow land was divided into long strips, the ends abutting on the sedge and separated by narrow lines where the grass had been trodden down or cut. Half of those strips were already mown.

'Hullo, you sportsmen!' shouted one of several peasants who were sitting beside a cart from which the horses had been taken out. 'Come and have something with us! A drink of vodka!'

Levin turned round.

'They are calling us to drink vodka. I expect they have been dividing the meadow. I should go and have a drink,' said Levin, not quite disinterestedly, hoping that the vodka would tempt Veslovsky and lure him away.

'Why are they offering it?'

'Oh, they are only making merry. Really, you should go to them. It will interest you. Go, you'll find the way to the mill!' cried Levin, and on looking round was pleased to see Veslovsky making his way out of the marsh toward the peasants, stooping and stumbling with his weary feet and holding his gun at arm's length.

'You come too!' shouted a peasant to Levin. 'Come! Have a bite of pie!'

Levin badly wanted a drink of vodka and a bit of bread. But the dog pointed. His weariness vanished, at once he went easily through the marsh toward the dog. Just at his feet rose a snipe; he fired and killed it. The dog continued pointing. Another bird rose before the dog. Levin fired, but that day he had no luck: he missed, and when he went to look for the bird he had killed, he could not find it. Even without Vasenka, whom he had blamed for his ill-luck, things went no better. Here, too, were plenty of birds, but Levin missed one after another. He tried to keep calm, but the same thing happened again. His finger pulled the trigger before he had taken aim. Things went from bad to worse.

He had only five birds in his bag when he came out of the marsh by the alder grove where he was to meet Oblonsky.

Before he saw him, he saw his dog. Krak, quite black with smelly marsh slime, sprang out from beneath the upturned root of an alder with the air of a conqueror and sniffed at Laska. Behind Krak, in the shade of the alders, appeared Oblonsky's stately figure. He came toward Levin red and perspiring, with his shirt unbuttoned.

'Well? You have been firing a good deal!' he said with a merry smile.

'And you?' asked Levin. But there was no need to ask, for he already saw the full bag.

'Oh, not bad!'

He had fourteen birds.

'A famous marsh! I expect Veslovsky was in your way. One dog for two people is inconvenient,' said Oblonsky, to soften his triumph.

9

When Levin and Oblonsky reached the peasant's hut where Levin used to put up, Veslovsky was there before them. He sat in the middle of the room, holding with both hands to a bench, from which a soldier—a brother of the mistress of the house—was tugging him by his slime-covered boots, and he was laughing with his infectiously merry laugh.

'I have only just got here. They fed me and gave me drink. What bread—wonderful! *Délicieux!* And the vodka ... I never tasted better! And they positively would not take any money.'

'Why should they take money? They were entertaining you, you see!

Do they keep vodka for sale?' said the soldier who had at last succeeded in dragging off one wet boot.

Despite the dirtiness of the hut, soiled by the sportsmen's boots, the dirty dogs that were licking themselves there, and despite the smell of bog and of powder and the absence of knives and forks, the sportsmen drank tea and ate supper with a relish known only when one is out shooting. Washed and clean they betook themselves to a hay-barn that had been swept out and where the coachman had made up beds for the gentlemen.

'Oh, what a night!' cried Veslovsky, gazing at the corner of the hut and the carts, visible in the faint afterglow through the now open barn-doors as in a frame. 'Just listen! It's women's voices singing, and not at all badly. Come, let's go for a walk! We shan't sleep, you know. Oblonsky, come along!'

'If only one could … go without getting up!' said Oblonsky, stretching himself. 'It's delightful to lie still.'

'Well, then I'll go alone,' said Veslovsky, rising quickly and putting on his boots. 'Good-bye, gentlemen! If it's jolly I will call you.'

'Isn't he a fine fellow?' said Oblonsky when Veslovsky had gone.

'Yes, fine,' answered Levin.

'Hasn't the fresh hay a strong scent!' remarked Oblonsky, sitting up. 'Nothing will make me sleep. Vasenka is up to something out there. Don't you hear the laughter and his voice? Shan't we go too? Let's!'

'No, I am not going,' answered Levin.

'Maybe you are stopping here on principle?' said Oblonsky, smiling, as he searched in the dark for his cap.

'No, not on principle, but why should I go?'

'D'you know, you will bring trouble on yourself,' said Oblonsky, having found his cap and getting up.

'Why?'

'Don't I see how you have placed yourself with your wife? I heard you discussing as a question of first-rate importance, whether you should go away shooting for two days or not! That's all very well for an idyll, but it can't last a lifetime. A man should be independent—he has his own masculine interests. A man must be manly,' said Oblonsky, opening the door.

'Is that to say, he should court the maid-servants?' asked Levin.

'Why not, if it's amusing? My wife won't be the worse for it, and I shall have a spree. The important part is to guard the sanctity of the home! Nothing of that kind at home; but you needn't tie your hands.'

'Perhaps!' said Levin drily. 'To-morrow one should start early.'

Levin could not fall asleep for a long time. And he began to think of the coming day.

'To-morrow I will start early in the morning, and make up my mind not to get excited. There are quantities of snipe and great snipe too. And when I come back, there will be a note from Kitty. Well, perhaps Stiva is right! I am not manly with her, I have grown effeminate. ... Well, what's to be done!'

Through his sleep he heard laughter and Veslovsky's and Oblonsky's merry talk. He opened his eyes for an instant: they were standing chatting in the open doorway, brightly lit up by the moon which had now risen. 'Gentlemen! To-morrow at dawn!' Levin mumbled drowsily, and fell asleep.

Waking at dawn Levin tried to rouse his companions. Vasenka, lying prone with one stockinged leg outstretched, was sleeping so soundly that it was impossible to get any answer out of him. Oblonsky, half asleep, refused to budge so early. Even Laska, sleeping curled into a ring on a corner of the hay heap, got up reluctantly, and lazily stretched and adjusted first one hind leg and then the other. Having put on his boots, taken his gun, and carefully opened the creaking barn doors, Levin went out into the street. The coachmen were asleep beside the vehicles, the horses were drowsing.

Laska ran ahead gaily along the footpath, and Levin followed at a brisk pace, continually glancing at the sky. He did not wish the sun to rise before he reached the marsh. But the sun did not tarry. The streak of dawn, previously so noticeable, now had to be looked for. Still invisible in the absence of the sun, the dew on the tall scented hemp wetted Levin's legs and his blouse to above his belt. In the translucent stillness of the morning the slightest sounds were audible. A bee flew past his ear, whistling like a bullet. The path led him straight to the marsh, which was recognizable by the mist rising from it, thicker at one spot and thinner at another, so that the sedge and willow bushes looked like islets swaying in the mist. Joyful and preoccupied, Laska started running across the bog, which swayed beneath her feet.

Noticing Laska's peculiar manner of searching, as lowering her body almost to the ground she appeared to be dragging her broad hind paws, he knew that she was pointing at snipe, and while running up to her he prayed inwardly for success, especially with the first bird. Having come close up to her he looked beyond, and from his height saw with his eyes what she had found with her nose. In the space between the hummocks, at a distance of about a sazhen, he could see a snipe.

With lusty cries and a sound of the beating of concave wings so peculiar to the great snipe, a bird rose; and, following the report of the gun, it fell heavily on its white breast ten paces from the first spot into the wet bog. Another rose behind Levin without waiting to be disturbed by the dog. By the time Levin had turned toward it, it had already gone far: but his shot reached it. After flying some twenty feet, the second snipe rose at an acute angle, and then, turning round and round like a ball, fell heavily on a dry spot.

'Now, things will go right,' thought Levin, putting the warm fat snipe into his bag. 'Eh, Laska dear, will things go right?'

When, having reloaded, Levin went on again, the sun, though still invisible because of the clouds, had already risen.

A boy ran up to Levin.

'Uncle, there were ducks here yesterday!' he shouted, following Levin from afar.

And Levin felt increased pleasure in killing three snipe one after another within sight of this little boy, who expressed his approval.

Tired, hungry, and happy, Levin returned to his lodging toward ten o'clock, having tramped some thirty versts and bringing nineteen red-fleshed birds, besides a duck tied to his girdle, as there was no room for it in his bag. His comrades had wakened long before, and had had time to get hungry and have their breakfast.

Oblonsky's envy gratified Levin. He was also pleased that a messenger had already arrived from Kitty with a note.

'I am quite well and happy. If you were uneasy about me, you may be quite at ease now. I have a new bodyguard—Mary Vlasyevna,' this was the midwife, a new and important personage in the Levins' family life. 'She has come to see me and finds me perfectly well, and we have got her to stay till your return. All are cheerful and well, so don't hurry and even stay another day if your sport is good.'

These two joys, his successful shooting and the news from his wife, were so great that two small unpleasantnesses which occurred after the shooting were easy to disregard. One was that the chestnut side-horse, having evidently been overworked the previous day, was off its feed and seemed dull. The coachman said it had been strained.

The other unpleasantness, which for a moment upset his good-humour, but about which he afterwards laughed heartily, was that of all the provisions that Kitty had provided so lavishly that it had appeared impossible to eat them up in a week, nothing was left! Returning tired and hungry from his sport, Levin so vividly anticipated the pies that on approaching his lodging he seemed to smell and taste them and he immediately ordered Philip to serve them. It turned out that there were no pies, nor even any chicken left!

'He *has* an appetite!' said Oblonsky, laughing and pointing to Vasenka Veslovsky. '*I* don't suffer from lack of appetite, but he's quite surprising ...'

'Well, it can't be helped!' said Levin, looking morosely at Veslovsky. 'Well then, bring me some beef, Philip!'

'The beef has been eaten, and the bone was given to the dogs,' answered Philip.

Levin was so annoyed that he said crossly: 'Something might have been left for me!' and he felt inclined to cry. 'Well then, draw the birds and stuff them with nettles,' said he in a trembling voice to Philip, trying not to look at Veslovsky; 'and ask at least for some milk for me.'

Later on, when he had satisfied his hunger with the milk, he felt ashamed of having shown annoyance to a stranger, and he began laughing at his hungry irritation.

In the evening they again went out shooting, when Veslovsky also killed some birds, and late at night they set off home.

The drive back was as merry as the drive out had been and Levin was glad not only to feel no hostility such as he had felt at home toward Vasenka Veslovsky, but on the contrary to feel quite friendly toward him.

10

Next morning at ten o'clock Levin, having made the round of his farm, knocked at the door of Vasenka's room.

'*Entrez!*' shouted Veslovsky. 'Excuse me—I have only just finished my ablutions,' he said smiling. 'I am really quite ashamed. I expect the ladies are already up? It would be fine to go for a walk now. You must show me your horses.'

When they had walked round the garden, visited the stables, and even done some gymnastics together on the parallel bars, Levin returned to the house with his guest and entered the drawing-room with him.

'We had fine sport, and so many new impressions!' said Veslovsky, approaching Kitty, who sat at the samovar. 'What a pity ladies are deprived of that pleasure.'

'Well, what of it? He must say something to the mistress of the house,' Levin told himself. He again thought he noticed something in the smile with which the visitor addressed Kitty. ...

The Princess, who sat at the other end of the table with Mary Vlasyevna and Oblonsky, called Levin and began a conversation about moving to Moscow for Kitty's confinement and taking a house there. Just as all the preparations for the wedding had been disagreeable to him, since they detracted by their insignificance from the majesty of what was taking place, so now the preparations for the coming birth, the time of which they were reckoning on their fingers, appeared to him yet more offensive. The birth of a son (he was certain it would be a son) which they promised him, but in which he still could not believe, so extraordinary did it seem, appeared to him on the one hand such an immense and therefore impossible happiness, and on the other such a mysterious event, that this pretended knowledge of what was going to happen and consequent preparations as for something ordinary, something produced by human beings, seemed to him an indignity and a degradation.

But the Princess did not understand his feelings and attributed his unwillingness to think and speak about it to thoughtlessness and indifference, and therefore gave him no peace.

'You must decide when you will move.'

Though this talk with the Princess upset him, it was not that but what he saw by the samovar which made him morose.

'No, this is impossible,' he thought, glancing occasionally at Vasenka, who was leaning toward Kitty and saying something, with his handsome smile, and at Kitty, blushing and agitated.

There was something impure in Vasenka's attitude, his look and his smile. Levin even saw something impure in Kitty's pose and smile; and again the light faded from his eyes. Again, as on the previous occasion, he suddenly, without the least interval, felt thrown from the height of happiness, peace, and dignity into an abyss of despair, malevolence, and degradation. Again everyone and everything became revolting to him.

'Well then, Princess, let it be just as you think best,' he said, turning away.

'"Heavy is the Autocrat's crown!"' Oblonsky quoted Pushkin banteringly, evidently alluding not only to the Princess's conversation, but also to the cause of Levin's agitation, which he had observed. 'How late you are to-day, Dolly!'

They all rose to greet Dolly. Vasenka only rose for a moment, and with the absence of politeness to women which is characteristic of modern young men, barely bowed and again continued his conversation, laughing at something.

'Masha has worn me out. She slept badly and is terribly capricious this morning,' said Dolly.

The conversation with Kitty begun by Vasenka again dealt with Anna and with the question whether love can rise above social conditions. This conversation was unpleasant to Kitty and upset her, both by the subject itself and by the tone in which it was carried on, but especially because she already knew the effect it would have on her husband. She wished to put an end to the conversation, but did not know how. Whatever she did, she knew, would be noticed by her husband and would all be construed into something wrong.

'Where are you going, Kostya?' she asked her husband with a guilty look as he passed by with resolute steps. This guilty look confirmed all his suspicions.

'The mechanic arrived during my absence and I have not yet seen him,' he answered, without looking at her.

He went downstairs, but had not had time to leave his study before he heard his wife's familiar footsteps following him with imprudent rapidity.

'What is it?' he asked drily. 'We are busy.'

'Excuse me,' she said addressing the German mechanic, 'I have a few words to say to my husband.'

The German was about to go out, but Levin said to him:

'Don't trouble!'

'The train is at three?' asked the German. 'I must not miss it.'

Levin did not answer him but went out with his wife.

'Well, what have you to say to me?' he asked in French.

He did not look her in the face and did not notice that she (in her condition) stood with her whole face twitching, and had a pitiful, crushed appearance.

'I ... I want to tell you that it's impossible to live like this—it's torture!' she muttered.

'The servants are there, in the pantry,' he said angrily; 'don't make a scene.'

'Well then, come into the garden!'

In the garden they came upon a man weeding a path, and without any longer considering that the man saw her tear-stained eyes and his excited face, or that they looked like people running away from some calamity, they went on with rapid feet.

'One can't live like this! It is torture! I suffer and you suffer. Why?' she asked, when they had at last reached a secluded seat at the corner of the lime-tree avenue.

'Only tell me this: was there something improper, impure, degradingly horrid in his tone?' he said, standing in front of her in the same attitude as on that night, with fists pressing his chest.

'There was,' she said in a trembling voice. 'But, Kostya, do you really not see that I am not to blame? From the time I came down I wanted to adopt a tone ... but these people ... Why did he come? How happy we were!' she said, choking with sobs that shook the whole of her expanded body.

The gardener saw with surprise that, though they could not have found anything very blissful on that seat, they passed him on their way back to the house with quieted and beaming faces.

After seeing his wife upstairs, Levin went to Dolly's part of the house. She was walking up and down the room and speaking angrily to a little girl who stood howling in a corner:

'You'll stand in that corner all day, and will have your dinner alone, and you will not see a single doll, and I won't have a new frock made for you!' she was saying, unable to think of any more punishments for the child.

'Oh, she is a horrid child!' she cried, addressing Levin.

'But you are upset about something? Why have you come?'

And by the tone of her question Levin knew that it would be easy for him to tell her what he meant to say.

'I have been in the garden alone with Kitty. We have quarrelled for the second time since ... Stiva's arrival.'

Dolly gazed at him with wise, comprehending eyes.

'Well, tell me, hand on heart—was there ... not on Kitty's side, but on that gentleman's ... a tone which might be unpleasant ... not unpleasant but terrible and offensive to a husband?'

'That is to say ... how am I to put it? ... Stop! Stop in the corner!' she said turning to Masha, who noticing a scarcely perceptible smile on her mother's face was turning round. 'The world would say he has behaved as all young men behave and a Society husband should be merely flattered by it.'

'Yes, yes,' answered Levin gloomily, 'but you noticed it?'

'Not I only, but Stiva too.'

'Well, all right, now I am tranquil. I will turn him out,' said Levin.

'What do you mean? Have you gone mad?' exclaimed Dolly, terrified. 'Consider!' she went on. 'No, if you like I will tell Stiva and he will take him away. One can say you are expecting visitors. Certainly, he does not suit your household ...'

'No, no; I'll do it myself. It will be a pleasure for me, a real pleasure,' said Levin with sparkling eyes.

Levin went in search of Veslovsky. Passing through the hall he ordered the *calèche* to be harnessed to drive to the station.

'One of the springs broke yesterday,' replied the footman.

'Well, then, the _tarantas_, but make haste! Where is the visitor?'

'He has gone to his room.'

Levin found Vasenka who was trying on a pair of leggings and preparing for a ride.

'You wear leggings for riding?'

'Yes, it's much cleaner,' said Vasenka, placing his fat foot on a chair, fastening the bottom hook, and smiling good-naturedly.

He was certainly a good-natured fellow, and Levin felt sorry for him and ashamed of himself as a host, when he noticed the shyness of Vasenka's look but, suddenly remembering Kitty and all that had happened, he said, looking Veslovsky firmly in the eyes: 'I have ordered the horses to be harnessed for you.'

'What do you mean?' Vasenka began with surprise. 'To drive where?'

'For you, to the station,' answered Levin gloomily.

'Why, are you going away, or has anything happened?'

'It happens that I am expecting visitors,' replied Levin more rapidly. 'Or no, I am not expecting visitors and nothing has happened, yet I request you to leave. You may explain my impoliteness as you please.'

Vasenka drew himself up.

'I ask _you_ for an explanation,' he said with dignity.

'I can't give you an explanation,' said Levin slowly, trying to control the trembling of his jaw, 'and it is better for you not to ask.'

Probably the sight of those gleaming eyes, low voice and trembling jaws, convinced Vasenka more than the words. He shrugged his shoulders, smiled contemptuously, and bowed.

'Can I not see Oblonsky?'

'I will send him to you at once.'

'What is this nonsense?' said Oblonsky, when he had heard from his friend that he was begin driven out of the house, and had found Levin in the garden, where he was awaiting the departure of his visitor.

'Please! I can't do otherwise! I feel ashamed before you and before him. But I don't think it will grieve him much to go away, and his presence is unpleasant to me and to my wife.'

'But he feels insulted! I never expected this of you!'

Levin turned away from him quickly and went far down one of the avenues, where he continued walking up and down alone. Soon he heard the rattle of the _tarantas_, and through the trees saw Vasenka, seated on hay (unluckily the _tarantas_ had no seat), with the Scotch bonnet on his head, jolting over the ruts as he was driven down the other avenue.

'What does that mean?' wondered Levin when the footman ran out of the house and stopped the vehicle. It was on account of the mechanic, whom Levin had quite forgotten. He bowed and said something to Veslovsky, then climbed into the *tarantas*, and they drove away together.

Oblonsky and the Princess were indignant at Levin's conduct. He himself felt not only that he was in the highest degree ridiculous, but quite guilty and disgraced; but recalling what he and his wife had suffered, and asking himself how he would act another time, he answered that he would do just the same again.

11

Dolly carried out her intention of going to see Anna. She was very sorry to grieve her sister and to do anything that was unpleasant to Levin, but felt it her duty to visit Anna and show her that the altered circumstances could not change her own feelings toward her.

On the appointed day Levin had four horses ready for his sister-in-law, as well as a relay—having made it up of farm and riding horses—not at all a handsome team, but one able to get her to her destination in a day. As horses were also required for the Princess, who was leaving, and for the midwife, it was inconvenient to Levin; but he could not be so inhospitable as to allow Dolly to hire horses while staying with him. Besides, he knew that the twenty roubles she would have had to pay for the journey were of importance to her, and he felt her distressing financial embarrassments as if they had been his own.

Acting on Levin's advice, Dolly started before day-break. The road was good, the *calèche* comfortable, the horses ran merrily, and on the box beside the coachman instead of a footman sat an office clerk whom Levin sent with her for safety. Dolly dozed, and only woke up when approaching the inn where the horses were to be changed.

At home her care of the children never gave her leisure to think, but now, during this four hours' drive, all the thoughts she had repressed crowded suddenly into her mind, and she reviewed her whole life from all sides as she had never done before. Her thoughts seemed strange to her. At first she thought of the children, about whom, though the Princess and especially Kitty (she had greater faith in Kitty) had promised to look after them, she still felt anxious. But then questions of the present began to be replaced by those of the immediate future. She began thinking that she would have to move into another house in Moscow for the winter, have the drawing-room furniture re-covered, and a new winter coat made for the eldest girl. Then came problems of a more remote future: how she should start her children in the world. 'With the girls it will be comparatively easy,' she thought, 'but how about the boys?'

'Of course Stiva is not to be counted on, but with the help of kind people I shall start them somehow. ... But in case of another child ...' And it occurred to her how inaccurate it is to say that woman's curse is the bringing forth of children. 'Travail, that's nothing—but pregnancy is torture,' she thought, with her last pregnancy and the death of her infant in mind. And once more the cruel memory rose that always weighed on her mother-heart: the death of her last baby, a boy who died of croup; his funeral, the general indifference shown to the little pink coffin, and her own heartrending, lonely grief.

'And what is it all for? What will come of it all? I myself, without having a moment's peace, now pregnant, now nursing, always cross and grumbling, tormenting myself and others, repulsive to my husband—I shall live my life, and produce unfortunate, badly brought-up and beg-gared children. Even now, if we had not spent this summer with Kostya and Kitty, I don't know how we should have managed. Of course Kostya and Kitty are so considerate that we don't feel it; but it can't go on so. They will have children of their own and won't be able to help us; as it is, they are put to inconvenience. Is Papa, who has kept scarcely anything for himself, to help us? ... So I can't even give the children a start myself, unless it's with other people's help and with humiliation. Well, suppos-ing the best: that none of the other children die, and that I somehow succeed in bringing them up; at the very best they will only escape being ne'er-do-wells. That is all I can hope for. And for this, so much suffering and trouble. ... My whole life ruined!' These thoughts frightened her.

'And they are all down on Anna! What for? Am I better than she? I at least have a husband whom I love. Not as I wished to love, but still I do love him; but Anna did not love hers. In what is she to blame? She wishes to live. God has implanted that need in our souls. It is quite pos-sible I might have done the same. I don't even know whether I did well to listen to her at that terrible time when she came to me in Moscow. I ought then to have left my husband and begun life anew. I might have loved and been loved, the real way. And is it better now? I don't respect him. I need him,' she thought of her husband, 'and I put up with him. Is that any better? I was still attractive then, still had my good looks,' she went on, feeling that she wanted to see herself in a glass.

Yet she thought it might not be too late even now. She remembered Koznyshev, who was particularly amiable to her; Stiva's friend the good-natured Turovtsyn, who had helped her nurse her children when they had scarlet fever and who was in love with her; and then there was a very young man who considered—so her husband told her as a joke—that she was the handsomest of the three sisters. And the most passionate and impossible romances occurred to Dolly's fancy. A roguish smile puckered her lips. Wrapped in such dreams she reached the turning from the high road, which led to Vozdvizhensk.

12

The coachman stopped the horses and looked round toward a field of rye on the right, where some peasants sat beside a cart. The clerk beckoned to a peasant. The breeze, which they felt while driving, died down when they stopped; and horse-flies settled on the sweating horses, which angrily tried to brush them off. The metallic sound of a scythe being hammered beside the cart ceased.

A curly-headed old man, with a piece of bast tied round his head, his rounded back dark with perspiration, approached the *calèche* and put his sunburnt arm on the mud-guard.

'Vozdvizhensk?' he repeated. 'There! When you have passed that bend turn to the left, and go right down the drive and you'll knock up straight against it.'

'Are they at home, my good man?' said Dolly vaguely, not knowing how to speak of Anna even to a peasant.

'I expect so,' said the peasant, shifting from one bare foot to the other, 'a while ago they passed by here on horseback, to see the reaper. Now they must be at home again. And who may you be?'

'We have come a long way,' replied the coachman, climbing back on to the box. But hardly had they gone round the corner when the peasant called out to them.

'Stop, friend! Stop!'

The coachman pulled up.

'They are coming! Here they are themselves!' cried the man, pointing to four persons on horseback and two in a char-a-banc coming along the road.

It was Vronsky with his jockey, Veslovsky and Anna on horseback, and Princess Barbara with Sviyazhsky in the char-a-banc.

When the *calèche* pulled up, the riders advanced at a foot pace. Anna's face immediately brightened into a joyful smile when she recognized Dolly in the little figure pressed back in a corner of the old *calèche*. She gave an exclamation, started in her saddle and touched her horse into a gallop. Riding up to the *calèche* she jumped unaided from the horse and, holding up her habit, ran toward Dolly.

'It's what I thought, but dared not expect! What a pleasure! You cannot imagine how delighted I am!' she cried, now pressing her face to Dolly's and kissing her, now leaning back to gaze smilingly at her.

'What joy, Alexis!' she said, turning to Vronsky, who had dismounted and was walking toward them.

Vronsky, taking off his grey top hat, approached Dolly.

'You can have no idea how pleased we are that you have come,' he said, putting peculiar emphasis into his words.

Vasenka Veslovsky, without dismounting, raised his cap and welcomed the visitor, joyously waving his ribbons above his head.

'That is the Princess Barbara,' Anna said, in answer to Dolly's glance of inquiry when the char-a-banc came nearer.

'Oh!' said Dolly, and her face involuntarily expressed displeasure.

The Princess Barbara was her husband's aunt, she had long known her and did not respect her. She knew that the Princess Barbara had all her life been a hanger-on to various rich relatives. Anna noticed Dolly's expression, became confused, blushed, let her habit slip out of her hands, and stumbled over it.

Dolly walked up to the char-a-banc and coldly greeted Princess Barbara. She was acquainted with Sviyazhsky too who, having glanced at the ill-matched horses and the patched mud-guard of the *calèche*, offered the ladies seats in the char-a-banc.

'No, stay as you are,' said Anna, who had also come up, 'and we two will go in the *calèche*,' and giving Dolly her arm she led her away.

When the two women took their seats in the *calèche*, both were seized with shyness. Anna was abashed by the attentively inquiring look Dolly bent upon her; Dolly, after Sviyazhsky's remark about the 'vehicle', felt involuntarily ashamed of the ramshackle old *calèche*. Philip the coachman and the clerk shared that feeling. The clerk, to hide his embarrassment, bustled about, helping the ladies in, but Philip became morose and made up his mind not to be imposed upon by this external superiority.

Anna was looking at Dolly's thin wan face with its dust-filled wrinkles, and wishing to tell her just what she thought: that Dolly looked thinner and worse. But remembering that her own looks had improved and that Dolly's eyes had told her so, she sighed and began talking about herself.

'You are looking at me,' she said, 'and wondering whether I can be happy, placed as I am? Well, what do you think? I am ashamed to confess it, but I … I am unforgivably happy! Something magical has happened to me. I have lived through sufferings and terrors, but for a long time past—especially since we came here—I have been happy! …' she said, looking at Dolly timidly and with a questioning smile.

'I am so glad!' answered Dolly, smiling. 'I am very glad for your sake. Why did you not write to me?'

'Why? … Because I did not dare … you forget my position.'

'To me? You dared not? If only you knew how I … I consider …' Dolly began; but it seemed out of place to begin to discuss this big subject in the *calèche*, so she briefly replied:

'I always loved you, and if one loves, one loves the whole person as he or she is, and not as one might wish them to be.'

Anna, turning her eyes away from her friend and screwing them up (this was a new habit of hers), grew thoughtful, trying thoroughly to grasp the meaning of the remark. Having evidently understood it in the sense she wished, she glanced at Dolly.

'If you had any sins,' she said, 'they would all be forgiven you for coming here and for those words!'

And Dolly noticed that tears had started to her eyes. She silently pressed Anna's hand.

'But what are those buildings? What a lot of them there are!' said she after a moment's silence.

'They are the employees' houses, the stud farm, and the stables,' answered Anna. 'And here the park begins. Everything had been neglected, but Alexis has had it all renovated. He is very fond of this estate, and—a thing I never expected of him—he is quite enthusiastic in managing the place. But of course his is such a talented nature! Whatever he takes up, he does splendidly! He has grown into a first-rate, prudent landlord, as I recognize; in farming matters he is even stingy, but only in farming. Where it is a question of thousands he does not count them,' she said. 'Do you see that big building? It is the new hospital. I think it will cost more than a hundred thousand roubles. And do you know why he started it? The peasants asked him to let them some meadows at a reduced rent, I think, and he refused, and I reproached him with being stingy. Of course it was not that alone, but one thing with another caused him to start that hospital, to show, you know, that he is not stingy. And now you will see the house in a moment. It was his grandfather's, and it has not been altered at all on the outside.'

'How fine!' said Dolly, looking with involuntary surprise at the hand-some house with a row of columns standing out among the variously tinted foliage of the old trees in the garden.

'It is fine, is it not? And from upstairs the view is wonderful.'

They drove into a gravelled courtyard surrounded by flowers, where two men were making a border of rough porous stones round a well-forked flower-bed, and stopped beneath a roofed portico.

'Ah, they've already arrived,' said Anna, seeing Vronsky and Veslovsky coming out to meet her.

'In which room are you putting the Princess?' Vronsky asked in French, addressing Anna, and without waiting for her answer he once more welcomed Dolly, and this time he kissed her hand. 'The large room with the balcony, I should think.'

'Oh no! That's too far off! The corner room will be better, we shall see more of one another there. Well, let's go in,' said Anna.

It was not the grand room that Vronsky had suggested, but one for which Anna apologized to Dolly. And this room needing an apology was full of luxuries, such as Dolly had never lived among, which reminded her of the best hotels abroad.

'Well, dearest! How happy I am!' said Anna, who in her riding-habit had sat down for a moment beside Dolly. 'Tell me about yourselves. I meet Stiva in passing, but he can't tell me about the children. How is my pet, Tanya? Grown a big girl, I suppose?'

'Yes, quite big,' answered Dolly shortly, and was herself surprised that she could talk so coldly about her children. 'We are very comfortable at the Levins',' she added.

'There now! Had I only known that you don't despise me ...' said Anna, 'you should all have come to us. You know Stiva and Alexis are old and great friends,' she added and suddenly blushed.

'Yes, but we are so comfortable ...' answered Dolly with embarrassment.

'However, my joy makes me talk nonsense! But really, dear, I am so glad to see you,' said Anna, kissing her again. 'You have not yet told me how and what you think about me, and I want to know everything. However, we will talk it all well over later. Now I will go and dress and send you the maid.'

13

Left alone, Dolly surveyed the room with a housewife's eye. All she saw when driving up to the house and passing through it, and now in her room, gave her the impression of abundance and elegance. Everything was new, from the French wall-papers to the carpet which covered the whole floor. The bed had a spring and an overlay mattress, with a specially-shaped bolster and small pillows with silk slips. The marble washstand, the dressing-table, the couch, the tables, the bronze clock on the mantelpiece, the curtains and door-hangings were all costly and new. The smart lady's maid with hair stylishly done, and wearing a dress more fashionable than Dolly's who came to offer her services, was as new and expensive as everything else in the room. Dolly found her politeness, tidiness, and attention pleasant, but did not feel at ease with her; she was ashamed to let her see the patched dressing-jacket, which as ill-luck would have it she had brought by mistake. She was ashamed of the very patches and darns on which she at home prided herself.

Dolly felt much relieved when Annushka, whom she had known a long time, came into the room. The smart maid had to go to her mistress, and Annushka remained with Dolly.

Annushka was evidently very pleased that the lady had come, and chattered incessantly. Dolly noticed that she wanted to express her opinion of her mistress's position, and especially of the Count's love of and devotion to Anna, but Dolly carefully stopped her whenever she began to speak about that subject. She was glad when Anna came in and thereby put an end to Annushka's chatter.

Anna had changed into a very simple lawn dress. Dolly knew what such simplicity meant and cost.

'An old acquaintance,' said Anna, pointing to Annushka.

Anna was now no longer embarrassed. She was free and at her ease. Dolly saw that she had quite got over the impression produced by her arrival, and had adopted a superficial tone of equanimity which seemed to close the door that led to the compartment where her feelings and intimate thoughts were kept.

'Well, and how is your little girl, Anna?' asked Dolly.

'Annie? Quite well. Would you like to see her? Come, I'll show her to you. ... I've had such trouble with the nurses,' she began.

'Well, and how have you arranged ...?' Dolly began, meaning to ask what name the little girl would bear; but seeing a sudden frown on Anna's face she changed the question and said: 'Have you already weaned her?'

But Anna had understood.

'That is not what you were going to ask? ... You wished to ask about her name? Am I not right? It troubles Alexis. She has no name. That is, her name is Karenina,' said Anna, screwing up her eyes till only the meeting lashes could be seen. 'However, we will talk about all that later,' said she, suddenly brightening. 'Come! I will show her to you. She can crawl already.'

In the nursery the luxury noticeable in the rest of the house struck Dolly still more strongly. Here were perambulators ordered from England, an apparatus to teach a baby to walk, a specially-constructed piece of furniture like a billiard-table for the baby to crawl on, swings, and baths of a new special kind. All these were English, strongly made, of good quality, and evidently very expensive. The room was large, very lofty and light.

When they entered the little girl was sitting in her chemise in a little arm-chair at a table, having her dinner of broth which she was spilling all over her little chest. A Russian nursemaid was feeding the child and evidently herself eating also.

On hearing Anna's voice a smart tall Englishwoman with an unpleasant face and an impure look came into the room, rapidly shaking her fair curls, and at once began excusing herself, though Anna had not accused her of anything. To each word of Anna's the Englishwoman quickly repeated, 'Yes, my lady!' several times.

The dark-browed, dark-haired, rosy little girl, with her firm ruddy little body, pleased Dolly very much, despite the severe expression with which she regarded the new visitor; she even felt a little envious of the child's healthy appearance. But Dolly did not at all like the general atmosphere of that nursery, especially the English nurse. Besides that, from a few words she heard, Dolly at once understood that the mother's appearance was not a usual occurrence. Anna wished to get the baby her toy and could not find it.

But the most astonishing thing was that when asked how many teeth the baby had, Anna made a mistake and knew nothing of the two latest teeth.

'I feel it hard sometimes that I am as it were superfluous here,' said Anna on leaving the nursery, lifting her train to avoid the toys that lay beside the door. 'It was quite different with the first one,' she said, screwing up her eyes as if peering at something far off. 'However, we will talk about that afterwards. Would you believe it, I am just like a starving woman to whom a full meal has been served, and who does not know what to begin on first? The full meal is you and the talks I am going to have with you, and which I could not have with anyone else, and I don't know on what to begin first! I must speak out about everything. Yes, I must give you a sketch of the people you will meet here,' she began. 'I will begin with the woman: Princess Barbara. You know her, and I know your and Stiva's opinion of her. Stiva says the one aim of her life is to prove her superiority to Aunt Catherine Pavlovna. That is quite true; but she is kind, and I am very grateful to her. There was a moment in Petersburg when I needed a chaperone. Just then she turned up. She made my position much easier. I see you do not realize the difficulty of my position ... there in Petersburg,' she added. 'Here I am quite tranquil and happy; but about that later on. I must continue the list. Then there's Sviyazhsky: he is a Marshal of the Nobility and a very decent fellow, but he wants something from Alexis. You see, with his means, now that we have settled in the country, Alexis can have great influence. Then there is Tushkevich: you have met him, he was always with Betsy. Now he has been deposed and has come to us. As Alexis says he is one of those men who are very agreeable if one takes them for what they wish to appear. Then there's Veslovsky ... you know him. He is a nice boy,' she said, and a roguish smile puckered her lips. 'What outrageous affair was that with Levin? Veslovsky told Alexis and we simply can't believe it. Men need distraction, and Alexis needs an audience; so I value all this company. Things must be lively and amusing here, so that Alexis shall not wish for anything new! Then you will also see our steward. He is a German, very good, and knows his business. Alexis thinks highly of him. Then there's the doctor, a young man, not exactly a Nihilist, but—you know, eats with his knife ... but a very good doctor. Then there's the architect ...'

14

'Well, here's Dolly for you, Princess! You wanted so much to see her,' said Anna as she and Dolly came out on to the large stone verandah where in the shade, before an embroidery frame, the Princess Barbara sat embroidering. 'I'll go and find Alexis and bring them all here.'

The Princess Barbara received Dolly affectionately but rather patronizingly, and at once began explaining that she was staying with Anna because she had always loved her more than did her sister Catherine Pavlovna, who had brought Anna up; and that now, when everyone had thrown Anna over, she considered it her duty to help Anna through this transitional and most trying period.

'Her husband will give her a divorce, and then I shall go back to my solitude; but at present I can be of use and I fulfil my duty, however hard it may be, not like others. ... And how kind you are, and how well you have done to come! They live like the best of married couples. It is for God to judge them, not for us. And then they do much good. Has he not told you about his hospital?'

Their conversation was interrupted by Anna, who had found the men in the billiard-room and brought them back with her to the verandah. As there was still plenty of time before dinner, and the weather was beautiful, several different ways of passing the next two hours were proposed.

'Let's walk through the garden and go for a row, to let Darya Alexandrovna see the banks,' suggested Vronsky.

All agreed to this. Veslovsky and Tushkevich went to the bathing-house, promising to get the boat ready there.

Two couples—Anna with Sviyazhsky and Dolly with Vronsky—walked down a garden path. Dolly was somewhat embarrassed and troubled by the quite novel circle she found herself in. Theoretically, she approved of Anna's action. As is frequently the case with irreproachably moral women who become tired of the monotony of a moral life, she from a distance not only excused a guilty love but even envied it. But actually seeing her among these people so alien to herself, with their fashionable tone which was quite new to her, Dolly felt ill at ease. In particular it was disagreeable to her to see the Princess Barbara, who forgave them everything for the sake of the comforts she enjoyed there.

Although in the abstract Dolly approved the step Anna had taken, it was unpleasant to her to see the man for whose sake the step had been taken. Besides, she had never liked Vronsky. She considered him very proud, and saw nothing in him to justify that pride, except his wealth. She experienced the same kind of shyness in his presence that she had felt when the lady's maid saw her jacket. With him she felt not exactly ashamed but ill at ease about herself.

Feeling embarrassed, she tried to think of something to talk about.

'I like the courtyard in front of the portico very much. Was it like that before?'

'Oh no!' he replied, and his face lit up with pleasure. 'If you had only seen that courtyard in spring!'

And he began, at first with reserve but more and more carried away by his subject, to draw her attention to various details of the adornment of the house and garden. One could see that, having devoted great pains to the improvement and decoration of his place, Vronsky felt compelled to boast of them to a fresh person, and was heartily pleased by Dolly's praises.

'If you care to see the hospital and are not too tired—it is not far. Shall we go?' he suggested, glancing at her face to assure himself that she really was not bored.

'Will you come, Anna?' he said, turning to her.

'We'll come. Shall we?' she asked Sviyazhsky. 'We must send to let the others know. Yes, it is a monument he is erecting here,' said Anna to Dolly.

The ladies opened their sunshades and entered the sidewalk. After several turnings they passed through a gate, and Dolly saw on the high ground before her a large, red, nearly completed building of a fanciful shape. The still unpainted iron roof shone dazzlingly in the sunshine. Another as yet surrounded by scaffolding was being built.

'How quickly your work gets on!' said Sviyazhsky. 'When I was last here there was no roof.'

'It will be finished by autumn. The interior is nearly completed,' said Anna.

'And what is this new building?'

'That will be the doctor's quarters and the dispensary,' replied Vronsky; and seeing the architect in his short jacket coming toward them, he apologized to the ladies and went to meet him.

Having finished talking with the architect Vronsky rejoined the ladies and led them to the hospital.

'This is the waiting-room,' said Vronsky. 'There will be a desk, a table, and a cupboard here: nothing more.'

'This way! We will pass here. Don't go near the window!' said Anna, feeling whether the paint was dry. 'Alexis, the paint is dry already,' she added.

From the waiting-room they passed into the corridor. Here Vronsky showed them the new system of ventilation which had been installed. Then he showed the marble baths and the beds with peculiar spring mattresses. Then he took them to one ward after another: to the store-room, the linen-room; showed the stoves built on a new plan, then some silent trollies to convey necessary articles, and much besides. Sviyazhsky appreciated everything like one who is acquainted with all the newest improvements. Dolly was simply surprised at what she had never before seen, and wishing to understand it all, asked for information about every detail, which evidently gratified Vronsky.

'But have a look at this ...' and he moved a chair for convalescents, just arrived from abroad, toward Dolly. 'Just look!' He sat down in the chair and began moving it. 'A patient is unable to walk—still too weak, or has something the matter with his feet; but he wants fresh air, so he goes out, takes a ride ...'

Everything interested Dolly and everything pleased her, especially Vronsky himself with his natural and naïve enthusiasm. 'Yes, he is a very nice, good fellow,' she thought again and again, not listening to him but looking at him, understanding his expression, and mentally putting herself in Anna's place. In this animated state she liked him so much that she understood Anna's being able to fall in love with him.

15

'No, I think the Princess Darya Alexandrovna is tired and horses do not interest her,' said Vronsky to Anna, who was suggesting that they should go to the stud farm where Sviyazhsky wanted to look at a new stallion. 'You go, and I will see the Princess back to the house and will have a talk with her—if you do not mind?' he added, turning to Dolly.

'I don't understand anything about horses, and shall be very pleased to,' answered Dolly, taken rather by surprise.

As soon as they had passed through the gate back into the garden, Vronsky glanced in the direction Anna had taken, and having assured himself that she could not hear or see them, he began.

'You have guessed that I want to talk to you,' he said, looking at her with laughter in his eyes. 'I know that you are a friend of Anna's.' He took off his hat, and with his handkerchief mopped his head, which was getting bald.

Dolly did not reply and only looked at him with alarm. Alone with him she suddenly felt frightened: his laughing eyes and stern expression scared her.

'As you have come to see us—and you are the only one of Anna's former friends who has (I do not count the Princess Barbara)—I feel you have done so not because you consider our position normal, but because, realizing all the hardship of that position, you love her as before and wish to help her. Have I understood you rightly?' he asked, turning toward her.

'Oh, yes!' answered Dolly.

'No one feels all the hardship of Anna's position more than I do; and that is naturally so, if you do me the honour of regarding me as a man with a heart. I am the cause of that position and therefore I feel it.'

'I understand,' said Dolly, involuntarily admiring him for the frank and firm way in which he said it. 'I understand that her position in Society is a hard one.'

'In Society it is hell!' he said quickly with a dark frown. 'It is impossible to imagine greater moral torments than those she endured for two weeks in Petersburg. ... I beg you to believe me!'

'Yes, but here, so long as neither Anna nor you ... feel that you need Society ...'

'Society!' he exclaimed with contempt. 'What need can I have of Society?'

'Till then, and that may be always, you are happy and tranquil. I see that Anna is happy, quite happy, she has already told me so,' said Dolly smiling; and involuntarily while saying it she doubted whether Anna was really happy.

But Vronsky, it seemed, did not doubt it.

'Yes, yes,' he said. 'I know she is happy in the present. But I? ... I am afraid of what is before us. ... Let us sit down here.'

Dolly sat down on a seat at the turn of the avenue. He stood before her.

'I see she is happy,' he repeated. 'But can it continue? Whether we acted rightly or wrongly the die is cast,' he said. 'And we are bound together for life. We are united by what are for us the holiest bonds of love. We have a child, we may have other children. Yet the law and the circumstances of our position are such that thousands of complications appear which at present, while resting after all her sufferings and trials, she neither sees nor wishes to see. But I cannot help seeing them. My daughter is not mine by law, but Karenin's. I hate this falsehood!' he said with an energetic gesture of denial, and looked at Dolly with a gloomy expression.

She made no answer, but only looked at him. He continued:

'Some day a son may be born, my son, and he will by law be a Karenin, and not heir either to my name or my property, and however happy we may be in our family life, and whatever children we may have, there will be no legal bond between them and me. They will be—Karenin's! Imagine the hardship and horror of this situation! I have tried to speak to Anna about it, but it irritates her. Now look at the other side of it. I am happy, happy in her love, but I need an occupation. I have found one. I am proud of it. The principal thing is that when working I want the assurance that the work will not die with me, that I shall have heirs; and that I have not got. Imagine the situation of a man who knows in advance that children born of him and of the woman he loves will not be his, but some one else's—some one who will hate them and will have nothing to do with them! You know it is dreadful!'

'Yes, of course. But what can Anna do?' asked Dolly.

'Well, this brings me to the point of my talk,' he went on, calming himself with an effort. 'Anna can do it; it depends on her. ... Even to be able to petition the Emperor for permission to adopt the child, a divorce will be necessary, and that depends on Anna. Her husband was willing to have a divorce—your husband had almost arranged it—and I know he would not refuse now. It is only necessary to write to him. I understand that it is painful for her, but the reasons are so important. I do not speak of myself, though it's very hard on me, very hard,' he said with a look as if he were menacing some one for making it so hard on him. 'And so, Princess, I shamelessly cling to you as an anchor of salvation! Help me to persuade her to write to him and demand a divorce!'

'Yes, certainly,' said Dolly thoughtfully. 'But how is it she herself does not think of it?' asked Dolly, suddenly remembering that strange new habit Anna had of screwing up her eyes. 'Certainly I will speak to her, for my own sake and for hers,' she said in reply to his expression of gratitude.

They got up and went back to the house.

16

Finding Dolly already returned, Anna looked attentively into her eyes as if asking about the talk she had had with Vronsky, but she did not ask in words.

'I think it's nearly dinner-time,' she said. 'We have not yet seen anything of one another. ... I am counting on this evening. Now I must go and dress, and you too, I suppose. We have dirtied ourselves on the buildings.'

Dolly went to her room, feeling amused. She had nothing to change into as she was already wearing her best dress; but to give some sign that she had prepared for dinner, she asked the maid to brush her dress, and she put on clean cuffs, pinned a fresh bow to her dress and placed some lace in her hair.

'This is all I was able to do,' she smilingly said to Anna, who came to her in a third dress, again extremely simple.

'Yes, we are very formal here,' Anna remarked, as if excusing her own smartness. 'Alexis is seldom so pleased about anything as he is at your having come.' She said. 'But aren't you tired?'

There was no time to discuss anything before dinner. When they entered the drawing-room the Princess Barbara and the men were already there. The men wore frock-coats, except the architect, who was in a dress suit. Vronsky introduced the doctor and the steward to his visitor; the architect had already been presented at the hospital.

The fat butler—his round, clean-shaven face and starched white tie shining—announced dinner. The ladies rose; Vronsky asked Sviyazhsky to take in Anna, and himself went up to Dolly. Veslovsky offered his arm to the Princess Barbara before Tushkevich could do so, so that the latter, the steward, and the doctor went in by themselves.

The dinner, the dining-room, the dinner-service, the servants and the wine and the food were not merely in keeping with the general tone of modern luxury in the house, but seemed even more luxurious and more modern than the rest. Dolly observed all this luxury and knew that so complicated and splendid an organization must have needed some one's careful attention; and from the way Vronsky surveyed the table, gave a sign with his head to the butler, and asked her whether she would take fish-broth or soup, she concluded that it had all been done by, and depended on, the master's care.

Anna was the hostess only in what concerned the conversation. And that difficult task for the mistress of a house with a small circle which included such people as the steward and the architect—people of quite a different world, who tried not to be abashed by the unfamiliar luxury and were unable to take any sustained part in the general conversation—Anna managed that task with her usual tact, naturally and even with pleasure, as Dolly observed.

The conversation among the diners—except the doctor, the architect and the steward, who sat in gloomy silence—was incessant, now gliding smoothly, now catching on something and touching one or other of them to the quick. Once Dolly was stung to the quick, and so aroused that she even flushed up, and afterwards wondered whether she had said anything superfluous and disagreeable. Sviyazhsky began talking about Levin.

'I am very fond of him, and we are great friends,' said Sviyazhsky with a good-natured smile. 'But he maintains that the Zemstvos and Magistrates are quite unnecessary, and he won't have anything to do with them.'

'That is our Russian indifference,' said Vronsky, 'not to realize the duties our rights impose on us, and to deny those duties.'

'I know no one who fulfils his duties more strictly,' said Dolly, irritated by Vronsky's superior tone.

'I, on the contrary,' continued Vronsky, who was evidently for some reason touched to the quick by this conversation, 'feel very grateful for the honour they have done me, thanks to Nicholas Ivanich'—he indicated Sviyazhsky—'by electing me Justice of the Peace. I shall consider it an honour if they elect me to the Zemstvo. It is only so that I can make a return for the advantages I enjoy as a landowner. Unfortunately people do not understand the importance the large landowners should have in the State.' To Dolly it sounded strange to hear how assured he was of being in the right, here at his own table. She remembered how Levin, who held the opposite opinion, was equally positive in his opinions at his own table. But she was fond of Levin, and therefore sided with him.

'And I rather agree with your brother-in-law,' said Anna, 'though I do not go to his lengths,' she added with a smile. 'I'm afraid we have too many of these public obligations nowadays. Formerly we used to have so many officials that there had to be an official for everything that was done, and now we have public workers for everything! Alexis has not been here six months, and I think he is already a Member of five or six different institutions. And I fear that with the multiplication of these positions they become a mere form. Of how many institutions are you a member, Nicholas Ivanich?' she asked, addressing Sviyazhsky; 'more than twenty, isn't it?'

Although Anna spoke playfully, irritation was perceptible in her tone. Dolly, who was attentively watching her and Vronsky, noticed it at once. She also saw that at this conversation Vronsky's face immediately assumed a serious and obstinate expression. Noticing these things, and that the Princess Barbara hastened to change the subject, she understood that with this question of public work some private difference between Anna and Vronsky was connected.

The dinner, the wine, the service were all very good, but they were all such as Dolly—though she had become unused to them—had seen before at dinner-parties and balls, and like those functions they bore a character of impersonality and strain; therefore on an everyday occasion and in a small gathering they produced an unpleasant impression on her.

After dinner they sat awhile on the verandah. Then they played lawn-tennis. The players, having chosen their partners, took their places on the carefully levelled and rolled croquet lawn, on the two sides of a net stretched between two small gilded pillars. Dolly tried to play, but was long unable to understand the game, and by the time she did understand it she was so tired that she sat down beside the Princess Barbara to watch the others. Her partner Tushkevich also gave it up; but the rest played for a long time. Sviyazhsky and Vronsky both played very well and seriously. Veslovsky played worse than the others. He was too eager, but to make up for that his gaiety inspired his companions. His laughter and shouts never ceased.

While they were playing Dolly was not feeling happy. She did not like the bantering tone between Anna and Veslovsky that continued during the game. All that day she felt as if she were acting in a theatre with better actors than herself, and that her bad performance was spoiling the whole affair.

She had come with the intention of staying two days but that evening during the game she resolved to leave next day.

When, after evening tea and a row in the boat at night-time, Dolly entered her bedroom alone, took off her dress and sat down to do up her thin hair for the night, she felt great relief.

Dolly was ready to get into bed when Anna in her night-gown came into the room. She sat by the window, looking at Dolly and mentally reviewing all those stores of intimate topics that had seemed inexhaustible, and could find nothing to say. It seemed to her at that moment as if everything had already been said.

'Well, and how's Kitty?' she asked with a deep sigh and a guilty glance at Dolly. 'Tell me the truth, Dolly: is she not angry with me?'

'Angry? No!' replied Dolly with a smile. 'But tell me about yourself. I have much to talk to you about and I have been talking with ...' Dolly did not know what to call him.

'With Alexis?' said Anna. 'I know you have. But I want to ask you frankly, what do you think of me and of my life?'

'How can I tell you all at once? I really don't know.'

'Oh, but all the same, tell me! ... You see what my life is. But don't forget that you see us in summer, when you have come and we are not alone. ... But we came here in early spring and lived quite alone, and we shall live alone again. I don't wish for anything better. But imagine me living alone, without him, *alone*, and that will happen ... everything shows that it will often happen,—that he will spend half his time from home,' she said, rising and taking a seat nearer to Dolly. 'Of course,' she went on, interrupting Dolly, who was about to reply, 'of course I won't keep him against his will! But think of me, imagine my position. ... But why talk of it!' She smiled. 'Well then, what did he talk about to you?'

'He talked about what I myself wanted to ask you, so it is easy for me to be his advocate: about whether it isn't possible ...' Dolly hesitated, 'to improve your position ... But all the same, if it is possible you should get married.'

'That is, get a divorce?' said Anna. 'Do you know, the only woman who called on me in Petersburg was Betsy Tverskaya? You know her, of course? She had a liaison with Tushkevich, deceiving her husband in the worst way, and she told me that she did not wish to know me as long as my position was irregular ...! Don't think I am making any comparison. ... I know you, my darling. ... But I could not help remembering. ... Well then, what did he say to you?'

'He said that he suffers on your account and on his own. Perhaps he wants, first of all, to legitimatize his daughter and to be your husband and have a right to you. And his most legitimate wish is that your children should not be nameless.'

'What children?' said Anna, screwing up her eyes and not looking at Dolly.

'Annie, and those that will come ...'

'He may be at ease about that: I shall not have any more children.'

'How do you know you won't?'

'I shan't, because I don't want them.'

And in spite of her agitation Anna smiled on noticing the naïve expression of curiosity, surprise and terror on Dolly's face.

'After my illness the doctor told me ...'

'Impossible!' said Dolly, with wide-open eyes. This discovery, which suddenly explained to her those hitherto incomprehensible families where there were only one or two children, awoke in her so many thoughts, reflections and contradictory feelings that she could say nothing, and only stared at Anna with wide-open eyes full of astonishment. It was the very thing she had dreamt of, but now on learning that it was possible, she was horrified. She felt that it was too simple a solution of too complex a question.

'Remember I have to choose between two things: either to become pregnant, that is ill, or to be the friend and comrade of my husband—for he is my husband all the same,' said Anna.

'Well, yes, of course,' said Dolly.

'For you and for others,' said Anna, as if guessing her thoughts, 'there may still be some doubt, but for me ... Remember, I am not a wife; he loves me as long as his love lasts! Well, how am I to keep his love? You forget my position. How can I desire children? Think who my children would be! Unfortunate beings, who would have to bear a stranger's name! By the very fact of their birth they would have to be ashamed of their mother, their father, their birth!'

'But that's just why a divorce is necessary!'

Anna did not listen. 'Don't forget the chief thing: that I am not in the same position as you! Don't you see that, situated as I am, I cannot desire them?'

'Then there is all the more need to regularize your position if possible,' said Dolly.

'Yes, if possible,' Anna said, in what had suddenly become quite a different—a quiet and sad—voice.

'Is a divorce not possible? I was told your husband had agreed ...'

'Dolly, I don't want to speak about it!'

'Well then, we won't,' Dolly hastened to say, noticing the look of pain on Anna's face. 'But I think you must do all that is possible.'

'But what is possible? Nothing! You say I must marry Alexis, and that I don't consider that. I not consider that!' she repeated, and flushed. She rose, drew herself up, sighed deeply, and with her light steps began pacing up and down the room, pausing occasionally. 'I not consider it? Not a day, not an hour passes without my thinking about it and blaming myself for what I think ... because those thoughts are enough to drive one mad! When I think of it I cannot fall asleep without morphia. They speak of divorce. For one thing, *he* would not agree now. *He* is now under the Countess Lydia Ivanovna's influence.'

Dolly, sitting upright in her chair, with a pained expression of sympathy turned her head to follow Anna's movements.

'One must try,' she said gently.

'Let's grant that. But what would it mean?' said Anna, evidently expressing a thought she had considered a thousand times and knew by heart. 'It means that I, who hate him but yet acknowledge myself to blame toward him—and I do think him magnanimous—I must humiliate myself by writing to him ...! Well, supposing I make that effort and do it: I shall receive either an insulting answer or his consent. Supposing I get his consent ...' Anna at that instant had reached the other end of the room and stopped there, doing something to the window curtain. 'I receive his consent, and my so ... son? They will not give him to me. He will grow up despising me, in the house of his father whom I have left. Understand that I love equally, I think, and both more than myself—two beings: Serezha and Alexis and the one excludes the other! I cannot unite them, yet that is the one thing I desire. And if I can't have that, nothing matters—nothing, nothing! It will end somehow, therefore I can't—I don't like speaking about it. So don't reproach me, don't condemn me for anything! You in your purity cannot understand all I suffer!'

She came and sat down beside Dolly, peering into her face with a guilty look, and took her by the hand.

'What are you thinking? What are you thinking of me? Don't despise me! I don't deserve contempt. I am simply unhappy. If anyone is unhappy, it is I!' she murmured, and, turning away, she wept.

Anna, returning to her boudoir, took a wine-glass and put into it some drops of medicine, the chief ingredient of which was morphia.

Having drunk it and sat still for a few moments, she entered her bed-room cheerfully and merrily.

When she came in Vronsky regarded her attentively. He tried to find some trace of the conversation which he knew, by her having remained so long in Dolly's room, must have taken place. But in her expression of restrained excitement, which concealed something, he detected noth-ing except that beauty which, though familiar, still captivated him, her consciousness of this, and her desire that it should act on him. He did not wish to ask her what they had been talking about, but hoped that she would tell him of her own accord.

He took Anna's hand and looked inquiringly into her eyes.

She, misunderstanding that look, smiled at him.

Next morning, in spite of her hosts' entreaties, Dolly prepared to go home. Levin's coachman in his by no means new coat, and a hat something like a post-boy's, with his horses that did not match and the old *calèche* with mended mud-guards, drove up gloomily but resolutely to the covered, sand-strewn portico.

Taking leave of the Princess Barbara and of the men was unpleasant to Dolly. After spending a day together both she and her host felt distinctly that they did not suit one another. Only Anna felt sad. She knew that when Dolly was gone no one would call up in her soul the feelings which had been aroused by their meeting. To have those feelings awakened was painful, but still she knew that they were the best part of her soul, and that that part of her was rapidly being choked by the life she was leading.

When they had driven into the fields Dolly experienced a feeling of relief, and she was about to ask the men how they had liked the Vronskys' place, when suddenly Philip the coachman himself remarked:

'They're rich, that they are, but yet they gave us only two bushels of oats. The horses had eaten every grain before cock-crow! What's two bushels? Only a bite. Nowadays oats are forty-five kopeks at the inns. When anyone comes to our place, no fear, we give their horses as much as they'll eat.'

'A stingy gentleman ...' confirmed the clerk.

'Well, and did you like their horses?' asked Dolly.

'The horses? Fine's the only word for them! And the food is good too. But it did seem so dull to me, Darya Alexandrovna! I don't know how you found it,' he added, turning his handsome, kindly face toward her.

'I felt the same. Well, shall we get back by evening?'

'We ought to.'

On returning home and finding every one safe and extremely nice,

Dolly gave a very animated account of her visit, of how well she had been received, of the luxury and good taste at the Vronskys', and of their amusements, and would not let anyone say a word against them, forgetting the indefinite feelings of dissatisfaction and embarrassment she had experienced there.

17

Vronsky and Anna went on living in the country in the same way, still taking no steps to obtain a divorce, all the summer and part of the autumn. They had agreed not to go away anywhere; but the longer they lived alone the more they both felt—especially in autumn when there were no visitors—that they would not be able to hold out and that a change was inevitable.

Their life seemed one that could not be improved upon: they had ample means, good health, a child, and both had occupations of their own. In the absence of visitors Anna read a great deal—both novels and such serious books as were in fashion. She studied also from books and from technical papers all the subjects with which Vronsky was occupied, so that he often came straight to her with questions about agriculture, architecture, and sometimes even horse-breeding or sport.

The arrangement of the hospital also interested her. There she not only helped, but arranged and planned many things herself. Nevertheless, her chief preoccupation was still herself—herself in so far as Vronsky held her dear and in so far as she could compensate him for all he had given up. Vronsky appreciated this, which had become the sole aim of her life, a desire not only to please him but also to serve him; but at the same time he was troubled by these love-meshes in which she tried to entangle him. As time went on, the oftener he felt himself caught in these meshes the more he desired, not exactly to escape from them but to try whether they really interfered with his freedom. Had it not been for this ever-increasing desire for freedom—not to have a scene each time he had to go to town to a meeting or to the races—Vronsky would have been quite content with his life.

In October there were the Nobility elections in the Kashin Province, in which Vronsky's, Sviyazhsky's, Koznyshev's, and also a small part of Levin's estates were situated. Vronsky had long ago promised Sviyazhsky to be present.

Before the elections Sviyazhsky, who often visited at Vozdvizhensk, called for Vronsky.

The day before, Vronsky, bracing himself for a struggle, announced his departure in a sterner and colder way than he had ever before used to Anna. But, to his surprise, Anna took the news very quietly and only asked when he would return. He looked at her attentively, not understanding this calm manner. She answered his look with a smile. He knew her capacity for withdrawing into herself, and knew that she only did it when she had come to some resolution in her own mind without telling him of her plans. He feared this; but he so wished to avoid a scene.

'I hope you won't be dull?'

'I hope not,' replied Anna. 'I received a box of books yesterday. No, I shan't be dull.'

'She means to adopt this tone—well, so much the better!' thought he, 'or else it would be the usual thing again.'

And so, without challenging her to a frank explanation, he left for the elections. It was the first time since their union that he had parted from her without a full explanation. On the one hand this fact disturbed him, but on the other hand it seemed the best way. 'At first there will be, as now, something uncertain, something concealed; but afterwards she will get used to it. In any case I can give her everything else, but not my independence as a man,' he reflected.

18

In September Levin moved to Moscow for Kitty's confinement. He had already been living there a whole month without occupation, when Sergius Ivanich Koznyshev, who had an estate in the Kashin Province and took a great interest in the forthcoming elections, prepared to attend them. He asked his brother, who had a vote for the Seleznev district, to accompany him.

Levin was still wavering, but Kitty, who had noticed that he was dull in Moscow and had advised him to go, without saying anything to him ordered for him the uniform necessary for the occasion, which cost eighty roubles. And it was these eighty roubles paid for the uniform which chiefly decided him. So he went to Kashin.

Koznyshev explained to him the meaning and importance of the changes anticipated as a result of the elections. The Marshal of the Nobility for the Province—in whose hands the law placed so much important public business—Snetkov, was one of the old type of nobles. He had run through an enormous fortune, was a kind man, honest in his way but quite unable to understand present-day requirements. He always sided with the Nobility in everything, openly opposed the spread of popular education, and gave a class character to the Zemstvo, which should have such enormous importance. It was necessary to put in his place a fresh, up-to-date, practical, and quite new man. In the wealthy Province of Kashin, always ahead of all others, such forces were now assembled that, if matters were here managed as they should be, it might serve as an example to other Provinces and to the whole of Russia. The affair was therefore of great importance. To replace Snetkov as Marshal, Sviyazhsky was proposed, or Nevedovsky, an ex-professor, a remarkably intelligent man, and a great friend of Koznyshev's.

The Session was opened by the Governor of the Province, who in his speech to the nobles told them that in choosing occupants for posts they should show no partiality, but should choose according to merit and for the welfare of the country, and that he hoped the honourable Nobility of Kashin would strictly fulfil its duty.

Having finished his speech the Governor left the hall, and the noblemen, noisily, vivaciously, some of them even rapturously, followed him out with enthusiasm, and stood around him as he was putting on his fur coat and talking in a friendly way with the Marshal of the Province. Levin, wishing to enter fully into everything and not to miss anything, joined the crowd.

In the cathedral Levin, with the others, raised his hand, repeating the words of the priest, and swore by the most awful oaths to fulfil all the things the Governor had hoped for. Church services always touched Levin, and when he was uttering the words, 'I kiss the cross,' and looked round at the crowd of men, young and old, who were repeating the same words, he felt moved.

On the second and third days matters were dealt with concerning the funds of the Nobility and the Girls' High Schools. On the fourth day the audit of the Provincial Funds was undertaken, and now for the first time there was a conflict between the new and old parties. The Commission entrusted with the task of auditing reported to the Assembly that the sums were all correct. The Marshal of the Nobility rose and with tears in his eyes thanked the Nobility for their confidence. The nobles loudly applauded him and pressed his hand. But at that moment one of the nobles of Koznyshev's party said he had heard that the Commission had not audited the Funds, considering that a verification would be an insult to the Marshal of the Province. Thereupon the members of the Commission withdrew their report and Koznyshev began very logically to prove that they must admit either that they had audited the accounts or that they had not done so, and to elaborate this dilemma. Levin was surprised that they disputed about it so long, especially as, when he asked Koznyshev whether he thought that money had been misappropriated, he received the reply:

'Oh no! He is an honest fellow, but this old-fashioned patriarchal management of the Nobility's affairs must be put a stop to!'

On the fifth day the election of the District Marshals took place. For some of the districts the election was stormy enough; but for the Selezensk district Sviyazhsky was elected without opposition, and he gave a dinner-party at his house that evening.

On the sixth day the Provincial elections were to be held. The large and small halls were full of noblemen in various uniforms. Many had come for that day only. Men who had long not met came together in those halls. At the Marshal's table, beneath the portrait of the Emperor, discussions were in full swing.

Both in the large and small halls the noblemen were grouped together in their parties, and from the hostility and suspicion of their glances, from the cessation of their conversations when a stranger approached, and from the fact that some of them even went whispering into the farther corridor, it was evident that each party had secrets it kept from the other.

Levin stood with his own group in the Small Hall, which was used as a refreshment and smoking room, listening to what was being said and vainly straining his mental powers to understand it all. Koznyshev was the centre around whom the rest were grouped.

Oblonsky, who had just had something to eat and drink, came toward them in his Chamberlain's uniform, wiping his mouth with his scented and bordered lawn handkerchief.

'We are holding the position, Sergius Ivanich!' said he, smoothing back his whiskers. And after listening to the conversation he backed Sviyazhsky's opinion.

'One district is sufficient, and Sviyazhsky evidently belongs to the Opposition,' he said, and every one but Levin understood him.

'Well, Kostya! You too seem to have got a taste for it?' he said, turning to Levin and taking him by the arm. Levin would have been glad to get a taste for it but could not understand what the point was.

Oblonsky briefly and clearly explained the matter to Levin who understood, but not fully, and wished to put some further questions when suddenly every one began talking at once, and moving noisily toward the Large Hall.

'What is it? What? Who? An authorization? To whom? What? Rejected! No authorization! Flerov is not admitted! What if he is being prosecuted? In that way they can exclude anybody! It's mean!'

Levin was standing some way off. He could hear only the distant soft voice of the Marshal, then the shrill voice of a venomous nobleman, and then Sviyazhsky's voice.

The crowd separated to make way for Koznyshev to approach the table. He waited for the venomous nobleman to conclude, and then said he considered the proper course would be to consult the wording of the Act and requested the Secretary to look it up.

Koznyshev read the Act aloud, and began to explain its meaning, but a tall, thick-set landowner interrupted him. Advancing to the table he struck his ring against it, shouting in a loud voice:

'Vote! Put it to the ballot! Enough talking! Vote!'

He was demanding the very thing Koznyshev was proposing; but he evidently hated Koznyshev and his party, and this hatred communicated itself to all those on his side, and in turn evoked a similar, though more decently expressed, feeling of conflicting anger from the opposing party.

Levin was astounded at the ardour with which they discussed the question whether Flerov's case should be put to the ballot or not. He forgot, as Koznyshev afterwards explained to him, the syllogism that for the common welfare it was necessary to displace the Marshal of the Province; but to defeat the Marshal it was necessary to have a majority of votes; to obtain that majority it was necessary to secure for Flerov the right to vote; and to secure Flerov's eligibility it was necessary to explain the meaning of the law.

But Levin had forgotten that, and it pained him to see these good men, whom he respected, in such an unpleasant, malevolent state of excitement. To free himself from this feeling he went, without waiting to hear the end of the discussion, into the refreshment-room, where there was no one except the waiters at the buffet. When he saw the waiters busily wiping crockery and arranging plates and wine-glasses, and saw their calm yet animated faces, he experienced an unexpected feeling of relief. He began pacing up and down the room, watching the waiters with pleasure, when the Secretary of the Court of Nobility, an old man whose speciality it was to know all the nobles of the Province by name and patronymic, diverted his attention.

'Please come, Constantine Dmitrich!' said he. 'Your brother is looking for you. The vote is being taken.'

Levin entered the Hall, was given a white ball, and, following his brother, Sergius Ivanich, approached the table at which Sviyazhsky stood with an ironical and impressive look on his face, gathering his beard into his fist and smelling at it. Koznyshev inserted his hand in the ballot-box and placed his ball somewhere, and making way for Levin paused beside him. Levin hastily thrust his hand under the cloth that covered the box, and, as the ball was in his right hand, dropped it on the right side. When he had done so he recollected that he ought to have put in his left hand also, and thrust it in, but it was too late; he hurried away to the very back of the room.

'One hund'ed and twenty-six fo'! Ninety-eight against!' came the Secretary's voice, dropping his *r*'s. Flerov was qualified and the new party had scored. But the old party did not consider itself defeated. Levin heard Snetkov being asked to stand; and he saw that a crowd of nobles surrounded the Marshal, who was speaking. Levin drew near. Replying to the nobles, Snetkov spoke of the confidence and affection of the Nobility, of which he was not worthy, his merit consisting only in his loyalty to the Nobility, to whom he had devoted twenty years of service. Several times he repeated the words: '*have served to the extent of my power—faithfully and truly—I appreciate and thank …*' Then suddenly, choked by tears, the Marshal disappeared through a sidedoor.

The most solemn moment had arrived. The elections were about to begin. The leaders of both parties were making estimates and calculating on their fingers the white and black balls they could reckon on.

The debate about Flerov had given the new party not merely his vote but also a gain in time, so that they had had a chance to bring up three more nobles who, by the machinations of the old party, were to be prevented from taking part in the election. Two of these noblemen, who had a weakness for wine, had been made drunk by Snetkov's agents, and the uniform of the third had been carried off.

The new party, having heard of this, had had time while Flerov's case was being discussed to send two of their men in a carriage to supply that nobleman with a uniform and to bring one of the tipsy ones to the Assembly.

19

The narrow room in which they were eating and smoking was full of noblemen. The excitement was ever increasing and anxiety was noticeable on all the faces. Especially excited were the leaders, who knew all the details and the estimates of votes. They were directors of the impending battle. The others, like the rank and file before a battle, though preparing for the fight, sought distraction meanwhile. Some of them ate, standing or hastily sitting down at the table; others smoked cigarettes, pacing up and down the long room, and talked to friends they had not seen for a long time.

Levin did not want to eat and did not smoke; he did not wish to join his own set—Koznyshev, Oblonsky, Sviyazhsky and the others—because among them, in animated conversation, stood Vronsky, wearing his uniform as an equerry. Levin had noticed him at the elections the day before and had carefully avoided meeting him. He went to the window and sat down, looking at the different groups and listening to what was being said around him.

Sviyazhsky approached, took Levin's arm and led him back to his own group.

This time it was impossible to avoid Vronsky. He was standing with Oblonsky and Koznyshev, and looked straight at Levin as he came up.

'Very pleased! I think I had the pleasure of meeting you ... at the Princess Shcherbatsky's?' said he, holding out his hand to Levin.

'Yes, I well remember our meeting,' said Levin, and blushing scarlet immediately turned and spoke to his brother.

Smiling slightly, Vronsky continued his conversation with Sviyazhsky, evidently having no desire to start a conversation with Levin; but Levin, while talking to his brother, kept looking round at Vronsky, trying to think of something to say to him, in order to mitigate his rudeness.

'What is delaying matters now?' asked Levin, glancing at Sviyazhsky and Vronsky.

'Snetkov. He must either decline or accept,' replied Sviyazhsky.

'Well, and has he agreed or not?'

'That's just it: neither the one nor the other,' answered Vronsky.

'And if he should refuse, who will stand?' asked Levin.

'Whoever likes,' replied Sviyazhsky.

'Will you?' asked Levin.

'Certainly not I,' said Sviyazhsky, becoming embarrassed and casting an alarmed glance at the venomous gentleman, who was standing beside Koznyshev.

'Who then? Nevedovsky?' said Levin, feeling that he had put his foot in it somehow.

'Not I, not on any account!' said the venomous gentleman.

So this was Nevedovsky! Sviyazhsky introduced him to Levin.

'Well, has it touched you to the quick too?' said Oblonsky, winking at Vronsky. 'It's like the races. It makes one inclined to bet on the result.'

'Yes, it does touch one to the quick,' replied Vronsky, 'and having once taken the matter up, one wants to carry it through. It's a struggle!'

he said frowning, and closed his powerful jaw.

There was a pause, during which Vronsky, since he had to look at something, looked at Levin: at his feet, his uniform, and then his face, and noticing the sombre eyes fixed upon him he remarked, just to say something:

'And how is it that you, living constantly in the country, are not a Justice of the Peace? You are not in the uniform of a Justice?'

'Because I consider that the Magistracy is an idiotic institution,' morosely replied Levin. 'We don't need any Justices of the Peace. I have not had a single case in eight years, and when I did have one it was decided wrongly. The Justice's Court is forty versts from my house. To settle a matter worth two roubles I should have to send an attorney who costs me fifteen.'

'Oh, he is such a crank!' said Oblonsky with his smoothest and most almondy smile. 'But come! I think the ballot has begun ...'

And they separated.

'I don't understand,' said Koznyshev, who had observed his brother's awkward sally, 'I don't understand how one can be so entirely devoid of political tact! Count Vronsky ... I do not make a friend of him; he invited me to dinner and I shan't go; but he is one of our party, so why make an enemy of him? Then you ask Nevedovsky whether he will stand. That kind of thing is not done!'

Levin remained silent and they entered the Large Hall together.

The Marshal of the Province, though he felt in the air that there was a plot prepared against him, and though he had not been unanimously asked to stand, had still decided to do so. There was silence in the hall, and the Secretary loudly announced that Michael Stepanich Snetkov, Captain of the Guards, was nominated for the post of Provincial Marshal, and that the ballot would now be taken.

The District Marshals carried little plates filled with ballot balls from their own tables to the Provincial table, and the election began.

'Put it on the right,' whispered Oblonsky to Levin as the latter, with his brother, followed the Marshal to the table. But Levin had forgotten the plan which had been explained to him, and was afraid that Oblonsky was making a mistake when he said 'right'. Surely Snetkov was their opponent! While approaching the box he had the ball in his right hand, but, thinking it was a mistake, he shifted it to his left hand just as he reached the box.

All became silent again, and one heard the balls being counted. Then a solitary voice proclaimed the number for and against. The Marshal had received a considerable majority. A clamour arose and every one rushed to the door. Snetkov entered and the noblemen thronged around him with congratulations.

'Well, is it over now?' Levin asked his brother.

'It's only beginning!' Sviyazhsky smilingly answered for Koznyshev. 'The other candidate may get still more votes.'

Levin had again forgotten about that. He was overcome by depression and wanted to get out of that crowd.

As no one was paying any attention to him, and he apparently was not wanted by anybody, he went up into the gallery.

The gallery was crowded with smartly-dressed women who leaned over the balustrade and tried not to miss a single word of what was being said below. Beside the women sat or stood elegant lawyers, spectacled High School teachers, and officers. Every one was talking about the elections and how tired out the Marshal was and how interesting the debates had been.

Having found a vacant place at the balustrade, Levin leant over and began to look and listen.

The noblemen were sitting behind partitions, arranged according to their districts. In the centre of the room stood a man in uniform, who announced in a loud shrill voice:

'As candidate for the post of Provincial Marshal, Captain Eugene Ivanich Apukhtin will now be balloted for.' Then followed a dead silence, and a feeble voice was heard saying:

'Declines!'

A similar announcement was made, and again followed by 'Declines'. So it went on for about an hour. Levin, leaning over the balustrade, looked on and listened. At first he was surprised and wanted to understand what it meant; then, coming to the conclusion that he could not understand it, he grew bored. Then, remembering the agitation and anger he had witnessed on all faces, he felt sad, and with the intention of leaving the place went downstairs.

The Secretary caught him. 'Please come, Constantine Dmitrich! They are voting!'

The candidate who was standing was Nevedovsky, who had so decidedly declined.

Levin went up to the door of the hall: it was locked. The Secretary knocked, the door opened and two landowners with flushed faces plunged out past Levin.

Then the head of the Provincial Marshal was thrust out at the doorway. His face was dreadful from its expression of exhaustion and fear.

'I told you to let no one out!' he shouted to the door-keeper.

'I was letting people in, your Excellency!'

'Oh, Lord!' said the Marshal of the Province with a deep sigh.

Nevedovsky had a majority as they had expected and he was now Marshal of the Province. When he left the hall the crowd surrounded him and followed him enthusiastically as it had followed the Governor of the Province on the first day, when he opened the meeting, and as it had followed Snetkov when he was successful.

The newly-elected Marshal of the Province and many of the victorious new party dined that evening at Vronsky's.

Vronsky had come to the elections because he felt dull in the country, in order to proclaim to Anna his right to freedom, to repay Sviyazhsky by supporting him at these elections for all the trouble he had taken for Vronsky at the Zemstvo elections, and most of all to perform strictly all the duties of the position he had taken up as a nobleman and landowner. But he had not at all expected that the election business would interest him so much and so touch him to the quick, or that he could do it so well. He was quite a new man in this circle of noble landowners, but he evidently was a success; and he was not mistaken in thinking that he had already gained influence among them. Now, at his own table, celebrating Nevedovsky's election, Vronsky experienced a pleasant feeling of triumph. Vronsky sat at the head of the table; on his right was the young Governor, a General of the Emperor's suite. On his left sat Nevedovsky with his youthful, dogged, and venomous look. Toward him Vronsky was simple and courteous.

Sviyazhsky bore his failure cheerfully. It was not even a failure for him; as he himself said to Nevedovsky, champagne glass in hand, no better representative of the new course which the Nobility ought to follow could have been found. And therefore all that was honest, as he remarked, was on the side of to-day's success and triumphed in it. Oblonsky too was pleased that he had spent his time merrily and that every one was satisfied.

During the dinner they continually spoke of Nevedovsky as 'Our Provincial Marshal' and addressed him as 'your Excellency'.

Nevedovsky pretended not merely to be indifferent to but to despise this title; but it was evident that he felt happy and exercised self-control to avoid betraying a delight ill-suited to the new Liberal circle in which they found themselves.

When they had already quitted the table and had all begun smoking, Vronsky's valet came up to him with a letter on a salver.

'From Vozdvizhensk, by express messenger,' he said with a significant glance.

The letter was from Anna. Expecting the elections to end in five days, he had promised to return on the Friday. It was now Saturday, and he knew that the letter he had sent off the evening before had probably not yet reached her.

The contents of the letter were just what he expected, but its form was unexpected and particularly unpleasant to him. 'Annie is very ill. The doctor says it may be inflammation. I lose my head when alone. The Princess Barbara is not a help but a hindrance. I expected you the day before yesterday, and yesterday, and am now sending to find out where you are and what the matter is. I wished to come myself, but changed my mind knowing that you would not like it. Give me some reply that I may know what to do.'

Baby was ill, and she wished to come herself! Their child ill, and this hostile tone!

The innocent mirth of the elections and this dismal burdensome love to which he must return struck Vronsky by their contrast. But he had to go, and he took the first train that night for his home.

20

Before Vronsky went to the elections Anna, having considered that the scenes which took place between them every time he went away could only tend to estrange them instead of binding them closer, resolved to make every possible effort to bear the separation calmly. But the cold, stern look on his face when he came to tell her he was going offended her, and even before he had gone her composure was upset.

Later on, meditating in solitude on that look—which expressed his right to freedom—she, as usual, came only to a consciousness of her own humiliation. 'That look shows that he is beginning to grow cold.'

Though she was convinced that this was the case, she could not do anything, could not in any way change her relation to him. Just as heretofore, she could hold him only by means of her love and attractiveness; and just as heretofore, only by occupations by day and morphia by night could she stifle the terrible thought of what would happen if he ceased to love her. True, there was one means, not of holding him—for that purpose she wished for nothing except his love—but of putting herself in such a position that he could not abandon her. That means was divorce and marriage. She began to wish for this, and decided to agree the first time he or Stiva should mention it to her.

With these thoughts in her mind she spent five days, the days she expected him to be away. But on the sixth day, when the coachman returned from the station without him, she felt that she was no longer able to stifle the thought of him and of what he was doing. Just then her little girl fell ill. Anna nursed her, but this did not divert her thoughts, especially as the illness was not dangerous. Try as she might she could not love that child and she could not make a pretence of love. Toward the evening of that day, being alone, Anna felt such terror on Vronsky's account that she decided to go to town, but after careful consideration she wrote that contradictory letter which Vronsky received, and without reading it over she sent it by express messenger. Next morning she received his letter and regretted her own. She anticipated with horror a repetition of that stern look he had thrown at her when leaving, especially when he should learn that the little girl was not dangerously ill. But still she was glad she had written. Let him feel weary, but let him be here with her so that she might see him and know his every movement.

She was sitting in the drawing-room, reading by lamp-light, listening to the wind outside, and expecting every moment the arrival of the carriage. At last she heard not only the wheels but also the coachman's voice and a dull rumbling in the portico. Even the Princess Barbara, who was playing patience, confirmed this, and Anna, flushing, rose, but stood still. She suddenly felt ashamed of having deceived him and still more afraid of how he might treat her. The feeling of injury had already passed, and she only feared the expression of his displeasure. She remembered that the child had been quite well since yesterday. She was even vexed with her for having recovered so soon as the letter had been sent. Then she heard his voice, and forgetting everything else ran joyfully to meet him.

'Well, how is Annie?' he asked timidly, looking up at Anna as she ran down to him.

He was sitting on a chair, and the footman was pulling off his warm boots.

'Oh, it's nothing! She's better.'

She took his hand in both hers and drew it to her waist, not taking her eyes off him.

'Well, I'm very glad,' he said, coldly surveying her coiffure and the dress which, he knew, she had put on for him.

All this pleased him, but it had already pleased him so often! And the stern and stony look, which she so dreaded, settled on his face.

'Well, I am very glad. And you are well?' said he, wiping his wet beard with his handkerchief, and kissing her hand.

'No matter,' she thought, 'if only he is here. When he is here he can't and daren't fail to love me!'

The evening passed happily and cheerfully in the company of the Princess Barbara. He told her about the elections, and Anna knew how by questions to lead him on to just what pleased him—his success. She told him about everything that interested him at home, and all her news was most cheerful.

But late at night, when they were alone, Anna, seeing that she had regained full mastery of him, wanted to efface the depressing impression of the look he gave her apropos of the letter, and said:

'But confess that you were vexed to get my letter, and did not believe me?'

As soon as she had said this she knew that, however lovingly disposed he might be to her, he had not forgiven her for that letter.

'Yes,' he answered. 'It was such a strange letter. Annie was ill, yet you wished to come yourself!'

'That was all true.'

'I don't doubt it. I am only displeased, really, that you seem not to wish to admit that one may have unavoidable business. Now, for instance, I shall have to go to Moscow about the house. ... Oh, Anna, why are you so irritable? Don't you know that I can't live without you? I am ready to give my whole life ...'

But she did not listen to him.

'If you go to Moscow, I shall go too! I will not stop here. Either we must separate or live together.'

'You know that that is my desire! But for that ...'

'A divorce is necessary? I will write to him! I see I cannot live like this. ... But I will go to Moscow with you.'

'You speak as if you were threatening me! Why, I don't wish for anything so much as not to be separated from you,' said Vronsky, smilingly. But the angry look of a hunted and exasperated man flashed in his eyes as he spoke those tender words.

Anna wrote to her husband asking him for a divorce; and at the end of November, having parted from the Princess Barbara, who had to go to Petersburg, she moved to Moscow with Vronsky. Daily expecting Karenin's reply, to be followed by a divorce, they now established themselves like a married couple.

PART SEVEN

1

The Levins had been more than two months in Moscow. The date on which Kitty should have been confined had long passed; but she had not yet been delivered. The doctor, the midwife, Dolly, her mother, and especially Levin began to experience impatience and anxiety; Kitty alone was perfectly calm and happy.

All whom she loved were with her, and all were so kind to her and so attentive, and everything was presented to her in so pleasant an aspect, that had she not known it must soon come to an end she could not have desired a better or pleasanter life. The only thing that marred the charm of this life was that her husband was not as she loved him best, not as he used to be in the country.

She loved his quiet, kindly and hospitable manner on his estate. In town he always seemed restless and on his guard, as if afraid lest some one should insult him or, worse still, her. There, on his estate, feeling that he was in his right place, he was never in a hurry to go anywhere and was always occupied. Here in town he was always in a hurry, as if fearing to miss something, and yet he had nothing to do.

The one advantage of this town-life was that here they never quarrelled. Whether it was that the conditions of town-life were different, or that they had both grown more careful and reasonable in this respect—at any rate, in Moscow they never had quarrels.

An event even occurred of great importance to them both in this respect, namely Kitty's meeting with Vronsky.

The old Princess, Mary Borisovna, Kitty's godmother, who had always been very fond of her, particularly wished to see her. Though Kitty was not going out anywhere because of her condition, yet she went with her father to see the venerable old lady, and there met Vronsky.

The only thing Kitty could reproach herself with when that visit was over was that for an instant, on recognizing Vronsky's once so familiar figure in his civilian clothes, she grew breathless, the blood rushed to her heart, and she felt a deep flush suffusing her face. But this lasted only a few seconds. Her father, purposely addressing Vronsky in a loud voice, had not finished what he was saying before she was quite ready to face

Vronsky, and if need be to converse with him just as she conversed with the Princess Mary Borisovna; especially so that everything down to the lightest intonation and smile might be approved by her husband, whose unseen presence she seemed to feel above her at that moment.

Levin blushed much more than she had done when she told him she had met Vronsky at the Princess Mary Borisovna's. It was very difficult for her to tell him this, and still more difficult to go on giving him details of the meeting, as he did not ask anything, but only frowned and looked at her.

'I am very sorry you were not there,' she said; 'I don't mean present in the room. ... I should not have behaved so naturally with you there. ... I am now blushing much more—much, much more,' she added, blushing to tears, 'but I am sorry you could not look in through a crack.'

Her truthful eyes told Levin that she was satisfied with herself, and in spite of her blushes he grew calm at once, and began questioning her, which was just what she wanted. When he had heard all, down to the fact that just for the first second she could not help blushing, but that afterwards she had felt as natural and easy as with anyone she might happen to meet, he became quite happy, and said he was very glad it had happened and he would try to be as friendly as possible with Vronsky next time he met him.

'It is so painful to think that there is a man who is almost my enemy,—whom I dislike to meet,' said Levin. 'I am very, very glad!'

2

Levin arrived at the club in good time. Members and visitors were driving up as he got there. He had not been there since the days when after leaving the university he had lived in Moscow and gone out into Society. He remembered the club and was enveloped in the old familiar atmosphere of the place, an atmosphere of repose, ease, and propriety.

'Let me have your hat, sir,' said the porter to Levin, who had forgotten the club rule that hats must be left at the entrance. 'It's a long time since you were here! The Prince entered your name yesterday. Prince Oblonsky is not here yet.'

This hall-porter not only knew Levin but knew all his connections and relatives as well.

Levin entered the noisy and crowded dining-room. He passed among the tables, which were nearly all occupied, surveying the guests. All seemed to have left their cares and anxieties behind them in the hall with their hats, and to be preparing to enjoy the material blessings of life at their leisure. Sviyazhsky and Shcherbatsky, Nevedovsky and the old Prince, Vronsky and Koznyshev, all were there.

'Why are you so late?' asked the old Prince with a smile, holding out his hand over his shoulder. 'How is Kitty?' he added, smoothing the table-napkin, which he had tucked in behind a button of his waistcoat.

'She's all right: they are all three dining together.'

'Ah! Well, there's no room at our table. Go to that table, and be quick and secure a seat,' said the old Prince, and turning away he carefully took a plate of fish soup that was handed to him.

'Levin! Here!' shouted some one a little farther off, in a kindly voice. It was Turovtsyn. He sat beside a young military man, and two chairs were tilted against their table. Levin joined them with pleasure. He always liked that good-natured spendthrift Turovtsyn; with him was associated the memory of his proposal to Kitty.

'These are for you and Oblonsky. He will be here in a minute.'

The military man, who held himself very erect, was Gagin, from Petersburg. Turovtsyn introduced him.

'Have you just come?' asked Oblonsky, hastening toward them. 'How do you do? Had any vodka? Well then, come!'

Levin rose and went with him to a large table on which stood various kinds of vodka and a very varied assortment of *hors d'œuvres*. They drank a glass of vodka each and returned to their table.

While they were still at their soup Gagin ordered a bottle of champagne and had four glasses filled. Levin did not refuse the proffered wine, and ordered another bottle. He was hungry, and ate and drank with great pleasure, and with still greater pleasure took part in the simple merry talk of his companions. They talked about horses, about that day's races, and how gallantly Vronsky's Atlasny had won the first prize. Levin hardly noticed how the dinner passed.

'Ah, here they are!' said Oblonsky, just as they were finishing, leaning back in his chair and stretching out his hand to Vronsky, who was approaching with a tall Colonel of the Guards. Vronsky's face too was lit up by the general pleasant good-humour of the club. Gaily leaning his arm on Oblonsky's shoulder, he whispered something to him, and with the same merry smile held out a hand to Levin.

'Very glad to see you,' he said.

'We were just speaking about your horse. I congratulate you!' said Levin. 'That was quick running!'

'He has been congratulated!' remarked the Colonel. 'It's the second time he's won the Imperial prize. If only I had the luck at cards that he has with horses! ... But why waste the golden moments? I'm off to the "infernal regions",' added he, and walked away.

'That's Yashvin,' said Vronsky in reply to Turovtsyn's question, as he took a vacant chair beside them. He drank a glass of champagne they offered him, and ordered another bottle. Whether influenced by the club or by the wine he had drunk, Levin chatted with Vronsky about the best breeds of cattle, and was very pleased to find that he had not the least animosity toward the man. He felt quite reconciled to him.

'Well, have you finished?' asked Oblonsky, smiling. 'Let's go!'

On leaving the table Levin, feeling that as he went his arms swung with unusual regularity and ease, passed with Gagin through the lofty apartments to the billiard-room. When they had traversed the Large Hall he met his father-in-law.

'Well, and how do you like our Temple of Idleness?' said the Prince, giving him his arm. 'Come, let's walk about a little.'

'Yes, a walk is just what I want, and to have a look round. It interests me.'

Chatting and exchanging greetings with acquaintances they chanced to meet, Levin and the Prince passed through all the rooms: including the large one, in which card-tables were already arranged and habitual partners were playing for small stakes.

'Will you come, Prince? Everything is ready,' said one of his habitual partners, finding him there, and the Prince went away. Levin went to look for Oblonsky and Turovtsyn.

Turovtsyn, with a tankard of something to drink, was sitting on the high sofa in the billiard-room, and Oblonsky was talking to Vronsky by the door in the far corner.

'She is not exactly dull, but that indefinite, unsettled position ...' Levin overheard, and was hastening away when Oblonsky called him.

'Levin!' said he; and Levin noticed that though in Oblonsky's eyes there were not actually tears, they were moist, as they always were when he had been drinking or when he felt touched. To-day it was both.

'Levin, don't go,' he said, holding him tightly by the elbow, evidently not wishing to let him go on any account.

'This is my true, almost my best friend,' he said to Vronsky. 'You too are even more near and dear to me; and I want you to be friends, and I know that you will be friendly and intimate because you are both good fellows.'

'Well, then there's nothing for it but to kiss and be friends!' said Vronsky, good-naturedly jesting and holding out his hand.

He quickly grasped Levin's outstretched hand and pressed it.

'I am very, very glad,' said Levin, pressing Vronsky's hand.

'Waiter! Bring a bottle of champagne,' said Oblonsky.

But in spite of Oblonsky's wish and theirs they had nothing to say to one another, and both knew it.

'You know, he is not acquainted with Anna,' said Oblonsky to Vronsky. 'And I particularly wish to take him to see her. Let's go, Levin.'

'Really?' said Vronsky. 'She will be very glad. I would go home at once, but I am anxious about Yashvin and want to stay here till he has finished.'

'Oh, is he in a bad way?'

'He keeps on losing and I alone can restrain him.'

'Well then, let us go to Anna's. Now, at once! She will be at home. I promised her long ago to bring you.'

Levin paid the club bill to an old footman who stood by the door and who seemed in some miraculous way to know what it came to, and, swinging his arms in a peculiar way, passed through the whole suite of rooms to the exit.

The carriage drove into the courtyard, and Oblonsky rang loudly at the front door, before which a sledge was standing.

Without asking the porter who opened the door whether Anna was in, Oblonsky entered the hall. Levin followed, unsure as to whether he was acting well or badly.

Glancing in the mirror, Levin saw that he was red in the face, but he was sure he was not tipsy, and he followed Oblonsky up the carpeted stairs. On the top landing a footman bowed to Oblonsky as to some one he knew well, and Oblonsky, asking who was with Anna Arkadyevna, received the answer that it was Mr. Vorkuyev.

'Where are they?'

'In the study.'

Passing through a small dining-room, panelled in dark wood, Oblonsky and Levin entered the study across the soft carpet. It was lit by a lamp with a large dark shade. Another reflector-lamp fixed to the wall illuminated a large full-length portrait of a woman, which attracted Levin's involuntary attention. It was Anna's portrait painted in Italy by Mikhaylov. While Oblonsky passed behind a screen of trellis-work—and the man's voice that had been speaking became silent—Levin looked at the portrait, which in the bright illumination seemed to step out of its frame, and he could not tear himself away from it. He forgot where he was, and without listening to what was being said gazed fixedly at the wonderful portrait.

'I am so glad,' he heard a voice saying near by, evidently addressing him, the voice of the very woman whom he had admired in the portrait. Anna had come out from behind the screen to meet him.

The tranquillity with which she extended to him her energetic little hand, introduced him to the publisher Vorkuyev, and, indicating a pretty red-haired child who sat in the same room doing needlework, spoke of her as her ward, showed the manners of a woman of good society.

'I am very, very pleased,' she repeated, and from her lips these simple words seemed to Levin to possess a peculiar meaning.

'We came into Alexis's room to have a smoke,' she said in reply to Oblonsky's question whether he might smoke; and glancing at Levin, instead of asking him whether he smoked, she drew a tortoiseshell cigar-case nearer and took from it a straw cigarette.

'How are you to-day?' asked her brother.

'Pretty well. Nerves as usual!'

'Isn't it wonderfully good?' said Oblonsky, noticing that Levin kept looking at the portrait.

'I have never seen a better portrait.'

'And it's a wonderful likeness, isn't it?' asked Vorkuyev.

Levin glanced from the portrait to the original. A special brightness lit up Anna's face when she felt his eyes on her. Levin flushed, and to hide his confusion asked whether she had seen Dolly lately.

'She was here yesterday. She is very angry with the High School because of Grisha. The Latin master, it seems, has been unjust to him. So you have been to the club?' she said, addressing her brother.

'What a woman!' thought Levin, and, quite forgetting himself, he gazed fixedly at her beautiful mobile face, which had now suddenly quite changed. Levin did not hear what she was speaking about while she leaned toward her brother but was struck by the change in her expression. After being so lovely in its tranquillity, her face suddenly expressed a strange curiosity, anger, and pride. She screwed up her eyes, as if she were remembering something.

Turning to the little English girl, she added in English, 'Please order tea in the drawing-room.'

The child rose and went out.

'Well, has she passed her examination?' inquired Oblonsky.

'Splendidly! She is a very capable girl, and has a sweet nature.'

'You'll finish by being fonder of her than of your own.'

'How like a man! There is no more or less in love. I love my child with one kind of love and her with another.'

'I was just saying to Anna Arkadyevna,' remarked Vorkuyev, 'that if she were to devote to the general business of educating Russian children a hundredth part of the energy she bestows on this English child, she would be doing a great and useful work.'

'Yes, but, say what you like, I can't do it. Count Alexis urged me very much.' As she spoke the words 'Count Alexis' she turned a timidly petitioning glance toward Levin and he involuntarily replied with a respectful and confirmatory glance. 'He urged me to take an interest in the village school. I went several times but I could not attach myself to the work. You mention energy. ... Energy is based on love; and where is one to get the love? One can't order it! I've become fond of this girl, you see, without knowing why.'

Again she glanced at Levin. And her smile and glance told him that she was speaking for him alone, valuing his opinion and knowing in advance that they would understand one another.

'Yes, I quite understand,' Levin replied. 'It is impossible to put one's heart into a school or an institution of that kind, and I think that is just why philanthropic establishments always give such poor results.'

After a pause she smiled and said, 'Yes, yes, I never could do it. However, won't you come and have some tea?' She rose and took up a book bound in morocco-leather.

'Let me have it, Anna Arkadyevna,' said Vorkuyev, pointing to the book. 'It is well worth it.'

'Oh no, it is so unfinished! My writings are something like those little baskets and carvings made in prisons,' she added, turning to Levin. 'And those unfortunate people achieved miracles of patience.'

And Levin perceived yet another feature in this woman whom he already liked so much. In addition to her intelligence, grace, and beauty, she also possessed sincerity. She did not wish to hide from him the hardships of her position.

She asked Levin and Vorkuyev to pass on into the drawing-room, and herself remained behind to speak to her brother. Levin was so excited about what she might be saying to Oblonsky that he hardly listened to what Vorkuyev was telling him about the merits of Anna's story for children.

Over their tea they continued the same kind of pleasant and interesting talk.

Levin all the time continued to admire her: her beauty, her cleverness, her good education, together with her simplicity and sincerity. And he, who had formerly judged her so severely, now by some strange process of reasoning justified her and at the same time pitied her and feared that Vronsky did not fully understand her. Toward eleven, when Oblonsky rose to leave (Vorkuyev had already gone), Levin felt as if he had only just arrived. He got up regretfully.

'Good-bye!' she said, retaining his hand and gazing at him with a look that drew him to her. 'Tell your wife that I am just as fond of her as ever, and that if she cannot forgive me my situation, I wish her never to forgive me. To forgive, she would have to live through what I have lived through, and may God preserve her from that!'

'Certainly, yes, I will tell her ...' said Levin, blushing.

3

Levin found his wife sad and depressed. The three sisters' dinner-party would have gone off very well, except that he did not come in as they expected and they all became dull. Then the sisters left, and she remained alone.

'Well, and what have you been doing?' she asked, looking him in the eyes, which had a suspicious glitter in them. But, not to hinder his relating everything, she masked her observation and listened with an appreciative smile while he told her how he had spent the evening.

'I was very pleased to meet Vronsky. I felt quite at ease and quite natural with him. You see, I shall now try to avoid meeting him again, but the constraint will no longer exist ...' said he, and remembering that whilst 'trying to avoid meeting him again' he had gone straight to Anna's, he blushed.

Kitty saw his blush and wanted to know the reason.

'Well, and where did you go then?'

'Stiva particularly begged me to call on Anna Arkadyevna.'

On saying this Levin blushed still more, and his doubts as to whether he had done right or wrong in going to see Anna were finally solved. He now knew that he should not have gone there.

Kitty's eyes opened in a peculiar manner and flashed at the mention of Anna's name, but making an effort she hid her agitation and so deceived him.

'Ah!' was all she said.

'I am sure you won't be angry with me for going. Stiva asked me to, and Dolly wished it,' continued Levin.

'She is very charming, very, very much to be pitied, and a good woman,' he said, telling her about Anna and her occupations and the message she had sent.

'Yes, of course she is much to be pitied,' said Kitty.

Misled by her quiet manner he went to undress. When he returned he found Kitty still sitting in the chair where he had left her. When he drew near she looked at him and burst into sobs.

'What is it? What is it?' he asked, well aware what it was.

'You have fallen in love with that horrid woman! She has bewitched you! I saw it in your eyes.'

It was long before Levin could pacify his wife. At last he managed it, but only by acknowledging that a sense of pity, after the wine he had drunk, had misled him, that he had yielded to Anna's artful influence, and he would avoid her in future. One thing that he sincerely confessed was that, living so long in Moscow with nothing but talk and food and drink, he was going silly. They talked till they were sufficiently reconciled to fall asleep.

4

When her visitors had taken their leave Anna did not sit down, but began pacing up and down the room. Though she had done all in her power to awaken love in Levin (as at that time she always did to all the young men she met), as he had left the room she ceased to think about him.

One thought, and only one, pursued her remorselessly in different forms. 'If I produce such an effect on others, on this married man who loves his wife, why is *he* so cold toward me? ... And it's not coldness, for I know he loves me, but something fresh now divides us. Why has he been away all the evening? He wishes to give me proofs that his love of me must not interfere with his freedom. But I don't need proofs; I need love! He ought to understand the hardship of my life here in Moscow. I do not live, but only wait for a solution which is deferred and still deferred. Again no answer! And Stiva says he can't go to see Alexis Alexandrovich; and I can't write again. He ought to pity me,' said she, feeling tears of self-compassion rising to her eyes.

She heard Vronsky's vehement ring at the front door and quickly dried her eyes. She even sat down near the lamp and opened a book, pretending to be tranquil. She might pity herself, but he must not pity her. She did not want strife and blamed him for wanting to fight, but yet she involuntarily took up a fighting attitude.

'Well, you've not been dull?' he asked cheerfully and with animation, coming up to her. 'What a terrible passion gambling is!'

'No, I have not been dull, Stiva and Lenin were here.'

'Yes, I knew they were coming to see you. And how did you like Levin?' he asked, taking a seat beside her.

'Very much. They left a short while ago. What did Yashvin do?'

'He was lucky and won seventeen thousand. I called him away and very nearly got him to come. But he went back and now has lost more than he had won.'

'Then what was the good of your staying with him?' she said, suddenly raising her eyes to his face. Her look was cold and hostile. 'You told Stiva you were staying to bring Yashvin away, but you have left him.'

A similar cold expression of readiness for strife appeared on his face.

'For one thing, I did not give him any message for you; and for another I never say what is not true. But chiefly, I wanted to stay, so I stayed,' he replied with a frown. 'Anna! Why? Why? ...' he asked after a short pause, bending toward her and opening his hand, hoping that she would place hers in it.

She was pleased by this appeal to tenderness. But some strange evil power prevented her from yielding to her impulse, as if the conditions of the struggle did not allow her to submit.

'Of course you wished to stay, and stayed. You always do what you wish. For you it's a matter of obstinacy,' she said, after gazing intently at him and suddenly finding a name for that look that irritated her so. 'Just obstinacy! For you it is a question whether you will conquer me, and for me ...' Again she felt sorry for herself and nearly burst into tears. 'If you only knew what it means to me! When I feel as I do now, that you are hostile toward me—hostile is the right word. If you knew how near I am to a catastrophe at such moments ... how afraid I am! Afraid of myself!' And she turned away to hide her sobs.

'But what is it all about?' he said, horrified at her expression of despair, and again leaning toward her he took her hand and kissed it. 'What have I done? Do I seek amusement outside our home? Do I not avoid the society of women?'

'I should hope so!' she said.

'Well then, tell me what I should do to make you easy? I am ready to do anything to make you happy,' he went on, touched by her despair. 'What would I not do to spare you such grief as this, about I know not what! Anna! ...'

'Nothing, nothing!' she replied. 'I don't know myself whether it is this lonely life, or nerves. ... But don't let's talk about it! What about the races? You haven't told me about them,' and she tried to hide her triumph at her victory, for the victory was hers after all.

5

At five in the morning the creak of an opening door awoke Levin. He jumped up and looked round. Kitty was not in the bed beside him, but on the other side of the partition a light was moving, and he heard her step.

'What is it?' he muttered, not quite awake. 'Kitty, what is it?'

'Nothing,' said she, coming candle in hand from beyond the partition. 'I only felt a little unwell,' she added with a peculiarly sweet and significant smile.

'What? Has it begun? Has it?' he asked in a frightened voice.

'No, no,' she said smiling, holding him back with her hand. 'I'm sure it's nothing. I only felt slightly unwell; but it is over now.'

At seven o'clock he was awakened by her touch on his shoulder and a soft whisper. She seemed to hesitate between regret at waking him and a desire to speak to him.

'Kostya, don't be frightened. It's nothing, but I think … We must send for Mary Vlasyevna.'

The candle was burning again. She was sitting on the bed holding in her hands some knitting she had lately been doing.

'Please don't be frightened! I'm not a bit afraid,' she said on seeing his alarmed face, and she pressed his hand to her lips. He had loved that face and known all its expressions and looks, but he had never seen her as she was now. How vile and despicable he appeared to himself before her as she now was, when he recollected the grief he had caused her yesterday! Her flushed face surrounded with soft hair that had escaped from beneath her night-cap shone with joy and resolution.

'I have sent for Mama. And you, go quickly and fetch Mary Vlasyevna. … Kostya! … No, it's nothing. It's past.'

She moved away from him and rang.

'Well, go now. Pasha is coming. I am all right.'

And Levin saw with amazement that she again took up the knitting which she had fetched in the night, and recommenced work.

As Levin went out at one door he heard the maid enter at the other. He dressed, and while the horse was being harnessed—for it was early, and no *izvoshchiks* were about yet—he ran back to the bedroom not on tiptoe but, as it seemed to him, on wings. Two maids were busy moving something in the bedroom. Kitty was walking up and down and knitting, and giving orders.

'I am going straight to the doctor's. They have already gone for Mary Vlasyevna. Is anything else wanted? Oh yes, to Dolly!'

She looked at him, evidently not listening to what he was saying.

'Yes, yes! Go,' she said rapidly, frowning and motioning him away with her hand.

He was already on his way through the drawing-room when suddenly a piteous moan, that lasted only a moment, reached him from the bed-room. He stopped and for a moment could not understand it.

'Yes, it was she,' he said and he ran downstairs.

'Lord have mercy! Pardon and help us!' he repeated the words that suddenly and unexpectedly sprang to his lips. And he, an unbeliever, repeated those words not with his lips only.

The doctor was not up yet, and the footman refused to wake him. Levin deliberately took out a ten-rouble note, and speaking slowly but without losing time, handed him the note and explained that Dr Peter Dmitrich had promised to come at any time, and that he would certainly not be angry and must therefore be called at once.

The footman consented and went upstairs, asking Levin to step into the waiting-room.

Levin could hear the doctor at the other side of the door walking about, washing, and speaking. Some three minutes elapsed; to Levin they seemed more than an hour. Two minutes more passed.

'Good morning!' said the doctor, holding out his hand. 'Don't hurry! Well?'

Trying to be as exact as possible, Levin began recounting every un-necessary detail of his wife's position, continually interrupting himself to beg the doctor to accompany him at once.

'Don't be in such a hurry. You see you are inexperienced, I am sure I shall not be needed, but I promised, and if you like I will come. But there is no hurry. Please sit down. Won't you have a cup of coffee?'

Levin gave the doctor a look which asked whether he was not laugh-ing at him. But the doctor had no idea of laughing.

'I know, I know,' he said with a smile. 'I am a family man myself. We husbands are the most miserable of creatures at those times.'

'Then you will come at once?' said Levin, looking angrily at the ser-vant who brought in the coffee.

'In half an hour.'

Levin got home just as the Princess arrived, and they met at the bed-room door. There were tears in the Princess's eyes and her hands shook. When she saw Levin she embraced him and began to cry.

'Well, Mary Vlasyevna, darling?' she asked, seizing the hand of the midwife who came toward them with a preoccupied expression.

Levin lost the sense of time. Sometimes minutes—those minutes when she called him to her and he held her moist hand, now pressing his with extraordinary strength and now pushing him away—seemed to him like hours; and then again hours seemed like minutes. He was surprised when Mary Vlasyevna asked him to light a candle behind the partition, and he learnt that it was already five o'clock in the evening. He saw her burning face, now bewildered and full of suffering, and now smiling and soothing him. He saw the Princess red, overwrought, her grey hair out of curl, and with tears which she energetically swallowed, biting her lips. He saw Dolly, he saw the doctor smoking thick cigarettes, and Mary Vlasyevna with a firm, resolute, and tranquillizing look on her face, and the old Prince pacing up and down the ball-room and frowning. But he did not know how they came and went, nor where they were. Then he was sent to fetch an icon with silver-gilt mounts from the Princess's bedroom.

He only knew and felt that what was happening was similar to what had happened the year before in the hotel of the provincial town on the deathbed of his brother Nicholas. Only that was sorrow and this was joy. And, as in that case, what was now being accomplished came harshly, painfully, incomprehensibly; and while watching it, the soul soared, as then, to heights it had never known before, at which reason could not keep up with it.

Every time the screams came from the bedroom, he succumbed to the same strange error that had possessed him in the first moments: every time, on hearing the scream, he jumped up and ran to justify himself, but recollected on the way that he was not to blame and that he longed to protect and help her. But when, looking at her, he again saw that to help was impossible, he was seized with horror and said, 'Lord, pardon and help us!'

At the same time both her sufferings and his feeling of the impossibility of helping her became more and more poignant. He would jump up, wishing to run away somewhere, but ran to her instead.

6

He did not know whether it was late or early. Suddenly there was a scream unlike anything he had ever heard. The scream was so terrible that Levin did not even jump up, but looked breathlessly with a frightened and inquiring glance at the doctor, who bent his head on one side to listen and smiled approvingly. Levin jumped up and rushed into the bedroom on tiptoe, past Mary Vlasyevna and the Princess, and stopped at his place at the head of the bed. The screaming had ceased, but there was a change; what it was he could not make out or understand, nor did he want to understand it; but he read it in Mary Vlasyevna's face. She looked pale and stern, and as resolute as before, though her jaw trembled a little and her eyes were fixed intently on Kitty. Kitty's burning face, worn with suffering, with a lock of hair clinging to her clammy forehead, was turned toward him trying to catch his eye. Her raised hands asked for his. Seizing his cold hands in her perspiring ones she pressed them to her face.

'Don't go! Don't go! I am not afraid, I am not afraid!' she spoke very rapidly and tried to smile, but all at once her face became distorted and she pushed him away.

'No, this is awful! I shall die ... die! ... Go! Go!' she cried, and again he heard that scream unlike any other cry.

Levin clasped his head in his hands and ran out of the room.

'It's all right, it's all right! All goes well!' Dolly called after him.

But say what they might, he knew that now all was lost. Leaning his head against the door-post he stood in the next room, and heard some one shrieking and moaning in a way he had never heard till then, and he knew that these sounds were produced by what once was Kitty. He had long ceased wishing for a child, and now he hated that child. He only longed that these terrible sufferings should end.

'Doctor, what is it? What is it? Oh, my God!' he cried, grasping the hand of the doctor who had just entered.

'It's coming to an end,' said the doctor, with a face so serious that Levin thought that *end* meant death.

Quite beside himself, he rushed into her room. The terrible screaming did not cease, but grew yet more awful until, as if it had reached the utmost limit of horror, it suddenly ceased. Levin heard a sound of movement, of rustling, of accelerated breathing, and her voice, faltering, living, tender, and happy, as it said, 'It's over.'

He raised his head. She lay, gazing silently at him, trying to smile.

And suddenly, out of the mysterious, terrible, and unearthly world in which he had been living for the last twenty-two hours, Levin felt himself instantaneously transported back to the old everyday world, but now radiant with the light of such new joy that it was insupportable. The taut strings snapped, and sobs and tears of joy that he had not in the least anticipated arose within him, with such force that they shook his whole body and long prevented his speaking.

'Alive! Alive! And a boy! Don't be anxious,' Levin heard Mary Vlasyevna say, as she slapped the baby's back with a shaking hand.

'Mama, is it true?' asked Kitty.

The Princess could only sob in reply.

And amid the silence, as a positive answer to the mother's question, a voice quite unlike all the restrained voices that had been speaking in the room made itself heard. It was a bold, insolent voice that had no consideration for anything, it was the cry of the new human being who had so incomprehensibly appeared from some unknown realm.

Toward ten o'clock the old Prince, Koznyshev, and Oblonsky were with Levin, and having talked about the young mother they had begun discussing other matters. Levin felt as if he were on some unattainable height, from which he painstakingly descended in order not to hurt the feelings of those with whom he was conversing. He talked, but never ceased thinking of his wife, of the details of her present condition, and of his son—to the idea of whose existence he painstakingly tried to accustom himself. That feminine world which since his marriage had received a new and unsuspected significance for him, now rose so high in his estimation that his imagination could not grasp it. He suddenly jumped up and left the room.

'Send and let me know whether I may see her,' said the old Prince.

'All right, directly!' answered Levin, and went to her room.

Made neat, her hair brushed, a smart cap trimmed with something blue on her head, she lay on her back with her arms outside the quilt, and met his look with a look which drew him toward her. That look, already bright, grew still brighter as he approached. On her face was the same change from the earthly to that which was beyond earth, as is seen on the faces of the dead; but in their case it is a farewell, in hers it was a welcome.

'And I have been dozing, Kostya!' she said. 'And now I feel so comfortable.'

She was gazing at him, but suddenly her face changed.

'Let me have him,' said she, hearing the baby's cry. 'Let me have him, Mary Vlasyevna, and he will see him too!'

'Well then, we'll let Papa have a look,' said Mary Vlasyevna, and stepped aside that Levin might see his son in all his beauty.

'A beautiful baby!' said Mary Vlasyevna.

Levin sighed bitterly. This beautiful baby only inspired him with a sense of repulsion and pity. These were not at all the feelings he had expected.

He turned away while Mary Vlasyevna laid the child to the unaccustomed breast.

Suddenly a laugh made him lift his head. It was Kitty laughing. The baby had taken the breast.

'Well, that's enough! That's enough!' said Mary Vlasyevna; but Kitty would not part with the baby. He fell asleep in her arms.

'Now look at him,' said Kitty, turning him so that Levin could see him. The odd-looking little face wrinkled up still more and the baby sneezed.

Smiling, and hardly able to keep back tears of tenderness, Levin kissed his wife and quitted the darkened room.

What he felt toward this little creature was not at all what he had anticipated. There was nothing merry or joyful in it; on the contrary, there was a new and distressing sense of fear. It was the consciousness of another vulnerable region. And this consciousness was at first so painful, the fear lest that helpless being should suffer was so strong, that it quite hid the strange feeling of unreasoning joy and even pride which he experienced when the baby sneezed.

7

Oblonsky's affairs were in a bad state. His whole salary went for household expenses and the liquidation of small pressing bills. He had no money at all.

This was unpleasant, inconvenient, and, in Oblonsky's opinion, ought not to continue. The cause, as he understood it, was that he received too small a salary. The position had certainly been a very good one a few years ago, but it was so no longer. He began pricking up his ears and looking around, and by the end of the winter he had discovered a very good post and begun an attack on it, first from Moscow through aunts, uncles, and friends; and then in the spring, when the matter had ripened, he himself went to Petersburg.

The post carried a salary of from seven to ten thousand roubles a year, and Oblonsky could hold it without resigning his official position. It depended on two Ministers, one lady, and two Jews; and it was necessary for Oblonsky to see all these people in Petersburg. Moreover, he had promised his sister Anna to obtain a decisive answer about the divorce from Karenin. So, having got fifty roubles from Dolly, he went to Petersburg.

Sitting in Karenin's study and listening to his article on 'The Causes of the Bad State of Russian Finance', Oblonsky only waited for him to conclude to speak about his own affairs and about Anna.

'Yes, it is very true,' Oblonsky agreed when Karenin, taking off the *pince-nez* without which he could no longer read, looked up inquiringly at his brother-in-law. Karenin was silent, thoughtfully turning over the leaves of his manuscript.

'Oh, by the way!' said Oblonsky, 'I wanted to ask you to take an opportunity, when you see Pomorsky, to put in a word for me, and to tell him that I should very much like to get the vacant post of Member of the Committee of the Joint Agency of the Mutual Credit Balance of Southern Railways.' The name of the post that was so near his heart was already familiar to Oblonsky and he pronounced it rapidly without any blunder.

'Certainly I could speak to him; but it depends chiefly on Bolgarinov, I think,' said Karenin.

'Bolgarinov quite agrees, as far as he is concerned,' returned Oblonsky with a blush.

He blushed at the mention of Bolgarinov, because he had that morning been to see the Jew and the visit had left an unpleasant impression on his mind. When Bolgarinov, with obvious intention, made him wait two hours in his waiting-room with other petitioners, he had suddenly felt uncomfortable. And when Bolgarinov at length received him with extreme politeness, evidently triumphing in his humiliation, and very nearly refused his request, Oblonsky hastened to forget it as quickly as he could; and only now on recollecting it blushed.

'Now there's another matter; you know what it is ... about Anna,' said Oblonsky after a short pause, when he had shaken off the unpleasant recollection.

Directly Oblonsky mentioned Anna's name Karenin's face entirely changed. Instead of its former animation it expressed weariness and lifelessness.

'Anna Arkadyevna's life cannot interest me,' interposed Karenin, lifting his brows.

'Allow me not to believe that,' Oblonsky rejoined gently. 'Her situation is tormenting to her and does not benefit anyone. She says plainly that she dare not ask anything. But I, and all her relatives, who all love her, beg and implore you! Her position is tormenting, and could be made easier by you, without any detriment to yourself. I would arrange everything for you so that you would not be bothered. You see, you promised!'

'The promise was given before, and I thought the question about my son had settled the matter. ... Besides, I hoped that Anna Arkadyevna would have generosity enough ...' uttered Karenin with difficulty, his lips trembling and his face turning pale.

'She leaves everything to your generosity! She asks, she pleads for one thing only: help her out of the intolerable position she is in! If you had not promised before, she would have grown reconciled to her position and have gone on living in the country. But as you had promised, she wrote to you and moved to Moscow. And now in Moscow where every time she meets anyone it is like a knife in her heart, she has been living for six months every day expecting your decision. Have pity on her …'

Karenin interrupted him. 'But perhaps I promised something I had no right to promise. I want time to consider in how far what was promised is possible.'

'No, Alexis Alexandrovich!' said Oblonsky, jumping to his feet. 'I will not believe that! She is as wretched as a woman can be, and you cannot refuse such a …'

'I beg you to stop … stop this conversation!'

'Well then, forgive me if I have pained you,' said Oblonsky with an embarrassed smile, holding out his hand.

Karenin gave him his hand, reflected, and then said:

'I must think it over and seek for guidance. The day after to-morrow I will give you a final answer,' he added, after consideration.

8

Petersburg acted pleasantly on Oblonsky physically. It made him younger. In Moscow he sometimes noticed some grey hairs; fell asleep after dinner; stretched himself; walked slowly upstairs, breathing heavily; felt dull among young women, and did not dance at balls. In Petersburg he always felt that he had shaken off ten years. He again felt quite a smart fellow.

Between the Princess Betsy Tverskaya and Oblonsky there existed long-established and very peculiar relations. Oblonsky in fun always paid court to her, knowing that she liked that more than anything. The day after his interview with Karenin, Oblonsky, calling on her, felt so youthful that he went accidentally to such lengths in this bantering courtship and humbug that he did not know how to get out of it, for unfortunately she was not merely unattractive but actually repulsive to him. This tone had sprung up between them because he was very attractive to her. So he had been very pleased when the Princess Myagkaya turned up, and put an end to their *tête-à-tête*.

'Ah, so you are here!' she said on seeing him. 'Well, how is your poor sister? Don't look at me like that,' she added. 'Since every one has been attacking her—all those who are a hundred thousand times worse than she—I have thought she has acted splendidly. I can't forgive Vronsky for not letting me know when she was in Petersburg. I would have gone to her and with her everywhere. Please give her my love. ... Well, tell me about her.'

'Yes, her situation is a hard one ...' Oblonsky began. But the Princess Myagkaya immediately interrupted him, as was her habit, and commenced telling her own tale.

'She has done what everybody, except myself, does secretly, and she would not deceive, and has acted splendidly. And the best thing she did was to leave that half-witted brother-in-law of yours! Excuse me. Every one used to say, "He is so clever, so clever." I alone said that he was stupid. Now that he has got so chummy with Lydia Ivanovna and Landau, every one says he is half-witted; and I should be glad not to agree with everybody, but this time I can't help it.'

'But do explain to me what it means!' said Oblonsky. 'Yesterday I called on him about my sister's affair and asked him for a definite answer. He did not give me an answer, but said he must think it over; and this morning instead of an answer I have received an invitation for this evening to go to the Countess Lydia Ivanovna's.'

'Ah, that's it, that's it!' Princess Myagkaya began joyfully. 'They will ask Landau and see what he says.'

'Ask Landau? Why? Who is Landau?'

'What? You don't know Jules Landau, the famous Jules Landau, the clairvoyant? He also is half-witted, but your sister's fate depends on him. See what comes of living in the provinces: you know nothing! Landau, you see, was a shop-assistant in Paris and went to see a doctor. He fell asleep in the doctor's waiting-room, and while asleep began giving advice to all the patients, and very strange advice too. Afterwards, Yury Meledinsky's wife (the invalid's wife, you know) heard of that Landau, and took him to see her husband. He is treating her husband. No good has been done in my opinion, for he is still just as weak, but they believe in him and take him about with them. So they brought him to Russia. Here every one rushed at him, and he began treating everybody. He cured the Countess Bezzubova, and she took such a fancy to him that she adopted him. He is now no longer Landau, but Count Bezzubov. However, that's not to the point; but Lydia—I am very fond of her, but her head is not screwed on right—naturally has rushed at this Landau, and now nothing is settled either by her or by Karenin without him, so your sister's fate is now in the hands of this Landau, *alias* Count Bezzubov.'

After an excellent dinner and a large quantity of brandy at

Bartnyansky's, Oblonsky entered the Countess Lydia Ivanovna's house.

'Who is with the Countess?' Oblonsky asked the hall-porter.

'Alexis Alexandrovich Karenin and Count Bezzubov,' the hall-porter replied.

'The Princess Myagkaya guessed correctly,' thought Oblonsky as he ascended the stairs. 'Strange! But it would be just as well to make friends with her. She has tremendous influence. If she would say a word to Pomorsky, the job is done.'

It was still quite light out of doors, but in the Countess Lydia Ivanovna's small drawing-room the blinds were down and the lamp alight.

At the round table beneath a lamp sat the Countess and Karenin, conversing in low tones. A short lean man, with hips like a woman's, knock-kneed, very pale, handsome, with beautiful shining eyes and long hair that hung over the collar of his frock-coat, stood at the opposite end of the room, looking at the portraits on the wall. After greeting the hostess and Karenin, Oblonsky involuntarily glanced at the stranger once more.

'Monsieur Landau!' The Countess addressed him with a softness and caution that struck Oblonsky. And she introduced them.

Landau hurriedly looked round, approached smilingly, laid upon Oblonsky's outstretched hand his own moist and motionless one, went back, and continued looking at the portraits. The Countess and Karenin glanced at each other significantly.

'I am very pleased to see you, especially to-day,' said the Countess Lydia Ivanovna, pointing to a seat beside Karenin.

'I introduced him to you as *Landau*,' she said softly, glancing at the Frenchman and then back at Oblonsky, 'but really he is Count Bezzubov, as you probably know. But he does not like that title.'

'Yes, I have heard,' replied Oblonsky. 'They say he has completely cured the Countess Bezzubova.'

'She called on me to-day, and was so pathetic,' said the Countess, turning to Karenin. 'This separation is dreadful for her. It is such a blow to her! He is going to Paris. He heard a voice yesterday,' said the Countess.

After a momentary pause the Countess Lydia Ivanovna, as if coming to the important point, turned with a subtle smile to Oblonsky.

'I have known you a long time, and am very pleased to know you more intimately. But to be a friend, one must enter into the state of the friend's soul, and I fear you will not do so in relation to Alexis Alexandrovich. You understand what I am speaking about?' she said, lifting her beautiful dreamy eyes.

'To some extent, Countess! I understand that Alexis Alexandrovich's position ...' said Oblonsky, not quite grasping what it was all about, and therefore wishing to keep to generalities.

'The change that has taken place in him cannot weaken his love for his neighbour; on the contrary, that change must strengthen his love. But I fear you don't understand me. Won't you have some tea?' she said, indicating with her eyes the footman who was handing tea round on a tray.

'Oh, certainly, Countess!' he said. 'But I think such changes are so very intimate that nobody, not even the closest friend, cares to speak about them.'

'On the contrary! We must speak, and so help one another.'

'Yes, of course, but there are such differences of conviction, and besides ...' said Oblonsky with a gentle smile.

'There cannot be any differences in what concerns the holy Truth!'

'Oh no, of course not! But ...' and, becoming embarrassed, Oblonsky stopped short. He realized that it was a question of religion.

'It seems to me he will fall asleep directly,' said Karenin in a significant whisper, approaching Lydia Ivanovna.

Oblonsky turned. Landau was sitting by the window, leaning against the arm and back of an easy-chair, with his head hanging down. Noticing the looks directed toward him, he smiled a childishly naïve smile.

'Take no notice of him,' said Lydia Ivanovna. 'Muscovites, men especially, are most indifferent to religion.'

'Oh no, Countess! I think Muscovites have the reputation of being the most steadfast believers,' replied Oblonsky.

'But, as far as I know, you unfortunately are one of the indifferent?' Karenin remarked to him, with a weary smile.

'I am in this respect not precisely indifferent, but rather expectant,' said Oblonsky with his most mollifying smile. 'I do not think that for me the time for those questions has yet come.'

Karenin and Lydia Ivanovna exchanged looks.

'We never know whether our time has come or not,' Karenin said sternly. 'We should not consider whether we are ready or not; grace is not influenced by human calculations. Sometimes it descends on the unprepared, as on Saul.'

'No, not yet, I think,' said Lydia Ivanovna, who was watching the Frenchman's movements. Landau rose and came up to them.

'You will allow me to listen?' he asked.

'Oh yes! I did not wish to disturb you,' said Lydia, looking tenderly at him. 'Sit down beside us.'

'Only one must not shut one's eyes, so as to deprive oneself of light,' Karenin continued.

'Oh, if you only knew the happiness we experience, feeling His continual presence in our souls!' cried the Countess Lydia Ivanovna with a beatific smile.

'But one may sometimes feel incapable of ascending to such heights,' remarked Oblonsky, conscious that he was in the presence of one who, by a single word to Pomorsky, might secure him the desired post.

'You mean to say, he is prevented by sin?' said Lydia Ivanovna. 'But that is a false view. For those who believe, there is no sin,' she went on.

'Yes, but faith without works is dead,' said Oblonsky, recalling that sentence from the catechism, and only by a smile maintaining his independence.

'You understand English?' asked Lydia Ivanovna, and having received an affirmative answer she rose and began looking among the books on a shelf. 'I want to read *Safe and Happy, or, Under the Wing*,' she said with a questioning look at Karenin. And having found the book and sat down again, she opened it. 'It is quite short. It describes the way to acquire faith, and the joy, higher than anything else on earth, with which it fills the soul. A believer cannot be unhappy, because he is not alone. It will be dull for you,' said the Countess Lydia Ivanovna, turning to Landau, 'as you don't understand English; but it is quite short.'

'Oh, I shall understand,' replied Landau with the same smile, and closed his eyes.

Karenin and Lydia Ivanovna exchanged significant looks, and the reading began.

In these strange surroundings he felt puzzled and dazed and could not take it all in. Listening to the Countess Lydia Ivanovna and feeling the fine eyes, naïve or roguish—he did not know which—of Landau fixed upon him, Oblonsky began to be conscious of a peculiar sort of heaviness in his head.

Suddenly he felt his nether jaw dropping irresistibly for a yawn. He smoothed his whiskers to hide the yawn, and gave himself a shake. But then he felt himself falling asleep, and nearly snored. He roused himself, just when the Countess Lydia Ivanovna uttered the words: 'He is asleep.'

Oblonsky was immediately comforted by noticing that the words did not apply to him but to Landau. The Frenchman had fallen asleep just as Oblonsky had done. But whereas Oblonsky's sleep would, he imagined, have offended them, Landau's sleep delighted them extremely, especially Lydia Ivanovna.

The Frenchman slept or pretended to sleep, leaning his head against the back of the chair, and his moist hand lying on his knee moved feebly, as if catching something. Karenin rose, and though he tried to be cautious he caught against the table. He went up to the Frenchman and placed his hand in his. Oblonsky also rose and, opening his eyes wide to wake himself up in case he was asleep, looked first at one and then at the other. It was all quite real, and Oblonsky felt his head getting worse and worse.

'Let the person who arrived last, the one who questions, go out! Let him go out!' the Frenchman said, without opening his eyes. 'Let him leave,' repeated the Frenchman impatiently.

'It's I, is it not?' And having received an answer in the affirmative, Oblonsky—forgetting the request he had wanted to make to Lydia Ivanovna, forgetting his sister's affairs, and with the one desire to get away from there as quickly as possible—went out on tiptoe, and ran out into the street as from an infected house.

Next day he received from Karenin a definite refusal to divorce Anna, and understood that this decision was based on what the Frenchman had said the evening before, in his real or pretended sleep.

9

Before any definite step can be taken in a household, there must be either complete division or loving accord between husband and wife.

Both for Vronsky and for Anna life in Moscow was intolerable; nevertheless they did not move to Vozdvizhensk, as they had long ago decided to do, but stayed in Moscow, which had become obnoxious to them both, because of late there had not been harmony between them.

For her he, with all his habits, thoughts, wishes, mental and physical faculties—the whole of his nature—consisted of one thing only: love for women, and this love she felt ought to be wholly concentrated on her alone. This love was diminishing; therefore, in her judgment, part of his love must have been transferred to other women, or to one other woman. She was jealous, not of any one woman, but of the diminution of his love. Not having as yet an object for her jealousy, she sought one. At the slightest hint she transferred her jealousy from one object to another. This last jealousy tormented her more than anything else, especially since in an expansive moment he had carelessly told her that his mother understood him so little that she had tried to persuade him to marry the young Princess Sorokina.

And being jealous, Anna was indignant with him and constantly sought reasons to justify her indignation. She blamed him for everything that was hard in her situation. The torture of expectation, living betwixt heaven and earth, which she endured there in Moscow, Karenin's dilatoriness and indecision, her loneliness—she attributed all to him. If he loved her he would fully understand the difficulty of her situation, and would deliver her from it. That they were living in Moscow, instead of in the country, was also his fault. He could not live buried in the country as she desired. He needed society, and so he had placed her in this terrible position, the misery of which he would not understand. And it was likewise his fault that she was forever parted from her son.

Even the rare moments of tenderness which occurred between them did not pacify her; in his tenderness she now saw a tinge of calm assurance which had not been there before and irritated her.

It was growing dusk. Anna, all alone, awaited his return from a bachelor dinner-party.

To-day he had been away from home all day, and she had felt so lonely, and it was so painful to feel herself at discord with him, that she wished to forget it all, to forgive and make it up with him. Wishing even to blame herself and to justify him, she said to herself:

'I am to blame; I am irritable and unreasonably jealous. I will make it up with him and we will go back to the country. There I shall be calmer.'

And not to continue thinking, and not to yield to irritation, she rang and ordered her trunks to be brought, to pack their things for the country.

At ten o'clock Vronsky returned.

'Well, have you had a good time?' she asked, coming out to meet him with a meek and repentant look on her face.

'Just as usual,' he answered, perceiving at a glance that she was in one of her pleasant moods. He was already accustomed to these transitions, and to-day was specially glad, because he himself was in the best of spirits.

'What do I see? Ah, that's right!' he said, pointing to the trunks in the ante-room.

'Yes, we must go away. I went for a drive, and it was so lovely that I longed to be in the country. There isn't anything to keep you, is there?'

'It is my only wish. I'll come in a moment and we'll have a talk. I will only go and change. Order tea.'

And he went to his room.

When he returned she told him, partly repeating words she had prepared, how she had spent the day and her plans for the move to the country.

'Do you know, it came to me almost like an inspiration?' said she. 'Why must we wait here for the divorce? Won't it do just as well in the country? I can't wait any longer. I don't want to hope, I don't want to hear anything about the divorce. I have made up my mind that it shall not influence my life any more. Do you agree?'

'Oh yes!' he answered, looking uneasily at her excited face.

'Well, and what have you been doing? Who was there?' she asked after a pause.

Vronsky named the guests. 'The dinner was capital, the boat-races and everything quite nice. ... Well then, when are we to be off?'

'Why, the sooner the better. We can't get ready by to-morrow; but the day after?'

'Yes. ... No! Wait a bit! The day after tomorrow is Sunday, and I must go and see *Maman*,' said Vronsky, and became confused, because as soon as he had mentioned his mother he felt an intent and suspicious gaze fixed upon him. His embarrassment confirmed her suspicions. She flushed and moved away from him. It was the Princess Sorokina who lived in the country near Moscow with the Countess Vronskaya who presented herself to Anna's imagination.

'You could go there to-morrow!' she said.

'No, I tell you! The things about which I have to go—to fetch a power of attorney and some money—will not have arrived by to-morrow,' he replied.

'If that's so, then we won't go at all!'

'Why's that?' said Vronsky, as if in surprise. 'There's no sense in that.'

'You see no sense in it because you don't care at all about me.'

For a moment she recollected herself and was horrified at having broken her resolution. Yet though she knew she was ruining her cause, she could not restrain herself, could not forbear pointing out to him how wrong he was, and could not submit to him.

'Dear me! This is becoming unbearable!' exclaimed Vronsky, rising from his chair. And standing before her he slowly brought out: 'Why are you testing my patience?' He looked as if he could have said much more, but restrained himself. 'It has its limits!'

'What do you mean by that?' she cried, glancing with terror at the definite expression of hatred on his whole face, and especially in the cruel, menacing eyes.

'I mean to say …' he began, but stopped. 'I must ask what you want of me!'

'What can I want? I can only want you not to abandon me, as you are thinking of doing,' she said, having understood all that he had left unsaid. 'But I don't want that, that is secondary. What I want is love, and it is lacking. Therefore all is finished!'

She moved toward the door.

'There are limits to one's endurance!' he exclaimed.

'He hates me, that is clear,' thought she, and silently, without looking round and with faltering steps, she left the room. 'He loves another woman, that is clearer still,' she said to herself as she entered her own room. 'I want love, and it is lacking. So everything is finished!' she repeated her own words, 'and it must be finished.'

'But how?' she asked herself, and sat down in the arm-chair before the looking-glass.

She remembered her illness after her confinement, and the feeling that never left her at that time. She remembered her words, 'Why did I not die?' and her feelings then. Yes, that was the thought which would solve everything. 'Yes, to die! Alexis Alexandrovich's shame and disgrace, and Serezha's, and my own terrible shame—all will be saved by my death. If I die *he* too will repent, will pity me, will love me and will suffer on my account!'

Sounds of approaching steps, his steps, distracted her thoughts. Pretending to be putting away her rings, she did not even turn round.

He came up to her, and taking her hand said softly:

'Anna, let us go the day after to-morrow, if you wish it. I will agree to anything.'

She remained silent.

'What is it?' he asked.

'You know yourself!' said she, and at the same moment, unable to restrain herself any longer, she burst into tears.

'Abandon me! Abandon me!' she murmured between her sobs. 'I will go away to-morrow. I will do more. … What am I? A depraved woman. A stone round your neck! I don't wish to torment you, I don't! I will set you free. You don't love me, you love some one else!'

'Anna, why torture yourself and me like this?' he said, kissing her hands. His face now wore a tender expression, and she thought she detected in his voice the sound of tears, and their moisture on her hand. And instantly her despairing jealousy changed into desperate, passionate tenderness. She embraced him, and covered his head, his neck, and his hands with kisses.

10

Feeling that they were entirely reconciled, next morning Anna began actively to make preparations for their move. Though it was not settled whether they would go on the Monday or on the Tuesday, as each the night before had yielded to the other's wish, Anna made all ready for their start, feeling now quite indifferent whether they went a day sooner or later. She stood in her room before an open trunk, sorting clothes, when he came in earlier than usual and ready dressed.

'I will go to *Maman* at once. She can send me the money through Egorov and I shall be ready to go to-morrow,' said he.

Good as the mood she was in might be, the reference to the move to the country pricked her.

'Oh no, I shall not be ready myself,' she said, and immediately thought: 'So it was possible to arrange things as I wished!'—'No, do as you wished to. Go to the dining-room. I will come directly. I will only sort out these things that are not wanted,' she said, placing some more articles on the heap of old clothes already piled up on Annushka's arms.

Vronsky was eating his beefsteak when she entered the dining-room.

'You would hardly believe how disgusting these rooms have become to me!' she said, sitting down to her coffee beside him. 'There is nothing worse than these furnished apartments! I think of Vozdvizhensk as of a Promised Land.'

Vronsky's valet came in to fetch a receipt for a telegram from Petersburg. There was nothing odd in his receiving a telegram, but, as if wishing to hide something from her, he told the man that the receipt was in his study.

'From whom was the telegram?' she asked.

'From Stiva,' he replied reluctantly.

'Why didn't you show it me? What secret can Stiva have from me?'

Vronsky called back the valet and told him to bring the telegram.

'I did not wish to show it you, because Stiva has a passion for telegraphing. What is the use of telegraphing when nothing has been settled?'

'About the divorce?'

'Yes, but he wires: "Could get no answer. Promises a decisive answer soon." But read it yourself.'

Anna took the telegram with trembling hands and saw exactly what Vronsky had said, but at the end were added the words: 'Little hope, but I'll do everything possible and impossible.'

'I said yesterday that it is all the same to me when I get the divorce, or even whether I get it at all,' she said, flushing. 'There was no need at all to conceal it from me.' And she thought: 'In the same way he may hide and is hiding from me his correspondence with women.'

'Oh, Yashvin wanted to come this morning with Voytov,' said Vronsky. 'It seems he has won from Pevtsov all and even more than Pevtsov can pay—about sixty thousand roubles.'

'But why do you imagine,' said she, irritated at his intimating to her so obviously, by this change of subject, that he saw she was losing her temper, 'that this news interests me so much that it is necessary to conceal it? I said that I don't want to think about it, and I wish that you were as little interested in it as I am. Why do you want it?'

'Oh God! Again about love!' he thought with a wry face.

'Don't you know why? For your own sake and for that of the children we may have!' said he.

'You want it for the children, but you don't think of me,' she pursued, quite forgetting or not hearing that he said: 'for *your own* sake and for the children.'

The possibility of having children had long been a subject of dispute, and it irritated her. She explained his desire to have children as showing that he did not value her beauty.

'Oh, I said *for your sake*! Most of all for your sake,' he repeated, his face contorted as with pain, 'because I am convinced that a great deal of your irritability is due to our indefinite position.'

'That is not the reason,' she said, 'and I can't even understand how what you call my "irritability" can be caused by that; I am entirely in your power. What indefiniteness of position is there? Quite the contrary!'

'I am very sorry you don't wish to understand me,' he interrupted, stubbornly intent on expressing his thought. 'The indefiniteness consists in your imagining that I am free.'

'You may be perfectly at rest on that matter!' she rejoined and was about to go away, but just then Yashvin entered. Anna said 'Good morning,' and stopped.

Why, when a storm was raging within her and she felt that she was at a turning-point which might lead to terrible consequences—why she need, at that moment, dissemble before a stranger who sooner or later would know all about it, she did not know: but immediately calming the storm within her, she sat down again and began talking to the visitor.

'Well? How are your affairs? Has the money been paid?' she asked Yashvin.

'Oh, I don't know. I don't think I shall get it all, and on Wednesday I must go. And you?' asked Yashvin, looking at Vronsky with half-closed eyes and evidently divining that there had been a quarrel.

'The day after to-morrow, I believe,' replied Vronsky.

'But you have been meaning to go for a long time past?'

'Yes, but now it's decided,' said Anna, looking straight into Vronsky's eyes with an expression that told him he must not think of the possibility of a reconciliation.

Voytov, who was buying a horse from Vronsky, arrived, and Anna rose and left the room.

All that day, except when she went to the Wilsons—which took her about two hours—Anna passed in doubting whether all was over or whether there was still hope of a reconciliation, and whether she ought to leave at once or to see him again. She waited for him all day, and in the evening when she went to her room, having left word for him that she had a headache, she thought: 'If he comes in spite of the maid's message, it means that he still loves me. If not, it means that all is over, and then I will decide what I am to do ...!'

At night she heard his carriage stop, heard him ring, heard his steps, and his voice talking to the maid. He believed what he was told, did not want to learn more, and went to his room! So all was over!

And death, as the sole means of reviving love for herself in his heart, of punishing him, and of gaining the victory in that contest which an evil spirit in her heart was waging against him, presented itself clearly and vividly to her.

Now it was all the same whether they went to Vozdvizhensk or not, whether she got a divorce or not—it was all useless. All she wanted was to punish him.

When she poured out her usual dose of opium she thought that she need only drink the whole phial in order to die.

In the morning a terrible nightmare, which had come to her several times even before her union with Vronsky, repeated itself and woke her. An old man with a tangled beard was leaning over some iron and doing something, while muttering senseless words in French; and as always in that nightmare (this was what made it terrible) she felt this peasant was paying no attention to her but was doing something dreadful to her with the iron. And she awoke in a cold perspiration.

When she got up, the previous day appeared in her memory as in a fog.

There had been a quarrel. It was what had happened several times before. 'I said I had a headache, and he did not come to see me. To-morrow we shall leave. I must see him and get ready for the move,' she thought. And hearing that he was in the study she went to him. As she passed through the drawing-room she heard a vehicle stop at the front door, and, looking out of the window, she saw a young girl in a lilac hat leaning out of the carriage window and giving an order to the footman who was ringing at the front door. After some talking in the hall, some one came upstairs and she heard Vronsky's step outside the drawing-room. He was going quickly downstairs. Again Anna went to the window. There he was on the steps, without a hat, going down to the carriage. The young girl in the lilac hat handed him a parcel. Vronsky said something to her and smiled. The carriage rolled away; he ran rapidly upstairs again.

The fog that had obscured everything within her was suddenly dissipated. Yesterday's feelings wrung her aching heart with fresh pain. She could not now understand how she could have humiliated herself so as to remain a whole day with him in his house. She went to his study to announce to him her decision.

'It was the Princess Sorokina with her daughter who came to bring me the money and documents from *Maman*. I could not get them yesterday. How is your head—better?' he said quietly, not wishing to see or understand the gloomy and solemn look on her face.

'Oh, by the way—' he said when she was already in the doorway—'we are definitely going to-morrow, aren't we?'

'You, but not I,' she said, turning round toward him.

'Anna, it is impossible to live like this ...'

'You, but not I,' she repeated.

'This is becoming intolerable!'

'You ... you will repent of this!' she said and left him.

Alarmed by the despairing look with which she had said these words, he jumped up, intending to run after her, but, recollecting himself, sat down again, tightly clenching his teeth and frowning. This—as it seemed to him—unbecoming and indefinite threat irritated him. 'I have tried everything,' he thought, 'the only thing left is to pay no attention,' and he began getting ready to go again to his mother's to obtain her signature to a power of attorney.

11

'Gone! Is it finished?' said Anna to herself as she stood by the window; and in answer to that question, the impressions left by the terrible dream filled her heart with icy horror.

'No, it is impossible!' she exclaimed and, crossing the room, she rang loudly. She was so terrified at being alone that she did not wait for the servant but went out to meet him.

'Find out where the Count has gone,' she said.

The man replied that the Count had gone to the stables.

'The Count told me to let you know that, in case you should wish to go out, the carriage will return very soon.'

'Very well. Wait a moment. I will just write a note. Send Michael with it to the stables at once. Quickly!'

She sat down and wrote:

'I was to blame. Come home. We must talk it over. For God's sake come; I am frightened.'

She stuck it down and gave it to the man.

Then, afraid to remain alone now, she followed him out of the room, and went to the nursery.

'How is this? That's not it—this is not he! Where are his blue eyes and his sweet timid smile?' was her first thought on seeing her plump, rosy little girl with curly black hair, instead of Serezha, whom, in the disorder of her mind, she had expected to find in the nursery. The little girl, sitting at the table, reminded Anna so vividly of Vronsky that, repressing her sobs, she hurriedly left the room. 'Is it really all over? No, it cannot be,' she thought.

She looked at the clock. Twelve minutes had passed. 'Now he has received my note and is on his way back. It won't be long; another ten minutes. ... But supposing he does not come? No, that's impossible! He must not find me with red eyes. I'll go and wash them. Oh! And did I brush my hair or not?' she asked herself; but could not remember. She felt her head with her hand. 'Yes, my hair was done, but I don't in the least remember when.' She did not even trust her hand, and went up to the mirror to see whether her hair really was done or not. It was, but she could not remember doing it. 'Who is that?' she thought, gazing in the mirror at the feverish, frightened face with the strangely brilliant eyes looking at her. 'Yes, that is I!' she suddenly realized, and looking at her whole figure she suddenly felt his kisses, shuddered, and moved her shoulders. Then she raised her hand to her lips and kissed it.

'What is it? Am I going mad?' and she went to her bedroom, where Annushka was tidying up.

'Annushka!' she said, stopping before the maid and looking at her, without knowing what she would say to her.

'You wished to go to see the Princess Oblonskaya,' said the maid, apparently understanding her.

'Darya Alexandrovna? Yes, I will go.'

'A quarter of an hour there, a quarter of an hour back; he is already on the way, he will be here in a minute.' She looked at her watch.

Just as she was going to compare her watch with the large clock some one drove up. Glancing out of the window she saw his *calèche*. But no one came upstairs, and she heard voices below. Her messenger had returned in the carriage. She went down to him.

'I did not find the Count. He had gone to the Nizhny railway station,' he said as he handed her back her note.

'Go with this note to the Countess Vronskaya's country house; do you know it? And bring back an answer at once,' she told the man.

'But what shall I do myself?' she thought. 'Yes, I will go to Dolly's, of course, or else I shall go out of my mind! And I can telegraph as well!' And she wrote out a telegram.

'*I must speak to you, come at once.*'

Having sent off the telegram, she went to dress. Ready dressed and with her bonnet on, she again looked at Annushka's placid and now still rounder face. Evident compassion showed plainly in those kindly little grey eyes.

'Annushka, my dear! What am I to do?' muttered Anna sobbing, as she sank helplessly into an arm-chair.

'Why take it so to heart, Anna Arkadyevna? Such things will happen. Go out and get it off your mind,' advised the maid.

'Yes, I will go,' said Anna, recovering and rousing herself; 'and if a telegram comes during my absence, send it to Darya Alexandrovna's ...' and she hurriedly went out and got into the *calèche*.

'Where to, ma'am?' asked Peter, before getting onto the box.

'To the Oblonskys', on the Znamenka.'

12

Sitting in the corner of the comfortable *calèche*, which rocked gently on its elastic springs to the rapid trot of the pair of greys, Anna—amid the incessant rattle of wheels and the rapidly changing impressions in the open air—again going over the events of the last days, saw her position quite differently from what it had seemed at home. Now the idea of death no longer seemed so terrible and clear, and death itself no longer seemed inevitable. She reproached herself now with the humiliation to which she had descended. 'I entreated him to forgive me. I have surrendered to him. I have confessed that I am to blame. Why? Can I not live without him? I will tell Dolly everything. She is not fond of Vronsky. It will be humiliating and painful, but I will tell her everything. She is fond of me and I will follow her advice. I won't submit to him; I won't let him educate me. ... How proud and satisfied he will be to get my note! But I will show him ...' At this point she recollected her past with Karenin and how she had effaced the memory of him. 'Dolly will think I am leaving a second husband and that I am therefore certainly unjustifiable. Do I want to be justified? I can't!' she said to herself, and wished to cry. 'I shall lose everything and shan't get him back. Yes, I shall lose everything if he does not return. He may have missed the train and be back already. Wanting to humiliate yourself again!' she said to herself. 'No! I shall go to Dolly's, and will tell her frankly: "I am unhappy, I deserve it; I am guilty, but all the same I am unhappy. Help me!" ... These horses, this carriage, how horrid it is of me to be in this carriage—they are all his, but I shall not see them any more.'

'Is anyone here?' she asked in the ante-room.

'Catherine Alexandrovna Levina,' answered the footman.

'Kitty! That same Kitty with whom Vronsky was in love,' thought Anna. 'She whom he remembered affectionately. He regrets not having married her. And of me he thinks with hate and regrets having joined himself to me!'

When Anna arrived the two sisters were consulting about feeding the baby. Dolly went out alone to meet the visitor.

'So you have not left yet? I was myself coming to see you,' said Dolly. 'I had a letter from Stiva to-day.'

'We also had a telegram from him,' replied Anna, looking round for Kitty. 'I thought you had a visitor. May I see the letter?'

'Yes, Kitty,' answered Dolly with embarrassment. 'She is in the nursery. She has been very ill.'

'I heard about it. May I see the letter?'

'I will fetch it at once. But he has not refused; on the contrary, Stiva is hopeful,' added Dolly, pausing at the door.

'What does it mean? Kitty considers it humiliating to meet me!' thought Anna when she was left alone. 'Maybe she is right. But it is not for her, who was in love with Vronsky—it is not for her to let me feel it, even if it is true! I know that no respectable woman can receive me in my position. I knew that from the first moment I sacrificed everything for him. And this is the reward! Oh, how I hate him! And why have I come here? It is still worse for me; it is harder than ever!' She heard the voices of the sisters conferring together in the next room. 'And what am I going to tell Dolly now? Console Kitty by letting her see that I am unhappy and letting her patronize me? No, and even Dolly would not understand. It is no use speaking to her. But it would be interesting to see Kitty and show her how I despise everybody and everything: how indifferent everything is to me.'

Dolly came back with the letter. Anna read and silently returned it. 'I knew it all,' she said, 'and it does not interest me in the least.'

'But why? I, on the contrary, am hopeful,' said Dolly, looking at Anna with curiosity. She had never seen her in such a strange and irritable mood. 'When are you leaving?' she asked.

Anna, screwing up her eyes, gazed straight before her without answering.

'Is Kitty hiding from me then?' she asked, blushing.

'Oh, what nonsense! She is nursing her baby and has difficulty with it, and I was advising her. … She is very pleased. She will come directly,' Dolly said awkwardly. 'Oh, here she is!'

When she heard that Anna had come Kitty did not wish to appear; but Dolly persuaded her. Having mustered up her courage, Kitty came in and, blushing, went up to Anna and held out her hand.

'I am very pleased—' she began in a trembling voice.

Kitty was confused by the struggle within her between hostility toward this bad woman and a desire to be tolerant to her; but as soon as she saw Anna's lovely and attractive face, all the hostility vanished at once.

'I should not have been surprised if you had not wanted to see me. I have got used to everything. You have been ill? Yes, you are changed!' said Anna.

Kitty felt that Anna looked at her with animosity. She attributed that animosity to the awkward position Anna, who had formerly patronized her, now felt herself to be in, and she was sorry for her.

'I came to say good-bye to you,' she said to Dolly, rising.

'When are you leaving?'

But Anna again, without replying, turned to Kitty.

'Yes, I am very glad to have seen you,' she said with a smile. 'I have heard so much about you from everybody, and even from your husband. He called on me and I liked him very much,' she added, with obvious ill intent. 'Where is he?'

'He has gone to the country,' answered Kitty, blushing.

'Remember me to him; be sure you do!'

'I will be sure to,' repeated Kitty naïvely, looking compassionately into her eyes.

'Well then, good-bye, Dolly!' And kissing Dolly and pressing Kitty's hand, Anna hurried away.

'She is still the same and as attractive as ever. Charming!' said Kitty when she was once more alone with her sister. 'But there is something pathetic about her, terribly pathetic!'

'Yes, but to-day there is something peculiar about her,' said Dolly. 'When I was seeing her out, I thought she was going to cry.'

13

Anna reseated herself in the *calèche* in a state of mind even worse than when she left home. To her former torments was now added a feeling of being affronted and repudiated, of which she had been clearly sensible during the meeting with Kitty.

'Where to, ma'am? Home?' asked Peter.

With these thoughts, she arrived at the porch of their house. Only when she saw the hall-porter coming out to meet her did she remember that she had sent the note and the telegram.

'Is there an answer?' she asked.

'I will look,' he replied, and glancing at his desk he took up and handed her the thin square envelope of a telegram. 'I cannot return before ten—Vronsky,' she read.

'And the man has not yet returned?'

'No, ma'am,' answered the hall-porter.

'Well, in that case I know what I must do,' said she to herself, and conscious of a vague sense of wrath and a desire for vengeance rising within her, she ran upstairs. 'I shall go to him myself. Before quitting him for ever, I will tell him everything. I never hated anyone as I hate that man!' thought she. Seeing his hat on the hat-rail, she shuddered with aversion. She did not realize that his telegram was in answer to hers and that he had not yet received her note. She imagined him now calmly conversing with his mother and the Princess Sorokina, and rejoicing at her sufferings. 'Yes, I must go at once,' she thought, not yet sure where to go to. She wished to get away as soon as possible from the feelings she experienced in that terrible house. The servants, the walls, the things in the house, all repelled and angered her, and oppressed her like a weight.

'Yes, I must go to the railway station, and if I don't find him, I must go *there* and expose him.' She looked at the time-table published in the daily paper. The train left at 8.20 p.m. 'I shall have time.' She gave the order to harness another pair of horses, and busied herself packing her handbag with things necessary for a few days. She knew she would not return. She vaguely resolved on one of the plans that passed through her mind. After what would occur at the railway station or at the Countess's estate she would go on by the Nizhny railway to the first town and remain there.

Dinner was served. She went to the table, smelt the bread and cheese and as the smell of everything eatable revolted her, she sent for the carriage and went out. The house already threw a shadow right across the street; the evening was bright, and the sun still warm. Annushka, who came out with Anna's things, and Peter, who put them into the carriage, and the coachman, who was evidently dissatisfied, were all objectionable to her and irritated her by their words and movements.

'I shan't need you, Peter.'

'But how about your ticket?'

'Well, as you like, I don't care,' she replied with annoyance.

Peter jumped up on the box, and with his arm akimbo told the coachman to drive to the station.

14

'There, again it is that girl! Again I understand it all,' Anna said to herself as soon as the carriage started and, rocking slightly, rattled over the stones; and again different impressions succeeded one another in her brain.

She remembered his words, the expression of his face, suggestive of a faithful setter's, in the early days of their union. Everything now confirmed her view. 'Yes, there was in him the triumph of successful vanity. Of course there was love too; but the greater part was pride in his success. He boasted of me. Now that is past. There is nothing to be proud of. Not to be proud but to be ashamed! He has taken from me all he could, and now he does not need me. He is weary of me and is trying not to act dishonourably toward me. Yesterday he betrayed himself—he wants the divorce and a marriage in order to burn his boats. He loves me, but how? *The zest is gone!*' she said to herself in English. 'That man wants to astonish everybody and is very well satisfied with himself,' she thought. 'No, I have no longer the right flavour for him. If I go away he will, at the bottom of his heart, be pleased.'

She saw it all clearly in the piercing light which now revealed to her the meaning of life and of human relations.

The clearness with which she now saw her own and every one else's life pleased her as she drove up to the low building of the Nizhny station, where the porters ran out to meet her.

'Shall I take a ticket to Obiralovka?' asked Peter.

She had quite forgotten where and why she was going, and only understood the question by a great effort.

'Yes,' she said, giving him her purse; and hanging her little red handbag on her arm, she descended from the carriage.

As she moved among the crowd toward the first-class waiting-room she gradually recalled all the details of her position and the resolutions between which she vacillated. And again hope and despair, alternately chafing the old sores, lacerated the wounds of her tortured and violently fluttering heart. She thought now of how she would reach the station and would write him a note, and of what she would write, and of how he was now complaining of his position to his mother, and of how she would enter the room and what she would say to him. And then she thought how happy life might still be, and how tormentingly she loved and hated him and how dreadfully her heart was beating.

The bell rang. Peter, in his livery and gaiters, with his dull animal face, came to her to see her into the train. She mounted the high step of the railway carriage and seated herself in an empty compartment on the dirty—though once white—cover of the spring seat. Peter with a stupid smile raised his gold-braided hat to take leave of her; an insolent guard slammed the door and drew the latch.

In order not to see anyone, she rose quickly and sat down at the opposite window of the empty compartment. A grimy, misshaped peasant in a cap from under which his touzled hair stuck out, passed that window, stooping over the carriage wheels. 'There is something familiar about that misshaped peasant,' she thought. And remembering her dream she went to the opposite door, trembling with fright. The guard opened it to let in a husband and wife.

'Do you wish to get out?'

Anna did not answer. Neither the guard nor those entering noticed the horror on her face beneath the veil. She went back to her corner and sat down. The couple sat down opposite her, attentively but stealthily examining her dress. Both the husband and the wife seemed to Anna disgusting. The husband asked if she would allow him to smoke, evidently not because he wanted to, but to enter into conversation with her. Having received her permission, he began speaking to his wife in French, about things he wanted to speak about still less than he wanted to smoke. They talked nonsense insincerely, only in order that she should hear them. Anna saw distinctly how weary they were of one another and how they hated each other. And it was impossible not to hate such ugly wretches.

She heard the second bell ring, and then a moving of luggage, noise, shouting and laughter. It was so clear to Anna that no one had any cause for joy that this laughter jarred on her painfully, and she wished to stop her ears, not to hear it. At last the third bell rang, the engine whistled and creaked. Anna looked out of the window at the people on the platform who had been seeing the train off, and who appeared to be gliding backwards. With rhythmic jerks over the joints of the rails, the carriage in which Anna sat rattled past the platform and a brick wall, past the signals and some other carriages; the sound of wheels slightly ringing against the rails became more rhythmical and smooth; the bright evening sunshine shone through the window, and a breeze moved the blind. Anna forgot her fellow-travellers; softly rocked by the motion of the carriage and inhaling the fresh air, she again began to think:

'Where did I leave off? At the point that I cannot imagine a situation in which life would not be a torment; that we all have been created in order to suffer, and that we all know this and all try to invent means of deceiving ourselves. But when you see the truth, what are you to do? I must escape! Why not put out the candle, if there is nothing more to look at? If everything is repulsive to look at? But how?'

When the train stopped at the station, Anna got out with the crowd of passengers, and shunning them as if they were lepers, stopped on the platform trying to remember why she had come there and what she had intended to do. Everything that had appeared possible before was now so difficult to grasp, especially in this noisy crowd of odious people who would not leave her in peace. Porters rushed up, offering their services. Young men passed along the platform, clattering their heels on the planks, talking loudly and gazing at her; and people she met tried to get out of her way on the wrong side. Recollecting that she meant to go on if there was no reply, she stopped a porter and asked him whether there was not a coachman bringing a note from Count Vronsky there.

'Count Vronsky? Some one from there was here just now, to meet the Princess Sorokina and her daughter. What is the coachman like?'

While she was talking to the porter, Michael the coachman, rosy and cheerful, came up in his smart blue coat with a watch-chain, evidently proud of having carried out his errand so well, and handed her a note. She opened it, and her heart sank even before she read it.

'Very sorry the note did not catch me. I shall be back at ten,' Vronsky wrote in a careless hand.

'Yes, I expected it!' she said to herself with a malicious smile.

'All right, you may go home,' she said softly to Michael. She spoke softly, because the rapid beating of her heart impeded her breathing.

'No, I will not let you torture me,' she thought, addressing her threat not to him nor to herself but to that which forced her to suffer, and she walked along the platform, past the station buildings.

Two maid-servants, strolling about on the platform, turned their heads to look at her, and made some audible remarks about her dress. 'It's real,' they said of the lace she was wearing. The station-master asked her in passing whether she was going on. 'O God! where am I to go?' she thought, walking further and further along the platform. She stopped at the end of it. Some ladies and children, who had come to meet a spectacled gentleman and were laughing and talking noisily, became silent and gazed at her as she passed them. She walked faster away from them to the very end of the platform. A goods train was approaching. The platform shook, and it seemed to her as if she were again in the train.

Suddenly remembering the man who had been run over the day she first met Vronsky, she realized what she had to do. Quickly and lightly descending the steps that led from the water-tank to the rails, she stopped close to the passing train. She looked at the bottom of the trucks, at the bolts and chains and large iron wheels of the slowly-moving front truck, and tried to estimate the middle point between the front and back wheels, and the moment when that point would be opposite her.

'There!' she said to herself, looking at the shadow of the truck on the mingled sand and coal dust which covered the sleepers. 'There, into the very middle, and I shall punish him and escape from everybody and from myself!'

She wanted to fall half-way between the wheels of the front truck, which was drawing level with her, but the little red handbag which she began to take off her arm delayed her, and then it was too late, the middle had passed her. She was obliged to wait for the next truck. A feeling seized her like that she had experienced when preparing to enter the water in bathing, and she crossed herself. The familiar gesture of making the sign of the cross called up a whole series of girlish and childish memories, and suddenly the darkness, that obscured everything for her, broke, and life showed itself to her for an instant with all its bright past joys. But she did not take her eyes off the wheels of the approaching second truck, and at the very moment when the midway point between the wheels drew level, she threw away her red bag, and drawing her head down between her shoulders threw herself forward on her hands under the truck, and with a light movement as if preparing to rise again, immediately dropped on her knees. And at the same moment she was horror-struck at what she was doing. 'Where am I? What am I doing? Why?' She wished to rise, to throw herself back, but something huge and relentless struck her on the head and dragged her down. 'God forgive me everything!' she said, feeling the impossibility of struggling. ... A little peasant muttering something was working at the rails. The candle, by the light of which she had been reading that book filled with anxieties, deceptions, grief, and evil, flared up with a brighter light, lit up for her all that had before been dark, crackled, began to flicker, and went out for ever.

PART EIGHT

1

Nearly two months had gone by. It was already the middle of the hot summer, but Sergius Ivanich Koznyshev was only now leaving to go to his brother's in the country. Katavasov, who had promised Levin to visit him, and had long been meaning to keep that promise, accompanied Koznyshev.

Hardly had they reached the station, got out of their carriage, and looked for the footman who had followed with their luggage, before some Volunteers drove up with four *izvoshchiks*. The Volunteers were met by ladies who brought them nosegays and who, with the crowd that rushed after them, accompanied them into the station.

One of the ladies who had met the Volunteers spoke to Koznyshev at the exit from the waiting-room.

'You too have come to see them off?' she asked in French.

'No, Princess, I am going to my brother's for a rest. And do you always come to see them off?' he asked with a slight smile.

'How can one help it?' replied the Princess. 'And what a telegram there is to-day! They have beaten the Turks again!'

'Yes, I read it,' he answered. They were talking of the latest telegram, confirming the report that for three consecutive days the Turks had been beaten at all points and were in flight, and that a decisive battle was expected next day.

'Do you know that the well-known Count Vronsky is going by this train?' remarked the Princess. 'Only his mother is seeing him off. After all, it is the best thing he could do.'

'Oh yes, certainly.'

While they were speaking the crowd rushed past them toward the dining-table. They too moved on, and heard the loud voice of a man who, with a glass in his hand, was making a speech to the Volunteers: 'To serve the Faith, humanity, and our brothers!' said the gentleman, raising his voice more and more. 'Mother Moscow blesses you in the great undertaking!' he concluded in a loud and tearful voice.

'Ah, Princess! What do you think of that!' said Oblonsky, beaming with a joyous smile, as he suddenly appeared in the midst of the crowd.

'Wasn't it finely and cordially expressed! Bravo! ... And Sergius Ivanich! Now, you should say something, so that ... just a few words, you know, of encouragement; you do it so well,' he added with an affectionate, respectful and solicitous smile, gently pushing Koznyshev forward by the arm.

'No, I am just going.'

'Where to?

'To my brother's in the country,' answered Koznyshev.

'Then you'll see my wife; I have written to her, but you'll see her sooner. Please tell her you have seen me and it's *all right*! She will understand.'

The Princess glanced at Koznyshev. But the fact that Koznyshev and the Princess seemed to wish to get rid of him did not abash Oblonsky in the least.

'You don't say so!' he exclaimed, when the Princess told him that Vronsky was going by that train. For a moment Oblonsky's face looked sad, but a minute later when, with a slight spring in his step and smoothing his whiskers, he entered the waiting-room where Vronsky was, Oblonsky had quite forgotten how he had sobbed with despair over his sister's corpse, and he saw in Vronsky only a hero and an old friend.

'With all his faults one must do him justice,' the Princess said to Koznyshev as soon as Oblonsky had left them. 'His is a thoroughly Russian, Slavonic nature! Only I'm afraid it will be painful for Vronsky to see him. Say what you will, that man's fate touches me. Have a talk with him on the journey,' said the Princess.

'Yes, I might if opportunity offers.'

'I never liked him. But this atones for much. Not only is he going himself, but he is taking a whole squadron at his own expense.'

'So I heard.'

The bell rang. Everybody thronged toward the door.

'There he is!' said the Princess, pointing to Vronsky who, in a long overcoat and a black broad-brimmed hat, was passing with his mother on his arm. Oblonsky walked beside him, talking.

Vronsky was frowning and looking straight before him, as if not hearing what Oblonsky was saying.

Probably at Oblonsky's indication, he looked round to where Koznyshev and the Princess were standing and silently raised his hat. His face, which was aged and full of suffering, seemed petrified.

Coming up to the train, Vronsky, letting his mother pass before him, silently disappeared into one of the compartments.

Having taken leave of the Princess, Koznyshev with Katavasov, who had joined him, entered the very crowded carriage, and the train started.

2

When the train stopped at the Provincial capital, Koznyshev, instead of going to the refreshment-room, walked up and down the platform. The first time he passed the Vronskys' compartment he noticed that the blind was down. But the next time he passed he saw the old Countess at the window. She beckoned to him.

'You see I am going with him as far as Kursk,' said she.

'Yes, so I heard,' replied Koznyshev, stopping by her window and glancing inside. 'What a fine action this is of his!' he added, noticing that Vronsky was not there.

'Yes, but after his misfortune what could he do?'

'What a dreadful occurrence!' remarked Koznyshev.

'Oh, what I have endured! But come in. … Oh, what I have endured!' she repeated when Koznyshev had entered and taken a seat beside her. 'You cannot imagine it! For six weeks he spoke to no one and ate only when I implored him to. One could not leave him a moment alone. We took away everything that he could kill himself with. We lived on the ground floor, but one could not tell what he might do. You know he had once before shot himself on her account?' she said. 'Yes, she ended as such a woman deserved to end. Even the death she chose was mean and low.'

'It is not for us to judge, Countess,' Koznyshev remarked with a sigh, 'but I understand how distressing it was for you.'

'Oh, don't speak of it! I was living on my estate and he was with me. A note was brought. He wrote an answer and sent it off. We had no idea that she was herself there at the station. In the evening I had only just gone to my room when my Mary told me that at the station a lady had thrown herself under a train. I knew it was she! The first thing I said was: "Don't tell him!" But his coachman had been there and saw it all. When I ran to his room he was beside himself—it was terrible to see him. He did not say a word, but off he galloped to the station. I don't know what happened there, but they brought him back like a corpse. I should not have known him. Then came raving madness, almost! … Ah, one can't speak of it!' exclaimed the Countess with a gesture of her arm. 'A terrible time! No, say what you will, she was a bad woman. Such desperate passions! She ruined herself and two splendid men—her husband and my unfortunate son.'

'And how about her husband?' inquired Koznyshev.

'He took her little girl. Alexis at first agreed to everything. But now he is greatly distressed at having given up his daughter to a stranger. But he can't go back on his word. Karenin came to the funeral; but we tried to arrange so that he and Alexis should not meet. For him, the husband, it is better. She has set him free. But my poor son had thrown up everything—his career, me; and then she did not even pity him, but deliberately dealt him a deathblow. God forgive me! I cannot help hating her memory when I see my son's ruin!'

'But how is he now?'

'It is a God-sent help for us, this Serbian war! Of course I, as his mother, fear for him; but it was the only thing that could rouse him. His friend, Yashvin, had lost everything at cards and was going to Serbia. He came to see him and persuaded him to go. Now it interests him. Please have a talk with him. I want him to have some distraction. He is so sad. Unluckily, too, his teeth have started aching. But he will be very glad to see you. Please have a talk with him. He is walking about on the other side.'

Koznyshev said he would be very pleased, and crossed over to the other platform.

Vronsky, in a long overcoat, his hat pulled down low and his hands in his pockets, was walking up and down like an animal in a cage, turning sharply every twenty paces. To Koznyshev as he approached it seemed that Vronsky saw but pretended not to see him. But Koznyshev did not care. He was above any personal considerations.

In his eyes Vronsky at that moment seemed an important worker in a great cause, and Koznyshev considered it his duty to encourage and cheer him. He went up to him.

Vronsky paused, looked at Koznyshev, recognized him, and advancing a few steps to meet him, pressed his hand very very hard.

'Perhaps you did not wish to see me,' said Koznyshev, 'but can I not be of some use to you?'

'There is no one whom it would be less unpleasant for me to meet than yourself,' returned Vronsky. 'Excuse me. There is nothing that is pleasant in life for me.'

'I understand, and I wanted to offer you my services,' said Koznyshev, gazing into Vronsky's face, which bore evident signs of suffering. 'I was very glad to hear of your decision,' he went on. 'The Volunteers are being very much attacked and a man like yourself will raise them in public opinion.'

Vronsky smiled with his lips, but his eyes retained their expression of angry suffering. 'As a man I have this quality, that I do not value my life at all and that I have physical energy enough to hack my way into a square and slay or fall—that I am sure of. I am glad that there is some-thing for which I can lay down the life which I not only do not want, but of which I am sick! It will be of use to somebody,' and he moved his jaw impatiently because of the incessant gnawing pain in his tooth.

'You will recover, I prophesy it,' said Koznyshev, feeling touched. 'To free one's brothers from oppression is an aim worth both dying and living for. God grant you outward success and inward peace,' he added, holding out his hand.

Vronsky grasped the hand warmly.

'Yes, as a tool I may be of some use. But as a man I—am a ruin!' said he, pausing between the words.

The acute pain in the strong tooth, filling his mouth with saliva, hindered his speaking. He remained silent, gazing at the wheels of the approaching tender, which was slowly and smoothly gliding over the rails.

Suddenly a quite different feeling, not of pain but of tormenting in-ward discomfort, made him for a moment forget his toothache. At the sight of the tender and the rails, and under the influence of conversa-tion with some one he had not met since the catastrophe, he suddenly remembered *her*; that is, remembered what was left of her when, like a madman, he ran into the railway shed where on a table, stretched out shamelessly before the eyes of strangers, lay the mangled body still warm with recent life. The head, left intact, with its heavy plaits and the curls round the temples, was thrown back; and on the lovely face with its half-open red lips was frozen an expression—pitiful on the lips and horrible in the fixed open eyes—an expression which repeated, as if in words, the terrible phrase about his repenting it—which she had uttered during their quarrel.

He tried to recall his best moments with her, but they were for ever poisoned. He could think of her only as triumphant, having carried out the threat of inflicting on him totally useless but irrevocable remorse. He ceased to feel the pain in his tooth, and sobs distorted his face. They returned to their respective carriages after the second bell had already sounded.

3

Koznyshev had not sent a telegram to his brother asking to be met at the station, and Levin was not at home when, toward noon, Katavasov and Koznyshev, dark as Arabs with the dust in the little *tarantas* they had hired at the station, drew up at the porch of the Pokrovsk house. Kitty, who was sitting on the balcony with her father and sister, recognized her brother-in-law and ran down to meet him.

'Aren't you ashamed of yourself for not letting us know?' she said, holding out her hand to him and offering her forehead for a kiss.

'We got here first-rate without troubling you,' replied Koznyshev. 'I am so dusty that I dare not touch you. I was so busy that I did not know when I could tear myself away. And you, as usual,' said he, smiling, 'are enjoying tranquil happiness outside the currents in your peaceful shallows. And here is our friend, Theodore Vasilyevich, who has come at last.'

'But I am not a Negro! When I have had a wash I shall look like a human being!' Katavasov said in his usual jesting way, holding out his hand and smiling, his teeth looking particularly bright in contrast with his black face.

'Kostya will be so pleased! He has gone to the farm. It is time he was back. I'll send for him. Papa is staying with us. He has not long returned from abroad.'

And having arranged that Levin should be sent for and that the dusty visitors should be shown where to wash, Kitty, exercising the right of moving quickly of which she had been deprived during pregnancy, ran up the balcony stairs.

'It's Sergius Ivanich and Katavasov, the Professor,' said she.

'Oh, how trying in this heat!' said the Prince.

'No, Papa, he is very nice, and Kostya is very fond of him. You go and entertain them, dear,' Kitty said to her sister. 'And I will run to Mitya. As ill-luck will have it I have not fed him since breakfast. He will be awake now and is certainly screaming.'

It was not a mere guess—she knew surely by the flow of milk within herself that he was wanting food.

She knew he was screaming before she reached the nursery. And so he was. It was a fine healthy voice, only hungry and impatient.

'Has he been screaming long, Nurse? Long?' she asked hurriedly, sitting down and preparing to nurse the baby. 'Be quick and give him to me! You can tie up his cap afterwards!'

The baby was convulsed with hungry yells.

'But one must, you know, ma'am,' said Agatha Mikhaylovna, who was almost always in the nursery. 'He must be properly tidied up! Goo! Goo!' she cooed to him, paying no attention to the mother.

The nurse brought the baby to his mother, and Agatha Mikhaylovna followed behind, her face softened with tenderness.

'He knows me, he does! It's God's truth, Catherine Alexandrovna, dear, he knows me!' cried Agatha Mikhaylovna, raising her voice above the baby's.

But Kitty did not listen. Her impatience was increasing with the baby's. As a result of their impatience matters were long in getting settled. The baby got hold in the wrong place and was angry.

At last, after desperate screaming and choking, matters went smoothly, and both mother and child felt calmed.

'Why do you think he knows you?' she asked, moving her eyes so as to see the baby's. They looked roguishly at her, she thought, from beneath his cap, which had slipped forward, and she watched the rhythmical rise and fall of his cheeks and the little hand with the rosy palm making circular movements.

'It's impossible! If he knew anyone it would be me,' Kitty replied to Agatha Mikhaylovna's statement, and smiled.

'Well, wait till he wakes up and you will see for yourself. When I do like that, he quite brightens up, the dear! He brightens up like a sunny morning,' said Agatha Mikhaylovna.

'Well, all right, all right! We shall see,' Kitty whispered. 'But now go away, he is falling asleep.'

Agatha Mikhaylovna went out on tiptoe; the nurse pulled down the blind, drove away the flies from under the muslin curtain of the cot and also a bee that was buzzing against the window-pane, and sat down, waving a birch branch above the mother and child.

Kitty sat softly rocking herself and tenderly pressing the little plump arm, which was still feebly waving while Mitya kept shutting and opening his eyes. At last the arm ceased waving and the eyes closed. Only now and then the baby, continuing his business, lifted his long curved lashes and looked at his mother with moist eyes that seemed black in the dim light. The nurse stopped waving the branch and began to doze. From upstairs was heard the roll of the Prince's voice and of Katavasov's laughter.

'I expect they've got into conversation in my absence,' thought Kitty, 'but all the same it's provoking that Kostya is away. I expect he has gone to the apiary again. He is more cheerful now than he was in spring. Then he was so gloomy, and suffered so much, that I was becoming alarmed about him. And how funny he is!' she whispered with a smile.

She knew what was tormenting her husband. It was his want of faith. Yet his lack of faith did not make her unhappy; she, who accepted the doctrine that salvation was impossible for an unbeliever, while loving her husband's soul more than anything in the world, smiled when she thought of his disbelief and called him funny.

Then a recent proof of his kindness came vividly to her mind. Two weeks before, Dolly had received a penitent letter from her husband. He implored her to save his honour and to sell her estate to pay his debts. Dolly was in despair; she hated her husband, despised him, pitied him, made up her mind to divorce him and to refuse; but ended by consenting to sell part of her estate. With an involuntary smile of emotion, Kitty remembered her own husband's shamefacedness after that, and his repeated awkward attempts to approach the subject he had on his mind, and how at length, having discovered the only way of helping Dolly without offending her, he suggested to Kitty that she should give her sister her own part of the estate, a device that had not occurred to her.

'How can he be an unbeliever with such a heart? Yes, only be like your father, only be like him!' she whispered, giving Mitya to the nurse, and touching his cheek with her lips.

When Levin returned to the country in June, he went back to his ordinary occupations—husbandry, intercourse with the peasants and with his neighbours, management of his house and of his sister's and brother's affairs, which were entrusted to him, relations with his wife and relatives, cares about his baby, and a new hobby—bee-keeping, which he took up with enthusiasm that spring—occupied all his time.

The day when Koznyshev arrived at Pokrovsk was one of Levin's most distressing days.

Early in the morning he rode to where the first rye was being sown, then to see the oats carted and stacked, and returning home when his wife and sister-in-law were getting up he drank coffee with them, and then walked to the farm where the new threshing-machine was to be started to thresh the seed corn.

All that day, when talking to the steward and the peasants and at home with his wife, Dolly, her children, and his father-in-law, Levin's thoughts were busy with the one and only subject, outside his farming, that interested him at this time, and in everything he sought its relation to his questions: 'What am I? Where am I? And why am I here?'

Standing in the cool shade of the newly-thatched barn watching the people bustling about in the dark and dust, he thought strange thoughts:

'Why is all this being done?' he wondered. 'Why am I standing here, obliging them to work? Why do they all make such efforts and try to show me their zeal? Why is my old friend Matrena toiling so? To-day or to-morrow, or in ten years' time, they will bury her and nothing will be left of her, nor of Theodore, who is feeding the machine, his curly beard full of chaff and his shirt torn on his white shoulder. Yet he loosens the sheaves and gives directions, shouts at the women, and quickly puts right the strap on the fly-wheel. And, moreover, not they only but I too shall be buried and nothing will be left. What is it all for?'

He thought this, and at the same time looked at his watch to calculate how much they could thresh in an hour. He had to know this in order to set them their day's task accordingly.

'They've been nearly an hour, and have only just started on the third heap,' thought he, approached the man who was feeding the machine, and shouting above its din, told him to put in less at a time.

'You put in too much at a time, Theodore! Don't you see, it gets jammed and that's why it does not go well! Feed it in evenly!'

Theodore, black with the dust that stuck to his perspiring face, shouted something in reply, but still did not do as Levin wished.

Levin went up to the roller, motioned Theodore aside, and himself began feeding the machine.

Having worked till the peasants' dinner-hour, which soon came, he left the barn together with Theodore and began chatting, standing beside the neat yellow freshly-reaped stack of seed-rye on the threshing-floor.

Theodore came from the farther village, the one where Levin had formerly let the land to be worked co-operatively. At present it was let to the innkeeper.

Levin got into conversation with Theodore about that land, and asked whether Plato, a well-to-do and worthy peasant of that village, would not rent that land next year.

'The rent is too high, Constantine Dmitrich,' answered Theodore, picking out the ears of rye from the front of his damp shirt.

'But how does Kirilov make it pay?'

'Why shouldn't Mityuka' (as he contemptuously called the innkeeper) 'make it pay, Constantine Dmitrich? That fellow will press hard, but he'll get his own! He will have no pity on a Christian! But as if Daddy Plato would ever skin a man! He'll lend, and sometimes he'll let a man off, and so run short himself. It all depends on the sort of man.'

'But why should he let anyone off?'

'Oh well, you see, people differ! One man lives only for his own needs: take Mityuka, who only stuffs his own belly, but Plato is an upright old man. He lives for his soul and remembers God.'

'How does he remember God? How does he live for the soul?' Levin almost cried out.

'You know how: rightly, in a godly way. You know, people differ! Take you, for instance, you won't injure anyone either ...'

'Yes, yes! Good-bye!' uttered Levin, gasping with excitement, and turning away, he took his stick and walked quickly away toward home. At the peasant's words about Plato living for his soul, rightly, in a godly way, dim but important thoughts crowded into his mind, as if breaking loose from some place where they had been locked up, and all rushing toward one goal, whirled in his head, dazzling him with their light.

4

Levin went along the high-road with long strides, attending not so much to his thoughts—he could not yet disentangle them—as to a condition of his soul he had never before experienced.

He felt something new in his soul and probed this something with pleasure, not yet knowing what it was.

'To live not for one's needs but for God! For what God? What could be more senseless than what he said? He said we must not live for our needs—that is, we must not live for what we understand and what attracts us, what we wish for, but must live for something incomprehensible, for God whom nobody can understand or define. Well? And did I not understand those senseless words of Theodore's? And having understood them, did I doubt their justice? Did I find them stupid, vague, or inexact?

'No, I understand him just as he understands them. I sought for miracles, regretted not to see a miracle that might convince me! A physical miracle would have tempted me. But here is a miracle, the one possible, everlasting miracle, all around me, and I did not notice it!

'If goodness has a cause, it is no longer goodness; if it has a consequence—a reward, it is also not goodness. Therefore goodness is beyond the chain of cause and effect.

'It is exactly *this* that I know and that we all know.

'What greater miracle could there be than that?

'Can I possibly have found the solution of everything? Have my sufferings really come to an end?' thought Levin as he strode along the dusty road, oblivious of the heat, of his fatigue, and filled with a sense of relief from long-continued suffering. That feeling was so joyous that it seemed questionable to him. 'Can this really be faith?' he wondered, afraid to believe in his happiness. 'My God, I thank Thee!' he uttered, repressing his rising sobs, and wiping away with both hands the tears that filled his eyes.

*

Levin looked straight before him, and saw the herd of cattle and then his trap and his horse Raven and the coachman who, having driven up to the cattle, was speaking to the herdsman; after that, close by, he heard the sound of wheels and the snorting of a well-fed horse; but he was so engrossed in his thoughts that he did not wonder why the coachman was coming for him.

That occurred to him only when the coachman drove up and called to him.

'The mistress has sent me! Your brother and another gentleman have come!'

Levin got into the trap and took the reins.

As if just awakened from a dream, it was long before he could collect his thoughts. He looked at the well-fed horse, lathered between the legs and on its neck where the reins chafed it—looked at Ivan the coachman sitting beside him, and remembered that he had been expecting his brother, that his wife was probably disturbed at his long absence, and he tried to guess who the visitor that had come with his brother might be. His brother, his wife, and the unknown visitor appeared in a different light to him now. It seemed to him that his relations with every one would now be changed. 'There will be no disputes; with Kitty never any quarrels again; with the visitor, whoever he may be, I shall be amiable and kind; and with the servants, with Ivan, everything will be different.'

Tightly holding in the good horse, who snorted impatiently and pulled at the reins, Levin kept turning to glance at Ivan, who sat beside him not knowing what to do with his unoccupied hands and continually pushing down his shirt as the wind blew it out. Levin tried to think of some pretext for beginning a conversation with him. He wanted to say that it was a pity Ivan had pulled the saddle-girth so tight, but that would have sounded like a reproof, and Levin desired an amicable conversation. But he could think of nothing else to say.

'Bear to the right, sir, there's a stump there,' said the coachman, taking hold of the rein.

'Please leave it alone and don't teach me!' said Levin, annoyed at the coachman's interference. Just as it always did, interference vexed him, and he immediately felt how wrong had been his conclusion that his spiritual condition could at once alter his manner when confronted with reality.

When they were still a quarter of a verst from the house, Levin saw Grisha and Tanya running toward him.

'Uncle Kostya! Mama is coming and Grandpapa and Sergius Ivanich, and some one else!' they cried, clambering into the trap.

'Who else?'

'An awfully dreadful man! And he goes like that with his hands,' said Tanya, standing up in the trap and mimicking Katavasov.

'Young or old?' asked Levin with a laugh, as Tanya's gestures reminded him of some one.

'Oh, if only it is not some one disagreeable!' he thought.

As soon as he had turned the corner of the road and saw those who were approaching he at once recognized Katavasov in a straw hat, waving his arms just as Tanya had represented.

After alighting from the trap and welcoming his brother and Katavasov, Levin asked where Kitty was.

'She has taken Mitya to Kolok,' which was a wood not far from the house. 'She wanted to let him sleep there; it's so hot in the house,' said Dolly. Levin always advised his wife not to take the child into the wood, considering it dangerous, and this news was disagreeable to him.

'She wanders about with him from place to place,' said the old Prince with a smile. 'I advised her to try taking him to the ice-cellar!'

'She meant to come to the apiary. She thought you were there. We are going there,' said Dolly.

'Well, and what are you doing?' asked Koznyshev, lagging behind with his brother.

'Oh, nothing particular. Busy with the estate as usual,' answered Levin. 'Have you come for a good stay? We expected you long ago.'

'For about a fortnight. I had a lot to do in Moscow.'

At these words the brothers' eyes met, and Levin felt ill at ease while looking at him. He dropped his own eyes, not knowing what to say. But he was suddenly struck by the calm and cheerful expression of Katavasov's face, and felt so sorry to lose the spiritual condition which he was evidently spoiling by his conversation, that recollecting his resolution he ceased speaking.

'However, we'll have a talk later on,' he said. 'If we are going to the apiary, it's this way, along this path,' he added, addressing the whole party.

When by the narrow footpath they had reached the unmown glade covered on one side by a thick growth of bright John-and-Maries, with tall spreading bushes of dark green sneezewort between them, Levin asked his guests to sit down in the deep cool shade of the young aspens—upon a bench and some tree stumps specially arranged for visitors to the apiary who might be afraid of bees—while he went to the hut to fetch bread, cucumbers, and fresh honey for the grown-up people as well as for the children.

He was glad of this opportunity to be alone and recover from reality, which had already so lowered his spiritual condition.

'Can it possibly have been but a momentary mood that will pass without leaving a trace?' he wondered.

But at that instant returning into that mood, he felt with joy that something new and important had occurred within him. Reality had temporarily veiled the spiritual tranquillity he had found, but it remained with him.

5

'Kostya! Do you know with whom Sergius Ivanich travelled coming here?' said Dolly, after she had distributed cucumbers and honey among the children. 'With Vronsky! He is on his way to Serbia.'

'Yes, and not alone, but is taking a squadron at his own expense!' said Katavasov.

'That is like him,' said Levin. 'But are Volunteers really still going?' he added with a glance at Koznyshev.

Koznyshev did not reply, but with the blunt side of a knife carefully extracted from a bowl in which lay a wedge of white honeycomb a live bee that had stuck in the running honey.

'Yes, I should think so! You should have seen what went on at the station yesterday!' said Katavasov, audibly biting into a cucumber.

'Well, how is one to understand it? In heaven's name, Sergius Ivanich, explain to me where all these Volunteers are going and whom they are fighting,' said the old Prince, evidently continuing a conversation that had been started during Levin's absence.

'Who has declared war on Turkey?'

'No one has declared war, but people sympathize with their suffering neighbours and wish to help them,' replied Koznyshev.

'But the Prince is not talking of help,' interposed Levin, taking his father-in-law's side, 'but of war! He says that private people cannot take part in war without the consent of the Government.'

Koznyshev said:

'It is a pity you put the question that way. There is no declaration of war in this case, but simply an expression of human, Christian feeling. Our brothers by blood and religion are being killed. Well, say they were not even our brothers or co-religionists, but simply children, women, and old people; one's feelings are outraged, and Russians hasten to help to stop those horrors. Imagine that you were going along a street and saw a tipsy man beating a woman or a child; I think you would not stop to ask whether war had or had not been declared against that man, but you would rush at him and defend the victim!'

'But I would not kill the man,' replied Levin.

'Yes, you would.'

'I don't know. If I saw such a thing, I might yield to my instinctive feeling; I can't say beforehand. But there is no such instinctive feeling about the oppression of the Slavs, nor can there be.'

'Perhaps you have none, but others have,' said Koznyshev with a dissatisfied frown. 'Among the people there live traditions of Orthodox Christians suffering under the yoke of the "Infidel Mussulman". The people have heard of their brothers' sufferings, and have spoken out.'

'Perhaps,' said Levin evasively, 'but I don't see it. I myself am one of the people, and I don't feel it.'

'Nor do I,' said the Prince. 'I was living abroad and read the papers, and must own that I could not at all understand why, even before the Bulgarian atrocities, all Russians suddenly grew so fond of their Slavonic brothers, while I don't feel any love for them. I was much grieved and thought I was a monster or that the Karlsbad waters had that effect on me! But on getting back I was relieved, for I see that there are others besides me who are only interested in Russia and not in their brother-Slavs. Constantine is one.'

'Personal opinions don't count in this matter,' said Koznyshev. 'It is not an affair of personal opinions, when all Russia—the people—has expressed its will.'

'But, forgive me, I don't see it. The people know nothing about it,' said the Prince.

'The people can't help knowing. A consciousness of their destiny always exists in the people, and at moments like the present it becomes clear to them,' said Koznyshev positively, glancing at the old beekeeper.

The handsome old man, with a black beard turning grey in places and thick silvery hair, stood motionless with a bowl of honey in his hand, gazing kindly and calmly down from his height at the gentlefolk, clearly neither understanding them nor wishing to understand.

'Yes, you'd better ask him! He neither knows nor thinks about it,' said Levin. 'Have you heard about the war, Mikhaylich?' he asked, addressing the old man. 'What they read in the church? What do you think? Ought we to fight for the Christians?'

'Why should we think? Alexander Nikolayevich, the Emperor, has thought for us, and will think for us on all matters. He can see better. …

Shall I bring some more bread and give the laddie a bit?' he asked Dolly, pointing to Grisha, who was finishing his crust.

'I have no need to ask,' said Koznyshev. 'We have seen, and still see, hundreds and hundreds of men who give up everything to serve the righteous cause, and who come from all ends of Russia and openly and clearly express their thoughts and aims. What does that mean?'

'It means, it seems to me,' said Levin, beginning to get excited, 'that in a nation of eighty millions there can always be found not hundreds, as is now the case, but tens of thousands of men who have lost their social position. ...'

'I tell you it's not hundreds, and not the happy-go-lucky people, but the best representatives of the people!' said Koznyshev, as irritably as if he were defending the last of his possessions. 'And the donations? There at any rate the whole people directly expresses its will.'

'That word *people* is so indefinite,' said Levin. 'Clerks in district offices, schoolmasters, and one out of a thousand peasants, may know what it is all about. The rest of the eighty millions, like Mikhaylich, not only don't express their will, but have not the least idea what it is they have to express it about! What right have we then to say it is the will of the people?'

Levin wanted to ask why, if public opinion is an infallible judge, is a Revolution and a Commune not as lawful as the movement in favour of the Slavs? But all these were thoughts that could not decide anything. One thing could be seen indubitably, namely, that this dispute was irritating his brother at the moment, and that therefore it was wrong to continue it, so Levin ceased to argue, and drew his visitors' attention to the clouds that were gathering and to the fact that they had better get home before the rain began.

6

The Prince and Koznyshev got into the trap and drove off; the rest of the party, hastening their steps, went home on foot.

But the cloud approached so rapidly that it was necessary to hurry still more to reach home before the rain came. When they were still about two hundred paces from the house the wind had already risen, so that at any moment a downpour might be expected.

The children, with frightened and joyful yells, ran on in front. Dolly, struggling with difficulty with the skirts that clung to her legs, no longer walked but ran, her eyes fixed on the children. The men, holding their hats, went on with long strides. They were just reaching the porch when a large drop broke against the edge of the iron gutter. The children, followed by the grown-ups, ran, talking merrily, under the shelter of the roof.

'And Catherine Alexandrovna?' Levin asked Agatha Mikhaylovna, who, carrying shawls and plaids, met them in the hall.

'In Kolok, I expect, and Nurse is with them.'

Levin snatched up the plaids and rushed to the Kolok.

In that short time the centre of the cloud had already so moved over the sun that it was as dark as during an eclipse. The wind obstinately, as if insisting on having its way, pushed Levin back and, tearing the leaves and blossoms off the lime trees and rudely and strangely uncovering the white branches of birches, bent everything in one direction: the acacias, the flowers, the dock leaves, the grass, and the crests of the trees. The girls who had been working in the garden rushed screeching under the roof of the servants' quarters. A white curtain of pouring rain was already descending over the distant wood and half the neighbouring field, and was advancing rapidly toward the Kolok. The moisture of the rain, shattered into minute drops, filled the air.

Lowering his head and fighting against the wind which was tearing the plaids out of his hands, Levin had almost reached the Kolok and could see something gleaming white behind an oak, when suddenly everything burst into flame, the earth seemed on fire, and just overhead the vault of heaven seemed to crack.

When he opened his dazzled eyes the first thing Levin saw with horror through the dense curtain of rain that now separated him from the Kolok was the strangely-altered position of the green crown of a familiar oak in the middle of the wood. 'Has it been struck?' he had barely time to think when, with quicker and quicker motion, the crown of the oak disappeared behind the other trees, and he heard the crash of a big tree falling on to other trees.

The flash of lightning, the sound of thunder, and the sudden cold sensation of his body that was being drenched, merged for Levin into one feeling of horror.

'Oh God! Oh God! only not on them!' he said.

And though it occurred to him at once how senseless was his prayer that they should not be killed by the oak that had already fallen, he repeated it, knowing that he could do nothing better than utter that senseless prayer.

Having run to the spot where they generally went, he did not find them there.

They were at the other end of the wood, under an old lime tree, and were calling him. Two figures in dark dresses (they had been light-coloured before) stood bending over something. They were Kitty and the nurse. The rain was already passing and it was growing lighter when Levin reached them. The bottom of the nurse's dress was dry, but Kitty's dress was wet through and clung close to her. Though the rain had stopped, they were still standing in the same postures that they had adopted when the storm began: they stood leaning over a perambulator with a green hood.

'Alive? Safe? Thank God!' he muttered, running up to them and splashing through the puddles with one shoe half off and full of water.

Kitty's wet and rosy face was turned to him, timidly smiling beneath her bedraggled hat.

'Well, aren't you ashamed of yourself? I don't understand how one can be so imprudent!' he reproached his wife in his vexation.

'Really, it was not my fault. I was just wishing to go when he became restless. We had to change his things. We had hardly …' Kitty began excusing herself.

Mitya was safe and dry and slept undisturbed.

'Well, thank God! I don't know what I am saying!'

They collected the wet baby-things, and the nurse took the baby in her arms and carried him. Levin walked beside his wife, feeling guilty at having been vexed, and stealthily, so that the nurse should not see, pressing Kitty's hand.

7

Throughout the whole day, amid most varied conversations in which he took part only with what one may call the external side of his mind, Levin, despite his disillusionment with the change that should have taken place in him, did not cease to be joyfully aware of the fullness of his heart.

After the rain it was too wet to go out walking, besides which the thunder-clouds had not cleared from the horizon, and, now here now there, passed thundering and darkening along the borders of the sky. So the whole company spent the rest of the day at home.

No more disputes arose; on the contrary, after dinner every one was in the best of spirits.

First Katavasov amused the ladies with his original jokes, which on first acquaintance with him always pleased people, and afterwards, encouraged by Koznyshev, he recounted his very interesting observations on the differences in character, and even in physiognomy, between male and female house-flies and on their life. Koznyshev too was in good spirits and at tea, led on by his brother, expounded his views of the future of the Eastern question, and did it so simply and well that every one listened attentively.

Only Kitty could not hear him to the end, she was called away to bath Mitya.

A few minutes after she had gone, Levin too was called to her in the nursery.

Leaving his tea and regretting the interruption in the interesting conversation, yet uneasy as to why he was sent for, as this only happened on important occasions, Levin went to the nursery.

All these considerations of the importance of the Slavonic element in universal history seemed to him so insignificant in comparison with what was going on in his soul, that he immediately forgot them all and returned to the frame of mind he had been in that morning. Now the feelings of joy and tranquillity were more vivid than before and his thoughts could not keep pace with them.

Just as he was entering the nursery he remembered what it was he had hidden from himself. It was that if the principal proof of the existence of a Deity is His revelation of what is good, why is that revelation confined to the Christian Church alone? What relation to that revelation had the Buddhist and the Mahomedan faiths, which also teach and do good?

It seemed to him that he had a reply to that question; but he had no time to express it to himself before he entered the nursery.

Kitty was standing, with her sleeves rolled up, beside the bath in which the baby was splashing about, and hearing her husband's step she turned her face toward him, beckoning him with a smile. With one hand supporting the head of the plump kicking baby who floated on his back, with the other she squeezed the water from a sponge over him, regularly exerting the muscles of her arm.

'There, come and look! Look!' she said when her husband came up. 'Agatha Mikhaylovna was right. He does recognize!'

The point was that Mitya had that day obviously and undoubtedly begun to recognize his own people.

Directly Levin approached the bath he was shown an experiment which succeeded perfectly. The cook, who had been called specially for the purpose, bent over him. He frowned and moved his head from side to side in a protesting way. Kitty bent over him, and his face lit up with a smile, he pressed his hand into the sponge and bubbled with his lips, producing such a contented and peculiar sound that not only Kitty but Levin too, went into unexpected raptures.

The nurse lifted the baby out of the bath with one hand and poured fresh water over him, then he was wrapped up and dried, and after a penetrating yell he was given to his mother.

'Well, I am glad you are beginning to be fond of him,' said Kitty to her husband, when with the child at her breast she had sat down in her usual place. 'I am very glad, for I was beginning to be grieved about it. You said you felt nothing for him.'

'No, did I say I felt nothing? I only said I was disillusioned.'

'What! Disillusioned with him?'

'Not so much with him as with my own feeling; I had expected more. I had expected that, like a surprise, a new, pleasant feeling would awaken in me. And then, instead of that, nothing but repulsion and pity ...'

She listened attentively, replacing on her slender fingers, across the baby, the rings she had taken off to bath Mitya.

'And above all, the anxiety and pity were far greater than the pleasure. But to-day, after that fright during the storm, I have realized how much I love him.'

Kitty brightened up with a smile.

'Were you very frightened?' she asked. 'I was too, but to me it appears more dreadful now that it is past. I shall go and look at that oak. But how nice Katavasov is! And in general the whole day has been so pleasant! And you are so nice to your brother when you like. ... Well, go to them. It is always hot and steamy here after the bath.'

8

When on leaving the nursery Levin was alone, he at once remembered the thought that had not seemed quite clear.

Instead of going back to the drawing-room, whence came the sound of voices, he stopped on the verandah and leaning on the balustrade gazed at the sky.

It had grown quite dark, and to the south, where he was looking, the sky was clear. The clouds were in the opposite direction. There lightning flashed and distant thunder rolled. Levin listened to the rhythmical dripping of raindrops from the lime trees in the garden, and looked at a familiar triangular constellation and at the Milky Way which with its branches intersected it. At every flash of lightning not only the Milky Way but even the bright stars vanished; but immediately afterwards they reappeared in the same places, as if thrown there by some unerring hand.

'Well, what is perplexing to me?' Levin asked himself, feeling in advance that the solution of his doubts, though as yet unknown to him, was already in his soul.

'Yes, the one evident, indubitable manifestation of the Deity is the law of goodness disclosed to men by revelation, which I feel within myself and in the confession of which I do not so much unite myself as I am united, whether I will or not, with other people in one community of believers which is called the Church. But the Jews, Mahomedans, Confucians, Buddhists—what of them?' he questioned, putting to himself the query that seemed to him dangerous. 'Is it possible that those hundreds of millions of people are deprived of that highest blessing, without which life has no meaning?' he pondered, but he immediately corrected himself. 'But what am I asking about?' he said to himself. 'I am asking about the relation to the Deity of all the different beliefs of mankind. I am asking about the general revelation of God to the whole universe with all those cloudy nebulae. What am I doing? To me personally, to my heart, has been indubitably revealed a knowledge unattainable by reasoning, and I obstinately wish to express that knowledge by reason and in words.

'Do I not know that it is not the stars that are moving?' he asked himself, looking at a bright planet that had already shifted its position by the top branch of a birch tree. 'But I, watching the movement of the stars, cannot picture to myself the rotation of the earth and I am right in saying that the stars move.

'And could the astronomers understand and calculate anything if they took into their calculation the whole of the complicated and varied motions of the earth? All their wonderful conclusions as to the distances, weights, movements, and disturbances of the heavenly bodies are based on their visible movement round a stationary earth—on this very movement that is now before me, and which has been the same to millions of people during the centuries, and that has been and will be the same and can always be verified. And just as astronomers' conclusions would be idle and uncertain were they not based on observations of the visible sky in relation to one meridian and one horizon, so would my conclusions be idle and uncertain were they not founded on that understanding of goodness which was and will be the same always and for every one, and which has been revealed to me by Christianity and can always be verified in my soul. The question of other creeds and their relation to the Deity I have not the right or possibility of deciding.'

'Oh, you've not gone?' suddenly asked Kitty, who was passing that way to the drawing-room. 'Nothing has upset you, has it?' she inquired, peering attentively into his face by the starlight.

But she would not have been able to discern its expression had not a flash of lightning that effaced the stars lit it up. By the light of that flash she saw the whole of his face and, noticing that he was calm and happy, she smiled at him.

'She understands,' thought he, 'she knows what I am thinking about. Shall I tell her or not? Yes, I will ...' But just as he was going to speak, she began:

'Oh, Kostya! Be good and go to the corner room and see how they have arranged things for Sergius Ivanich! I can't very well do it myself. Have they put in the new washstand?'

'Yes, certainly I will,' said Levin, standing upright and kissing her.

'No, I had better not tell her,' he thought when she had passed out before him. 'It is a secret, necessary and important for me alone, and inexpressible in words.

'This new feeling has not changed me, has not rendered me happy, nor suddenly illuminated me as I dreamt it would, but is just like my feeling for my son. It has not been a surprise either. But be it faith or not—I do not know what it is—this feeling has also entered imperceptibly through suffering and is firmly rooted in my soul.

'I shall still get angry with Ivan the coachman in the same way, shall dispute in the same way, shall inopportunely express my thoughts; there will still be a wall between my soul's holy of holies and other people; even my wife I shall still blame for my own fears and shall repent of it. My reason will still not understand why I pray, but I shall still pray, and my life, my whole life, independently of anything that may happen to me, is every moment of it no longer meaningless as it was before, but has an unquestionable meaning of goodness with which I have the power to invest it.'

About this Compact Edition

Tolstoy began Anna Karenina in 1873, four years after he had completed *War and Peace,* and it was serialized between 1875 and 1877. In the abridged edition published here the language of the translation is adhered to, but cuts are made in a number of areas in the novel. These include some descriptions of society life in Moscow and Petersburg – overlong dialogue is reduced in the interests of narrative directness – while some minor characters are either eliminated or have a diminished emphasis. Philosophical and political sections of the novel are outlined rather than given at full length, and detailed descriptions, from characters' reactions to particular events, are cut back while retaining the essential spirit of the narration. The central focus is on the ill-starred love affair of Anna and Vronsky, the marriage of Dolly and Stiva, and the coming together of Kitty and Levin, with the latter's struggle towards an essential belief in human goodness contrasted with Anna's despair.